Maidenhair

Mikhail
Shishkin

Maidenhair

Translated from
the Russian by
Marian Schwartz

OPEN LETTER
LITERARY TRANSLATIONS FROM THE UNIVERSITY OF ROCHESTER

Library of Congress Cataloging-in-Publication Data:

Shishkin, Mikhail.
    [Venerin volos. English]
    Maidenhair / Mikhail Shishkin ; translated from the Russian
  by Marian Schwartz.
      pages ; cm
    ISBN-13: 978-1-934824-36-8 (paperback : alkaline paper)
    ISBN-10: 1-934824-36-4 (paperback : alkaline paper)
    1. Refugees—Switzerland—Fiction. 2. IUr'eva, Izabella—Fiction.
    3. Women singers—Russia—Fiction. 4. Translators—Soviet Union—Fiction.
    I. Schwartz, Marian. II. Title.
    PG3487.I7525V4613 2012
    891.73'5—dc23
                       2012022669

Published with the support of the Institute for Literary Translation (Russia).

Translation of this publication and the creation of its layout were
carried out with the financial support of the Federal Agency for
Press and Mass Communication under the federal target program
"Culture of Russia (2012-2018)."

Partially funded by a grant from the
National Endowment for the Arts, a federal agency.

NATIONAL
ENDOWMENT
FOR THE ARTS

Printed on acid-free paper in the United States of America.

Text set in Caslon, a family of serif typefaces based on the designs of
William Caslon (1692–1766).

Design by N. J. Furl

Open Letter is the University of Rochester's nonprofit, literary translation press:
Lattimore Hall 411, Box 270082, Rochester, NY 14627

www.openletterbooks.org

Maidenhair

And your ashes will be called, and will be told:
"Return that which does not belong to you;
reveal what you have kept to this time."
For by the word was the world created, and by the word shall we be resurrected.
—Revelation of Baruch ben Neriah. 4, XLII

Darius and Parysatis had two sons, the elder Artaxerxes and the younger Cyrus.

Interviews start at eight in the morning. Everyone's still sleepy, crumpled, and sullen—employees, interpreters, policemen, and refugees alike. Rather, they still need to become refugees. For now they're just GS. That's what these people are called here. *Gesuchsteller.*[1]

He's brought in. First name. Last name. Date of birth. Thick lips. Pimply. Clearly older than sixteen.

Question: Briefly describe the reasons why you are requesting asylum in Switzerland.

Answer: I lived in an orphanage since I was ten. Our director raped me. I ran away. At the bus stop I met drivers taking trucks across the border. One took me out.

Question: Why didn't you go to the police and file a statement against your director?

Answer: They would have killed me.

---

1. A person who has filed for asylum. *(Ger.)*

Question: Who are "they"?

Answer: They're all in it together. Our director took me, another kid, and two girls, put us in a car, and drove us to a dacha. Not his dacha, I don't know whose. That's where they all got together, all the bosses, the police chief, too. They were drinking and made us drink, too. Then they put us in different rooms. A big dacha.

Question: Have you cited all the reasons why you are requesting asylum?

Answer: Yes.

Question: Describe your route. What country did you arrive from, and where did you cross the border of Switzerland?

Answer: I don't know. I was riding in a truck and they put boxes around me. They gave me two plastic bottles—one with water, the other for piss—and they only let me out at night. They dropped me off right here around the corner. I don't even know what the town's called. They told me where to go to turn myself in.

Question: Have you ever engaged in political or religious activity?

Answer: No.

Question: Have you ever been tried or investigated?

Answer: No.

Question: Have you ever sought asylum in other countries?

Answer: No.

Question: Do you have legal representation in Switzerland?

Answer: No.

Question: Do you consent to expert analysis to determine your age from your bone tissue?

Answer: What?

During breaks you can have coffee in the interpreters' room. This side looks out on a construction site. They're putting up a new building for a refugee intake center.

My white plastic cup keeps sparking right in my hands. In fact, the whole room is lit up by reflected sparks. A welder has set himself up right outside the window.

There's no one here. I can read quietly for ten minutes.

And so, Darius and Parysatis had two sons, the elder Artaxerxes and the younger Cyrus. When Darius was taken ill and felt the approach of death, he demanded both sons come to him. At the time the elder son was nearby, but Darius had sent for Cyrus to another province, over which he had been placed as satrap.

The pages of the book are flashing in the reflected sparks, too. It hurts to read. After each flash, the page goes dark.

You close your eyes and it penetrates your eyelids, too.

Peter peeks in the door. Herr Fischer.[2] Master of fates. He winks: it's time. And a spark lights him up, too, like a camera flash. That's how he'll be imprinted, with one squinting eye.

Question: Do you understand the interpreter?
Answer: Yes.
Question: Your last name?
Answer: ★★★.
Question: First name?
Answer: ★★★.
Question: How old are you?
Answer: Sixteen.
Question: Do you have a passport or other document attesting to your identity?
Answer: No.
Question: You must have a birth certificate. Where is it?
Answer: It burned up. Everything burned up. They set fire to our house.
Question: What is your father's name?

---

2. Mr. Fischer. *(Ger.)*

Answer:	★★★ ★★★. He died a long time ago. I don't remember him at all.
Question:	The cause of your father's death?
Answer:	I don't know. He was sick a lot. He drank.
Question:	Give me your mother's first name, last name, and maiden name.
Answer:	★★★. I don't know her maiden name. They killed her.
Question:	Who killed your mother—when, and under what circumstances?
Answer:	Chechens.
Question:	When?
Answer:	Just this summer, in August.
Question:	On what date?
Answer:	I don't remember exactly. The nineteenth, I think, or maybe the twentieth. I don't remember.
Question:	How did they kill her?
Answer:	They shot her.
Question:	Name your last place of residence before your departure.
Answer:	★★★. It's a small village near Shali.
Question:	Give me the exact address: street, house number.
Answer:	There is no address there. There's just one street and our house. It's gone. They burned it down. And there's nothing left of the village, either.
Question:	Do you have relatives in Russia? Brothers? Sisters?
Answer:	I had a brother. Older. They killed him.
Question:	Who killed your brother—when, and under what circumstances?
Answer:	Chechens. At the same time. They were killed together.
Question:	Do you have other relatives in Russia?
Answer:	There's no one else left.
Question:	Do you have relatives in third countries?
Answer:	No.
Question:	In Switzerland?

Answer: No.

Question: What is your nationality?

Answer: Russian.

Question: Confession?

Answer: What?

Question: Religion?

Answer: Yes.

Question: Orthodox?

Answer: Yes. I just didn't understand.

Question: Briefly describe the reasons why you are requesting asylum in Switzerland.

Answer: Chechens kept coming over and telling my brother to go into the mountains with them to fight the Russians. Otherwise they'd kill him. My mother hid him. That day I was coming home and I heard shouts through the open window. I hid in the bushes by the shed and saw a Chechen in our room hitting my brother with his rifle butt. There were a few of them there, and they all had submachine guns. I couldn't see my brother. He was lying on the floor. Then my mother lunged at them with a knife. The kitchen knife we use to peel potatoes. One of them shoved her up against the wall, put his AK to her head, and fired. Then they went out, poured a canister of gasoline over the house, and lit it. They stood around in a circle and watched it burn. My brother was still alive and I heard him screaming. I was afraid they'd see me and kill me, too.

Question: Don't stop. Tell us what happened then.

Answer: Then they left. And I sat there until dark. I didn't know what to do or where to go. Then I went to the Russian post on the road to Shali. I thought the soldiers would help me somehow. But they were afraid of everyone themselves and drove me away. I wanted to explain to them what happened, but they fired in the air to make me go away. Then I spent the night outside in a destroyed house. Then I started making my way to Russia. And from there to here. I don't want to live there.

Question: Have you cited all the reasons why you're requesting asylum?

Answer: Yes.

Question: Describe your route. What countries did you travel through and by what means of transport?

Answer: Different ones. Commuter trains and regular ones. Through Belarus, Poland, and Germany.

Question: Did you have money to buy tickets?

Answer: How could I? I just rode. Avoided the conductors. In Belarus they caught me and threw me off the train while it was moving. Good thing it was still going slowly and there was a slope. I fell well and didn't break anything. I just tore the skin on my leg on some broken glass. Right here. I spent the night in the train station and some woman gave me a band-aid.

Question: What documents did you present upon crossing borders?

Answer: None. I walked at night.

Question: Where and how did you cross the border of Switzerland?

Answer: Here, in, what's it . . .

Question: Kreuzlingen.

Answer: Yes. I just walked past the police. They only check cars.

Question: What funds did you use to support yourself?

Answer: None.

Question: What does that mean? You stole?

Answer: Different ways. Sometimes yes. What was I supposed to do? I get hungry.

Question: Have you ever engaged in political or religious activity?

Answer: No.

Question: Have you ever been tried or investigated?
Answer: No.
Question: Have you ever sought asylum in other countries?
Answer: No.
Question: Do you have legal representation in Switzerland?
Answer: No.

No one says anything while the printer is printing out the interrogation transcript.

The guy picks at his dirty black nails. His jacket and filthy jeans stink of tobacco and piss.

Leaning back and rocking on his chair, Peter looks out the window. The birds are chasing down a plane.

I draw crosses and squares on a pad, divide them into triangles with diagonal lines, and fill them in to create relief.

There are photographs on the walls around us—the master of fates is crazy about fishing. Here he is in Alaska holding a big old fish by the gills, and over there it's something Caribbean with a big hook poking out of its huge gullet.

Over my head is a map of the world. All stuck with pins with multicolored heads. Black ones are stuck into Africa, yellow ones poke out of Asia. The white heads are the Balkans, Belarus, Ukraine, Moldova, Russia, and the Caucasus. After this interview one more pin will be added.

Acupuncture.

The printer falls silent and blinks red. It's out of paper.

My good Nebuchadnezzasaurus!

You have already received my hasty note with my promise of details to come. Here they are.

After a day spent in a place with bars on the windows, I came home. I ate macaroni. I read your letter, which made me so happy. I began looking out the window. The wind was driving the twilight. The rain fell and fell. A red umbrella lay on the lawn, like a slit in the grass pelt.

But I don't want to get ahead of myself.

It is not every day, truly, that the postman spoils us with missives from foreign lands! Especially one like this! Amid the bills and ads—unexpected joy. Your letter. In which you describe in detail your Nebuchadnezzasaurus realm, its glorious geographic past, the ebbs and flows of its history, the ways of its flora, the habits of its fauna, its volcanoes, laws, and catapults, and the cannibalistic inclinations of its populace. It turns out, you even have both vampires and draculas! And so, this means, you are emperorizing. I am flattered.

True, your writing abounds in grammatical errors, but really, what does that matter? You can learn to correct your mistakes, but you may never send me a missive like this again. Emperors grow up so quickly and forget about their empires.

I cannot get my fill of the map you included of your island homeland, the painstaking labor of your inspired imperial cartographers. And you know, I just may pin it up here on the wall. I'll look at it and try to guess where you are there right now, among those mountains, deserts, lakes, felt-tip bushes, and capitals. What have you been up to? Have you already moved from your summer residence to your Autumn Palace? Or are you already asleep? Your unsinkable navy guards your sleep. There go the triremes and submarines in file around your island.

What a glorious name for a benevolent sovereign! And in multicolored letters! I even have a few guesses as to where you got the idea, but I will keep them to myself.

In your missive, you ask me to inform you about our distant power, which is as yet unknown to your geographers and explorers. How could I fail to answer your question!

What shall I tell you about our empire? It is promised, hospitable, skyscrapered. You can gallop for three years without galloping all the way across. For number of mosquitoes per capita during the sleepless hours, it has no equal. For fun, the squirrels run along my fence.

Our map abounds in white patches when snow falls. The borders are so far away no one even knows what the empire borders on: some say the horizon; according to other sources, the final cadenza of the angels' trumpets. We know for a fact that it is located somewhere to the north of the Hellenes, along the coastline of the ocean of air where our unsinkable cloud fleet sails in file.

There is still flora, but all that's left of the fauna are the tops of those trees that resemble schools of fry. The wind frightens them.

The flag is a chameleon, every law has a loophole, and I personally have no knowledge of any volcanoes.

The main question that has occupied imperial minds for more than a generation is this: Who are we and why are we here? The answer to it, for all the apparent obviousness, is muddled: in profile, Hyperboreans; en face, Sarmatians—in short, either Orochs or Tungus. And each is a fiddle. I mean riddle.

The beliefs are primitive but not without a certain poeticism. Some are convinced that the world is an enormous elk cow whose fur is the forest, the parasites in its fur are the taiga beasts, and the insects hovering around it are the birds. Such is the universe's mistress. When the elk cow rubs up against a tree, everything living dies.

In short, in this empire, which someone has deemed the best in the world, your humble servant—do you care if I'm not a chief?—well, I'm no chief. How can I explain to you, my good Nebuchadnezzasaurus, what we do here? All right, let me try this. After all, even these fry out the window, who form a school and have no inkling that it's just the wind, are convinced that someone is waiting for each of them, remembers them, knows their face—every last vein and freckle. And there's no convincing them otherwise. And here each of the celestial beasts pushes forward, two by two: blunderers and glowerers, truthseekers and householders, lefties and righties, mobsters and taxidermists. And no one understands anyone. And so I serve. An interpreter in the chancellery for refugees in the defense ministry of paradise.

And each person wants to explain something. He hopes they'll hear him out. But here we are with Peter. I'm interpreting the questions and answers, and Peter is taking notes and nodding, as if to say, Of course I believe you. He doesn't believe anyone. Some woman comes and says, "I'm a simple shepherdess, a foundling, I don't know my parents, I was raised by an ordinary goatherd, poor Drias." And so the hoodwinking begins. The trees are in fruit; the plains in grain; there are willows on hills, herds in meadows, and everywhere the crickets' gentle chirp and the sweet scent of fruit. Pirates lie in wait, the enemy at the gates. Well-groomed nails blaze up in the lighter's flame. "After all, I grew up in the country and never so much as heard the word 'love.' I pictured her IUD looking something like a couch spring. Oh, my Daphnis! They separated us, ill-starred that we were! It was one showdown after another. First the Tyre gang attacks, then the Methymna hosts insist on their rights. Daphnis accompanied me like a guard when I went to see clients. A hairstyle affects how your day goes—and your life as a result. But do you see what they did to my teeth? My teeth weren't all that great to begin with. But that's from my mama. She used to tell me how she would flake plaster off the stove when she was a child and eat it. She wasn't getting enough calcium. And when I was carrying Yanochka, I'd walk off with the teachers' chalk at the institute and gnaw on it. Love is like the moon: if it's not waxing, it's waning, but it's the same as the last time, always the same." Peter: "That's it?" She: "That's it." "Well then, madam," he proposes, "your fingerprints." "What for?" She's dumbfounded. "You've been tracked down in our imperial-wide card file." And he knees her up the ass. But she's already shouting from the elevator, "You aren't human beings; you're still cold clay. They've sculpted you but they haven't breathed a soul into you!"

Whereas another couldn't string two words together properly at all. And his diction was like a water faucet's. I agonize, trying to sort out what he's gushing about, while Peter, still at his desk, is laying out pencils and toothpicks in a row, as if on parade, as if he were the desk marshal reviewing a parade. We're on the clock. No one is in any hurry. Peter likes order. And this GS is muttering something about open sesame and shouting for someone to get the door. He's babbling about white circles on gates, then red ones. He starts assuring us that he was sitting by himself in the wineskin, not touching anyone, not bothering anyone, but he got the boiling oil treatment. "There," he shouts, "you see? Is that really right? Boiling oil on a live person?" But all that's necessary to refuse the rogue is to find discrepancies in his statements. Peter gets a little book off his caseload shelf and things start moving. "Tell me, dear man, how many kilometers from your Bagdadovka to the capitals? What is the piaster's rate of exchange against the dollar? What national holidays are celebrated in the country that abandoned you besides the Immaculate Conception and the first snowman? What color are the streetcars and wineskins? And how much is a Borodinsky loaf?"

Or say the Jews are returning from Babylonian captivity, and they start singing the chorus from the third act of *Nabucco*, and our chief asks them: "What language do they speak in the Chaldean kingdom?" They: "Akkadian." He: "What is the temple to the god Marduk in Babylon called?" They: "Esagila." He: "And the Babylonian tower?" They: "Etemenanki." He: "To what goddess are the northern gates dedicated?" They: "Ishtar, the goddess Venus. And the Sun is personified by Shamash, the Moon by Sin. Mars is Nergal. The scoundrel Babylonians see Ninurt in Saturn, Nabu in Mercury, and Marduk himself is identified with Jupiter. By the way, the seven-day week comes from these seven astral gods. Did you know that?" He: "I ask the questions here. The illegitimate daughter of Nebuchadnezzar, second letter 'b,' seven letters." They: "What kind of fools do you take us for? Abigail!"

Before Peter, Sabina was our chief. She, on the contrary, believed everyone. And didn't ask questions from the omniscient book. And never used her stamp "Prioritätsfall." So she was fired. But Peter lets nearly everyone have it. On the first page of their file. This means an expedited review of the case in view of its obvious rejection. Here the GS signs the transcript, says goodbye, smiles ingratiatingly at the master of fates, at the interpreter, and at the guard with the halberd who has come for him, and hopes that now everything will be all right, but as soon as the door closes, Peter stamps it.

This paycheck was not for Sabina. When the interpreter used to go to the café across the street with her during break, she would complain that when she got home from work and sat down to eat, she would see the woman who had wept at the interview that afternoon telling her how they had pulled out her son's nails while this same little nail-less boy was sitting next to her in the waiting room. Children are questioned separately from their parents.

"You can't take pity on anyone here," Sabina said once. "But I take pity on them all. You just have to know how to detach, be a robot, question-answer, question-answer, fill out the form, sign the transcript, send it to Bern. Let them decide there. No, I have to find another job."

Sabina was very young to be our chief. After she was fired, she left for the opposite end of the empire and sent the interpreter a bizarre postcard. But none of that matters. Maybe I'll explain later someday. Or not.

I think we've been sidetracked, my good Nebuchadnezzasaurus.

What else makes our empire glorious? Just imagine, we have submarines, and deserts, and even a Dracula—not a vampire, the real thing. Basically everything here is the real thing.

What else? The wound in the grass scabbed over—darker.

Oh yes, I forgot to say that cannibalism has not gone out of style here. Moreover, people are consumed not just by anyone but by the autocrat personally—I don't know if it's a he or she, I haven't checked the court calendar in a long time, and after all, gender is all a matter of dialect. In short, there's just one Herod the Great, but if you don't think about it all the time, then you could burst into song for sheer joy. At the streetcar stop by the train station today, someone got out, whistling.

It's funny. Years from now you'll receive this letter and may not even remember that there was once an emperor of this marvelously pin-studded empire.

Notepad, pen, glass of water. Sun outside. The water in the glass lets a sunbeam in—not just a little sunbeam but a big fat one. It spills over the ceiling and suddenly, for a second, looks like an ear. Also an embryo. The door opens. They bring the next one in.

Question: Briefly describe the reasons why you are requesting asylum.

Answer: I used to work in customs on the Kazakhstan border. Soldiers would bring in drugs in their vehicles, and my superior was in cahoots with them. We were supposed to look the other way and write them up properly. I wrote a letter to the FSB. A few days later a truck ran over my daughter on the street. They called me and said this was my first warning.

Question: Briefly describe the reasons why you are requesting asylum.

Answer: I actively supported the opposition candidate in the gubernatorial elections and took part in protest rallies and collected signatures. I was called into the police, and they demanded that I stop coming out with revelations against the provincial leadership. I was beaten up several times by plainclothes police. Attached to my application for asylum I have medical certificates about my broken jaw and arm and other consequences of the beatings. Now, as you see, I'm disabled and can't work. My wife, who came with me, has stomach cancer.

Question: Briefly describe the reasons why you are requesting asylum.

Answer: I have AIDS. Everyone in town shunned me. Even my wife and children. I got infected when I was in the hospital, during a blood transfusion. I have nothing now: no job, no friends, no home. I'm going to die soon. This is what I decided. If I'm going to croak anyway, why not do it here, with you, in humane conditions? After all, you're not going to kick me out.

Question: Briefly describe the reasons why you are requesting asylum.

Answer: There was a voivode by the name of Dracula in the Orthodox land of Wallachia. One day, the Turkish pasha sent envoys to him, and they demanded that he reject his Orthodox faith and submit to him. While speaking with the voivode, the envoys failed to remove their hats, and when asked why they were insulting the great sovereign in this way, they replied: "Such is the custom of our land, sovereign." Then Dracula ordered his servants to nail the caps to the envoys' heads and sent their bodies back, ordering that the pasha be told that God is one, but customs vary. The enraged pasha came to the Orthodox land with an enormous army and began plundering and killing. The voivode Dracula assembled his entire modest host and attacked the Muslims one night, killed many of them, and put them to flight. In the morning, he organized a review of his surviving soldiers. Anyone wounded in the front had great honor bestowed upon him and the title of knight. Anyone wounded in the back was ordered impaled, as he said, "You are a wife, not a husband." Learning this, the pasha pulled the remnants of his army back, not daring anymore to attack this land. So the voivode Dracula went on to live on his possessions, and at that time there were many poor, destitute, sick, and feeble people in the Wallachian land. Seeing how many unfortunate people were suffering in his land, he ordered them all to come see him. A multitude without number—unfortunates, cripples, and orphans, hoping for great mercy from him—gathered, and they each began telling him of their misfortunes and pains: one about a lost leg, another about an eye poked out; one about a dead son, another about an unfair trial and an innocent brother thrown in prison. Great was the lamentation, and a wail hung over the entire Wallachian land. Then Dracula ordered them all assembled in a single edifice, built for the occasion, and ordered that they be given fine comestibles and plenty of drink. They ate, drank, and made merry. Then he came to them and asked, "What else do you want?" They all replied, "Only God knows, and you, great sovereign! Do with us as God instructs!" Then he told them, "Do you want me to make you without sorrow in this world, so that you want for nothing, so that you do not bemoan your lost leg or poked out eye, your dead son or unfair trial?" They were hoping for some miracle from him, and they all answered, "We do, sovereign!" Then he ordered the building locked, surrounded with straw, and set on fire. And the fire was great, and all in it burned.

My good Nebuchadnezzasaurus!

I checked my mailbox. Nothing from you.

True, you have other things on your mind besides us. Not that we are complaining. After all, matters of state significance await you. God forbid you should declare war on anyone or extraterrestrials should attack. An eye for an eye for everyone, for sure. This is no time for letters.

Here everything is the same as of old.

The universe is expanding. The interpreter is interpreting.

You go home, but you can't empty your head of all that transpired during the day. You've brought it all home with you.

You just can't rid yourself of those people and words.

All is the same as ever there. What could be new in the interpreting service? Everything follows a well-beaten path. Everything goes according to the form approved in the upper echelons. Each question according to the established model; likewise each answer. Peter doesn't even waste his voice on the standard greeting; he lets the interpreter read it off the page to the intimidated GS. Which the interpreter does: "Hello! How good you're here! Please, come in, and let us while away this endless day together! Have a seat. You must be weary from your journey. Take a load off your feet. We'll have the samovar put on right away! Bring your boots, your boots over here, closer to the stove! Well, how do you like our best of all possible blank spots on the map, where a man is what he is and says what he keeps silent? You haven't had a look around yet? You'll have time! Maybe you'd like to move over here, away from the window, so you don't catch a draft. You never know. Will you tell me if there's a draft? That's just hunky-dory. Now what were we about?" So you see, we get all kinds here, and they're all pretty crumpled, and none too clever, and they have bad teeth—and they lie. They assure us they've mislaid their documents so we won't send them straight back. They tell horrific stories about themselves. No one here tells any that aren't. Complete with details. They keep bringing up their elephantine wrists, into which molten vaseline was supposedly injected. Bogeymen and horror flicks. The things they come out with make you want to sit down and pen detective novels. As if their mama hadn't taught them to tell the truth when they were children. Sob stories! They wanted to live in paradise! Martyrs we get! But it's not about compassion. It's about clarifying circumstances. In order to keep them out of paradise, we have to ferret out what really happened. But how can you if people become the stories they tell? You just can't. That means it's all very simple. Since you can't clarify the truth, you at least need to clarify the lie. According to our instructions, improbability in statements is grounds for affixing this very stamp. So you'll have to come up with a better legend for yourself and not forget what is most important: the minor details, the trivia. Who would have believed in the resurrection had it not been for the detail about the finger placed in the wound, or about how they ate baked fish together? A stamp's all well and good, but can you really swear that the landscape is as black as you paint it? Take a look around! There go the clouds crawling on their belly. Over there someone has had a bite to eat on the bench and left his newspaper, and now a sparrow's pecking the letters. The neck of a broken bottle glitters on the dam—see?—and the mill wheel's shadow is black. The lilac smells like cheap perfume and believes everything's going to be all right. The stones are alive, too, multiplying by crumbling. You're not even listening. It's like talking to a wall. They only know their own story: they attacked me, tied me up, took me into the forest, beat me up, and left me there. Maybe they were right to beat you up! Did you have debts to pay or not? There you go! Or here there were two guys on the same day; they surrendered together, one supposedly from an orphanage outside Moscow, the other from Chechnya. A week later, the police sent over their passports. They'd hidden their documents in a concrete pipe near the rails where workers came across them. Both were from Lithuania. They'd come for vacation. The hotel was too expensive, so here they had a roof over their head and three squares a day. Results of bone analysis showed they were way past sixteen. Stamp. Stamp. Or here's a family surrendering: papa, mama, and a daughter of Zion. They assure us they'd fled their Anatevka; they couldn't take the villagers' persecution anymore. Those weren't the native inhabitants, they said, those were real fascists! May God save the Jews, and if He can't, then at least let Him save the goyim! They started telling stories about how the Christians there beat them. The husband and wife had their front teeth knocked out, and their daughter—she wasn't even twelve yet—was raped. As he was supposed to, Peter questioned each one separately. The papa and mama said approximately the same thing, as if from a memorized text: threats through the mail, nighttime phone calls, attacks at their front door, et cetera. Then they asked the girl in. Through the open door, you could see her clinging to her mama. She didn't want to, but her mama told her, "Go on, don't be afraid!" The girl went in and sat on the edge of her chair. Peter offered her chocolate for courage. He keeps chocolates in his right-hand desk drawer for just such occasions. This is not provided for by the instructions, but who would forbid it? Now Peter asked her whether her family was religious, and she answered, "Honest to God! We go to church all the time." And for greater proof, she crossed herself. She got it all mixed up, she was so frightened. Her dad was probably a failed merchant whose deals with his villager partners had gone south. They'd taken a standard story for surrendering, a sure thing. Who would dare not take pity on Jews? They thought they'd get away with it. After all, you can't simulate missing teeth, and according to a medical examination, the child's rape really had taken place. Stamp. You see how people sign the interrogation transcript! One, nodding obediently, as if to say, we are ignorant people, we'll sign what you say to sign; another checks even the spelling of geographical names. A third, who arrived with a stack of certificates from all his houses of sorrow, bonesetters, and lockups and assured us that he didn't believe anyone in the world anymore, demanded even a written translation of the interrogation transcript—because an oral one wasn't good enough, don't you know, and he wasn't about to put his signature on who knew what, on principle. Peter gave him a stamp straight away. And the guy started protesting then and there. We had to whistle for the guard. They threatened him with a halberd. Even in our neighborly country a guy like that will get to the bonesetters before too long. And a fourth up and asks us to put in the transcript that it's nice here with us, not too cold and not too hot, whereas they have four seasons: winter, winter, winter, and winter. We know you! You surrender as martyrs of winter and then you steal! So many times it's happened. First we introduce ourselves at the interview— hello-hello—and then the inevitable meeting at the police when they catch him for stealing—after all, the interpreter moonlights for the police, too—ah, old friends! It's been ages! And the creepy stories start up again. He says he definitely didn't bite the Migro mart manager at the exit by the cashier, and if he did, then it was only because the other tried to strangle him. So let's get back to our sheep. Take a look at yourself! You've lived to have gray hair and you're still on the run! Where's your passport? You don't know? But we do: at the train station's left luggage. Or the refugee shelter with your homeboy who surrendered before. We're going to write you up, you'll get an official travel pass under an invented name, and once you're out, you'll go straight for your documents. What? You won't? Then you'll have all your needs provided for—and onward: steal and sell the stolen goods for cheap. No matter his grief, he's still a thief. Neither cardsharp nor cheat, but a journeyman of the night, who is he? Hungry, even a bishop would steal. And you can save your breath about working! Who needs people like you? There are plenty of takers here as is. Many are called, darky, but few are chosen. What you rob from our stores here, you sell in your stalls there. That's the full extent of your working. So what if everything's hooked up to an alarm! Don't you know how to make bags? It's very simple. You take aluminum foil and glue it to the inside, and it's like a reflective sack and no alarm goes off. Take out whatever you want. Then send it on. How? By mail even. You write it's a gift, say, used items, all kinds of rubbish. The main thing here is the return address. Find someone nice and respectable in the phone book. Even better, some philanthropic organization. No one's going to pick on you then. Get it? What do you mean you're not up to it? The eyes are afraid but the hands obey! You aren't the first, and you won't be the last! So tell the truth, the whole truth, and nothing but the truth! And don't forget that no one has believed your blood-curdling stories for a long time. After all, life also consists of love and beauty, and because I sleep and my heart keeps vigil, there, the voice of my beloved knocks—Open up, sister mine, my beloved, my darling, my pure!—because my head is covered with dew and my curls with the damp of night. Have you understood your rights and responsibilities and that no one gets into paradise anyway?" GS: "Yes." Peter, taking the greeting text from the interpreter: "Any questions?" GS: "Those speaking may be fictitious, but what they say is real. Truth lies only where it is concealed. Fine, the people aren't real but the stories, oh, the stories are! It's just that they raped someone else at that orphanage, not fat-lips. And the guy from Lithuania heard the story about the brother who burned up and the murdered mother from someone else. What difference does it make who it happened to? It's always a sure thing. The people here are irrelevant. It's the stories that can be authentic or not. You just need to tell an authentic story. Just the way it happened. And not invent anything. We are what we say. A freshly planed destiny is packed with people no one needs, like an ark; all the rest is the floodgates of heaven. We become what gets written in the transcript. The words. You have to understand. The divine idea of the river is the river itself." Peter: "Then let's get down to it." And we were off: question-answer, question-answer. And snowflakes coming through the window pane. How could that be? It was just summer, and the snow's already begun? I can see the courtyard out the window. Some African there is shoveling snow from the path with a big iron shovel under a policeman's watchful eye. The thin iron scrapes the asphalt, just like in Moscow. Look, they've brought in this morning's second set of frozen GSs for interviews. They're wrapped up in jackets and scarves, mainly Africans and Asians, they're stamping over the fresh-fallen snow, and someone's child, a little Arab or Kurd, or maybe an Iranian—who can tell those five year olds apart?—keeps trying to scoop up a handful and make a snowball while his mother clucks at him, dragging him by the arm. Question-answer, question-answer. Then a break and coffee from a plastic cup. In another window, another courtyard, more snow, and the little Indians are having a snowball fight. But weren't these same little Indians just having a snowball fight, or has a year flown by? And once again question-answer, question-answer. It's like talking to yourself. You ask yourself the questions. And answer them.

Before going to sleep, the interpreter tries to read in order to clear his head. Before he turns off the light and puts a pillow over his ear, he would also like to speed off to the other end of the empire and travel with Cyrus through the desert, keeping the Euphrates on his right, in five crossings of thirty-five parasangs. The land there is a plain, as flat as the sea, and grown over in wormwood. The plants you encounter—the bushes and reeds—all give a marvelous scent, like incense. There is not a single tree, but the animals are quite varied: you encounter wild asses and large ostriches. You come across mouflons and gazelles, too. Often horsemen are chasing these animals. The asses, when they're being chased, run ahead and then stop—they run much faster than horses. When the horses get close, they take off again, and there is no reaching them unless the horse-men are in different places and hunt in turn. The meat of the asses is like venison, but tenderer. No one has ever caught a single ostrich, and the horsemen who chase after them quickly give up. The ostrich runs off and breaks away, using both its legs and its wings, raised like sails, during its flight.

You close the book and try to fall asleep, but your head again hears question-answer, question-answer. Again plainclothes police-men trying to break down a door, bursting into an apartment, turning everything upside down, punching you in the kidneys, and breaking your arm or rib. But Peter asks, When you were a child, did you and your parents ever take the *Rossiya* across the Black Sea and in the most unexpected places—for instance, in the overhead fans—suddenly notice "Adolf Hitler" in embossed Gothic letters? Answer: Yes, I did. Question: Your son, when visitors came over, did he crawl under the table out of boredom and start removing everyone's slippers, and did their feet feel around blindly over the parquet? Answer: Yes, he did. Question: Your mother, when she was buried, they put a slip of paper with a prayer on her forehead, and all of a sudden you thought, Who is going to read that and when? Answer: Yes, I did. Question: Is the River Styx in Perm? Did it freeze overnight? Did you toss a stick that took a hop on the ice, and did the ice boom, hollowly, lightly? Answer: Yes, it did. Question: Where did that girl swim to at night, one arm forward, under the pillow, the other back, palm up, and you so wanted to kiss that palm but you were afraid to wake her up?

In the wee hours the interpreter woke up bathed in sweat and with a pounding heart: he had dreamed of Galina Petrovna—except the boys all called her Galpetra, out of sheer meanness—and it had all come back to him—the lesson, the blackboard—as if all these decades lived had never been. He lay there looking at their brightening ceiling and returned to himself, clutching at his heart.

Why be afraid of her now?

And what exactly was in your dream—you forget right away and are left with just your schoolboy fear.

It's a nasty feeling, too. You never know what empire you're going to wake up in or who as.

The interpreter had switched off the computer but now he turned it back on to write down how he'd tossed and turned, unable to fall asleep, and how he'd remembered Galina Petrovna leading us on a field trip to Ostankino, to the Museum of Serf Art. It was still September, but the first snow had fallen, and the Apollo Belvedere was standing in the middle of a circular, snow-covered lawn. We were firing snowballs at him. Everyone wanted to hit where the leaf was, but no one could, and then Galpetra shouted at us and we started our field trip to the museum. I remember the echo in the cold dark rooms hung with time-blackened pictures. Reflections from the windows flowed over the waxed parquet like ice floes. We glided as if we were on a skating rink, in the oversized felt slippers we put on directly over our boots, and we stepped on each other's heels, so whoever was walking ahead of you would fall. Galpetra hissed at us and doled out clips to the back of the head. I see her as if it were today, the dark mustache at the edges of her mouth, in her violet wool suit, white knit mohair cap, and winter boots with the zipper half down so that her feet wouldn't get too funky, with museum slippers that resembled Lapp snowshoes over them. From the guide's stories I remember that if a serf ballerina danced badly in the theater, then her skirt was ripped off and she was thrashed in the stables. Doubtless I remembered it because of that: her skirt was ripped off. I also remember how they did thunder. If they needed thunder during the play, they would sprinkle peas down the top of a huge wooden pipe. This attraction was part of the excursion, and someone invisible at the top sprinkled a packet of peas into the pipe. But I remember the field trip mainly because someone whispered to me that our Galpetra was pregnant. This seemed so impossible to me at the time, so unimaginable, that our ageless, mustachioed teacher could get pregnant. After all, for that to happen, what happened between a man and woman—a woman, not our Galpetra!—would have to happen. I looked closely at the stomach of the old maid, who fought so fervently in school against mascara and eye shadow, and noticed nothing. Galpetra was just as fat as ever. I didn't want, simply couldn't, believe it. After all, there's no such thing as immaculate conception, but I was convinced by these words: "The whole school already knows she's going on maternity leave." So we were standing there listening to peas being transformed into peals of distant thunder, while something inexplicable was growing inside Galpetra, and out the window, through the snowfall, you could see the Ostankino television center, and the Apollo Belvedere was walking toward it through the snow without leaving tracks.

This Tungus morning, the interpreter chanced to wake up as an interpreter in a one-room apartment across from the cemetery. Maybe that was why the rent was cheap. Green as green could be. Finely drawn, fizzy, feathery. And since morning, everywhere, not only in the next apartment, the radio reported the murders and robberies of the previous night in a brisk voice. You didn't notice the crematorium right away. It looked like someone's villa on the hillside. And there was never smoke, although they operated indefatigably, as everyone here was expected to. It was all in the filters. They were installed in the chimney to keep from sullying the rain.

I've already written about the squirrel running along the fence.

For a long time my neighbors were nowhere to be seen. Just their linen. They did their laundry in the basement, where there were several washing machines. The machines were almost always in use, and laundered socks, old ladies' darned stockings, and prewar drawers awaited their bodies on lines in the drying rooms.

Until what war?

The interpreter thought there was something strange about this building when he came here the year before—no, it was a year and a half now. At first, he didn't realize that something was wrong with this huge building, where it was always quiet. He only noticed that he never heard children's voices. Then he noticed that there were only one-room apartments here and only old people lived in them. They seemed like decrepit walking stockings and socks.

The interpreter got a little apartment on the first floor, with a door that let out on the lawn, where there was always something lying on the ground. Right now the grass was stirring under the drops, and a tube of Colgate was getting wet under his window.

He could hear but not see his neighbors to the left and right. The one on the left kept whistling to his key so it would whistle back. The one on the right was talkative. He chirped to himself like a bird. He went around at night in long johns and a T-shirt, winter and summer. One day the interpreter was getting home very late, around two in the morning, and his neighbor was sweeping the path.

The toothpaste was from the seventh floor. In the first few days after he moved in, various items started falling on the lawn right in front of his window—but it wasn't garbage. One time a telephone fell, then sets of sheets, then a radio, food items, ladles, openers, office supplies, different notepads, a box of staples, envelopes. Not every day. Sometimes nothing would fly for a week and then you look—scissors. The interpreter collected it all in black garbage bags, and anything useful he simply pocketed. If it fell from the sky, it was lost. In his desk drawer lay those heaven-sent pencils, glue, and scissors. The interpreter simply could not understand who was throwing all this or why. Then one windy day the lawn was covered in dropped sheets of white paper, as if fall had come to a paper tree. They turned out to be ballots. After all, they had referendums here at the drop of a hat. And indicated on these ballots were a name and address. Where: to the best of all possible worlds, to whom: Frau Eggli. The interpreter went out to look at the list of residents' names and everything fell into place. Frau Eggli lived directly above him on the seventh floor. He went upstairs and rang her doorbell. Who knew, there could just have been a draft and all her papers were blown off her windowsill. He just wanted to return them. No one opened for a long time. The interpreter was about to go away when he heard a shuffling inside. Finally the door cracked open. First his nose was struck by the smell, but then in the darkness the interpreter made out an eight-hundred-year-old lady. He was actually amazed that so much smell could come from such a wizened creature. He apologized and started explaining about the ballots, that they had fallen, he said, and he had brought them up. She was silent. He asked, checking the plaque by her doorbell one more time, "Sie sind ja Frau Eggli, oder?"[3] She mumbled, "Nein, das bin i nöd!"[4] and she slammed the door. No is no. Maybe she was switched at birth. And from time to time something fell from above.

Before this the interpreter had lived in another building, and not alone, with his wife and son. And it came to pass that his wife was now someone else's wife. This can happen in our empire, and in every other one, too. It's nothing special.

Over the telephone the interpreter asked his son each time, "How're you doing?"

And he always answered, "Fine."

For Christmas, when the interpreter called to find out whether he liked the present he'd sent, a young magician's set, his son said, "Everyone else only gets presents from one papa, but I get them from two! Isn't that great?"

"Yes, it is," the interpreter replied.

His son also sent him amusing letters from time to time with pictures included. One time he invented his own country and drew a map.

The interpreter pinned the map to his wall.

Question: So you say you're searching for a haven for your weary, wounded soul, which is exhausted from the humiliations and trials, from boors and poverty, from scoundrels and fools, and that everywhere you go you're threatened by the impending danger of becoming evil's toy and victim, as if an inescapable curse lay on your line, and on

---

3. Aren't you Mrs. Eggli? *(Ger.)*

4. No, that's not me! *(Swiss Ger.)*

everyone else, too, and how your grandmothers and grandfathers suffered, and how the current generation is suffering, too, and how the unborn are going to suffer to the seventh generation, and possibly even beyond. As substantial proofs you've shown your ticket from Romanshorn to Kreuzlingen, punched by the sleep-deprived conductor, a page torn from a school notebook with doodlings, and your body worn to holes. One thing at a time, though. You earned your living—after all, you have a family and an old mother on your neck, too, and an unmarried sister—by working as a bodyguard for a high-flying journalist, a smart guy, really wicked, who anchored a killer TV show that mortals adored because it brought them hope and a smidgeon of light to their hovels and palaces. God knows how, but said journalist got his hands on materials about the source of evil. Something to do with a needle. A needle hidden in an egg, that was in a drake, that was in a hare, that was in something else, and all of it in turn was stuffed into a briefcase. The fearless journalist planned to take out the contents publicly, live on the air, break off the needle's tip, and thus destroy evil. Not that the powerful of this world (evil, after all, always thinks it's good, and good, vice versa, evil) were asleep at the wheel. The daredevil read the anonymous threats he'd received out loud, in front of everyone, and immediately tore them to shreds, demonstrating his contempt for his invisible but omnipresent enemies. Then one day, in a wet snowfall, you said goodbye to him for the day, he got into his snow-covered car with his new wife—he'd divorced half a year before wipers swept aside this slushy mess—and you thought that you were seeing him for the last time. Actually, no one ever gave a rat's ass what you thought. They sat there, and while the car was warming up, they wanted to live a long and happy life and die on the exact same day at the exact same minute. She said, "To hell with the truth. There is no truth, Slavik, my beloved. I'm afraid for you and for me. Please, I beg of you, don't do this!" Before he could answer her, the car blew up. The investigation began working on the mistake theory: the bomb had been planted in the wrong automobile, and the agents studied data on the owners of all snow-whitened BMWs who had left their cars by Ostankino that slushy day, where living pyramids of snowflakes rose in parking places under every streetlight. They even searched for the briefcase with the truth, but they didn't find it. The deceased's former spouse, insulted and crushed in her feminine nature, had tried to forget the man who had betrayed her love while he had still been alive, but from time to time she called him and just listened. Oh, how alike all lonely discarded women are, stifling their rage as they breathe heavily into the receiver! For fear of going mad, she went to see a psychotherapist and sobbed for two hours straight. They'd lived together for years, after all. Waiting for her to finish, the psychotherapist, who had a glass eye, which he often covered with his hand, suggested she picture her past happy life as a video she'd seen and said she needed to relax, close her eyes, view the tape once more quickly, at fast-forward, so that everyone looked funny mincing along and kissing as if they were pecking each other with their nose and made love with the briskness of hamsters, and then pull the tape out of the player and throw it down the rubbish chute. "Our building doesn't have a rubbish chute," the woman replied. Finally, when she learned what had happened, she commenced to bellowing, but in a completely different way. Now she could allow herself to think about how he'd loved her, remember the good, and take pleasure in those memories. Now these were god-sent tears that washed her soul and brought relief. After all, when he'd been alive, if she'd thought of him at all, she thought of him only in the past tense, as if he'd died. Now that he had, and for real, she didn't have to pretend anymore. One day, returning to her empty apartment, she sensed that someone had been in the room in her absence. Nothing was out of place, but she was gripped by a strange burning sensation. Her feet ached from exhaustion, she lay down and suddenly smelled something on her pillow—his cologne. So he'd come. That made sense. The soul of a murdered man is reluctant to quit this world because the woman who loves him is still there and she needs his protection. We so want to believe that the people we care about but who have quit this life are not lost to us forever, that they're nearby and in a difficult moment can come to our aid. Much has been written about the relativity of death, when all of a sudden it becomes clear that the dead man is alive—as is everyone ever killed or dead. After all, the grass's roots live on, oblivious to the fact that someone has already eaten it. Another time, coming home she saw in her grandmother's half-blind mirror, which was covered with old-age spots, a sweeping inscription in red lipstick done in his hand. The deceased said that his murderer was—you. That made sense, too, basically. Opportunity knocked. No surprise the bodyguard was hired for the murder. That's obviously the simpler, surer way. But you ended up between a rock and a hard place. It's hard to agree but not so easy to refuse. Say what you like, but you came in handy. Sure, the dead can be wrong, too, but you get the picture. Now the investigation took a new turn, and you were charged with the journalist's murder. You had to go into hiding. The story took on a life of its own, and now, to clear yourself, you had to find the real murderer, or even better, the vanished truth. It was getting to be a regular detective novel. Meanwhile, the dead man's ex-wife went to see a clairvoyant, who had just finished with a woman who'd asked her to lift a curse from her family. In a single year she'd had her husband die an untimely death, her daughter, son-in-law, and granddaughter perished in an auto wreck, her grandson, now an orphan, had been seriously ill since birth, and there'd also been a fire in her apartment. The seer's room smelled of smoked tar, and outside, a beetle's gnawed writings were hidden in an old tree, under the bark, writings describing his beetle-ish life that no one would ever read. The clairvoyant took the agreed-upon fee in an envelope and counted the money, and when she asked how to get in touch with her husband, who was both gone and there at the same time, gave her the address of an Internet chat room where he would come to her online at first star light. At the appointed time, there was a single visitor to the chat room. Him. She kept jabbing her finger. All she wanted to know was: "My beloved, why did you leave me?" He answered her about some locker number in left luggage at the Belorussky train station, but she went on and on: "I just want to know. Why?" Let us leave them to themselves, though, and take a look at what was happening at that time with you. You couldn't go home, where an ambush was doubtless lying in wait. You were afraid they might do something to your wife and son, although the child, who wasn't yours, was already grown, but for

34

love and plot development that doesn't matter. So you went to see your army friend who never got his fill of toy soldiers as a kid and had assembled a tin panorama of the Battle of Waterloo. Army friendship, you decided, was sacred. People who were once together and fairly close, meeting after many years, seek out that lost intimacy, although they've become completely different people. You might compare it to the water that was in a vase and later turned into steam or rain. You told him your story while your friend smoked, and the smoke streams from his nostrils struck his plate of macaroni. He realized it was a losing proposition and that he might have to die helping you, but this was exactly what got him so stirred up. Dostoevsky, I think it was, said that sacrificing your life might be the easiest sacrifice of all. The next day your friend put on his striped vest and went to see the journalist's former wife, in order to make contact, through her, with the dead man's spirit and tease out the secret of the missing briefcase. Hearing shots, workers at the laundry across the street called the police, but the on-duty squad got stuck in traffic and so arrived only when rush hour was over, and they detained the noble daredevil after surreptitiously planting silver spoons in his pocket during a desperate struggle, although he tried to vindicate himself, saying he had found the woman's dead body on the bed in the room, sniffing the pillow. She was dead—shot through the heart. He had rushed to her to see whether he could bring her around, and that was how her blood ended up on him. That was when he took the revolver out of her hand. It had been put there by someone to make it look like suicide, and the gun went off, shooting her in the leg, because the safety was off, and your friend didn't know how to use a firearm. This was by way of explaining her blood on him, the powder residue, and his fingerprints on the gun. But that didn't matter. What mattered was that your faithful comrade was able to read on the screen of the computer, which had been left on, and tell you over the phone, before his arrest, the code and locker number at the train station, where you finally got the ill-starred case. The arrest of an utterly innocent man, who got into trouble because of you, merely lent the action a certain tension and drama. Now you were walking down the street with the evil in the case and thinking about what you should do. Everyone turned around at the sound of glass clinking and grinding—it was an old woman pulling a sled over the asphalt with a bassinet full of empty bottles. On the square the young mamas with strollers were discussing the best way to wean, and one was telling how her mother, when she was breastfeeding her younger child, rubbed her nipples with mustard, and her son, who had already begun to talk, squirmed and said, "Titty poo-poo!" If the child nurses for a long time, he'll be late learning to talk and won't enunciate well. The pensioner who had been looking out the window at them went into the kitchen, tore off the calendar page, and sighed: tomorrow Pushkin would be killed. By midday the snow had become mealy, spongy, and the drifts had been eaten away as if by locusts, and under the elderberry the pimply crust had melted around the edges. Near the restaurant entrance an African in livery did a little jig, rejoicing at the sun and flashing his gold buttons; he'd probably come here at one time to study. In the kindergarten, when the children sat on the potties, the nanny opened the window to increase colds and reduce attendance. A crooked poster in the candy shop window: "You were slime yesterday, you'll be ashes tomorrow." Lion cubs nursed by a dog frolicked in the zoo. At the beauty salon the hairdresser hiccuped after dinner, thinking about how she would practice her guitar again that evening—she'd put foam rubber under the strings to dampen the chords. Across the street, at the art school, a life model was posing with a sock on his phallus; he didn't have the special little lace-up pouch. The cross on the church's crown was secured with chains, so it wouldn't fly away. The service was over, and women in scarves had roped off the passage to the altar and were washing the trampled floor and grumbling. The beggar on the parvis knew it was bad to give to anyone who was bald, so he always wore a cap. At the home for disabled children, the instructor was shaking out the mattresses in the girls' bedroom, digging around in the beds, and rummaging in the cubbies in search of contraband mascara, but the cherished box was hanging out the window, wound round by string. In the market they were selling half-sours in aquariums. An unshaven native of the Caucasus was wiping his apples with a dirty rag. At school they were covering Gogol. The young teacher was explaining that the nose's flight was a flight from death, and his return was a return to the natural order of life and death. Lovers were taking a bus to go conceive a child. They were pressed up close in the crush, doing a little jig on the back platform along with all the other passengers. Later, at home, coming to a stand-still with the fragrant coffee grinder in her hands, she would think, "Lord, how simple it is to be happy!" while he opened a can of sardines, winding the lid around the key as if he were winding the world up like a clock. And it was someone else who had to unload the sides of beef hanging on hooks and sparking rime in the refrigerator car, where the frost fogged and a hazy, shining rim flickered around the light bulb. No one in town knew the secret anymore of the cavalry guard's white leg chamois—you had to put them on wet and dry them on your naked body. In despair, you went to a well-known philanthropist and human rights activist—let's call him Wynd—signed up for an appointment, and sat in the waiting room, drumming your fingers on the case's artificial leather. Wynd was the only person in the whole windy world who could help you get the truth out and punish the evil that was triumphing outside. After all, someone had to break off the tip of evil on a live broadcast! Lots of people probably thought that way because the waiting room was filled with refugees from Central Asia wearing torn and faded robes. It was an old mansion that a certain oil bank had coveted for a long time. The ceilings were decorated with antique molding, and no one was surprised anymore that Apollo, the god of the arts, had killed all Niobe's children one after the other and then turned her to stone, thereby putting an end to the mother's sufferings. But you waited in vain. Wynd had mysteriously vanished from his office, and his body was found in the neighbor's garden, hanging from a branch. There you have it, the mystery of the closed room so beloved by all. So what if the press came out with wimpy conjectures about mysticism and unknown otherworldly forces? It all turned out to be very simple. Three tramps, former tank crew, outraged at the realm's humiliation, had decided to take their revenge on liberals. They were remembered by specific traits: their rotten teeth shone in the darkness. They also liked to recall how piles of bananas were dumped on Leningrad in early

1938. And one of them said that if he knew there was no death, that you didn't die but simply "shifted" to some other life, that is, you died but not really, for pretend, then all this was unworthy. You had to die with dignity, like a man, in earnest, knowing that death existed. But here's what happened. One fired an old dueling pistol as he was walking down the street after noticing Wynd standing there by the open window, thinking, for some reason, about Turgenev's boots, which he had seen years ago in a museum. The boots had stood behind glass, dried up and dead, and he could not believe they had ever been alive and smelled of feet and leather and that after the hunt, oats had been sprinkled in them to draw out the damp, and they had been carried outdoors to air out and then smeared with tar. At the shot Wynd looked out. The second tank tramp dropped a noose over him from the upper floor, jerked the old man up, and then flung him into the other window which looked out on the park, which was saturated with ripe evening light, and signed, like a verdict, with the flourish of a swift. The third accomplice hooked him on to a tree. It grew dark quickly. You headed for the train to Podlipki, where your aging mama and your sister, a literature teacher, lived. At the station they kept announcing over the loud-speaker that life was a drawn bow and death was the flight of the released arrow. On the train—heated, stuffy, and sweaty—you hugged the briefcase and imagined your mama and sister right then sitting at the table, drinking tea, eating pancakes with pot cheese, and watching the news. They had just shown a bus with hostages in Nazran flying into the air and the human bits soaring, skillfully shot in slow motion, like scraps of red snow. The whole train was reading detective novels. Which

39

was understandable. A detective novel assumes that before the crime was committed, before the first corpse
showed up, there was a primordial harmony in the world.
Then this was violated and the detective not only found
the murderer but also restored order to the world. This
was the ancient function of the cultural hero. He waded
through the uncertainty. Yet it was also clear where good
was and where evil, because good always won out and
there was no getting it wrong. If it won out, that meant
it was good. Basically they were reading because it was
scary to squeak through life like a mosquito, somewhere
in the darkness, unseen and unheard. A detective novel
was the same kind of horror as in the newspapers, the
only difference being that it ended well. It simply couldn't
end any other way. First came the sufferings, fears, worries, tears, and losses, and in the end it was all behind
you. Like in the fairy tale: a beast from the netherworld
seizes the island and rules the people, who are imperfectly drawn, imperfectly written. He gnaws off their
heads. They're afraid but alive. Somehow they have to
live. Then a hero shows up, brimming with valor and
oriental wisdom, and he gives the beast a boot in the
balls. As to newspapers, better not to open them at all.
It's not the news, it's a report of especially dangerous
crimes that chill the soul and blow on the weathervane
of public opinion: according to the latest surveys, everyone is again demanding the introduction of, first, public
executions for the rape of their daughters and sons and,
second, Sharia law, in order to chop off thieves' hands:
the next time they get the urge to steal something, they
won't have anything to do it with. Sitting next to you
was an ugly young woman with hair growing everywhere it shouldn't, dying at night for want of love, and

reading about a Jewish sect called the Sadducees. Squinting, you ran your eyes over the lines, which said that the Sadducees asserted that in the future there would be neither eternal bliss for the righteous nor eternal torment for the impious. They rejected the existence of angels and evil spirits, as well as the future resurrection of the dead. "I guess that means we're Sadducees," you sighed. The commuter train was pulling into Podlipki. Out the window, half of a dog some little boys had tied to the rails flashed by on the embankment. You could take a bus from the station, but you decided to proceed on foot and get a little air. As you approached the five-story apartment building, you greeted the babushkas on the bench and thought, You're about to get killed, and they're going to be discussing the funeral details, just like you'd expect—what kind of coffin and how loudly the widow wept. You walked through the front door, and instead of dashing up the stairs as usual, to keep from breathing in the smells seeping from the corners, you began climbing the stairs slowly, cautiously, listening closely, peering into the darkness, and crushing the empty syringes. And you stopped. Upstairs, on the next flight, someone was standing there and talking quietly, and when you stopped, the conversation broke off. The clank of a jerked bolt. You realized this was for you, and at this the description of nature began. It was a quiet summer morning. Though the sun had risen fairly high in the clear sky, the fields still glittered with dew. A fragrant freshness blew in from the recently awakened valleys, and in the forest, still damp and noiseless, the early birds were singing their cheery songs. In the millpond, sky-striders ran over the clouds' reflections. A storm-battered aspen, the color of slate. A glassy halo around a dragonfly stuck to a sunbeam. Ticks swarming in the oak's crown. An elm turned bronze. The wind parting the spruce's hair. According to Dante, the forest was made of sinners turned into trees. The dried meadow crunched underfoot. Your ears were blocked by the squawk of grasshoppers. The stream was creeping along, infantry-fashion, and dragging the algae by the hair. It never occurs to anyone to name the sky, although it too, like the oceans, has its straits and seas, trenches and sandbars. The bolt's clank turned out to be the sound of a tossed empty beer can. The conversation on the staircase resumed, and someone picked up his story about his dog with the human eyes. The dog and its owner were on the same wavelength. The dog seemed like a person to him, except with fur and paws. But when the dog had puppies, something happened to it. One time he came home and saw the dog had bitten off its puppies' heads. Something in nature was out of kilter. This couldn't, shouldn't be. He was forced to shoot the dog. "Made it through that one." You heaved a sigh of relief and climbed upstairs. You opened the door with your key and took a step back at the spectacle that unfolded before you, gripped by horror and consternation. As the investigation later established, since three in the morning the peaceful sleep of the block's inhabitants had been disturbed by terrific shrieks, but frightened by the times, which were evil and brigandish, the neighbors had kept mum. The apartment was in the wildest disorder—the furniture broken and thrown about in all directions. On a chair lay a razor, smeared with blood. On the hearth were two or three long and thick tresses of grey human hair, also dabbled in blood, and seeming to have been pulled out by the roots. Upon the floor were found four

Napoleons, a topaz earring, and two bags, containing the old jubilee rubles, which all the vending machines here accept for the five-franc William Tell. By the window was a smashed three-liter jar of mash made from mushrooms that had dried and shriveled. Of your mother and sister no traces were seen; but an unusual quantity of soot being observed in the fire-place, a search was made in the chimney, and (horrible to relate!) the corpse of the daughter, head downward, was dragged therefrom, it having been thus forced up the narrow aperture for a considerable distance. The body was quite warm. Upon examining it, many excoriations were perceived, no doubt occasioned by the violence with which it had been thrust up and disengaged. Upon the face were many severe scratches, and, upon the throat, dark bruises, and deep indentations of finger nails, as if the deceased had been throttled to death. Most interesting, moreover, was that your sister was discovered in a room locked from the inside, and the windows were latched shut. The mystery of the closed room again! Let's see how you squirm out of it this time. After a thorough investigation of every portion of the house, without further discovery, the party made its way into a small paved yard in the rear of the building, where the garbage that rotted slightly spread a foul smell when it thawed, lay the corpse of the old lady, with her throat so entirely cut that, upon an attempt to raise her, the head fell off. The body, as well as the head, was fearfully mutilated—the former so much so as scarcely to retain any semblance of humanity. Traces had been left everywhere in the room: the uneaten remains of cheese blinchiks, which the murderers had tasted, which meant they had left saliva, lipstick-stained butts, a burned match with a charred tip in the ashtray, glasses with fingerprints, tracks from a size forty-five right boot, which led to thoughts of the scoundrels' one-leggedness, but the investigators did not find any evidence or clues, and the press release read at the briefing asserted that the murderer was a gigantic Ourang-Outang, which climbed out the window—which closed of its own accord when the beast fled. I am skipping ahead in the interest of brevity—after all it's mealtime soon, and my stomach is growling already—but we are only at the very beginning, which is why the description of the murders of people about whom we know virtually nothing does not give rise to any particular grief, anger, or burning protest. We'll all be goggle-eyed when we turn our toes up, so I'm skipping, I repeat, the further misadventures of the briefcase, the encoded letter, the twins alike as two drops of water, the secret passages, and the window broken from the outside, if the shards are inside, and from the inside if out, and although the dog that did not bark when it should have leads you to think that it knew the murderer, we will move on to your closing statements, the final chase, where the rather unsophisticated storyline reaches its apogee. You were running with the case that all the fuss was about, through a field, rosy buckwheat, blue flax, but right there you got confused and later made corrections to the transcript, you allegedly remembered the dusty road through the strawberry field. After the hot day it smelled keenly of berries. They were in hot pursuit. On the one hand, law enforcement agencies; on the other, the Mafia, which as you realized, were one and the same, and there before you was a river filled with reflections from above, but with time on the inside, filling it to the brim. An upturned stump went into the water up to its waist and let a cabbage white butterfly perch on its proffered elbow. Behind the bushes, a boy was fishing. He cast his hook, the long rod's flexing tip ripping the air. The bait smacked the river and circles rippled through time. A ping-pong ball bounced, surfacing gradually, deliberately. Somewhere downstream you could hear a wolf howling, a goat bleating, an oarlock creaking. There were mosquito thickets by the shore. A spider was catching a chill in its net and laying it up for the fall. You touched the spider with your finger, and it climbed skyward over its web. Majestic clouds had come to a halt above the river, where summer people were dragging sacks of cabbages from the field, having taken in with their mother's milk the saying: You're only a thief if you get caught. Someone had rigged a piano lid for a fence. A hose was coiled in its shadow, heavy from the water it held. There was a couple in the sand on the opposite shore. From far away you couldn't tell what was going on there, a kiss or artificial respiration, but there was no time to ponder that because the spetsnaz was behind and you could hear them shouting, "The Lord knows where he leads us, but we shall find out at the end of our journey!" The leather throats were chanting: "It's not so terrible for life to end, but if life doesn't start up again, that's bad!" You removed your boots to make the swimming easier, lowered your foot into the black water, and it went immediately up to your knee. Stalks crept slickly under your soles, bubbles took off and burst, and it stank of decay. You stepped on your other foot—and a little white ball started rocking on the circles and hopping just as it reached you. You jumped in and started swimming, but the shore, that had seemed just a couple of strokes away, started playing keep-away with you. You swam for a long time, but it was still those same couple of strokes away. You were nearly to your breaking point because you had to stroke with one hand while the case was dragging you to the bottom. Floundering, you swallowed a mouthful of water and a watery ceiling closed overhead. You opened your eyes: a yellow wall with a sprig of algae and the sun's circle through the radiant turbidity. You struggled until you suddenly felt an incredible lightness. You were care-free, delighted. All of a sudden you thought, "Why was I struggling if this is so easy and marvelous!" You were saved by Captain Nemo in his *Nautilus* and put to shore at Romanshorn. There you bought this ticket here and boarded the train for Kreuzlingen. Seating yourself by the window so you'd have a view of Lake Bodensee, you started checking how much money there was in your wallet, and you came across your son's drawing, the very same doodle he'd drawn for your birthday, and you had carried that scrap around with you ever since, and out the window stretched bare trees leaning to the right, like letters written in a woman's hand, and you realized that this was your wife writing you a letter saying she loved you and was waiting for you. You fell asleep, but then you had to get off. You jumped out on the platform and suddenly realized you'd left your briefcase, as well as all the documents attesting to your identity, but it was too late. The train was gone. That's the straight goods?

Answer: Yes. I think so. I don't know. Maybe I got something mixed up. You have to forgive me, I'm upset.

Question: Just calm down. It's all behind you now. Do you want some water? I realize you're having a hard time of it right now.

Answer: Thank you! Word of honor, I tried to tell you every-thing the way it was, and you see what came of it.

46

Question: It's nothing terrible. Everyone tells his story the best he can.

Answer: I didn't make anything up. That's how it all was. Do you believe me?

Question: It makes no difference whether I do or don't.

Answer: Maybe you thought it was over the top, well, the part about the fireplace or the clouds and the stolen cabbages, but that's all how it was, the way I told it, why should I make anything up?

Question: Don't take it so hard! People tell all kinds of stories here. It's all fine. And the fact that it sounds like a detective novel, well, you yourself said you just hope it all ends well. That's all there is to it.

Answer: Yes, that's all there is to it. Exactly. You want so badly for it all to end well. Tell me, will it?

Question: Listen, you're a grown man. You're graying at the temples. You've lived some. Do you really not understand that what you told me is ultimately irrelevant to our decision?

Answer: Irrelevant how? Why? What is relevant then?

Question: Well, it's all irrelevant. What difference does it make who dragged a cabbage from the field or where the case went missing? It just did. You don't really believe, in fact, in the drake, the hare, and some rusty pin, do you?

Answer: No, of course not.

Question: There, you see?

Answer: But what is relevant?

Question: Tell me, the part about the doodle and the trees on the shore like cursive handwriting, is that true?

Answer: Yes.

Question: Do you love her?

Answer: What, is this necessary for your report?

Question: What naïve people they are when it comes right down to it! They arrive thinking someone needs them. Here they are pushing and swarming so, you can't question them all. And who needs you? The main thing is they believe in this foolishness. One, kind of like you, he even looks a little like you, gray hair, shabby, scruffy, with the same faded, washed out eyes, tried to assure me he'd read somewhere, in some free newspaper, that we had all in fact already lived once in the past and then died. And here they were resurrecting us at this very trial, and we had to account for how we'd lived. That is, our life was the story itself because not only did you have to tell it in detail, you also had to make it understandable. You see, each coin jangling in your pocket was relevant, each word swallowed by the wind, each silence. It was like an investigative experiment that restored the sequence of events. I was standing right here, in the kitchen, next to the rimed window, looking through a hole in the frost, while someone in the yard was scraping off the snow that had accumulated on their car overnight with a yellow plastic dustpan, and she came out of the bathroom wrapped in her robe with her wet hair wound in a towel, turned on the hairdryer, unwound the towel, and started drying her hair, combing it with her fingers, and I asked, "Do you want a child from me?" She asked me to repeat myself: "What? I can't hear a thing!" And he had to show how he stood by the window, felt the glass on his skin, heard the sound of the hairdryer, saw her tangled wet hair and her fingers pushing through it, and to imagine that yellow dustpan in the snow. At this trial no one was in any hurry, since everything had to be carefully sorted out, and therefore a night took an entire night to show and a life an entire life. So they reconstruct everything the way it was, without rushing:

today, cirrus clouds; tomorrow, cumulus. The smells and sounds—to a T. And you show how a pebble landed in your kasha and you broke a tooth—here it is, the yellow chip. Or how he determined from the vomit on the subway car floor that the person had been eating vermicelli, which stank. How he fell in love while he was asleep and woke up before dawn happy. There, do you hear the janitor scraping the asphalt?

Answer: But this was in the yard, look, a freezing African was scraping the snow into a pile with an iron shovel! While over there the little Indians were having a snowball fight!

Question: There he goes again, really, this is all the real deal, even the sounds. In short, everything everywhere is this story. You can't hide anything. Here's how I was born, here's how I lived all those years, here's how I died. But it's all nonsense. In fact, that's not how it was at all. You can't be so naïve as to think that someone is going to agree to listen to you your whole life! Actually, excuse me, I lost my temper, I got sidetracked.

Answer: You mean nothing's going to come of it?

Question: You know yourself, it's easier for a camel to pass through the eye of a needle.

Answer: That's it? Can I go?

Question: Wait a minute! Sit down.

Answer: But still I see what interesting work you have. Just like an investigator. What, where, and why. Spill it, this second. Like it or not, make your case.

Question: I wish I had something to make it out of. The investigator has a body, an ax, clues, eyewitnesses, and identification. Up until the last moment you still have no idea who put the poison fish in the pool. A riddle! A mystery! What's the mystery here?

Answer: What do you mean, what's the mystery? What about us? We once lived somehow and now we've come here. Aren't we the mystery?

Question: The only mystery is that you came into this world at all. Everyone is amazed by immaculate conception, and no one believes in it, but a sinful one doesn't surprise anyone. Now here's a mystery: everything has already been, but you haven't yet, and here you are. And afterward, once again, you'll never be. Everything else is known.

Answer: What's known?

Question: Everything. What was and will be.

Answer: But who knows it?

Question: How can I make this easier for you . . . Imagine you get invited to Indian Island. And you're pleased. You're expecting something good, otherwise why invite you at all? You're on your way there and dreaming of love. The woman who happens to be sitting across from you by the window has skin the color of an immature July ash berry, but you feel awkward staring straight at her, and you turn away and look out the window the whole time, while there the evening sky also shines the color of an immature ash berry. It's the sunset driving its color to match her skin. Later, at the shore, the sea seems soapy and the air littered with the cries of seagulls. Wagtails run along the very edge, their little legs mincing. A smelly sort of scum washes to shore. A small pier. The waves beat against its legs, throws grape-like spray on you. Seagulls are perched on the iron railings. The birds are blown up by the wind—one rises for a second and settles back down—and they chirp drearily. Sea and sky run together, like a sweating window, and then the horizon suddenly appears once again, as if it had been drawn with a sharpened pencil and ruler. And here you arrive and there in your room, on the wall, is a counting rhyme. And it's all written there. About the little Indians having a snowball fight outside, and about you. Because you're a little Indian, you go out to sea, you drown, and Captain Nemo rescues you. He brings you back to his wheelhouse, lets you turn all the levers and wheels, push all the shafts, bolts, valves, and buttons, explains what's for what, and puts his sweat-stained, salt-logged captain's cap on your curly head. Do you understand what I'm talking about?

Answer: I'm not a child. It's all about the counting rhyme. But I didn't figure that out until later.

Question: And then, all the stories have already been told a hundred times. But you—this is your story.

Answer: What kind of story?

Question: Oh, any kind. Some simple, banally sentimental story always goes well, you know, there was a princess and she became Cinderella.

Answer: I became Cinderella?

Question: That's just a manner of speaking. A metaphor!

Answer: Then you should have said so right away, otherwise I'm some kind of Cinderella.

Question: Fine then, you don't like Cinderella, let's do something different. Some unpretentious little device working to increase the tension and acuity of situations, like one against all, one good man among all bad. A knight roaming the subway, fighter for justice, defender of the downtrodden, consoler of orphans, and even more of widows, and he himself unjustly persecuted and suffering for what someone else did. It's tawdry, but it never fails. People invariably sympathize with that combination of good and fists. They thirst for his victory with all their heart.

Answer: And now you're going to tell me how you've made a knight of me . . .

Question: So what? You dreamed of being a fearless truth seeker since you were a boy! You wanted to grow up and be a detective, fight criminals, punish evil. Or go into the taiga like a Robin Hood and rob tourists of their ill-gotten gains—since no one ever got anything justly—and give it all to an orphanage. Or like that Captain Nemo guiding his submarine on a ram attack, to drown the bad and save the good!

Answer: I don't remember anymore. Well, I did dream.

Question: But you do remember sitting next to a pit, or a quarry, or a ravine, and all of a sudden a child started crying. You rushed over—and it was a kitten.

Answer: Yes, my buddies and I were sitting by the fire. There was a big dump there. People carted stuff in from all over town. You take a broken record and fling it into the air. Or ripped hot water bottles—rubber makes great slingshots. Burned out lamps explode like grenades. There we were sitting by the fire, and the older guys were talking about reform school. A scary place to end up, and there we were listening about what you could and couldn't do there. For instance, if you didn't have anything to smoke in a holding cell but you wanted to, what did you do? So they stripped the bark from broom-birch branches and dried it. But to light up—there weren't any matches— they took some stuffing out of a mattress or pillow, put it on the lamp, and waited for it to start smoldering. But that's hearts and flowers compared to the scary things I remember I heard about "registration." That's when they beat you with a wet towel that has dominos tied up inside it. And you can't scream. And then the main ordeal, a kind of game: Who do you want to be? You can choose:

pilot or tankist. If you choose pilot, you climb up, take a leap, and go flying headfirst. You were the one who said pilot. And you have no choice. You said pilot, and that means you have to answer for your words. No one there says a word lightly. You want to be a tankist? Then smash your head into the steel door, like a battering ram. And you can't take back what you said or they'll defile you right away. But if you run right out of the box, that means you're one of them and at the last second they can slip a pillow in. And you have to go through that, and not be scared, and run head first at the steel door.

Question: You were in Afghanistan, right?

Answer: Where did you come up with that?

Question: By deduction. Like Sherlock Holmes. Dr. Watson comes to see him, and Holmes immediately picks up on the fact that he's come straight from Afghanistan. From a drop of water, a logician could infer the possibility of an Atlantic or a Niagara without having seen or heard of one or the other. By a man's finger-nails, by his coat-sleeve, by his boots, by his the crease in his trousers, by the calluses on his forefinger and thumb, by his expression, by his shirt cuffs—by each of these things a man's calling is plainly revealed. He was also wounded in the left arm by an antediluvian rifle. The grandson loaded it, and the grandfather fired. That is elementary. But this is simply the laws of the genre. First Afghanistan, then the harsh day in-day out of peacetime: the fight against evil, injustice, and corruption. Unjustly condemned. Then you lost your way, were broken, became a killer. A lost generation, little lead boys. The heroes and victims of someone else's war. You said to them, How can that be? I'm a veteran! I shed my blood! And they replied, We didn't send you there.

Answer: Humph!

Question: That humph was made a-purpose, the djinn told the camel that could not crawl through the eye of the needle and ran down the tracks away from your father. Think about when they were transporting you on the train. The military echelon had been on the move for a long time, through the heat, and when you saw your first camel you suddenly thought of your father. He was an engineer, and he used to tell you how early one morning he was driving a train across the steppe in Central Asia and saw camels up ahead, right on the tracks, and they were licking the dew from the tracks. Your father blew the whistle and they ran off helter-skelter, but one ran down the rail bed instead, away from the train. The train couldn't stop and your father ran over it. Remember?

Answer: Yes, but how do you know that?

Question: How do I know? The camel told me so. The very one. He couldn't climb through the needle's eye and there he was running down the tracks away from your father.

Answer: But that has nothing to do with you. My father. That camel.

Question: If you don't want it to, fine. No need. So be it. But do you really not see that, other than me, no one in or out of the world is interested in your father or that camel? Well, go on, now you're going to tell me about the third toast.

Answer: What does the third toast have to do with this?

Question: Come on now, for those who died. Now you're going to tell me that just as you were getting ready to drink a third toast to the dead, shots rang out. You looked through your night vision goggles to see who was shooting, and it's that same grandfather and grandson who that morning brought you a melon and you gave cans of food.

The grandfather's shooting and the little kid is loading for him—the same rifle that wounded Dr. Watson. But it's only there, where you live, that you're heroes and victims. Here you're invaders and murderers. And it's not someone else's war, it's yours.

Answer: That's not true. Nothing there was mine. From the very first. When we arrived it was winter, absolutely no snow, the wind chilled me to the bone, we're wearing quilted jackets and we're still freezing—and they're walking around barefoot. That was the first time I saw people selling wood by the kilo. Weighing and arguing. The houses in the kishlaks are practically made of sand. The peasants wear torn robes, there are no women at all, and squatting around the dukans are either beggars or the stalls' owners. But you can't imagine what was on the shelves: Japanese tape recorders, televisions, watches of every stripe, and French perfume. At first there wasn't any particular hostility. Everything was just foreign. I remember feeling uneasy when I saw a peasant singing something plaintive while plowing with bulls, a tape recorder swinging on its horns. Only later do you realize it's all wrong: the boys aren't boys and the peasants aren't peasants. A gang of barefoot kids runs after an APC: "*Shuravi, bakshish,* give!" At first we would toss them a can of stewed meat or condensed milk. Then we saw our first dead: a boy of about twelve with nine notches on his submachine gun—that meant nine of our guys. And then, when guys I'd had time to make friends with started buying it, that's when it started. I was dying for revenge. Especially for our guys who got captured, for what they did to them. And I was terrified of getting captured myself. The guys we captured looked absolutely thrilled that they were going to die soon. I remember the

first well. He's sitting, dirty face, wounded, hands tied
behind his back with barbed wire, and is totally unafraid.
He's all submission to fate. Aloof and calm. This cast a
real chill over us. So we would explode. Either someone would kick him with his boot, or hit him with his
rifle butt, and it was contagious—the others caught it.
Then we saw that they only died calmly, with dignity,
from bullets, while they lived in sheer panic of a bloodless death—drowning, strangulation, or hanging. So
we would put them under the wheels, or drown them,
which is exactly what they were afraid of. Right away
they'd start wailing, shouting something, struggling. But
this just provoked us. We would twist his arms and put
him in a swallow—that's when you tie him from behind
with his turban so he can't move his arms or legs. You're
living in a state of such constant tension you have to
find some release. When we weren't on a mission we
lived in temporary units, and every day you had to play
some trick on the unit next door. One time we smeared
their ceiling with condensed milk. There were so many
flies . . . They balanced a wash bucket overhead near the
door. Open the door and it pours all over you. Or you
test their reactions: you paint a training grenade green
and toss it into someone else's room to see who reacts
how. Hilarious! One guy covers up with a sheet, another
with a newspaper. You can't get by there without prac-
tical jokes. Because at night you get up and you don't
know where you're going. One time at night we blocked
a gorge and were waiting for something. Here came a
caravan with laden asses. We opened fire on them. But
it was the residents of the kishlak taking their apples to
market. They were warned about the curfew, but they
went anyway. They wanted to get to the bazaar as early

as possible. So we walked up and saw the scattered apples, ripe and handsome, and it was so irritating that civilians were lying there, that it was a mistake. None of us even picked up those apples. No one took a single apple. We just left them lying there.

Question: They all rotted a long time ago, those apples, and there's nothing left of them!

Answer: I know. But it's there they rotted. Here they were lying on the stones as if lit up from the inside.

Question: Where here?

Answer: You were the one who said we've all landed on Indian Island. It's where we aren't that things have form. Here they have essence. Didn't I understand you correctly? There, in that mountain valley, the apples have rotted, but here, on this island, they can't. Nothing happens to them. They'll keep on lying like that.

Question: And you'd realized that good and evil were this one werewolf? Right?

Answer: No. Not yet. I hadn't realized anything then. All I'd realized was that there was someone leading you who could save you, like a sign or a talisman. In the army there used to be a custom of putting on clean underwear before battle, but now it's the exact opposite. You don't wash, shave, or change your underwear before battles. Otherwise you'll get killed. There are these prohibitions about what you shouldn't do to cheat death. It's as if you're bargaining with it: I won't do this, and in exchange you won't touch me today. If an injured man who's nearly unconscious, when his mind's fuzzy, if he puts his hand here, between his legs, and touches it—that means he's going to die. Under no circumstances should he do that. You have to hold his hands so he doesn't. You shouldn't wear a dead man's things or take his place.

You shouldn't show on yourself where someone else was wounded. And each man there had his own personal talisman or rule, and all that had to be kept secret. I for one never took anything from the dead, not even a watch. And I noticed that as soon as someone else broke my rule, he died. But later I realized it was all nonsense. Whatever the counting rhyme has in store for someone, that's what's going to happen to him.

Question: And the little Indian lived to be demobbed and return to that place on the island where the sky was pale, trains tried to arrive in the morning, and the churches were stuffy and prayerful?

Answer: Sort of. The first few days it was all kind of bizarre. You walk down the street, forget yourself, and check out the roofs. A car backfires and you nearly fling yourself down on the grass. Peacetime started. And everything was out of whack. I was dying to set everything to rights. Everyone started getting whatever jobs they could and making money. I got all kinds of offers. But I was proud—proud, honest, and naïve. For a while I worked in the market as a guard. Then I realized I couldn't go on like that. There was a hell of a lot of scum around. I realized they needed cleaning up.

Question: So peacetime started, becoming a battlefield between light and dark, like they told you when you were hired. At first you thought you weren't the only one, that there were lots like that, an order of light bearers, knights, battling the beast of gloom with your flashlights. But just try to deal with it if the dark is so dark you can't see anything. The bogeyman was everywhere you turned. You even had an emblem on your sleeve depicting a little Indian, and the light from his flash pierced the monster's maw like a spear, lighting up his tonsils. In short, the little Indian went and became a cop. Right?

Answer: Why ask if you know everything?

Question: I know the counting rhyme. But you tell your own story. In the counting rhyme the little Indian boys bought apartments from lonely old people and killed them. That was your first case. Remember?

Answer: And how. I thought I'd seen everything in Afghanistan, and this was plain murder in an ordinary apartment. We arrive and the stink is so bad there's no airing it out. The soured potato on the plate has gray fuzz growing on it. A glass of kefir—the white walls are cracked. And an old woman is lying on the blood-spilled parquet floor wearing a flannel robe, pink panties, and ripped stockings. Her leg is bent unnaturally. Her green, wrinkle-covered face grimaced in pain. All of a sudden I felt the bile rise in my throat, forcing me to leave the apartment for a minute. I stood on the landing and smoked until I calmed down.

Question: On the way back, your high beams poked into the night's flocky, disheveled fog—after all, this was the fur of that beast—and the light bearers were discussing a newspaper article about whether or not you should help the terminally ill die. And you decided it was probably all for the best. After all, the old lush would have sold her apartment for a currant leaf and ended up on the street and frozen to death in the gutter. Tramps brought nothing but plague.

Answer: Not only that, she was living on the courtyard right next to mine. The next day, I had a day off, I went out to the pastry shop, I'm walking past the rubbish heap and I see they've taken her bed out into the courtyard and a bundle of her linen. Five minutes later I'm walking back and someone in slippers is already wrenching off the legs, and next to him a woman in curlers is giving him orders, but the linen bundle is gone.

Question: In short, after you went to work for the police, you turned your own life into a detective novel, and each day read like a freshly written page. In the morning at breakfast you glance at the counting rhyme to see what's on for today, and in the afternoon that's just what happens.

Answer: What detective novel! You're checking the counting rhyme, but outside it's drunks and domestic scandals. Or guttersnipes making a mess. The whole detective novel. Once, some boys decided they'd plan a train wreck, to take people's valuables, they later explained. So on a forest stretch they started unscrewing the bolts. They also got the idea of turning off the signals—they used wire cutters on the wire under the rails. But they just couldn't loosen the main butt screws. Then they went to the workshop of one of their fathers and brought a huge special key. That was when a trackman discovered them. I asked the boys, Didn't you feel sorry for the people? They snickered. And you say it's a detective novel.

Question: But you did arrest someone, right?

Answer: Yes. I remember my first arrest. We burst into an apartment at night, wake up the kids, they start screaming, the wife is scared out of her wits, in her robe, takes some pills, and the one who's the criminal, he's nervous, he goes to the closet in his pajamas to get dressed, and when he comes up to the rug slips out of his house shoes and then slips them back on when he comes off the rug.

Question: And the beast? Where was the beast? You wanted to fight a beast.

Answer: Where was the beast? You yourself said it, the beast was
              the fog. It came right up to the windows and rubbed its
              hide on the balcony grating. And we went out in it on a
              raid. They were demanding that we falsify records. After
              each raid you had to turn in reports. So everyone would
              see the raid hadn't been for nothing. But in fact there
              was nothing but fog. My partner taught me to draw up
              reports on the weekdays for all kinds of violations and
              leave the date off. So when there was a raid, you'd pull
              the reports out of the safe and add the right date. But
              that was only in the beginning. Later I ended up in a
              special group. Big Daddy took me in. That's what we
              called him.

Question: Was this a group involved in covering up major crimes?

Answer: Yes. But I didn't realize that right away.

Question: Tell me about Big Daddy.

Answer: What's there to tell? He came and went.

Question: Tell me because he liked you. He only had daughters,
              but he'd dreamed of a son. And here you were with your
              crosswise personality.

Answer: He just had this nickname. He was a father to everyone
              in the group. The department's walking legend—the old
              man even wrote a letter to the Turkish sultan and caught
              Grishka Otrepiev, the thief of Tushino. People used to say
              that once he rescued an old woman from an ice hole, but
              the old woman climbed back in. She belonged to some
              sect and believed that if someone was baptized again and
              climbed under the ice along a rope in winter, from one
              ice hole to the next, he would become a new person, and
              all his old sins would stay behind in his old life, while in
              his new one he'd be a newborn babe. So when I real-
              ized what was up, I started to look through Big Daddy's

closed cases in the archive. I looked and simply could not believe my eyes. I take a file and page through, and it's a put-up job, clear as day! Judge for yourself. A man's in handcuffs—and his head's been gnawed off. And it goes through as a suicide. Not only that, but in the photographs there are paw prints everywhere. It's him, the beast! He got away. I drove to the crime scene and there was a bloody trail. Right across the fresh snow. I follow the footprints, and the tracks lead straight across the streetcar rails to the House on the Square! That's where all the municipal offices are—police, court, mayor's office, savings bank, post office. That's what it's called, the House on the Square, where they drink powdered coffee and there's a powdered road out the window. And there the tracks go right to the steps. And everyone on the street saw those tracks. They're all witnesses. I ask them, Do you see that? They nod: You bet! The beast! I wrote a report, saying this and that and demanding the case be reopened for further investigation.

Question: Did you feel like a hero?

Answer: No. Well, maybe a little. It wasn't until later that I realized what I'd done. At the time it was even kind of exciting. As if I really had woken up to be the hero in some detective novel. All of a sudden getting up in the morning was interesting. This wasn't your usual beer stand raid! At the time I still believed that life should consist of events.

Question: Did they reopen the case?

Answer: Yes, but not right away. Big Daddy called me in. I'd never seen him so terrified. According to the counting rhyme a big bear was supposed to hug him. And here he was scared the jig was up.

Question: What did he say?

Answer: He said, "We eat beef, the cow eats grass, and the grass eats us."

Question: That's it?

Answer: No. He also said that if a rock possessed awareness it would think it fell to earth freely, but if it didn't think that it would fall anyway.

Question: But did he shout? Make threats?

Answer: No, he sat by the window, looked at the square, and talked as if I weren't there. He said, "Just yesterday I was helping my wife—we were shredding cabbage. But at night I couldn't get to sleep. I was lying with my eyes open, and the branches in the window were shredding the moon. And I kept thinking about you—because you're going to be lost." He sighed and then added, "Anatoly Batkovich, maybe I don't quite fit between my cap and boots either. But since you live here and now, you have to understand, you have to live like a river— flow without knowing you're going to freeze come winter. But then winter comes and the river freezes. Tolya, you have to live level with your times and not spill over its banks."

Question: What about you?

Answer: I said, "No, Pavel Efimich, you have to live level with yourself!"

Question: Why be like that with an old man? He was just wishing you well.

Answer: Oh, I know. I know. Right then he nearly broke down crying. "You've been like a son to me. Do you think I don't understand you? I was young, too, and wanted to solve crimes, terrible, inhuman crimes, guided by a sense of anger and justice. I too wanted to work with charred scraps of paper and ascertain who was where at that rainy moment when the mail carrier flashed by on her bicycle with a plastic bag on her head and determine who broke the branch off the old arbutus that blooms under the library window! You think I didn't want to make a sweep of all the scum, if not from the entire island then at least from our Tsarevokokshaisk, catch vipers, crush degenerates? But later it was explained to me in a way I could understand that my enthusiasm was superfluous. What difference did it make who the killer was? Who cared, since everyone understood that he was a mediocre, minor, insignificant person! If not Petrov, then Sidorov. Listen, Anatoly, I was a soldier in the desert, and we used to catch scorpions out of boredom. You catch them and throw them into a ring of fire. We morons wanted to see them commit suicide—a poisonous sting to the back of their own head. But you know, not one of them even thought of that. They all wanted to live to the very last—until they burned up. Get it?" But again I didn't get anything then. I told him, "I've seen blood, pain, and death. I've killed, the righteous and the guilty. Scare tactics don't work on me. So they kill me. On the other hand, it's no shame to live." Then he really screamed: "You're still a pup, but I have a wife and three daughters! And there's nothing dearer to me in the world! And you're talking to me about shame and no shame! First hold your child's hand in yours. Then you can talk to me about scare tactics!" And he clutched his heart. I made a move toward him, but he rasped, "Get the hell out, you snot-nosed kid!" We called his wife, she came, and we took him home together. When we got there we put him on the couch. She said to me, "Wait a minute. Don't go. I'll give you tea." The children weren't there. The older was at the institute, where she was studying programming; and the younger hadn't come home from school yet. They had tomato seedlings in milk cartons on their windowsills and photographs on the walls. She started telling me about all their relatives. His father was a priest, then he fell ill and went blind, but his son had to hide his background and wrote in all the forms that his father was disabled, and he was always afraid of being found out. His granny on his mother's side buried four children—all sons—and used to tell him that he had to do her for four. During the war, evacuation, and famine his mama saved him. She got a job as a milkmaid and stole milk, carried it out in a hot water bottle hidden on her belly. Before her death, when she was an old woman, she said, "Don't you dare bury me in my rings. Remove them all or they'll steal them. Better you sell them!" And Big Daddy's wife herself, when she was breastfeeding their youngest, she had so much milk, she would strain it in thin blue streams into a glass, cover it with cheesecloth, and call to the older children through the open window. But they wouldn't drink it. They thought it was too warm and sickly sweet. She drank it herself, reluctant to let good go to waste.

Question: What happened with the case you reopened?

Answer: They squashed the suicide story. On the other hand they did accuse the dead man's wife. They said she'd been planning to divorce him and he didn't want to give her anything. In those days they held on to cases for months. People languished in holding, and here everything turned around in a second. Trial. Prison colony.

Question: And witnesses? There were witnesses, right?

Answer: Yeah, but they all got out of it. Wouldn't you be afraid to go testify, considering what that would mean?

Question: I don't know.

Answer: There you go!

Question: What happened then?

Answer: I went home.

Question: A weak little woman was waiting for you there, and you needed her to support big strong you?

Answer: I guess so. Once she said I was a real man: a bunker on the outside and a nursery in.

Question: How did it come about that she, still a little girl, treated you, a grown man, like a kitten?

Answer: She only looked like Thumbelina. I did pick her up in the clink, the one at the train station. They brought her in drunk. Our guys wanted to have a little fun with her and then let her go without writing her up. They felt sorry for the girl. I told them, "Leave her be. This one's mine." I took her home. Brought her there and put her in the shower. I stood there and watched black mascara streaks run down her breasts, stomach, and legs. She had tiny breasts, no bigger than a puffed cheek, but strong nipples, tall, they poked out like two gooseberries. And she kissed greedily, clicking her teeth. She ended up staying with me.

Question: But you loved her?

Answer: Yes. I don't know. I guess I probably thought I did. After all, I'd never had much of anything before her. She taught me everything. And she shouted every time the neighbors started banging on the pipe. One time after that I went to the sink to wash my hands—my fingers had been inside her, every hole—and I thought, looking at her little bottles in front of the mirror, that she wasn't like the others really. I thought I'd understood something about women in Afghanistan. They went there willingly, after all. It was a foreign country and they were paid by check. They could save up for an apartment and bring something back—clothes, a television. We didn't have anything. Times were like that. Everything was just for people with pull, through closed distributors. What were you going to do if you were nobody and no one was going to bring you in and you wanted to live like a human being, too? So they went to war for the paycheck. They worked in hospitals, warehouses, laundries. They'd hook up with some colonel. Or a warrant officer, which was just as good because a warrant officer had a warehouse, but a colonel could order the warrant officer to bring him something from the warehouse. They lived in a dorm—the cat house. But they wouldn't have anything to do with us ordinary soldiers. Who were we to them? What could a woman get from us? A torn puttee? It just seemed to me that Lenka wasn't like that. Who am I, after all? Nobody. A cop with a crummy salary. But she got attached to me. She grew on me imperceptibly. And she was cheerful. She regaled me with her story of running away from her Old Believer parents. She went to work at a thread factory where the work was hazardous—the thread dust—but on the other hand she got a place in a dorm. Later she quit and got a waitressing job in a café. She told me how she'd scrape the dirt from under her nails and add it to the ice cream—tell me while she was dying laughing. I liked the way she jutted her lower lip and blew the hair out of her eyes. She got a job at a beauty salon—and was always cutting my hair. The minute it grew out, she'd cut it. I really liked the way she cut my hair. I also liked to watch her put on makeup. I kept asking, What's this for? And this? She'd laugh and show me. Look, to make my dyed eyelashes even longer, you need powder and soap. The tips of her eyelashes stuck together like little rays. One time I came back from duty late, walked into the room, and she was asleep with the blanket over her head—just her hair flowing over the pillow. The guys in the department warned me that Thumbelinas like that think fast, like lizards, and she could enter a stranger's life like a knife, up to the hilt. I didn't listen. I thought they were envious. They were. One time she and I went out of town to go boating. A path led to the lake between blackberry bushes. Lenka was wearing a long full skirt, flowery, made of some kind of thin, light fabric. So her skirt caught on a blackberry branch and nearly ripped. Lenka freaked out like a kid. At the time I told her, "Lenka, what's the matter? I love you." I'd never said that before.

Question: Were you planning to get married?

Answer: Yes. But we never got around to it. We already had our license. She'd chosen a wedding dress and asked me to stop by the seamstress's to see it, but I never had the time.

Question: But according to the rhyme, Thumbelina was supposed to marry a mole.

Answer: And that's what happened. But I found that out later.

Question: So you came home.

Answer: I came home. She was hanging on my neck. All of a sudden she whispered in a kind of strange and serious way, "I waited for you so long!" We sat down to eat. Under the table, she slipped off her slippers and stroked my knee with her foot. Then she asked, "Tolik, did something happen?" I smiled. "Everything's fine. Eat!" She stood up, walked around the table, and sat in my lap. She grabbed my ears—she liked to grab them like that and twist them like a steering wheel—looked at me and said, "I can feel it. Something happened. Tell me, what?" Then I told her the whole thing, about the beast and the tracks.

Question: What about her?

Answer: She got scared. I told her something had to be done. Otherwise there was no saving anyone. This beast would gnaw everyone's heads off. I hugged her. "Lenka, tell me, what should I do?" She pressed very close and tight. "My sweet, my dearest! You're so strong. You can do anything! Go to the square, kneel, cross yourself in front of the bells, and say that you're just a strand of wool in his hide. And everything will be fine."

Question: What about you?

Answer: All of a sudden I felt very much alone. I'd never felt that so keenly before. Here I stood, alone. Even in her arms. Alone.

Question: Were you expecting something else from her?

Answer: Yes. It's probably wrong and stupid, but I was expecting something else. She ran from the kitchen into the room and shouted, "Maybe I don't have a brain, but I do have a womb, and I want to have a child from a father who's by my side and loves me!" Then she started crying. I left and spent the night at the department. I tossed and turned on the wooden bench. I kept thinking about what I should do. In the morning Big Daddy called me in and sent me on some trip. A trip nobody needed. Go there, anywhere, and bring back something, anything.

Question: He just plain saved you. Got you the hell out until everything could settle down, cool down, be forgotten.

Answer: Probably. Now I think so, too. I got home and Lena was gone. That was fine. I didn't want to see her. I started getting ready, I had to go. Then the doorbell rang. I open up and it's some woman, not young, smart-looking, in a hat, carrying a purse. Turned out to be the mother of the one who had been convicted after the case was reopened. I asked her, "What do you want?" She: "Nothing. I just wanted to look into your eyes." I slammed the door.

Question: And you disobeyed the order to go out of town and started investigating the case on your own because you could still see that woman standing in front of you and you had to bring her daughter back from prison? One good man against all the bad? A solitary hero against the fog? Did it bring out the beast in you?

Answer: No. Or rather, yes. I mean, that wasn't it at all. I don't know where I went, but I really did keep seeing that woman, her eyes. I left the winter and arrived the next morning to spring. I was lying on the upper berth watching the trees make love out the window. And my thoughts kept snagging on that blackberry branch. The next morning it wasn't spring anymore. It was summer. Really nothing. A desert. Not a sandy desert, a rocky one. I was walking over the rocks and searching for something, I don't know what. In the night I saw fires in the distance and went to see who that might be. First I thought it was a gypsy camp. But then, what kind of gypsies could it be? It had to be refugees. There were wagons and horses. A big camp. It was late and everyone was probably asleep by then. Someone had lingered by the fire. I came a little closer. When the flame flared, the man's black silhouette in front of the fire shrank. I came even closer and was astonished. They were dressed like ancient Greeks. And speaking some foreign language. Shooting a movie, probably. They do that a lot now. Everything's so expensive over there, but here they do it for cheap. So they come.

Question: But time and space are decrepit, worn, shaky. What if they suddenly snag on something—your blackberry branch? And it snaps off? Anyone could fall into that hole, even ancient Greeks.

Answer: Maybe. I don't know.

Question: Did they notice you?

Answer: One heard my steps and jumped up and started looking in my direction, but he couldn't see me in the dark. I continued on my way. That night I realized what I had to do. It all came down to the counting rhyme. I had to stop it. How can I put it . . . I had to stand up to the counting rhyme.

Question: So the little Indians wouldn't go out to sea?

Answer: Yes, I had to stop the little Indians. Make everything stop. Make everything be different. So I could look that woman in the eye. And bring back her daughter. So I wouldn't have to be afraid of anyone or anything. So life would be clear and good.

Question: But you knew that according to the rhyme one little Indian wanted to stop the rhyme, got in chancery, where they defiled him because he was a cop.

Answer: Yes. And that's why the rhyme had to be stopped.

Question: But how did you propose to do that?

Answer: Very simply. I had to go out on the square and say, "I am not a strand of wool!"

Question: Yes, but . . .

Answer: Don't interrupt! There I was, coming back on the train. The other people in my compartment never stopped eating: crushed, cracked eggs on newspaper, a split tomato in bread crumbs, salt in a matchbox. Someone was reading an article out loud from the wet, greasy newspaper spread on the table, about how our island was in first place for number of abortions per capita, but in prison it was the opposite, none of the imprisoned women would get rid of their babies. Everyone kept them and tried to get pregnant, if only by the guard—anyone really. An immaculate conception, so to speak. The one man sitting across from me and dipping potatoes into a heap of damp salt on the article, on those same women, said that for them a child was a way to get better food. Not only that, they didn't work. But most of all was the amnesty for maternity. They were released first. Later, according to statistics, when they left prison and were at liberty, the majority of those mothers abandoned their children. Later he started telling us about his buddy, a priest, who had a dog with human eyes. The dog really was a person, except with fur. And it had bitten off its children's heads. Then this priest killed it. He sipped his tea and looking out the window said, "What can you expect of a country where mothers kill their own children?" The train was on a bridge slowly crossing a river, and on the frozen river, in the snow, two people—a he and a she—were stomping out big letters, huge letters, so they could be seen from far away, from the passing trains, from our window, in fact.

Question: What did they stomp out? What words?

Answer: I don't know. They'd just started, and the train had already gone by.

Question: But this is important!

Answer: I couldn't exactly stop the train!

Question: Oh, all right. So you returned, took the streetcar, and rode to the House on the Square.

Answer: I returned, took the streetcar, and rode to the House on the Square. I'm walking from the stop. From a distance I can see Big Daddy waving to me in the window. He's shouting inaudibly, rapping his knuckles on the glass, showing me something with his hands. He saw I'd come back without permission and understood everything. So I come out to the middle of the square and he runs out the front door and shouts, "Anatoly! What are you doing! Quiet! Don't do it! You won't change anything, but you'll ruin yourself!" He ran down the steps, and the entrance is right under the courtroom windows. Right then a huge clock fell out the window and landed on top of him. A white marble bear with the dial in its belly.

Question: There it is, the big bear's hug.

Answer: Yes. I ran over to him. The old man was still breathing, or rather, rasping, whistling almost. And looking me in the eye. As if he understood everything but there was no point anymore to speaking. The funeral wasn't until Tuesday—due to the autopsy and due to the fact that Saturday and Sunday are days off. There were lots of people, all our guys, the bosses, some veterans. His widow and three daughters, all in black kerchiefs. There was a frost, so first they put on hats and tied the kerchiefs over the hats. And the men were all wearing caps with earflaps, or rather, dancing around to keep warm. The coffin slipped its ropes and went in vertically, so they had to drag it back out and lower it again. They'd dug the grave beforehand, but the night before the funeral a frost struck and everything froze solid. They couldn't close it up. They hacked at the ground with crowbars and shovels. You can't leave a grave open. Big Daddy stretched out in his coffin as if he were on parade. Some woman next to me—I don't know who she was to him— heaved a sigh. "Look, Pasha. Even in your grave you're handsome. Not a dead man, a groom." And I looked at him and remembered them saying on television that in the old days they buried people sitting, posed like a fetus, legs pressed to the chest, as if they could be born a second time. And the grave was like the womb. That is, plunging into a grave was a copulation with the earth, like fertilizing the earth with a person. Big Daddy ended up as the earth's groom. On the one hand—for us—it was a funeral; but on the other hand—for him—it was a wedding. That's why they wash the deceased and dress them up. Even the band on Big Daddy's head was like the wreath a groom wears. In the old days, the Greeks thought that the dead married and kept living in their graves and eating what was brought to them and drinking the wine spilled on them. We do the same thing. I looked at the nearby graves and saw all kinds of things placed by the cross, even apples and bananas. Then I came to my senses. Lord, what am I thinking! Three little girls here have lost their father because of me.

Question: And then?

Answer: Then at the funeral meal I drank a hundred grams to his soul's rest, had a bite of pancake, and took the streetcar. There. I went out on the square and said what I should have said. I'm standing at the stop and saying, "I am not a strand of wool!"

Question: And?

Answer: After that it all followed the rhyme. Went in for law. Got in chancery.

Question: And did the judge have a round stained mark on his high bald forehead, was he robed in scarlet—the red bathroom curtain—and a wig made from a skein of gray knitting-wool?

Answer: Yes. How did you know?

Question: I guessed. And the trial was all according to Hoyle? No rules broken?

Answer: It was all exemplary.

Question: And what did he say, the one in the curtain?

Answer: What could a judge say? He said that experience cleanses the soul, but overpowering grief tempers it, that you cannot behold truth or you will go blind, that people want good for each other but don't know how. Then he really shouted: "How can you not get it? This isn't just eeny, meeny, miney, mo, this is the life force! Do you really want to get in life's way?" I said to him, "Don't you raise your voice to me. I'm not your strand of wool anymore. And I don't recognize your court or life according to your rhyme anymore. Do what you want with me." He flew into a rage. "It's just a few smart alecks who think the universe is as simple as an old shoe: here's the wool, here's the hide, here's the bloody trail across the streetcar tracks, here's the tail poking out of the pipe in the frosty sunset. Except here there is no hero! Where are we supposed to get one in this world? In novels he strikes the beast in the balls, but we're not in a novel! And who are you to go against the rhyme? It makes the world go 'round! And it's there in black and white: the little Indian refused and told the rhyme he wouldn't go to sea and it seized him by the scruff of the neck. Whether you like it or not, everyone goes to sea! You're not going to sea, you're flying, and you're going to kiss the beast's balls! Get it, you bastard?" And he read out the verdict, which consisted of a single sentence: "Only savages believe in the struggle between good and evil." And personally he added that it made no sense to have a conversation with a savage, trying to prove that a wooden doll was just a doll, not a god. And also, as he left, he said, "Sorry for the masquerade, buddy. But you know yourself it's not about the wig."

Question: And that was the whole trial?

Answer: You want more?

Question: So that was justice.

Answer: They allowed me a last visit with my mother and sister and shipped me off. Lenka didn't come.

Question: You couldn't forgive her for it?

75

Answer: At first I couldn't, then I did. A whole different life began after that. There you're all fresh, you still smell of freedom, you don't understand anything yet, but you have to know everything. And no one's going to tell you or explain. I stuck a spoon in my breast pocket—but you shouldn't do that, it means you're a fag. Or I go to the chow hall and sit down on a bench—but no, that's the table where the fags eat.

Question: But what do you want? There not to be any fags? In prison, they rape men convicted of gang-raping minors. It's violence, but that way justice prevails. An eye for an eye. Not everyone believes in punishment on Judgment Day. That means you have to answer for what you did here. And you were a cop. So it's all basically in a day's work. And then, the fags are people, too, and somehow they get by. Everything has its own rules. Raped cons are just part of those rules. Wasn't that how it was for you?

Answer: Yes. In prison we had about a thousand men and fifteen or twenty fags. They sat at separate tables but slept in the common barrack. Maximum security means you can't get out of your barrack, fag or not. But they slept in their own fag corner. They were needed, of course. They cleaned the parade ground and latrine. The dirtiest and smelliest you've ever seen. And every person who walked by had to kick them, so they tried not to get in anyone's way. And the fact that they were dirty, well, that's understandable. For a fag, even washing is a problem. He's not going to go into the bathhouse with an ordinary inmate. It's not even that easy for him to move around the prison. Let's say you're a fag and you're going up the stairs to the second floor of the barrack and someone's walking toward you. When you see him, you're supposed to back into a corner and wait for him to pass, so in no instance, even accidentally, would you touch a full-fledged inmate. And if he thought you weren't following the rule all the time, he'd kick you. It's no dishonor to kick. Touching a fag with your fists is humiliating, but kicking him is just the ticket. And you can't pick anything up from the parade ground. If someone dropped something, that was it. You couldn't pick anything up because the fags swept the parade ground. If you were going to the cafeteria and dropped your spoon on the ground—no more spoon. And most importantly, make sure you have no contact. The bowl in the cell fell on the floor—that's it, it's considered defiled. After that you can't eat out of it. If you're eating and a bite falls on the floor, you have to say right away, "It fell on the newspaper," although, of course, there's no trace of any newspaper there.

Question: You're not a little kid, though. All that has its own deep meaning, after all, a hygienic one! Life requires hygiene. But on the island, life is everywhere. It's all so natural.

Answer: Yes, that's what I'm talking about. That's why they take the cots closest to the door, to minimize contact. But you're still going to have contact one way or another. Say the fags are sleeping on their cots. Then those fags leave the unit—they're released or transferred somewhere. But their cots stand there empty, and for a long time. According to prison camp laws, empty cots are dismantled and carried off to the storehouse. So do the defiled cots remain defiled after they've been in the storehouse? That's the question! After all, they could be issued to any other inmate. Or take this debate: Can iron be defiled or not? One time I threw up. I found some fag to clean up my vomit. Then I decided, purely out of human feeling, to support him. I gave him bread and smokes. Strictly by the book, of course. I would never hand him something. I put it on the floor and said, Here, take it. All of a sudden I saw this gratitude in his eyes. Just like a dog's. You couldn't put it any other way. He looked at me like a beaten dog that's been petted. They told me, Great, you've found someone to pity. Dogs are just that. Dogs. If he gets told to spit on you in the cafeteria, it's all over. Which is true, too, of course. It is what it is. Fags have their own hierarchy, and everyone's afraid of the head fag. If he takes a dislike to you, you'll be raped by tomorrow. He'll tell one of his punks to kiss you in front of everyone, and that'll be the end. After that they'd beat the punk mercilessly, tromp on him, and break his bones, but you're already defiled.

Question: Tell me, what's important there?

Answer: What's important? Family. The same as here. People there are just living, after all, like you and me. What's important is that piece of the world where someone's waiting for you and is happy to see you. Well, people there live in families, too, from a kitty. Families protect each other, heal you, and if anything happens, they meet you when you come out of solitary. The family is supposed to get you new clothes and stock up on tea. A person needs warmth. And someone to smile at him. In the camp you can't smile, after all. Because a smile is the sign of the weak ingratiating himself with the strong. If anyone approaches you with a smile, your first reaction is revulsion—you take it as a ruse, some secret dirty trick. But it's so important to smile at someone! At night you lie there and remember how when you were a kid and you couldn't get to sleep you'd play a game with yourself. You'd warm one hand under the pillow so it's hot and hold something cold with the other. Then you'd play as if two little men were walking on their finger-legs up the knee-mountains across the folds in the blanket and the pillow. As if one had gone missing and the other was wandering around searching for him. And the warm hand always found the cold one, and the little men were so happy and they hugged. The warm hand warmed and saved the cold one and took it along under the blanket—get warm, get warm! I thought of Lenka all the time, too. The way she jutted her lower lip and blew the hair out of her eyes. Putting her in my bath and sponging her, as if she were a little girl, then wrapping her up, combing her hair, and taking her to bed. A few times, I even dreamed I'd been released and gone home and it was already late. I opened the door with my key, tiptoed into the room, and watched her sleep with the blanket over her head—just her hair flowing over the pillow. After that it was really scary to wake up in the barrack.

Question: How did they feed you?

Answer: It wasn't about the grub! Do you know what else was important there? Your word.

Question: What word?

Answer: Just in general, your words. What you said. It's just you had to answer for every word. There aren't any laws there except your word, and you answer for it. There you are, the new guy in the cell. The feeding trough is small, but there are lots of people, and there's always pushing and shoving during dinner and supper. You push someone and he spills his gruel. Pushed him accidentally, of course. But there is no such word as "accidentally" there. You left him without a meal. So you offer him yours, as if to say, it's my fault, eat. But the answer you

79

get is, "I'm going to eat your shit-ass food?" You've been called a shit-ass, you're defiled. If you don't respond, that means you've defined your place for yourself. You've been accused of something, and if you don't object, object with every fiber of your being, that means the accusation is true. No one's going to help you. You have to defend yourself. There has to be a fight, and you have to stick it out. If you agree to a word, you are that word. Now they have to defile you. And then there's no living for you. Just words, you say.

Question: But when you arrive, doesn't someone have to explain what you should and shouldn't do?

Answer: No one's going to explain anything. You're not supposed to explain at all. It's like the air you breathe. You start breathing it and you learn. If you ask, "Can I?" you don't have to ask again. They'll tell you no. A person can only do what he believes he can. Put simply, you have the right to everything. Except that you have to account for everything you do and say, every step and every word. I realized there what freedom is. It's not the absence of barbed wire. No. It's the absence of fear. It's when no one can get to you. When you have nothing. When you're not afraid of losing anything. When you say something and stick with it to the end.

Question: Did you ever feel free there?

Answer: Once. For real. The bosses knew all about me, who I was, where I was from. So they called me in and said I was going to be a stoolie. If I didn't inform, they'd rat me out. At that moment I suddenly felt the kind of freedom I'd never in my life had. I told them, "I'm not a strand of wool."

Question: Well, why have you stopped?

Answer: What's there to say?

Question: What happened afterward?

Answer: You know very well. Why ask futile questions?

Question: I realize you don't want to tell me how it was.

Answer: No.

Question: You don't have to. Don't tell me if it's too hard. I'll just write it into the report from the rhyme.

Answer: Write whatever you want.

Question: Fine, I'll write this. It's not that easy to rape a strong, healthy man. They sent you to the punishment cell. At night, when you fell asleep, they stuck a sperm-smeared towel in your face. You jumped up, but before you could get your shiv they started beating you over the head with something heavy. The toilet in the cell was partitioned off by a small metal shield, a little bridge. They bent you over the bridge and started taking turns raping you. Then they stuck a broom handle up your asshole, too. You spent a few days in the prison clinic until your rectum stopped bleeding. Is that how it happened?

Answer: What difference does it make?

Question: Then, before they sent you to prison, you cut yourself open. Right?

Answer: So I did, so what. I didn't want to go back. I wanted to be sent to the district hospital. A couple of weeks before me one guy slit himself open, and they sent him. The colony's deputy chief for security operations—number two after the boss—came, looked at me, and said, "No hospital." They called in the doctor, right there, in the corridor, bandaged the stitches, and sent me back to the punishment cell. I slit myself open again. You can always find something in the cell to slit yourself up with. I broke a lamp. I cut my belly. You've got to cut so your guts poke out, in which case the local doctors won't risk sewing you up themselves. The deputy chief comes again and says, "I don't care if you croak here. We're not sending you anywhere." They sewed me up haphazardly and left me alone, handcuffed to the pipe.

Question: Did you want to die?

Answer: Why? I wanted to live. I'm lying there half-delirious and that night I can tell someone's come. It's the deputy chief again. He sits down on the stool. He says, "You think I'm some beast? Put yourself in my place. You think I don't feel sorry for you? Of course I do! A man gets driven to dumping his guts in his hand. But think about it. If you get sent to the district, another twenty men are going to cut themselves open! You have to be thinking about others, not yourself! I had to show them this act wouldn't work. So they wouldn't cut themselves anymore and cripple themselves! And you say I'm a beast! I'm saving you, you fools!"

Question: Did he save you?

Answer: Yes.

Question: Did he send you to the hospital?

Answer: No. This wasn't about the hospital. There, that night, I must have been raving, and I kept remembering my Romka and me decorating the tree for New Year's. I would put him on my shoulders and he would hang the ornaments from the top branches. Or how after bathing him I would wrap him up in a sheet and toss him on the couch, on the pillows, and cut his nails. After his bath they softened up, and his fingertips got all puffy and wrinkled. And how later, when the child was already snuffling sweetly, I would move him to his little bed, and she would be waiting for me in bed, my beloved, my only, all hot, she'd whisper to me, "Come quickly!"

82

Question: Wait, but you still didn't have them then, that woman or your son, right?

Answer: That's just the point. I didn't. I don't even know how to explain it to you. I didn't have these precious people at all, but I was already prepared to do anything for their sake. Just to be able to live with her, day in and out, taking root in each other. For my son to draw a doodle for me for my birthday and write in big letters in his shaky hand: "TO PAPA."

Question: You mean, that's what they picked you up for, for doodling?

Answer: Yes.

Question: You didn't need your freedom?

Answer: No.

Question: That's why they released you?

Answer: Yes. I wrote an appeal: "Strand of wool. Counting rhyme acknowledged. Flying to sea. Kissing." And that's it.

Question: What happened then?

Answer: It all went according to the rhyme. The little Indian became a strand of wool in the hide. He started making good money and got married.

Question: And what did your job consist of?

Answer: You know, there used to be this custom. When a king was buried, they strangled his favorite concubine, cupbearer, equerry, falconer, steward, and cook at his graveside. In short, everyone who had been responsible for his life. They explain to schoolchildren that this shows a desire to provide the king with everything he needs in the next world. But in fact there is no such next world. And every schoolchild knows that. The living king killed them at the graveside for his own sake, not the dead king's. So the serving staff would realize what was what. A guarantee of his safety and care, so to speak.

Question: Did the people close to you know about your job?

Answer: As soon as I started making money, I wanted to give my mother some kind of present. What good had she ever seen in her life? After all, she was an orphanage kid and worked her whole life in a rubber factory. When I was a boy and started whining for some toy, she would always tell me about the orphanage. There weren't any notebooks, so they used every scrap of paper for writing, even the margins of old newspapers. There wasn't any ink, so they diluted soot with water. But the children were constantly stealing it from each other. The stronger ones just took away the younger ones' pens, pencils, and bread. When I didn't want to eat my soup, she would remember how she'd been brought to the orphanage, how the first night they gave her a bowl of soup that had a dozen flies swimming in it and she wouldn't eat it. Later, she ate whatever they served and licked out the bowl, even if her neighbor spat in her dish. During the war the orphanage wasn't evacuated. All the bosses fled, leaving just the nannies and children. The Germans demanded lists of children, and the nannies gave them, but then they realized that it listed nationalities. The Germans came and started collecting the Jewish children, according to the lists. At first everyone thought they were going to the ghetto, but later they found out they were all shot. For me this was all ancient history. But for her it was like now. She also used to tell me about working at the rubber factory. She dipped the molds in the rubber to make galoshes. When my father died she couldn't stop herself at work, she'd start to cry and the tears would fall on the mold. She knew they would be defective, but she couldn't stop. Wherever a tear falls, the rubber won't stick no matter what. The ventilation was bad and they started getting

84

poisoned, especially those who had anything to do with glue. One would start laughing and the entire line would start laughing. They had to stop the conveyer belt immediately to let people calm down. Here I was going to visit her. She was still living alone then. It was only later that she moved in with her older daughter in Podlipki. My sister's a teacher, so there's no talking with her about anything. She starts right in about her school and the horrors there with drugs. She says, "It just makes you not want to have children. They grow up and some creep lets them shoot up in some entryway. The people who get our children hooked on drugs should be publicly hanged! Publicly! On the squares!" In short, I went to see my mother wearing my good suit and an expensive watch. My boots alone cost more than her whole assembly line earned in its whole life, and I said, "Mom, here, I bought you a trip to Egypt. Fly off and see the world!" She was in tears. I hugged her and stroked her head. She'd gotten so small in her old age, she buried her face in my belly. I said, "Mom, what's the matter?" She answered, "Tolichka, my sweet son, I don't need anything. I already have everything. As long as everything's good with you, I don't need anything more!" I said to her, "Mom, what are you saying? This is Egypt! The cradle of civilization! Pharaohs! Pyramids! Mummies!" She never did go anywhere. She had a three-liter jar of mushroom mash on her windowsill. She kept offering it to me so that I would have it, too, but I didn't feel like dealing with jars. You stop in for five minutes—and hightail it out. I was constantly telling her, "Next time!" And I'd fly. She would be left standing there in the doorway holding the jar.

Question: You married a woman with a child. Did you know his story?

Answer: No. I didn't want to know any story. I'd been waiting for this person, my Tanya, for so long, I didn't care about all her stories. And she'd been waiting for me so long that nothing else mattered. It was so important to drift off to sleep knowing she was by my side, looking at me, her elbow propped on the pillow. Or to take her hand and put it over my eyes. And in the morning to wake up from the smell of ironing because she was ironing and that fragrant steam rose from the ironing board. I would call her from work and ask, "Any news?" She would say, "Yes. I love you even more." When I would go away somewhere, she would pack my things and slip in little notes. She would just write a couple of words, silly things: "Kisses." Or "I miss you, come back soon." Or "Stand up straight, don't slouch." Or "I dreamed of you today." She knew how to be dreamed.

Question: Was it hard with her child? He is someone else's after all . . .

Answer: You mean Romka? I fell in love with him immediately. At first he was surly, naturally. He'd shrink into a corner and not say anything. My wife told me that when he was five he announced he was going to marry her. He couldn't stand her talking to another man. Right away there'd be a scandal, tears, hysterics. Her defender. He wouldn't let anyone insult her. Once at the bus stop he rushed at some drunk with his fists. But I said to him, "Are you going to make ships out of soap with me?" So we started making our navy: ships of the line, destroyers, submarines. You take a piece of soap, cut it into slabs a finger thick. Use a broken off razor blade to neatly cut the hull, deck superstructures, gun towers, and life-boats out of the slabs. The masts and gun barrels are made of wire. The tackle from thread. When the soap dried a little, we painted the ship with black ink. And a whole squadron with submarines sailed across the table! I couldn't tear him away. He kept sighing, "If only I could go inside, into the mess room!" He had red hair, and sometimes I called him carrot top for a joke—and he'd sulk. When we went to register, I adopted him. He'd just learned his letters, and he would read everything nonstop, all the signs. He took the adoption decree, too, and started reading it loudly, syllable by syllable. Then he said, "Tolya, you're what, my papa now?" And I said to him, "Why now? I was your papa before, too. This is just a piece of paper."

Question: But was it important for her to tell you what happened then?

Answer: Probably. Yes, I think so. She was tormented by the fact that she couldn't. That's why I didn't ask her any questions.

Question: Do you want to know?

Answer: Yes. After all, she wanted me to. It's just that no one but her could tell it. Do you know what happened then?

Question: No. I don't know anything about her. I only know about the little Indians. The little Indians went to sea. There was a village nearby where other little Indians lived. The newly arrived little Indians were warned to be on the lookout. So she knew and understood everything. In that village, though, there was one little Indian, Ruslan, who wasn't like that at all. When he met her he said, "Tanya, none of ours have offended you, have they? If anything happens, tell me. There are all kinds of people!" He brought her fruit from his orchard. He also told her that people said things about the little Indians from his village, and he felt hurt and ashamed, but they weren't all like that. On the last day he invited her to the sea for a picnic. His army friend had come, and for little Indians, hospitality and friendship among men are sacred. That was when Tanya suddenly realized she absolutely could not refuse. That meant showing him that all of them were monsters no one could trust. She went with a girlfriend, Lyusya. Lyusya liked Ruslan a lot. So did your Tanya, for that matter. She told herself, Under no circumstances was she to fall in love with him—but she did just that. But she took an immediate dislike to the army buddy. Red hair, cruel eyes, grating voice. Anxious little hammers started pounding inside her suddenly, too: "Ruslan and Red were talking Indian to each other, and we didn't understand." They got to a stream, set themselves up by a fire, ate shashlyk, and drank wine. Ruslan kept making toasts, and after each they had to toss one back—to motherly love, to the health of the children-to-be. She could already sense danger lurking nearby, but you couldn't just get up and leave. They were sitting like lambs to the slaughter. Lyusya was completely out of her mind, guffawing, shouting to her, "Why are you being like that? Tanya, relax!" We finally started back, but it was already late and dark. She felt a little more at ease now that it was all winding up. All of a sudden they veered off. They should have gone straight, but they were heading for the sea. They started trying to persuade them. "Let's sit a little longer. It's such a fine night!" They stopped at the shore. Ruslan and Lyusya suddenly went into the woods. At first you could still hear her laughing, but then they got quiet. Your Tanya was left alone with Red. The little Indian tried to get fresh and take off her jersey. She pushed him away. He tried again, pawing her all over. She told him, "No!" All of a sudden the little red Indian punched her right in the nose.

No one had ever hit her like that before. The blood was spewing, but she felt no pain. She didn't feel anything at all. It's was if she were paralyzed. He didn't do anything more to force her, didn't take off her clothes, just beat her to make her say she wanted it, too. Tanya told him, "No!" Then he kicked her in the belly. She doubled over and the thought flashed: "How can this be happening? They were like human beings all evening, and all of a sudden he kicks me in the belly! My gosh, it hurts so much!" He asked again, "Want it?" She shook her head. Then he really hissed: "Are you going to make a fool of me for long?" He grabbed a bottle by the neck, smashed it on a rock, came toward her, and said, "I'm going to slice up your face now." At this Tanya was genuinely frightened. He broke her with this fear. All of a sudden she stopped being a human being. There was no Tanya, there was just a frightened animal howling at the hurt and fear, which would now hurt even more. This animal said, "Yes! I want it!" He gave it to your Tanya in every orifice. Afterward she crawled to the stream to wash herself. Right then Ruslan and Lyusya returned, content and happy. Tanya was dirty and her face was all bruised. "What happened to you?" She answered, "Nothing. Everything's fine."

Answer: Why did you tell me this?

Question: So you'd know what happened.

Answer: Did she want an abortion?

Question: No. She just told her mama she'd been in the south, gotten pregnant, and now wanted to have the child. They were standing in the kitchen. Her mama was smoking in silence. She wasn't supposed to smoke, she was already sick, but she hadn't told anyone this. Then she put out the cigarette under the tap and said, "This is good.

You'll have a baby for us and we'll love him. God doesn't give us more than we can handle." She got a chance to fuss over her grandson. What's with you?

Answer: I'm sorry, my eyes just stuck shut. I was looking at the phone and suddenly I thought, What if Tanya were to call here right now—miracles do happen in this world—and ask, "Any news?" I know what I'd answer. I'd say, "Yes. I love you even more."

Question: Did you want a child with her?

Answer: Of course. Both of us did. At first nothing came of it. She just couldn't get pregnant, and I was afraid it was because of me, that something was wrong with me, since she already had a child. But then she did get pregnant. It happened the same day she held the fragrant coffee grinder tight and I was opening a can of sardines. We'd bought a test at the pharmacy and she went into the toilet—we'd just been strolling down Gogolevsky Boulevard. It was winter and there was snow and slippery ice trails everywhere. She scampered up to me and bowled me over like a little girl. Laughing and waving her arms. She slipped right into my arms. She didn't say anything. She didn't have to.

Question: Did you know she had kidney problems?

Answer: How could I? At first everything was fine. I remember, we went to her doctor's visit together, I definitely wanted to go with her, I don't know why. All of a sudden I was afraid for her. I took a dislike to everything there right away. They started a case history on Tanya, as if pregnancy were a disease. When you go to the doctor, you have to bring your own towel and slippers or else put plastic bags on your feet. Once on television there was a program about giving birth in the sea. They showed pregnant women going to the sea and giving birth there.

They invited people to come and gave out a telephone number to call. Later Tanya suddenly asked me, "Maybe I should go give birth in the sea, too?" But this was a kind of sect, and the women later were supposed to eat the afterbirth, like dogs. I said, "Don't worry, I'll pay whatever's necessary and everything will be all right." Tanya got a chill in her kidneys and was supposed to lie down. She spent weeks in bed, drank a lot of fluids, and got so bloated you'd think she was having twins. She thought she'd lost her looks and so kept placing used teabags on her eyes, believing they helped her edema. Or two cucumber slices. But all this was when I was out. She was afraid I'd see her like that, with cucumber eyes.

Question: And her son? Was he jealous?

Answer: On the contrary. Romka was glad he was going to have a little brother or sister. I remember the three of us lying around one evening stroking her belly—me on one side and Romka on the other. I said, "Grow, little sister!" And Romka said, "Grow, little brother!" I wanted a girl, he wanted a boy. Later, at the ultrasound, they said it was going to be a boy. Romka was so happy. "Hurray! I won!" We put the screen image behind the bookshelf glass. You wake up in the morning a few minutes before the alarm and look, and its like looking through interference from outer space: here's the head, here's the arm. As if he were sending us greetings from some spaceship, as if he were already speeding toward us from some other planet where he'd been living all these thousands and millions of years, waiting for us. Later they admitted her for observation. She couldn't live without books and took several with her to the hospital. She tried to read there, but the female chatter was too distracting. I stopped by every day, and we would take a walk through the hospital corridor, then I'd run to pick up Romka at kindergarten. She opened the book she was reading and asked, "Look, here it says that the human body is extended in time, and in that way fills the space with itself everywhere. How is that?" I shrugged. How was I supposed to know? If it said so, then maybe it was true. They know better. I asked, "Do you understand?" She shook her head. "Not yet. But someday I will." I laughed. "So will I." The aide was washing the floor there and kept muttering, "Here we live our whole life in constant fear. First you're afraid of getting pregnant, then of giving birth, and then to your grave for your child."

Question: Did she come home without the child?

Answer: Yes. She stopped feeling it moving inside her. The child was already dead, inside her.

Question: Did they explain what happened?

Answer: Yes. I didn't really understand. I was afraid for Tanya. She took it very hard. And mainly, I didn't know what to say to her. I wanted to reassure her, console her, but in a situation like that it's impossible. The whole time all I could say was, "We're together and that's the main thing. We have Roman. And we'll have another child. Definitely! You'll see!"

Question: What did you tell the boy?

Answer: What's there to say? We said his brother didn't get born. That he died. Tanya took Romka to church school on Sundays. He would come back and serve up a maxim like, "Saying there's no God is like trying to convince children that they've never had parents." Now he came home and said, "No, he didn't die! He's just waiting for us somewhere." I was afraid for Romka, that it would be hard for him, that the other boys would hit him. It was with his mother that he would fight to the point of hysterics. With other children he was quiet as a mouse. He was afraid of swimming in the pond, that he'd swallow tadpoles or leeches would stick to him. And he felt sorry for everyone. Once in the winter, in the freezing cold, he brought a bird home that he'd picked up on his way. It was frozen and hard, and he thought he'd warm it up and it would revive. And the imagination on that kid! He'd be playing by himself, as if the two teapots with raised spouts were two elephants talking to each other, a big one and a little one. He and I went to the bathhouse, where it was hot and noisy. He said, "Papa, do this!" He stood there and closed his ears with his hands, then opened them, and closed them again, and it sounded as if someone's making a smacking sound in his ears. So he and I are standing there smacking our ears. At bedtime I put him in bed and read him something. He and I were always rereading—*Robinson Crusoe*, *Gulliver*, *Munchhausen*, and Jules Verne. He made Captain Nemo's submarine out of soap himself. He and I had this ritual before bedtime, trying to guess who would like to wake up where. On a desert island or somewhere else. One time he guessed Captain Nemo's submarine, where his little brother was waiting for him. But more often I fell asleep faster than he did. Tanya would come in, I'd be asleep, and Romka would be sitting playing Legos or looking at a book. I was afraid of losing all that. I was afraid something might happen to them. All kinds of things might happen to them. I was afraid for them.

Question: Everything will be fine.

Answer: It will?

Question: Believe me, it will all turn out.

Answer: You think so?

Question: I know so.

Answer:	How do you know?
Question:	Everything always ends well. It happens every time, you know. First the sufferings, fears, worries, tears, and losses, but ultimately it's all in the past. You can't even believe it ever was. Like a bad dream. It's over—and gone.
Answer:	But I just fell asleep, and I dreamed we were lying in our bed again, Romka had slipped under the blanket with us, and he and I were stroking her belly from either side, and I was asking her, "You mean he didn't really die there?" And Tanya replied, "Of course not. Listen!" And I stroked her belly and wanted to put my ear to it and listen, and all of a sudden I got so afraid that it was all a dream and inside her was death and I was going to wake up now in the chilly cell, handcuffed, and they were sending me stitched up haphazardly back to the barracks.
Question:	What are you talking about! There's nothing to be afraid of. Everything's fine. It's all in the past! You don't have to be afraid of anything anymore! Everything that was bad, all that was just a nightmare, and now you're going to wake up where you were thinking of waking up with your son. You and he wanted to wake up in your soap mess room! And your Tanya and Romka would be there. And his little brother had already given up on you there. Same for your mama. And sister. And everyone near and dear to you. And all of a sudden everything became so simple and understandable about the human body, which is extended in time and in that way fills the space with its love. And what freedom for Romka there—an entire submarine! You could touch everything, turn the handles and wheels, press the knobs, bolts, valves, buttons, levers. And Captain Nemo himself would put his sweat-stained, greasy cap, still hot on the inside, on his head.

In the morning the army advanced on Babylon. The hour had come when the bazaar became crowded, and the place where Cyrus had proposed making a halt was not far off when Pategyas, a Persian, a trusty member of Cyrus's personal staff, came galloping up at full speed on his lathered horse, and to every one he met he shouted in the languages of the barbarians and Greeks that the king was approaching with a large army prepared to do battle. Cyrus heard him out and said, "Men, my father's empire is so great that it stretches southward to a region where men cannot dwell by reason of the heat, and northward to a region uninhabitable due to the cold. If victory attends us, it will be mine to bestow on my friends power over those lands. My fear is not that I may not have enough to give each of my friends, but lest I may not have friends enough on whom to bestow what I have to give."

Cyrus, alighting from his chariot, donned his armor, mounted his horse, took up his spear, and ordered all be armed in full and take their place in formation. Cyrus himself went into battle with bared head.

It was now mid-day, and the enemy had yet to show itself. Only after mid-day did a pillar of dust appear, like a bright cloud, and after a considerable time on the plain, at a far distance, there rose what looked like a black pall. When the enemy did approach, their brass and spear points glinted, and the regiments could be distinguished. In front were the scythed chariots. Their scythes were fitted to the wheel axles and turned under the chariots with edges facing the ground, so as to slash to pieces all they encountered. The barbarian army approached with even tread, while the Greek stood their ground and formed up, adding suitable contingents. Cyrus rode past his soldiers in formation and looked in first one direction and then the other, observing his enemies and his friends. Clearchus galloped up to him and endeavored to convince him to remain behind his men and not expose himself to danger. "What is that you say, Clearchus!" Cyrus exclaimed. "I seek a kingdom, yet you advise me to show myself unworthy of being king!" The army of the enemy came on calmly and slowly, without shouts, in perfect silence.

My good Nebuchadnezzasaurus!

This is our mail night, so I am hurrying to dash off a few lines.

I don't know how it is with you, but here words take shape at night, coalescing out of the word-fog. The word dust is transformed in some fashion—this was explained to us in school, but I've forgotten everything, possibly with the participation of our Liebig refrigerator or under the influence of climatic fluctuations—into tiny seeds on the tongue.

Or maybe it's simply the law of insomnia.

By the way, did you receive my previous letter in which I told you about hunting for woodcocks, the groom-less wedding, the shredded note on the moon-lacquered piano, the war, the ball, the duel, and the university porter who played checkers artistically, with beaker stoppers? Truly, one grows weary of blaming the mails! You send it express, ask them to hurry, tickle the beanpole-postmaster's humongous palm, my dear fellow, you say, for old times' sake, we won't hold you up, while he, instead of harnessing his well-fed huskies to the dogsled, sends his goners. And after the tundra comes the taiga. There you have to cross the ice of the frozen Tunguska. And then only if the occasion arises.

It is no surprise that you may receive my letter with news only years hence. It's half past twelve here now. My half-past twelve will be conveyed to you. Actually, I think I already told you that something is wrong with the time in our boundless expanse.

My half-past twelve is blocked by banana crates. They were never sorted after the move. They're stacked by the wall. At the time I was just leaving them there temporarily, for the first few days, to be unpacked afterward, but the first few days stretched out and subsumed the seasons, nature's snow-cycle, the mosquito's buzz.

They come in very handy for moving. At Denner's then I took a few excellent crates. But here I wanted to find something. I didn't remember where it might have been, so I had to take everything apart. All kinds of junk, old notebooks, newspapers, magazines, drafts, clippings, excerpts, antepulvian Egypt, a filling that fell out, the four horses' opening on the Anichkov Bridge across the Fontanka River, the dents in the parquet from sharp heels.

I also found papers from that very same antepulvian Egypt, when the interpreter was the young teacher of Orochs and Tungus, earning kopeks, and after school dashed here and there giving private lessons. At the time, the young teacher had just had his first story published in a certain journal, a story that was supposed to turn the world on its head but, contrary to expectations, didn't. Fortunately, nothing can. On the other hand, as consolation, one rainy winter's day—half the winter had passed without any frosts or snow, and the discarded New Year's trees lay about the yard on the sere grass—the young teacher had a call from a certain publishing house, such as were then opening up in every basement, offering him a job writing a book about a once famous singer of love songs for their biography series.

When he heard her name, he immediately thought of the basement on Starokonyushenny, the antediluvian electric record player with a broken arm that his father, a former submariner, had bandaged up with dark blue electrical tape. The future young teacher had played his records about Cippolino and Uncle Styopa endlessly, while his father played his old, black, heavy ones, and then it had to be switched from 33 rpm to 78. Naturally, the naughty troublemaker adored listening to everything sped up, and then Lord Tomato chirped something in Lilliputian, and on his father's records the women's voices sounded like Uncle Vitya's, their neighbor, who'd had his jaw shot off in the war and who went around—as people said—with a silver straw inserted in his throat.

The former submariner had had one record by this very same singer. When he came home drunk, that was the one he always

97

played. His mama would go to the neighbors' or into the kitchen, and his father would slam the door behind her, grab the future young teacher in his arms, sit on the couch where all three of them slept—the woman put their son to bed there between her and her husband although he had his own little bed, probably to barricade herself with the child—and talk about someone named Zosya who gave him that record when their submarine was docked after the war at the base in Libau. The part about Zosya was boring, and the future young teacher asked him to tell him about the watermelons. Then the father would recall how as boys they would steal watermelons and cantaloupes from the railroad. The future teacher pictured it all, like in a movie: there's the train slowing down, his hero-father running it down and leaping onto the watermelon car's step, making his way, flat against the car's shaking side, to the hidden windows just under the roof, and throwing watermelons or cantaloupes out of the full moving car. Sometimes the watermelons break and explode like bombs. Then he leaps neatly halfway between two poles and somersaults down the slope. The future young teacher was very proud of his father and those watermelons.

Even now, as I write all this, all of a sudden I really wanted a watermelon, as if I, not my father, were making my way along, flattened against the side of the thundering train car, toward the open window. It's dark there, and I already know it isn't watermelons in the car because I catch the smell of cantaloupe rinds coming out of the hot, stuffy darkness.

And here they were asking the young teacher to write about the same singer from the record who sounded like Uncle Vitya with the silver straw in his throat. It turned out she was still alive, though everyone thought she'd died long ago. The publisher had been given her reminiscences and diaries. I had to meet with her and tape her stories.

Naturally, the poor young teacher agreed straightaway, especially since they promised him an advance—a fabulous three hundred dollars. He couldn't earn that much in a year at school. For some reason I remember that outside, in the yard, when I was talking on the phone, two girls were playing New Year's, having stuck a half-shredded tree with silver tinsel into a pile of dirt next to the garbage, and were giving each other presents, putting something no one but they could see into each other's empty hands.

On the appointed day, when he was supposed to come for the contract, a frost struck and everything was chilled and glassy, both the street and the streetcar. People's hair turned gray at the temples. Everyone's mustaches and beards were silvered, and each carried his breath in front of him, like cotton candy on a stick. From far away he could see a huge, solid cloud of steam near the subway entrance. Half a meter of ice had built up over the doors, on the station signs, on the façade, and on the columns.

In the basement where the publishing house was, there was a draft coming from all the windows, which were covered with a thick layer of frost, and people were sitting around the rooms in their fur coats. The editor who was in charge of the book was standing on a chair, closing the gaps in the frames with wide tape. A white thread had stuck to the back of her skirt, and the young teacher caught himself realizing he had a sudden urge to pluck that thread, cautiously, and wrap it around his finger: Alexei, Boris, Cyrill . . . The lady was wrapped in a shawl. She was coughing and sniffling into the handkerchief pressed to her nose and telling him not to look at her.

"I'm a fright. Look at Sinai instead!"

There were some sun-burned mountains on the wall calendar. The editorial lady's eyes really were oozing pus, and the young teacher, embarrassed, obediently looked at Sinai. It was a hot day there, the air was scorching, trembling, streaming.

While the future biographer was filling out the agreement, she, sniffing constantly, complained how hard it was to work with old people and told him about some film director who had also had a book written about him in this series and who kept forgetting that his son had died long before and from time to time would ask, "But where's Vasya?" Each time they told him he had gone to the store. Satisfied with this answer, the old man continued to talk about his own youth, omitting no detail.

They wouldn't give him the actual diaries to take home. The young teacher could only take photocopies, but he looked through the notebooks that same day, installing himself on the icy leather couch in the publishing house's chilly corridor, next to some stunted plant in a tub that probably wasn't frozen only because they smoked around it and used the tub as an ashtray. His fingers stiffened so he had to put on gloves, which made turning the pages awkward. The pages slipped and didn't want to turn, and a couple of times the precious notebooks even jumped out of his hands onto the filthy floor, but fortunately no one was in the corridor at the time.

The diaries, in their motley, antediluvian bindings, smelled of the old cigarette butts from the tub, and through this musty stink came the smell of the time compressed in these full pages. There was also the faint smell of something feminine, or rather, old lady-ish, some kind of old perfume. The ink had faded, and sometimes she had written in pencil. Some entries had dates, others didn't. Her handwriting was fairly slovenly and kept changing. Some pages went along as if embroidered with satin-stitch; others were scribbles. Some spots were simply smeared with thick black paint. Sometimes there was a run of blank pages, as if she'd intended to fill them in later. Then her disorderly entries again. Some pages had been torn out. Judging from the notebooks' numbering, three of them had disappeared altogether.

Frozen stiff, the young teacher returned to the editor's office and once again began to look at Sinai bathed in sun and languishing from the heat. It occurred to him how right it was that it was there that the sky, deep blue from the haze, gaped and the Chosen People had been given the tablets, not in a steam cloud by a Moscow subway entrance overgrown with ice. The editor, sniffling, gave instructions to go meet with the heroine as soon as possible because she was well past ninety and was already mixing everything up and tuning out, but she did have moments of clarity, and he needed to hit on one of those moments and get her talking. She had begun writing her memoirs long ago, but she had never been able to get past her childhood, and then she'd abandoned it altogether.

"It will be some help to you," the lady said, "but don't get your hopes up. I tried to read it and it was all wrong. The main thing is, try to get her to talk. You could at least nod."

The young teacher nodded obediently, carelessly thrusting the hundred-dollar bills, which he had never held in his hands before, in his pocket.

"How can I explain what I would like from you?" she continued. "The essence of the book is a kind of rising up from the grave. Seemingly she died and everyone forgot her, and now you're telling her, Come out! Do you see?"

He nodded.

"Yes yes, of course. What's there not to understand?"

Later, in the subway, as he was riding home, he kept checking to make sure the three cherished pieces of paper were there. He thought everyone could see how lucky he was, and he was afraid the money might be lifted in the sweaty underground crush.

The future biographer looked through the packet of photocopies of her diaries and memoirs that same night. The old woman had indeed written in great detail about all kinds of superfluous people only she cared about, endlessly recalling various unimportant details, and for the book he'd been asked to write, it was all useless.

The next day during class change the young teacher called the number he'd been given at the editorial office. He was told that Bella Dmitrievna was feeling unwell and could not meet with him for an interview. They asked him to call back the next week. The next week the same thing was repeated. Finally they made an appointment and he headed for Trekhprudny Lane.

It was spring by now, and all the trash that had collected over the winter peeked out from under the snow in the courtyard, which was filled with rusty Zhigulis and foreign makes splashed with Moscow slush. The buzzer in the lobby was broken and the elevator wasn't working, so he had to take the stairs, which were heaped with pieces of brick, from an extended renovation, newspapers, and sardine heads. It was the Moscow entryway spirit: the smell of urine, cats, and damp whitewash. The bell didn't work. The young teacher knocked. They looked through the peephole for a long time and then the door opened a crack. They told him the old lady had been taken to the hospital the night before. In the darkness of the corridor, all he could see were flour-sprinkled hands. As the young teacher was talking to the flour-white hands, which sprinkled dust, he realized nothing would come of this book about the singer.

Later he called several times. His heroine had returned from the hospital, but it made no sense to meet with her—there were no more moments of clarity. He asked for at least one meeting, just to try, maybe something would come of it.

"She doesn't recognize anyone, though," he was told. "Have a conscience, young man! Leave the sick old woman in peace. You shouldn't do this!"

Time passed. The young teacher found out that the biography series he was supposed to be writing the book for had been halted before it ever began. Then a certain major bank went bust, and the publishing house vanished with it. Then there was a lot of everything, and the packet of useless photocopies wrapped in a bakery bag lay around for several years somewhere among his other papers and books.

When Bella Dmitrievna died, he was already far away, interpreting. He just happened to hear of her death when he flew to Moscow.

The official funeral, the articles in the newspapers, and the television broadcasts had already come and gone. And so it happened that the interpreter was going about his business and found himself on Trekhprudny. The building was barely recognizable. It was all spit and polish, and sturdy crew-cut men in expensive suits were lounging beside freshly washed limousines sparkling in the June sun. Two young mamas had left their strollers and were breaking off branches of lilac in bloom. The interpreter stood by the fragrant cracking. Then for some reason he decided to stop in. The buzzer was broken. The entryway smelled of paint after a newly completed renovation, and mixed in with this new smell was the old one—cats, urine, and damp whitewash.

He rang the doorbell. The same woman the young teacher had spoken with a few years before opened up. Only now she was holding a cell phone in her floury hands. Apparently someone had bought the apartment, and things packed for the movers crowded the hall. The uninvited visitor began explaining that he had once spoken to her on the phone, he had intended to write about Bella Dmitrievna, and he had even been here. He was interrupted.

"What do you want?"

He himself had no idea what he wanted or why he'd come. Surely not to explain to her about the old, taped-up record player on Starokoniushenny, Lord Tomato, Uncle Vitya's voice, and the smell of melon rind.

For some reason he asked, "Were you with her when she died? How did she die?"

The woman grinned.

"Is this for publication or how it really was?"

He shrugged. "For real."

"Then here's the deal. The poor thing hadn't been able to shit lately. What do you want, at a hundred! One night I hear what sounds like thunder. I run in and the lamp on her nightstand is lying on the floor, smashed, and Bella Dmitrievna has fallen from the bed—and she's covered in shit, Lord forgive me. She had already consigned her soul to God. May she rest in peace."

There's a piglet with a funny little tail running around the kitchen. I play with him and we make friends. He grunts so contagiously. We grunt in the steam and squeal from piggy delight. Later I see him, with the same funny and lively little tail, in the dining room on a platter. I sob and want to flee the table. I remember being especially frightened because they wanted to put the detached tail on my plate so I would calm down. That was probably my first experience of death.

How old was I? Three? Four? Not me, of course, old, muddle-headed, and now foolish, but that distant little girl.

The fifth, late, unplanned child.

I remember my brother Sasha, the eldest of all us children, ill with scarlet fever. He was quarantined from us, and I'm talking to him through the closed door. My brother assures me that his skin is coming off. I don't want to believe it for anything, and he sticks a piece of it through the keyhole.

My sister Anya, my favorite, who I called Nyusya, is studying arithmetic, doing problems, her nose in her textbook. I stand close to her, she puts me in her lap, and I fall still, seeing her pen draw amazing, incomprehensible little marks. Nyusya tells me about addition and subtraction. On Easter we go to the cemetery, and suddenly I discover that dead people have plus signs over them.

My mama takes the younger children—Masha, Katya, and me—to the French bakery on Bolshoi Prospect. I like the name of the tarts that melt in my mouth—petit fours. We say the seltzer water is boiling because it bubbles and tickles our tongue.

When we quarrel and fight, Mama forces us to make up before we go to bed, so the anger isn't left over for tomorrow.

Mama's perfume is Muguet de mai.

At the table we're not supposed to wiggle and squirm, our hands must not under any circumstance be in our laps but on the table, and not just any which way but so that our two index fingers touch the edge of the plate. For some reason the sovereign emperor is believed to hold his hands that way.

Mama says that every person must plant trees and dig wells. Each child is given a row in our front garden and we plant something there and water it. I run over every day to see whether my peas have poked through to the light and my green shoots are growing. Later, at night, little boys from Temernik slip over to our house and trample everything. Mama tries to convince us that we need to replant, but I don't want to.

In the morning mama wears her robe with the wide sleeves, and I like sticking my head in her sleeve. After breakfast the adults drink coffee and she gives the children a chunk of sugar in a spoon after dipping it in the black coffee from her cup. But I also try to lick Mama's hand because she calls me a lickspittle. I took this literally, which is why I say it's a licker, not a tongue.

I like it when she writes letters. She lets me put exclamation points at the end of lines.

Mama plays Tchaikovsky for us, "The Children's Album." "The Doll's Funeral" touches me especially. I remember taking my Liza, who could close and open her eyes, and putting her in a box. I weep because she's died. Then I grow bored without her. I want to open the box but keep stopping myself. No, you can't, because Liza died. She's gone. At that, everything inside me rebels against this impossibility. Why can't I? Here she is, my beloved Liza. Here are her luxurious blond tresses. Here are her pink cheeks. Here is her little silk dress. Here she is opening her eyes and coming out of the box as if nothing ever happened! Don't be afraid, Liza! There is no death!

The day will come and I will let one little girl play with my Liza, and when we fight she will poke the doll's eyes out in a fit of malice.

The glass balls will rattle around noisily in the empty china head with the black eye sockets.

The kitchen is the realm of my nanny, who also acts as cook. There my nanny receives her suitors. In the evenings policemen show up, and sailors with accordions. I still don't know the word "exploitation," but this is just that, what my nanny does with them, having them beat rugs in the courtyard or mop floors. For the floors she prefers her suitors to be professional floor polishers. They show up once a month, and she flirts with them in the kitchen and entertains them zealously. For my mama this is a nightmare of a day, and she leaves the house. I, on the contrary, love the fact that everything in the house is turned upside down, and also the smell of the polish.

On birthday morning my nanny is already waiting in the door for you to wake up so she can give you a present the moment you open your eyes.

On Soroki, March 9, she bakes lark cakes with spread wings, as if they were flying, and raisin eyes. We don't eat them all but leave the heads for our parents—we just dig out the eyes and suck the sweet raisin. We shout, Larks, come fly, come take away, the winter's cold, we pray, and bring a warm, spring day, the cold fills all of us with dread, the winter's eaten all our bread. Every day we have a fresh, fragrant loaf from the bakery on the table, but at that moment it seems to me that after the long winter we really don't have a crumb left and only the larks can bring us salvation. Before putting them in the oven, my nanny always hides a coin or ring in a few of them. I always get the special lark. Obviously my nanny, remembering exactly which one she put the kopek in, slips it to me. I'm convinced that this holiday is somehow connected with magpies—*soroki*—and am very surprised to learn that this is how we celebrate the Day of the *Soroki*—the Forty Martyrs of Sebaste. I remember my nanny in church pointing to some dark icon where I couldn't make out anything, only the saints' heads with halos merged into a cluster of grapes, and whispering into my ear how the unfortunates were led out onto the ice unclothed and froze.

I like the smell of pitch in the lamp and the incense in church, especially in winter when there's driving snow and frost outside. My nanny explains that they light the pitch so that God will have something nice to sniff. I'm sure that God lives in the church, and my nanny supports me in this. After all, in winter it's cold outside, and everyone has their own home, and here's the church, and this is the home where He keeps warm.

From Christmas to Epiphany she chalks a white cross against evil spirits on every door and object. Then she consecrates everything with holy water from the river and after that you don't have to be afraid of any devilry. After Christmas God rejoices that his Son was born to him, and he opens all the doors and lets the devils out to play.

In my nanny's world devils and angels are as real as stockings or galoshes. She and I together do not doubt that each person is presented with a devil and an angel at birth, and neither leave you for a moment. The angel stands on your right side, and the devil on your left. Therefore you mustn't spit to the right and you must sleep on your right side, to keep your face turned toward your angel and not dream of something bad. The angel writes down all your good deeds, your devil the bad ones, and when a person dies the angel will argue with the devil about your sinful soul. A ringing in your left ear means the tempter has flown to Satan to report the sins the person committed that day and now he's flown back in order to stand guard again and wait for an occasion and argues for temptations. During a storm, a demon pursued by lightning bolts hides behind a person. Felling a demon, Ilya the Prophet might kill an innocent as well. Therefore, during a storm, you must cross yourself.

Before falling asleep I imagine what my Guardian Angel looks like, what snowy white wings he has, soft and fragrant, like Mama's powder puff.

My nanny is taking me somewhere. On the way we see little boys throwing rocks into the bushes. My nanny is distressed and grumbles that they shouldn't. There are angels in the air everywhere and they might hit one by accident. Something rustles in the bushes we're walking by. The boys holding the rocks are waiting for us to leave. In the bushes I see a bird, a dove, with a broken wing. We take it with us. It lives in our kitchen until evening, but the next day it disappears. My nanny tells me it recovered and flew away. I don't believe her, but I keep quiet. Before I go to sleep I imagine my Guardian Angel having a broken wing and me healing him.

Somewhere under the floor lives the house spirit, our invisible lodger, guardian of all who live here. You can't see the house spirit—that is beyond man's powers—but you can hear him and even touch him—or rather, feel his touch. He talks like the rustling leaves and strokes those sleeping at night with his soft paw.

My nanny is teaching me to pray. She has lots of icons in a corner, but my favorite is the icon of the Virgin of the Three Hands. I love it when my nanny tells me about her. When Herod wanted to kill the little Christ, the Virgin fled with him to Egypt, and once along the way brigands chased her. Carrying the Infant, she ran and ran and suddenly before her was a river. She plunged into the water to swim to the other shore and escape her pursuers. But how could she swim carrying a baby? How could she paddle with a single hand? This is when the Virgin prayed to her own son. My son, my own, give me a third hand, or swimming will be more than I can bear. The infant heard his mother's prayer—and she grew a third arm. Then it was easy to swim. She climbed out on the other bank and was saved.

I'm afraid of Judgment Day. I even know it will happen before Shrovetide—Judgment Day week. A fiery red sunset is growing outside in the frosty evening, and I decide it's already begun. I run into the kitchen and give nanny back the caramels and toffees I'd hidden.

For cuts, she thinks spider webs are the best way to stop the bleeding. One day I take Papa's penknife without asking—and blood spurts from my finger. My nanny runs to the shed to collect a spider web in the corners, covers the cut with it, and binds it with rags. Papa thinks this is all absurd, and when he finds out what's wrong, he shouts in vexation at my savior. He wants to treat the wound with iodine, but I won't let him and I weep until he asks my nanny's forgiveness. She sits there scowling, then sheds a few tears, makes the sign of the cross over him, and reconciliation ensues—though not for long.

Returning from church on Easter, Papa is indignant that everyone takes communion from the same spoon. After all, this is the direct path to getting sick! My nanny objects that the child is baptized!

I remember him recounting how in childhood he studied the flute and stopped, could not go on, after his teacher, demonstrating, played his instrument and then Papa had to put the mouthpiece in his mouth after him.

The blessing of the water. My nanny is certain that consecrated water is curative and that the earlier you collect consecrated water, the holier it is. The peasant women and workers, old women and old men, swarm toward the ice hole, crushing one another. Immediately they wash someone's diseased eyes. Some woman pours water with ice into the mouth of a sick child. I'm afraid of the crush, the maddened crowd, and start wailing. Flushed and disheveled, my nanny picks me up and makes me take a sip straight from the bottle. I wince. We go home. My nanny takes a few sips and sprinkles the whole building—certain this will turn away misfortune and the evil eye. Before I go to sleep she tells me that the night before a baptism Christ himself bathes in the water, which is why the water sloshes. If you come to the river at midnight and wait by the ice hole, a wave will come. That's Christ immersing himself in the water. Papa, who turns out to be standing in the doorway and listening, starts to laugh. He asks how water can be curative if they bathe their mangy piglet in it?

When I think of Papa I get a lemon taste in my mouth right away. He always drank freshly squeezed lemon juice and made us children drink it, too. Here we are at dinner in the sun-filled dining room taking turns coming up to him and taking our jigger. The sun's rays bounce off its facets and jump all around the walls and ceiling.

I know I'm Papa's favorite. Sometimes he takes me along without my sisters. To visit some friend of Papa's—a boat on wheels, but with real oars. I sail down the wide corridors in it.

Papa is famous in the city as a specialist in skin diseases. He works at the municipal hospital but often sees patients at home, too, especially public figures, who like to avoid excessive publicity in such delicate matters. One time, left unmonitored, I start rummaging around in his cupboard in search of picture books, and soon after they found me sitting on the parquet floor examining color illustrations of male genitals richly adorned with every possible kind of awful ulcer. For a long time after that I look with revulsion at the men walking by. I imagine them all having ulcers like that. After this I look with even greater horror, despair practically, at Papa and my brother Sasha. I still can't believe that they have such a horrible growth between their legs.

Since that incident Papa has always had innocent picture books at the ready. He subscribes to all the books published by Knebel in Moscow, and the first time I go to the Tretyakov, I'm gripped by the sensation of returning to my childhood.

Papa is interested in history and subscribes to specialized journals. One summer he takes the children to a dig at an ancient Greek town. Ancient Greece turns out to be quite nearby. Tanais, founded by Greek colonists from Kerch, lies next to the Don, in the village of Elizavetovskaya. All I remember is the noonday oven, some pits, and distant barrows in the steppe. My father is talking about philosophers and winemakers, chitons and peploses, and I'm whining that

I'm dying of heat and thirst. I wait for us to leave this Tanais, which consists of pits and scattered rocks. I don't believe in any ancient Greeks. When I hear that the town stood on the edge of the known world, between education and savagery, between light and dark, and was destroyed by barbarians, I'm amazed that the boys from Temernik destroyed it, the ones who trampled our flowers. After all, Mama called them barbarians, too. A child's insight flashes through my mind. Might people someday think about us the same way we do about the ancient Greeks who lived among the barbarians?

Later, in a trap with a bench so scorching hot from the sun that I burn myself, we ride for a long time toward a Scythian barrow where scientists have found gold. I'm being rocked, and my head is swimming from the searing sun. I want to see the gold, but here, too, disenchantment strikes. All I remember is some men showing my Papa some strange goblets. They turn out to be sliced-off skulls, which they've made into ashtrays. They also joke that this is revenge for Prince Svyatoslav, whose skull the Pechenegs made into a wine goblet for themselves. My father doesn't smoke, but later there will be an ashtray like this on his desk.

At night I adore sneaking out of my room and slipping into the bed in my parents' bedroom. It's a kind of game. Mama hides me under the blanket, and Papa searches for me and shows me the door, talking about certain mysteries, entrée to which children are not allowed. I mix everything up and say "ministries." They laugh, and Mama shakes her head and carries me off to the nursery to put me to bed.

Later, many years later, I learned that by then Papa already had another family.

He rarely went to church and almost never to the cemetery. It enraged him that people went to wish the dead a happy Easter, exchange triple kisses with the cross, feed eggs to the dead buried in the ground, leave blini on the grave, and pour vodka on the ground. He admired the Germans, who had invented crematoriums. He read an article in *Niva*, and showed it to everyone, about how to build ovens, and he sighed as a joke: "If only I live long enough to see a Rostov crematorium!"

At the same time, it seems to me he deeply believed. I don't know how all that got reconciled in him. One day, after I'd learned the alphabet, I was reading everything I came across out loud: "Again I will be with you at that very time, and Sarah shall have a son, though it ceased to be with Sarah after the manner of women. Sarah did laugh, and the Lord told Abraham, 'Is anything too hard for the Lord?'" I thought it was funny, too—like Sarah. I read it to my father. He said, "I don't see anything funny in that."

I never knew my grandfathers and grandmothers. They died before I was born.

Every spring we go to the bazaar in Nakhichevan. On Georgievskaya, where the Armenian Church of St. George is, they hold a huge, week-long bazaar on some vacant land between Nakhichevan and Rostov. I remember the swings and carousels decorated and painted with these fantastic animals that twirled to the organ. A show booth—and at the entrance the actors and clowns tout the show to the crowd. We buy halvah and oranges, kvass and all kinds of sweets.

Many years later I learn that, on the order of Catherine the Great, the Armenians and Greeks were deported from the Crimea and left high and dry on the wild steppes. Thousands perished, but the monument to the empress in Nakhichevan said, "From the Grateful Armenians." When they caught a ladybird, Russian children would sing, "Ladybird, ladybird, fly to the sky, bring me some black bread, bring me some white." And the Armenians, "Ladybird, ladybird, show me the way to Crimea today." But all this would come later. Right now at the bazaar I'm eating walnut halvah. If you take a bite of it, the piece that's left in your hand doesn't unstick from your teeth right away. It stays stuck until the tip starts to look like an elephant's trunk.

During a religious procession we're met by an old woman and a small boy. My nanny and I are walking down the street singing about Christ. I see the old woman hastily cover his face with her scarf so he doesn't see us. My nanny grumbles spitefully, "Look! So we don't soil them!" That's how I learn about Jews for the first time.

My nanny tells us how on their Day of Atonement the Jews make sacrifices. The men swing a tied up rooster over their head, the women a hen, and they ask God to bring the punishment for the sins of those praying down on the bird. "Fancy that!" My nanny shakes her head. "It was the rooster and hens that crucified Christ!" I also learn about circumcision and that at the moment of circumcision the boy's blood is sucked out by someone called a mohel. This frightens me. And I don't understand why it is they're cutting the poor little boys!

There are more and more places I don't want to go anymore. Once at the bazaar they caught a thief right in front of me and started beating her. I'm with Mama and Nyusya. Mama shoos us aside so we can't see. After a while we return to finish buying what we hadn't had time for. I see the janitor sprinkling the blood with sand.

I also don't like the bazaar because of the knackers who prey on stray dogs. The knackers throw them strychnine pills. Several times we've seen a dog suffering as it died. But the number of homeless mutts is not going down. There are cowardly dogs from Nakhichevan on unused land, their tongues hanging out to the side, their tails curled. That's where they're poisoning the dogs; the Rostov ones are directed there.

I'm six. I learn the words "strike," "revolution," and "pogrom."

Nyusya and Masha, who already go to school, run back home one morning and tell us how in the middle of a lesson they heard shouts and gunfire outside. Someone fired into the window of the main hall where the portraits of the sovereign and the tsar's whole family hang, easily seen from the street. Lessons are canceled often now. The strike keeps the teachers from arriving on time.

There is unrest in the city. Everyone has anxious faces. No one wants to explain anything to me. I hear that Jews fired on a religious procession and killed the boy up front carrying the icon. I feel terribly sorry for the boy and weep inconsolably.

The New Bazaar goes up in flames. A column of black smoke rises over the city, straight up, because there is no wind, like someone's giant boot.

I hear the word "pogrom" constantly. My nanny exchanges agitated whispers with someone. A white cross on the gates—does that mean they should or shouldn't smash everything? She displays icons and crosses in the windows and carries an icon out past the gates herself. I'm being kept in the nursery under Katya and Masha's watch. They're searching for Sasha, but he ran off to town, everyone's worried about him, and Mama is taking her drops. Papa is at the hospital all the time. Nyusya sits down at the piano as if nothing were happening. She wants to study at the conservatory and become a famous pianist. They pounce on her, telling her to stop immediately. She shouts, "I can't miss a lesson because of those scoundrels!"

Mama brings a dark little girl we've never met into our nursery. Her name is Lyalya. She's frightened and trembling. Mama explains that Lyalya is a Jew. A terrifying word, but the girl isn't terrifying at all. On the contrary, we feel terribly sorry for her. She is so unfortunate. She's been deceived. They've told her there was no Christ. We want to do what we can to help her and try to convince her that there was a Christ. She starts to cry. Glancing into the nursery, Mama thinks we're insulting Lyalya and gets angry at us.

Later, Lyalya will be my best friend. Her brother, Efrem Zimbalist, who is ten years older and a violinist, will go to America and become a famous musician.

The pogrom lasts a few days. Sasha shows up and disappears again, even though Mama begs him not to go anywhere. There's gunfire throughout the city. In the nursery he tells us what he's seen. They carried the body of that boy who was the first killed through the streets. They tossed bottles of sulfuric acid out the window of a pharmacy. My brother says he found two severed fingers and they're in his eyeglass case. He wants to open it and show us but we run away, wailing. He laughs.

We've been told to stay away from the window, but one of my sisters stands watch there all the time, and we peek out cautiously, hiding. Sometimes people with armfuls of things come running by. I still remember muzhiks in derby hats, factory hands in every style of jammed-on hat—and someone carrying an armful of peaked caps. A raggedy boy is wearing a nice new school cap. There was a hat store not far away.

In the evening we eavesdrop as Papa, back from the hospital, talks about how many bodies they brought in that day. The dead had serious injuries. They were killed with clubs, stones, and shovels.

Finally they let us outside. Now the crowds are walking through the streets and looking at the smashed up stores. We stand in front of a synagogue that has been burned down. Next to it is the home of Volkenshtein the barrister, which was also smashed and burned. It occurs to me that it was right here that Papa and I visited and took a ride in the boat on wheels. I think about the boat in horror. Could it really have burned? I look around fearfully. What if some of the people around me, the people who were walking down the streets with me, were the ones who smashed and burned that amazing, wonderful boat?

Life goes on. One day I ask why I was named Isabella. Papa answers, In honor of the Spanish queen. I like that. I pretend I am the Spanish queen. Or rather, I know I am she. It's not about the long dress made from Mama's shawl, or the crown I craft for myself out of gold foil, it's about my secret knowledge that I am a queen. In the mornings I spend a long time washing, making myself long, elbow-length ball gloves out of soap.

My sisters are cramming for history and a familiar name reaches me, so I listen closely. Horrors! All of a sudden I find out that

Isabella of Spain drove out the Jews. How could that be? That's utterly impossible! My queen—and now pogroms! Once again I recall the severed fingers in the eyeglass case. It turned out Sasha had not been lying. Papa silently confiscated the fingers from him and in the morning took them along to the hospital.

I go running to see my papa, burst into his study, and ask him with worry and hope about my Isabella. Only he can save me now. Papa is not alone. He's seeing someone. There's a man sitting at his desk. I'm afraid Papa is going to get angry and drive me out, but he takes me in his arms and explains in a calm voice that yes, indeed, Isabella did issue that edict, but you also had to think about the fact that the same year Columbus, whom she had sent off, discovered America. So if she hadn't sent Columbus, who would ever have discovered America there? Maybe to this day there'd be no such thing as America. Maybe there isn't. For some reason Columbus and the absence of the America he discovered consoles me.

The point isn't the persecutions against the Spanish Jews or Columbus but that I love my wonderful, smart, and admirable Papa and I know he loves me. All the rest, besides my loving and being loved, has no importance whatsoever.

The thundering of cannons has stuck in my mind as well from that terrible year. It's December. Dark, frosty December. Everyone says "Temernik" with horror. It's dangerous to walk the streets because of Temernik. Sasha and my sisters aren't allowed to go to school—because of Temernik. There's a real battle under way in the city. A Cossack battery is firing on Temernik from the old Jewish cemetery. At dawn, a terrible explosion shakes the entire city. A shell has hit the cafeteria at the Aksai factory, where there was a store of ammunition. Many people die. Someone says he saw pieces of bodies and clothing in the trees.

When I'm outside I see filthily dressed people with gloomy faces, and I know this is Temernik. On holidays they're drunk, and then they're even more frightening. On Shrovetide my sisters and I go to a fête that turns into a slaughter when the different ends of Temernik get into a brawl. We flee.

In the spring, the gypsies arrive in the city. Sasha and his friends run to look at their camp. He says that the gypsies inflated a hedgehog through a pipe, to force the pelt and needles off, and then they baked it in clay. We don't believe him, but the grownups confirm that hedgehogs are a famous gypsy delicacy. I declare I don't like gypsies. Mama objects: You eat chicken, and they eat hedgehogs. For a while after this conversation I can't eat my favorite drumstick, which my nanny gives me after wrapping a napkin around the bone.

An argument flares up between my nanny and Papa over the origin of the gypsies. My nanny heard that gypsies are the Jews who came out of Egypt with Moses, but they're a cursed, fallen branch of Jews who failed to obey the prophet and went on to worship the golden calf, that they always did the dirtiest jobs among the Jews, blacksmithing, and they forged the nails used to crucify Christ. For this the Lord sentenced them into permanent exile.

Papa objects that this is all nonsense, that they came from India, but in fact no one really knows why they don't have literacy. If you don't write down what in fact happened, Papa says, everything disappears and nothing remains, as if it never was. "Here, do you remember what happened to you a year ago?" he asks me. I don't remember what happened yesterday, let alone a year ago. "There, you see?" Papa continues. "For that you have to keep a diary and write down absolutely everything."

Papa gives us all handsome notebooks for diaries, even me, though I'm still just learning how to write.

When I go to the pastry shop with Nyusya, on the way, on Nikolskaya, a gypsy woman accosts her. "I'll tell your fortune! Who your fiancé will be!" Dusty floral skirts. She grabs her with her grimy hands. Nyusya pushes her away and laughs. "I already have a fiancé." This is how I first learn of Kolya's existence, Nyusya's future husband. The gypsy clings to her and won't back off. Nyusya gives in. "All right, tell my sister's fortune!" I'm holding a juicy pear I've just bought from a stall. The gypsy reads my palm. I find out I'm going to live a long time, I'm going to be a queen, I will have a knight and true love to the grave, and that I will give birth to a miracle. Then she takes my barely eaten pear and quickly spits on all sides of it. Then she holds it out to me, as if to say, take it, now it will all come to pass. I hide my hands behind my back. The gypsy leaves with my pear, her skirts raising dust.

Now before I go to sleep I think about my knight and the miracle to be born to me one day. I already know where babies come from, but I still can't imagine a baby crawling out of such a small hole.

Sasha reads endless novels about knights. At school masquerades he dresses in cardboard armor and a helmet glued with silver foil.

A conversation over evening tea about Pushkin's duel. Mama hates Natalia. I hate her, too. After all, Pushkin died because of her. The comment slips out that Pushkin was a genuine knight. I can't imagine him in armor and a visor and I laugh. Papa says, "You certainly don't have to wear steel armor to be a knight. Knighthood is the state of your soul." I ask, "Papa, are you a knight?" He smiles in embarrassment. My mama suddenly jumps up from the table and runs away. She's always so calm and gentle, and this is the first time I've seen her in that state. Soon after my sisters tell me in secret that we have another little brother now, but he's not Mama's.

For some reason I don't like to draw. The white pencil irritates me in particular as incredible foolishness, but on the other hand I adore playing theater. They buy us a toy theater: a box with a pediment and a curtain that goes up. There are boxes drawn on the sides and sitting in them are children wearing dresses in a style practically from Pushkin's times. Inside there are sets: backdrops and wings for five acts based on the fairy-tale about the golden fish. The moralizing fish quickly bores us and we think up our own sets and cast. Katya and Masha cut them out and paint them, and I set out the little figures. I talk and sing for nearly all of them. We put on shows for the little children we know—I'm big already. Outside is the winter's frosty twilight, but here there is a magical forest and fragrant flowers. The little ones listen with bated breath.

In the summer we set up a real theater, not a puppet one. We stretch a rope between birches and hang a sheet on it for a curtain. We bring chairs and stools and invite the children we know and the neighbors. We rummage through chests of drawers and hatboxes. Any object that might work for our performance vanishes from the house: hats, gloves, umbrellas, blankets.

But more than anything in the world I love to sing. Not just sing, but portray everything I'm singing about. "Down the Old Kaluga Road" is always a sure-fire success. I portray a fine young man striding at verst forty-nine carrying a bludgeon, and then I transform myself into a female image and show how

> *A brave miss through the forest went,*
> *Went through the darkness, praying,*
> *The miss's arms were wrapped around,*
> *Her precious newborn baby.*

My doll plays the baby. Passions rise, and I get carried away showing the fierce brigand grabbing the poor woman by her braid and killing her! But when he kills my doll and lightning strikes the evildoer, I throw myself to the ground and finish my song lying on the floor:

> *A mighty arrow strikes full force.*
> *Thus the brigand dies.*
> *Here 'neath that very broken pine*
> *That very brigand lies!*

Mama doesn't like my masterpieces, and I can't understand why. On the other hand, Papa is always thrilled, no matter what I've cooked up. He picks me up, kisses me, and calls me Queen of Rostov and All Nakhichevan. His kiss tickles because of his beard. When we have guests, he always asks me to perform something. I'm not the least bit afraid of an audience. On the contrary, singing for myself is boring. I need fellow sufferers. Everyone around me says I have a natural-born voice and admires the powerful chest tone that the vocal cords of this very little girl produce.

I am constantly looking through Papa's albums of reproductions of paintings by Russian artists, and all of a sudden I catch myself thinking that I'm trying on the people depicted in the paintings for size. Becoming them in a way. Here is Queen Sofia. I stand in the middle of the room, like her, hair lowered over my shoulders, arms crossed over my chest, and rage at someone. She was locked in a room, the way they lock me in the nursery whenever I do something bad. But the Strelets strung up out her window frightens me. I ask Sasha about the Streltsy. My brother tells me about both the uprising and the window on Europe. "Understand?" "Yes."

Amazingly, I did understand it all then. Now that I'm old and have lived my life, now I don't understand anything. It turns out that life is living from understanding to not.

Sasha also reassures me so I won't be afraid. There haven't been Streltsy for a long time and no one is going to chop off anyone's head anymore. Times have changed.

I'll write later about how Sasha was killed.

Answer: What mitt?
Question: The story is the hand, and you're the mitt. Stories change
             you, like mitts. You have to understand that stories are
             living beings.
Answer: What about me?
Question: There is no you yet. Look: blank sheets of paper.
Answer: But look, I've arrived. I'm sitting here. I'm looking out
             the snow-covered window. The storm's died down.

Everything is whiter than white. I see photographs on the wall: he's got someone by the gills. Some kind of bizarre map. I can't even make out the continents' outlines. It's not a map, it's a little hedgehog. It squeezed in between the wild strawberry and whortleberry bushes and the berries were speared on its needles.

Question: No really, there's no one here yet.

Answer: What do you mean no one? Then whose shadow is this? You see? On the wall? Here's my palm. And now a dog's head. Arf arf! If I use both hands, then look, a flying eagle. Here's a wolf snapping its teeth.

Question: Wrong. A dog. A wolf. None of this is the real thing. Your story is the groom and you're the bride. Stories choose the person and start wandering.

Answer: I see. If that's the case, then write this down. I didn't want to tell my wife anything, but she could tell something was wrong. I tried to pretend nothing had happened, that everything was all right. Later it turned out she'd found out about everything from her girlfriend. My wife was telling her over the phone that I'd started coming home in a bad mood, snarling, and she was told, "You mean you don't know? Your guy's in a jam. He borrowed big-time and the meter's running!" She didn't say a word to me. She rushed over to where she shouldn't, and they explained to her she should butt out. There I was holding out to the very last. I laughed off all her questions and even managed to reassure her it would work out. But then I lost it, got drunk to forget myself, and it just burst out of me, I dumped it all on her: how I'd borrowed money from the bank and given it to another bank, the Chechens shook them down, and I had to borrow money again to get it back in circulation—and they stiffed me. All she understood was that the money was gone, the interest was mounting by the day, and they wanted to kill me. She started blubbering: "Why would they kill you? A dead man doesn't pay anything back!" I screamed, "You really don't understand?" I'd never raised my voice to her before. Selling the apartment, dacha, and car was pointless. Nothing was enough, and I had until Friday.

Question: Wrong.

Answer: Yes, I realize that.

Question: Where are you from? A country where people moan in bed and don't speak, where all the words are dirty and there aren't any clean ones?

Answer: I just want to be free of fate and homelands.

Question: Has Friday come?

Answer: Yes.

Question: Who owned the bank, Tunguses or Orochs?

Answer: Orochs.

Question: What did you know about these people?

Answer: Not much. They believe the first woman fell into a lair and later gave birth to two children, a cub and a boy. The two brothers grew up and one killed the other and that was the beginning of the world. When that boy grew up, he became a hunter.

Question: What happened after?

Answer: Then a huge elk stole the sun, and the hunter went after him to recover it.

Question: Did he?

Answer: No. I mean, yes. They went very far away. The elk, anyway, runs across the sky with the sun in its teeth. But it keeps coming back. Moebius put the sky together his own special way. And the Milky Way is the hunter's ski track. There, up above, they travel on skis, too. There are ski tracks all across the sky. The hunter travels in a circle, first along the visible, and then along the invisible side of the Moebius sky. There are three worlds: upper, winter, and lower, which is the most important one, the *mlyvo*. When the upper people cut animal hides for shoes and clothing, the scraps fall on the ground and turn into foxes, hares, and squirrels. The upper people hold people's souls by threads, the upper trees the trees', and the grasses the grasses'. If this thread breaks for any reason, the person falls ill and dies, the tree dries up, and the grass withers. The way to the upper world lies through an opening in the sky, and *nyangnya sangarin* is the North Star. In the lower world, the *mlyvo*, life differs in no way from earthly life: the same winter, only the sun shines when it's night on earth, and the moon when it's day. The winter passes into the *mlyvo*, or rather, it is the person leaving for the *mlyvo* who takes the winter along with him. There people live the same winter life—they hunt, they fish, they make sledges, they repair harnesses, they sew clothes. They marry when the spouse who remains on earth enters into marriage; they bear children, fall ill, and die, that is, they are born again here, having awakened as a man or woman in the middle of winter. In the *mlyvo* everything is and isn't the same. A living person there is invisible to those here and his words are mistaken for the crackling of the hearth.

Question: You mean there, in the *mlyvo*, there's this same room where they're fishing for fish on the walls and men on the chair, where there's a parade of fasteners and a map's pinned where stories remained but people were driven out, and a snowy landscape is leaning on the windowsill?

Answer: I don't know. We're not Orochs. We don't believe in anything except winter.

Question: What kind of beginning of the world do you have?

Answer:	We have two brothers, too. But in the beginning there was water everywhere. Nothing but water. And it was impossible to live anywhere. Then winter came, the water froze, and there was solid ground.
Question:	And the brothers?
Answer:	One was good, the other bad. One sculpted the Tunguses out of snow, the other the Orochs.
Question:	And the *mlyvo*?
Answer:	The *mlyvo* is the *mlyvo*.
Question:	And those two who woke up in the middle of winter, who were they when they woke up? Daphnis and Chloe?
Answer:	Yes. Chloe is an Oroch. Daphnis is a Tungus.
Question:	Goats, sheep, and reed? And warm winters, do those come in pairs, too?
Answer:	No one has ever avoided love and no one ever will, as long as there is beauty and eyes to behold it.
Question:	But who wants to be a shepherd's wife for a few apples?
Answer:	You don't know? It's like a disease. Bad for man and good for viruses. For them it's the golden age of civilization. And so it is with love. Chloe stopped eating, couldn't sleep at night, neglected her flock, would laugh then cry, doze off and jump back up. Her face would turn pale and then blaze up. A heifer suffers less when a gadfly stings it. Her gaze hardened and the wallpaper moved. I'm sick, but I don't know what kind of disease it is. I'm suffering but I have no wounds. I'm languishing, but I haven't lost a single sheep. She closes her eyes and her toes grope for the seams in the wallpaper.
Question:	But it's winter. The cold penetrates to the fasteners on her bra. And no one wants to marry a snowwoman.
Answer:	There is something more powerful than winter in the *mlyvo*. They hadn't met for a thousand years. And so they pined away. All of a sudden they wanted each other.

That was when the ice drift started. One night the entire town was awakened by thunder, protracted and rolling: it was the ice on the river breaking up. In the morning everyone went out to see how the road they had strolled down just yesterday had moved. For three days the blocks of ice broke off and thundered, fat and translucent. They cracked, sending up hefty sprays, stood on end, crawled over each other. They crept ashore and nearly swept away the huts perched at the very edge. A river of ice blocks piled up cliffs, which the daredevils climbed, scrambling to the very top and floating past, as if on a huge, sparkling ship. Among those desperate heads was Chloe. She ripped off her hat and her hair fanned back on the wind.

Question: As she floated past on the ice, Chloe's hat flew off. Chloe went after the hat. And Daphnis after Chloe.

Answer: Yes, I can see for myself that it's all wrong.

Question: Only there's no need to invent anything. It's all there already. The winter and the *mlyvo*.

Answer: But what can I do if that's how it all happened? She tumbled into the water and he pulled her out by the collar, saved her. But in their infancy they were switched. It was all predicted for them in a prophetic dream, from the first snow to the last. Some lady who'd been waiting by the school door after the second shift would silently put a ring in her hand and drive away in an expensive car; someone would deposit a whole lot of money in his savings account when he could still walk under a table, and then the reforms would begin and it would all turn to dust. The children would grow up and their hormones would come into play. Love-over-blood. She would swear on her heifer that she would save herself for him and would tell him, "Swear on this herd and the goat that has fed you that you will not abandon Chloe so long as she is faithful to you. If she sins against you, run from her, hate her, and kill her like a wolf!" He would swear, one hand on the she-goat, the other on the billy, that he would love Chloe so long as she loved him, and if she preferred someone else to him then he would kill himself but not her. She rejoices and believes him. After all, she is born a shepherdess and is certain that the goats and sheep for them, the shepherds, are the true gods. Later, brigands would separate them and she would marry their marshal with the carbuncle on his upper lip. She would feed the pigeons in winter—so cold—and they have such thin legs, like twigs. While Daphnis, certain that Chloe is dead—for he himself heard the streetcar's warning bell, the rusty squeal of brakes, the shouts of the passersby, and saw the body in a pool of blood, motionless, except for her twitching wrist—would set to wandering and arriving in capitals, and would share a room with a medical student who would hit the books from morning 'til night and auscultate and tap the unkissed shepherdess body. For some reason he remembered "musculus cremaster." One day he would be lying on his cot with his hands behind his head, looking at the frozen window with the ferns and hieroglyphs sparkling in the sun, and thinking about his people, that it was the sheep that got tangled in the bushes that Abraham sacrificed instead of Isaac, when his neighbor returned from his exam in a foul mood. He couldn't find a certain muscle, and the professor actually mocked him. He said, "I'm amazed your corpse doesn't have a muscle as big as that. Congratulations, young man, this has never happened before!" Later Lycaenion, a nurse, comes to desire Daphnis, and she steals alcohol

	from the operating room and trades it at the flea market. She has a long braid.
Question:	Wait a minute!
Answer:	Well?
Question:	So both were switched?
Answer:	What about it?
Question:	Does that really happen?
Answer:	Lord, anything can happen! She was switched in the palace and he in the maternity hospital.
Question:	What palace?
Answer:	Why don't you ask what maternity hospital? That's what it is! Everyone wants to know how they make the switch in palaces, with their polished parquet floors, where veterans slipped in the waiting room, holding on to each other, especially the one-legged, and the Prussian emperor ate so fast and as soon as he finished one dish they changed everyone else's plate, too. No one cares about the district hospital. There was no doctor on duty, and the night nurse was dead-drunk. They didn't want to admit her—until they promised to repair the roof over the midwifery department. They'd run out of medicine a long time ago, and whatever did come in, the chief physician sold on the side or through relatives to the same patients. You had to have your own everything: sheets and robes. And coughs were soothed with dog fat rendered from stray dogs they caught. Do you hear me?
Question:	I'm sorry. I got to thinking about something. Look out the window. See the antenna in the distance, in the sunset, like an insect in amber? Never mind, it just caught my eye. But why switch?
Answer:	What do you mean why? Her father might have been a king, but he was an Ethiopian, and she was a white

child. The father would call the mama to account, so what could she do? Tell him that at the moment of conception she'd been looking at the snow-white image of Andromeda? Quite the Aethiopica, brother.

Question: Fine, but in the maternity hospital?
Answer: There it was just the opposite. Look, he's not an Oroch, he's a little Indian! What could they do? And all of a sudden a fire! Started at Tsarevo Zaimishche and half the town burned down. That's how dry it was! In the confusion she snatched someone else's child—its mother had died in the fire—and out the window. Left her own baby high and dry. All the documents burned. The investigation established that the fire was caused by carelessness. One biddy who'd been carrying off an egg a month was combing her hair, she was in a hurry, and in her haste forgot to put out the spirit lamp she used to heat her curling iron on the table, and the muslin curtains, blown aside by a draft, touched the fire and went up in flames. But it's a savage people we have, all they want is to make short work of someone. They blamed everything on some actors who'd run out of the hotel next to the tavern in just their undergarments, dazed and half-asleep. The would-be Leonidovs and Moskvins packed their suitcases haphazardly, piled into a wagon, and started making their way to the river through the fire. The glow lit up everything as bright as day. Wailing, shouting, and drunks all around. The firemen ran, primarily to save the taverns and wine cellars; they cared little about the townspeople. They accosted the actors: Are these things stolen? The women, embittered at being left homeless with small children, surrounded them. They held the wagon back, grabbed the horse by the bridle, and began calling to their husbands. "Over here. Here they are, the

arsonists. Here they are! Beat them! Beat them!" Ultimately, these poor women—the fire's victims—weren't hard to understand. The drunken men ran up and started grabbing them by the throat and throwing them in the dirt. The women hurried past with buckets—and started beating them with the buckets. They beat them to death. Their crippled bodies were dragged to the river to drown. One woman spat into a dead man's open mouth.

Question: But didn't it come out later that it wasn't them?

Answer: Of course. It obviously wasn't them. But once it got started, it was hard to stop. The peasants started setting fire to the landowners' grain. The huge ricks burned for two, even three days, lighting up the night—enough so you could read.

Question: But didn't you yourself say something about a curling iron and a spirit lamp?

Answer: Oh, the investigation cooked all that up so their people could beat the rap. That's the Orochs—hand in glove. One woman wanted to sell her house. Buyers came and that night there was a fire and the house burned down. Her relatives lit the match. They didn't want her to be richer. They wanted her to be as poor as they were. What's there not to understand?

Question: But what really happened?

Answer: No one will ever know what really happened. One retired captain fell in love with a vile creature kind of like this Chloe, trying to pass herself off as innocent, left his wife, who'd spent her life dragging herself from one taiga garrison to another, cursed his grown son, who took umbrage at this attitude toward his mother, and the fact was the inheritance wasn't all that great—but still it hurt to have it stolen from under her nose—and he went through all his savings with that mattress acrobat anyway, and afterward, instead of bookmarks in *The Jew-ish War*, where it talks about how Antiochus died and his throne and hatred for the Jews was handed down to his son, Antiochus, she slipped him a note with spelling errors saying I really loved you, and you really were my first, not like you thought at the time, as if I'd pricked my finger with a pin to drip on the sheet. I'm not like that. But I've fallen in love with someone else. You know yourself how this happens, my dear, my only, my little snort. A hurricane is suddenly unleashed without anyone ever asking you. It picks you up by the nape and flings you skyward. He found the note and read it, but he had very little life left with a heart like that. He decided to sell his little house. But it was insured for a tidy sum. The captain went to pray to St. Nicholas and got down on his knees before the icon: "Help me. I am christened with your name, after all. Show me a way out!" He looked up and saw it: a candle. The flame flickered. He went to the store and bought a candle that weighed a couple of pounds. He went home and calculated it would burn an inch an hour. He measured the candle—enough for eighteen or so hours. He put it under the staircase, covered it with all kinds of flammable trash, and doused it with kerosene. He lit the wick, crossed himself, and went to Moscow. Now the matter is in Your hands! He calculated it would burn down at two in the morning. In Moscow he went to eat at the Yar, drank champagne, went to the toilets at about one in the morning, and as he was walking down the hall he met someone and socked him in the kisser. Scandal, police. They drew up a report stating that tonight this sinner, guilty of love, committed violence and would be held legally responsible. By that time the house was already ablaze. For three rubles to the officer a copy of the report went straight into his pocket. He received the insurance payment without comment. He sent all the money to his son. He took nothing for himself. Not a ruble. Not a kopek.

Question: They were switched, and so? Maybe we've all been switched.

Answer: But that all happened later, whereas nine months before that there was an immaculate conception.

Question: No such thing.

Answer: The newspapers even wrote about it.

Question: You mean that case in the pipe?

Answer: Yes. Daphnis's mother was working at a ship works. The rust had to be cleaned off the pipes. The outside wasn't so bad, but there was the inside to do, too. The pipes were exactly a person in diameter. She crawled inside on all fours and then started backing out. Her ass was already outside, but the rest of her was still in the pipe. That's when it all happened. She tried to jerk away, but where are you going to go in a steel squeeze? She screamed, but her voice was carried to the other end of the pipe—the draft. She climbed out, pulled up her panties and hose, her warm leggings, and her quilted pants, and around her—no one. Just the snow falling. There weren't even any tracks, just snow-powdered ones. Fat snowflakes had fallen, as big as a child's hand. They're the ones who have golden beams, rains, swans, and doves, while we have winter—and snowfalls.

Question: Wait a minute. This is going in the wrong direction. This way you're going to go all the way back to your grandpas and grandmas, to the ancestor taking the grape treatment at Lac Leman who met Paganini, who was already suffering from general enfeeblement and the beginning of paralysis in his breathing instrument and

131

who when he was talking held his nostrils with two fingers, which looked fairly ridiculous, and how at that time your ancestors on the other side, the line that died out, would catch crayfish—take a dead cat, cut off its paws, and stick them in the crayfish holes.

Answer: You're right. Time can be a slippery thing in winter. Your foot takes a step and you have no idea where or when you're going to plop down. Lo and behold, you're in the Russo-Turkish war! It's also good if you're in a snowdrift in the Shipka pass. Or else you might wind up in some obscure hole where newspapers arrive only rarely and stacked. You snatch up the latest issue and shout to your old lady, "Masha! Masha! General Ganetsky took Plevna! Osman Pasha surrendered unconditionally!" But she always reads them in order and hisses, "You're always in a rush! I'm still far away. I'm just to Dolna Dubnyak, they're about to lay siege to the fortress."

Question: Listen, this way we'll be going all the way back to the ancient Greeks! Before you know it, Xenophon'll show up. But first there's supposed to be a battle and the Hellenes still have to sing their paean. Do you at least understand that? We're going in the opposite direction time-wise! Let's take this all in order. We were in the *mlyvo*. Right?

Answer: We are in the *mlyvo*. Here time has no other aspects, and the season isn't entirely clear anyway, but outside it's winter.

Question: What happened then?

Answer: Brigands fell on them. I mean, us. Me and Chloe. We, you—what's the difference. After all, everyone's been switched anyway. You aren't you. I'm not me. We're not us. You said yourself that we're just mitts for stories to put on in winter to keep warm in the cold.

Question: Let's take a break.

Answer: What do you mean? Don't you believe brigands fell on us?

Question: I don't know. There's no finding out who you really are anyway. You walk into this fishery office, you tell us what did and didn't happen, you stammer, gasp, sniffle, and weep, you show your notes from hospitals, you roll up your sweater and shirt to show your scars, as if someone could believe you were hung up on a hook, you ask for a drink of water, you wipe your tears and snot with tissues, a pack of which is always in front of you on the table, you don't know what to do with your hands, you chew your nails and dig at your hangnails, scratch the mosquito bite on your ankle, but in actual fact there is no real you. How much better the Greeks! Even from here, from the height of the third floor, I can see the barbarians' army like a dark crust on the earth. And here the ranks of Hellenes have fallen still in tense anticipation, and the soldiers are still standing, holding their shields up against their leg. On the right flank by the Euphrates are Clearchus' Lacedemonians, he is joined by the Boeotian proxenos, and Menon and the Thessalians are on the left wing of the Hellenic host. Cyrus and his barbarians are even farther to the left. A light murmur runs through the phalanx's ranks, like a gust of wind. They are passing along the call that is already making the host's rounds for a second time: "Zeus the savior or victory!" The final agonizing minutes before battle pass insufferably. The distance to the Persians, who are advancing in silence, is now less than three stadia. And now, at last, having sung their paean, the Hellenes are moving against the enemy. The phalanx's left section has moved slightly ahead and those behind are shifting into

133

a run. Here everyone raises a shout in honor of the god Enyalios and runs forward. The soldiers strike shield on spear to frighten the enemy's horses. The armies collide, intermingle, and grapple, like two combs.

Answer: Do you think if I'm a mitt I don't understand anything? Nothing at all? Maybe I am a mitt—but I'm a thinking mitt! What, you think I don't understand that winter is one thing and *mlyvo* something entirely different? In winter, life, like drifting snow, ran across the street on the red light, and it's gone with the wind, but in the *mlyvo* last year's snow—well, there it is, wet and malleable, you can make a snowball, crumbly, fragrant, with ash seeds and a dirty earthen side—even build a fort. An impregnable one. One no one could take. And everything, including a supply of snowballs for driving little boys off the Oroch-infested streets, is still kept in that fort. Everything in winter was lost. Everything gets lost in winter. Even the summer. And childhood. Here they took your Daphnis and Chloe to the same zoo. Bread crusts and candy wrappers were floating in the duckweed-filled pool. Ice cream trickled down their elbows. Fornication in the monkey house. Sawdust that smelt of urine. A dense animal stink. In the rusty cages, the maddened beasts suffered from longing and the heat. The cashier in the booth, equally maddened in her narrow confinement, raged behind her small window. And now in winter, now that there had been a thaw, this entire zoo—all its animals, cages, and smells and the cashier in the booth—thawed out. They all died—the animals, the smells, and the cashier. But here, in the *mlyvo,* everything remained, the entire zoo, and nothing would happen to the animals, or the bread crusts turning sour in the black water, or the ice cream in laps, and the cashier would always rage in her booth and would never die. In winter there may no longer be any Chloe, but in the *mlyvo* she is still feeding her doll scraps of paper. There are wild strawberries at the cemetery, and her grandmother says she mustn't pick or eat anything that grows here because that angers the dead, and they might punish her, and there in the cemetery, amid the graves and corpses, she suddenly feels endlessly alive. On the first day of vacation she jumps from the porch and lands barefoot on a rake lying in the grass. She fashions a little house out of a shoebox, cuts out a door, hides her hand in the house, knocks with the other, and asks, "May I come in?" And she won't let the second hand into the house. She holds a piece of crumpet out to Mama on a fork and, indulging her, pops it into her mouth so that the tines jab her palette—and there's blood. She dreams of her father putting her to bed and telling her at night that if you set your slippers out all neat and tidy they'll run off to savage lands and bring back dreams and put them under children's pillows. She learns to dive. Her grandmother is against it, but her grandfather says that this is wonderful and that a young girl ought to be as strong and fearless as a young boy. It will stand her in good stead. She always left her key under a brick to the left of the porch where the phlox were. When she picked up the brick, there was a centipede there. In the night the dog rose tries to creep through the open window. Her left breast is growing but not her right. She examines herself with a hand mirror. How disgusting all that there is, and her finger smells like a zoo. She thinks, where am I and not I? Is my skin the boundary? Or my double? Or a sack I've been stuffed into for dragging off somewhere? And what remains of me minus my body?

At the dacha, if she whistled across the fence, the pimply shepherd would climb over. He was embarrassed, he could tell from her eyes that she had seen him at night, when she was getting ready for bed, peeking in the window from behind the lilac bushes. There were racquets but no shuttlecocks. They tried to use pine cones—which flew off ringingly and never returned. A ping-pong ball was located. The wind blew it straight into the nettles. What are you gawking at? Go on! He climbed in, hissing at the stinging. He started thrashing at the evil green with his racquet. He stuck the ball in his pocket and they headed for the river. They spat from the creaking, half-rotted bridge as they leaned over the railings, still wet from the rain, into the slimy Klyazma. A cloud of mosquitoes could be seen in the sunbeam above the surface. If you spat simultaneously, figure-eights scattered across the water. The names carved into the railings were rotting along with the wood. He wanted to take out his knife—but the little ball slipped from his pocket, flicked on a log, and smacked the water right in Chloe's reflection, right where her panties glimmered. But this is not Daphnis. Daphnis could not fall asleep and saw his mother undressing in the dark, removing her slip, which gives off blue sparks. He and the boys came up with their own weapon, they took a cork-tumbler, drove a nail into the heavy end, sawed off the head, and filed it to a point. They cut a cross in the tilting doll's hollow plastic head and inserted a piece of cardboard for plumage. If you threw it like a rock you could drive the nail through a board at ten paces. His granny mended the holes in his trousers and grumbled about everyone being so picky now. Next door to the labor camp where she worked as a medic in the work release section, there

· 136 ·

was a children's home and the children kept running over to them, to the edge of the prison zone, asking for something to eat and something to wear, and she would take pity on them: she would take the quilted jackets off the dead and give them to the children. They were taken to the museum, where "The Last Day of Pompeii" shows people just before their death; in a few minutes they would all be gone. A year later they were brought to the museum again, and there, in the picture, they were still a few minutes from death. The first of September every year are the ritual brawls between schools. Sometimes the Orochs win, sometimes the Tungus. On the holiday everyone attends the shaman's *kamlanie*. On the tribune is the provincial shaman next to the statue in the central square where a granite sculptural group has been erected: a hero, the commander he has saved, and a horse. Someone once saved a commander for some reason, carried him off the battlefield, and here they were making their way back to us. For two days they had no water, and the hero found a few swallows for his commander while he himself drank horse urine. After the *kamlanie* the shaman speaks into the microphone, still panting and waving the tambourine at himself like a fan. "Everyone searches for something, but later it turns out that all it takes for happiness is a little winter." He learns about the *mlyvo* from a neighbor lady. She has thick lenses—as if her eyes were sealed inside. And if she took off her glasses they would stay right there, in the glass. Daphnis tells her, "There is no such thing as the *mlyvo!* There's only winter." She: "There is. You just can't see it from here. After all, everything that's far away seems nonexistent. God, for instance, or the chicken whose feathers you're keeping in your pillow until chicken resurrection, or Tierra del

Fuegans. They're just very far away. You'd have to take the *Beagle* to reach them. Here, read this!" Her tired mother has dragged herself home from work. She washes her blue hands. She'd been opening cans. She makes extra money working as a cleaner in the parish Sunday school, and when they receive humanitarian aid, they first open the cans and only then pass it out, or else people would sell everything and drink up the proceeds. Her son was growing up in a one-room apartment and she had no private life. While next to them municipal housing was going up. She'd got in line, but the line wasn't moving. She sent her son to summer camp and made her decision. She dressed up, put on makeup and perfume, and went to see the deputy director. He received her curtly: "Leave your application!" And he added that he had to stop by to take a look at her living conditions. He stopped by on the appointed day with his briefcase. "Everything's already on the table, Dmitry Dmitrievich. You must be hungry after work, and tired. Here, have something to eat. I whipped up stuffed cabbage rolls, I'm a good cook, but I don't have anyone to cook for!" He opened his briefcase and took out a bottle of brandy. She put glasses on the table. He poured. "Let's drink, you know to what, Tatiana Kirillovna? Not to an apartment. What does an apartment have to do with this? Let's drink to here's what. Someone once said that every person has a hole in his soul the size of God, but that's just silly. Every person has a hole the size of love!" He swore at her and used vulgar words, then he went limp and slumped to his side, panting and swallowing and swallowing. He had swallowed a long hair of hers and couldn't get it down or dredge it up. He stuck his finger down and nearly threw up. Then they lay there, thighs touching, stuck to each other. "I'm so sorry, Dmitry Dmitrievich. I'm sweating so badly!" He started licking the sweat off her. He slithered in again. She got a two-room.

Question: The Persians' chariots are racing back, into the very thick of the enemy host, sweeping the ranks aside and splashing the blood of the fallen under their scimitars. The barbarians shudder and flee. The Hellenes pursue the enemy with all their might, calling on each other not to scatter but to proceed in formation. Seeing that Clearchus has vanquished the foes who stood against him and is pursuing them, Cyrus lets loose a joyous cry, and those around him bow to him to the ground, as to their king. Cyrus and his suite rush into the very thick of the enemy host, where the king's golden halo gleams on the spear's long shaft in the rays of the now setting sun. When Cyrus finds the king and his numerous suite, he immediately cries out, "I see him!" and gallops toward Artaxerxes, looking for an opportunity to join battle with his brother. Tossing his spear, he wounds the king through his armor, so that the point enters two fingers' deep into his chest. The blow throws Artaxerxes from his horse, and confusion and flight ensues immediately in his suite, but the king rises to his feet and with his few escorts climbs a neighboring hill and from there follows the course of battle in safety. Meanwhile Cyrus, who has fallen into the thick of the foe, is carried off farther and farther by his fiery horse. It is already growing dark, and his enemies do not recognize him, his friends are searching everywhere, and he, proud of his victory and full of bold ardor, gallops ahead with a shout: "Off the road, you ragged men!" But at this a young Persian by the name of Mithridates runs up from the side and hurls a javelin that strikes Cyrus in the temple. Blood gushes from the wound, and Cyrus, deafened, falls to the ground. His steed spins to the side and is lost in the gloom, but the blood-stained saddlecloth slips from the horse's back and is picked up by Mithridates' servant.

Answer: No, that's all wrong! You need to begin very differently! You know what? Cross out everything up to here! You should start with the interesting part. About Daphnis and Lycaenion, and Chloe and Pan. Yes, from right there! So Daphnis was making extra money working nights. He unloaded beef carcasses from refrigerator cars at a meat factory, and here he was, just before dawn, coming back to his room, which he shared with a medical student, when a premature rosy-fingered Eos had nearly begun. The student was gone, but Lycaenion was here. He found the nurse languishing on his bed, and her eyes were moist with love. Her loosened hair took up half the bed. But before this, I forgot to say, he hadn't been able to get Chloe to do that. Chloe said that his hair was like the berries of a myrtle tree, he had taught her how to play the pipes, but when she began to play he took the pipes away and let his own lips slide over all the reeds, so it looked as though he was teaching her, correcting her mistake, but in fact, by these pipes, he was modestly kissing Chloe. Later when they embraced and lay down but rose again without achieving anything, they were hungry and drank wine, mixing it with milk. Lycaenion lit a cigarette and said, "Daphnis, you love Chloe. I found that out one night from the nymphs. They appeared in my dream and told me about her tears and yours and ordered me to save you by teaching you about matters of the heart. These matters are not just kisses and embraces, or what the goats and sheep do. You love words; for you, words are sweeter than kisses. But words only spoil everything. Come here!" He was about to say something, but she put her hand on his lips. "I know everything!" When she rose from him, drops of sperm trickled out of her and onto his belly. She gathered them in her palm and started smearing them over her breasts. She smiled. "The best cream!" She got up, clothed herself in her hair, and went to the window, clattering oddly over the parquet floor. She flung the curtains open. Only now did he notice that she had goat's hooves. She went back and sat on the bed, tossing her hair behind her and crossing her legs. She lit another cigarette, swinging her hoof. Releasing a stream of smoke, she said, "I'm not at all what you thought. I'm not just a girl with a braid. I'm a sister of mercy. Mercy is a brother to me, and I a sister to it. So what if I'm cloven-hoofed? It's just that not all your feelings come at the right time and some have room for growth. You are going to love many women—more than there are reeds in your pipes. Believe me, after all I am older than Cronos and all his lifetimes." Daphnis would go on to seek out his Chloe because a thinking mitt is always lost. It's there, in the winter, that a lost mitt is always going somewhere, I don't know where, to search for something, I don't know what. But in the *mlyvo* everything is supposed to be distinct. Here is the beginning, and here is the end. Everything has been predetermined in a prophetic dream. Because prophesy is not the cause of an event, but a flight into Egypt serves as cause for prophecy. If in the end what is prophesied is to return to winter, that means we will return. Yes, exactly, absolutely everything has to be done differently! Change both the mitt and history! Above all, the heroes. It's in winter, in a thaw, that a mitt can land in a puddle and allow itself to go limp until the nighttime frosts turn it to steel. The *mlyvo* is no place for going limp! Here mittens set themselves unattainable goals and move toward them with a doggedness inaccessible to mortals, like that hunter who set out after the elk that stole the sun. That is the only way to leave behind a ski track of stars! Daphnis is supposed to attempt the impossible, to resist the good-evil empire alone, and conquer! It's in winter that mitts simply search for each other, in order to press close, to be stuffed in the same pocket, but here you have to stake everything! He is not only supposed to deliver a baby in a stranded subway car with a random nocturnal mother-to-be, a drunken homeless woman, cut the umbilical cord with his pen knife after disinfecting it with vodka from the bottle the woman hadn't finished, and wrap the subway's new citizen in his own jacket—that anyone can do. No, something immeasurably more important will depend on him, on his action, on his good eye, swiftness, attack, and store of knowledge, and primarily on his readiness to sacrifice himself not for the sake of some Chloe but for the sake of something important—immortality, for example, or for the sake of that commander on the square who died of thirst anyway but refused to drink horse urine. For instance, Constantinople and the straits—return those to the Orochs or not? What about Alaska? Naturally, the act must come before the war, so that events ultimately touch everyone. So Daphnis sacrifices himself, and coming out of the elevator and happening to find himself at the epicenter of world events, he thwarts an attempt on the life of the English envoy and saves thousands of lives on the fields of an unnecessary war! A loving heart is more powerful than the good-evil empire! Or, at worst, he can simply try to save his own skin, which is no less human. But it's there, in the winter, that Daphnis can abandon his Chloe and flee to the back of beyond, jamming in behind crates in a trailer, taking sleeping pills, with his arms wrapped around plastic bottles—one for drinking, the other for piss. Whereas here, in the *mlyvo,* he has to go somewhere, I don't know where, and find something, I don't know what, in order to vanquish death, and he has until Friday. And he will find it, you'll see! One other not insignificant point. What kind of heroes can there be without a description of their appearance? After all, this shepherd and shepherdess are so easily confused with other shepherds and shepherdesses! You have to introduce the cast so they can be remembered, not like at a winter cocktail party, when they introduce fifteen people to you at one time and never in your life are you going to remember their names or lips! As far as Daphnis' appearance goes, that's pretty easy. Look at me! As for Chloe, how can I describe her? Maybe like this. Imagine the portrait of a young woman by Lorenzo di Credi, Florence, 1459/60-1537, oil on wood, and go upstairs in the Metropolitan, not by the main staircase but by the next one, after passing through the Middle Ages, and there you have to go not toward Titian but take an immediate left, by the doors letting out on the second floor—and pay attention, it's easy to miss it and walk past. This is her exact half-length portrait. She is depicted wearing black, sitting half-turned, and holding in her fingers a ring that is obviously going to play some important role since it has appeared in this story twice already. Something else very important: given this abundance of characters, it should be made clear right away which of them is the main character, so there's no confusion and no one thinks it's the word. Here is Chloe. This isn't just anyone saying one shouldn't hold evil inside, that cancer can come of this, therefore one must get rid of it, pass it on; nor is this the one who gathers ox-eye stems in the swamp, weaving them into cricket cages, and often getting so caught up in doing this she forgets her sheep. No! This is the one whose nipples jutted out like two gooseberries and who stealthily dug the dirt out from under her nails in the café and slipped it into the ice cream. She's the one who shouted she had no brains but did have a womb and therefore wanted to have a baby conceived in love. Or rather, she's the one who would later shout, when he would put another story on her hand, but for now Chloe says this: Only those who live for tomorrow believe in God, whereas I live only right now. I do not regret in the slightest choosing this path; it has made me independent and strong. And the *mlyvo* performs miracles with Chloe! If in the winter she is unattractive, then here she is even more unattractive, hates more fiercely, loves more passionately. If there she is a nobody, then here she is even more of a nobody and wants even more for people to love her, and the loneliness at night in the *mlyvo* is even more unbearable than in the winter. She isn't obliged to anyone to be ideal: irreproachable mitts are boring. Working in a hair salon on rich old biddies, she might resent life and believe that she, so young and ephemeral, ought to have everything, not these fat old fools. Actually, when the object of envy is young and beautiful, then the torments are even worse. Who in the depths of his soul could fail to understand poor Chloe? Taking a short break from her client and walking past an expensive fur coat hanging on a hanger, she stealthily flicked

144

her razor over it. No one ever suspected her. And all those train station stories! But she took pleasure in the role she'd invented for herself and played it to the hilt: the little orphan angel fallen on the garbage heap of life. The legend: she came here to go to school, was robbed, was raped. Face paint is layered over her good makeup; she is a trained makeup artist. A little blue on her lower lids, to demonstrate slight emaciation without affecting her beauty and attractiveness. A touch of mourning to her irreproachable manicure. Her puffy lips whitened slightly with toner. A slight but not repulsive dishevelment to her clothing. In the most visible place—her fragile shoulder—a shoulder seam unpicked, and through the gap a visible bruise. It is in the winter that Chloe marries the bird in the bush every time, whereas in the *mlyvo* she strives for something unfeasible. Daphnis is supposed to find the secret of immortality by Friday, and she must find Daphnis. Each time she thinks, here he is, my beloved, my dearest, my one and only, my little snort, and in her arms, Daphnis turns out to be Pan, who loves Pitys and loves Syrinx as well and is always pestering the dryads and pursuing the nymphs. Once, when Chloe was minding her sheep, playing and singing, Pan appeared before her as Daphnis and tried to seduce her, leading her toward what he wanted, and he promised her that in return all her goats would give birth to two kids at once. She let him, and once he got what he wanted, he started doing pushups and leaping around the room, as if it were a boxing ring and he were sparring with an invisible opponent. His shoulders and chest gleamed like armor from sweat. His gloves hung on a nail over the sofa, and his trophies were in a glass display case. "Daphnis," she called to him, "my beloved!"

And Pan said to her, "Why didn't you tell me it was your first time, fool?" When Chloe realized his deceit, she commented drily, "Give me the gloves!" Grinning at her maidenly daredevilry, Pan helped Chloe pull them on, huge and heavy, like a leather sofa's bolsters. He raised his palm. "Hit me!" All of a sudden Chloe struck him not in the hand but the face, over and over, with all her might, desperately, spitefully. Disconcerted, Pan leapt back, feeling his nose, and then burst out laughing. "You've got to be kidding!" He started dodging her blows, jumping around the room-ring, lunging to the left, then the right, giving her a spank. He shouted, "Come on, Lenka, do it!" She became furious that she couldn't land one on his face anymore. By accident she knocked a glass off the table. But she smashed the vase off the television on purpose. Then she started breaking the glass in the display case and the trophies. Pan decked her with a jab to the jaw. She dragged herself home all blubbery, holding her cheek. She applied snow to it. Light, bright snow was sprinkling down from a gray sky. On her way, she also stopped at a store to buy milk for her cat. Chloe had a cat that loved visitors and flowed from one pair of arms to the next. Now, when no one was home, the cat jumped to the window, made herself comfy by the open hinged pane, and tried to catch snow-flakes with her paw. Then she yawned, and no one saw what a big ribbed cat gullet she had. After all, one is always attracted by what can't be seen. In talking about the mitt, you have to know what about it can and can't be seen. So now one needs to talk about what can't be seen. Without seeing Chloe, to know everything about her, the merest trifle, even how she goes to the Tungus-ka for water and takes along an ax to break up the ice in the frozen hole. And so they don't have to go every time, Chloe and her mother keep chunks of ice in the cold shed, in a Cuban sugar sack, which they cram into a barrel in a corner of the kitchen, where the ice melts. Soon after the ice breaks up you can't go anywhere without a mosquito net. They put on their quilted vests and smear themselves with grease. When you go into the forest, even as you approach, you can hear the dense drone. On windy days, clouds of mosquitoes are driven into the town. They swarm the walls, as if the huts were growing fur. Three or four times a summer they have to be smoked out. People light dry bark and chips in a holey bowl, let it get going, and then layer on moss and green resinous fir branches. This produces a heavy, acrid smoke. And still they swallow mosquitoes with their pottage right up until the freeze. But for heaven's sake, who cares about hovels? Let's forget pestilences and the dislike of the winter! No, we must shift the action somewhere to the south, which, as we know, dulls one's thoughts but heightens the senses. There, you see how the sunset pulses on the revolving glass door of the expensive hotel on the shore of the Euxeinos Pontos, which, for the illiterate, means "hospitable sea"? After all, it's nicer for your heart to bleed over heroes in a town that was once second after Athens. Not for nothing did Strabo write that trade in Dioscura was conducted with the mediation of three hundred interpreters. And how could that happen without a beach photographer, wearing shorts and sombrero, a monkey on his shoulder and an inflated yellow crocodile under his arm? Or we could head for the bazaar in Damascus, where they sell little boys for next to nothing and teach them everything. They'll even castrate them, if that's what

you like. The dead season on Crete—and the tangerines
and oranges lie strewn under trees in the parks, but they
don't taste good. It seems odd that the children of cy-
clopses and cicadas are islands. And if your drop-dead
deadline really is Friday, why are you lollygagging! On
your way! Follow your nose! You have to find something to ward off death, after all, be it an amulet or a
plot. Magic words. Say them and no death can frighten
you. Daphnis will come out of the house, and everything in the yard is whiter than white from the snow
that fell overnight. The streetcars aren't running and the
trains are experiencing delays. The snow piles up thick
and slow, last year's. The huge, newly constructed apartment building looks like it's rising into the snowfall, like
a Zeppelin. When he walks by the gynaeceum, he raps
on the window. Daphnis stops and takes a closer look.
It's Lycaenion waving, summoning him through the
hinged pane, as if to say, Come quickly and I'll tell you
something very important. Daphnis shakes his head.
"Busy!" There's a crackling sound as Lycaenion flings
open the shutters of the window, which has been sealed
for the winter. She shouts, "You can't return an eye to
every socket or a person to every skull! But I have one
secret! Come here!" She pokes her head in and tosses her
braid through the window like a rope. "Well, what's
taking you so long?" She rests her hands on the windowsill for stability. "Grab on and climb, my beloved,
my one and only, my little snort!" Daphnis hightails it
out of town without stopping, and he will keep running
until the first green, green grass pokes through, since
everything secret becomes manifest. Daphnis will keep
on walking. The leaves' shadow turns the road ribbon to
guipure. A swift flits by. A snail races its own shadow.

Water lives out its days in a puddle. A pebble gets into his sandal. An impasto sunset. Shelter. You can burrow into the hay for the night. A kopek moon. Daphnis lays his head toward where he came from and his feet into the starry ski track. The mosquitoes eat him up at night. A sleep sweaty and disturbed. All night Daphnis tosses and turns, and in the morning he awakens with his feet toward where he came from and his head toward where the sun keeps dragging the balking elk. Daphnis rises and continues on his way, amazed at the inside-out landscape. The closer he comes to his hometown, the more intense his amazement. As the spires, cupolas, and domes begin to reveal themselves, a man with a bloodied head, clutching something in his fist, runs past Daphnis from the direction of the city. Daphnis thinks, "It's just amazing how much this city looks like mine!" And he picks up his pace. In the city, meanwhile, while Daphnis was absent, the following occurred. Summer came. Two Oroch masons were working for a certain Tungus, and while the latter was going to the temple it began to rain. In the rain you can see the threads that stretch from the upper trees to the trees, from upper grass to grass, from upper people to umbrellas. And while their boss was gone, the Orochs saw much silver and gold ware in the underground storage and they wanted to steal it. Which they did. They found their way into the underground space and took all the silver and gold they found. Then the one who crawled out first thought, "Why should I share the loot? I could have it all for myself!" He went right up to his buddy as he was coming through the narrow access and struck him on the head with a hammer so that he fell down dead. The Oroch grabbed all the loot and was out of there. As soon as the rain stopped and

steam started rising on the river from the sand, the boss
came home and saw the corpse lying in his cellar. The
poor Tungus began quaking with fear. What should he
do? First he wanted to hide the body, so no one would
know, because he greatly feared Oroch retribution. But
the murderer had hidden the silver and gold and was
already running through the streets crying, "The Tunguses butchered an Oroch! Everyone come quick! The
Tunguses butchered an Oroch!" At this, an enraged
crowd rushed from every quarter to the banks of the
Tunguska, where bitterness and hope found shelter in
squalid little houses, and were about to initiate a slaughter. The Tunguses brought their shaman out on a stretcher. At the sight of the elder the crowd fell silent. "What
are you trying to do, you unfortunate people?" he began
in a weak voice, but his every word could be heard. Even
the river fell quiet. "Kill the living over a dead man? He
died, yes, he did. It's not so terrible. How could anyone's
death be a surprise? Life is a string and death is the air. A
string makes no sound without air. And then, he hasn't
left for good, he's just away for a while. And that the
murderer was not a Tungus, that is clear. But I see you
need some kind of proof. You will have it right now!
And so, there were two Oroch masons working in the
house. While it was raining, they crawled into the cellar.
When the rain stopped, the thread that connected one of
them to the sky broke. That was it. Now the dead man
himself will show us who the murderer is. Bring the
dead man!" And so it was done, they brought the Oroch
with the smashed head and set him at the shaman's feet.
The crowd took a step back. The elder looked around
and saw Chloe in the back ranks of Orochs. He sum-
moned her with a gesture. The crowd parted. Looking

around in fright, Chloe stepped forward. Nervous, she kept blowing the hair out of her eyes and jutting her lower lip. The elder held his hand out palm up, as if in anticipation of her putting something in it. Understanding nothing, looking around, Chloe shrugged, smiling in dismay. The elder said, "The ring!" She: "What ring?" He: "*The* ring. Why else did it appear in this story? This must be the amulet we've been searching for!" Chloe attempted to remove the ring, but in her fright it got stuck on her finger and wouldn't come off. She started licking her finger. Finally the ring slipped off; the elder placed it in the dead man's hand and closed his fingers around it tight. The crowd held its breath. The dead man revived. The crowd gasped. The dead man sat up and began looking for his killer. He saw him immediately, hiding behind other people's backs, and shouted, "You are my killer!" The stunned crowd rushed at the evildoer with a shout, in order to tear him apart, and the dead man, taking advantage of the general confusion, meanwhile fled unnoticed. And here Daphnis comes walking through the streets, and everything seems familiar, only the bridges are lower because the water rose after the rains. All of a sudden he sees the gynaeceum. Exactly the same. Exactly the same Lycaenion stuck her head out the window. Someone is climbing up her braid to see her. Everything's the same but somehow different. As if everyone's been switched. All of a sudden it occurs to Daphnis that maybe he simply turned around in his sleep and is now coming into his own city. He is going home to Chloe. The house looks the same. And the smells in the entryway are the same. So is the bell. Chloe opens up—exactly the same, only alien somehow. She asks, "Who do you want?" Daphnis notices, on the coat rack in the vestibule, a policeman's greatcoat with shoulder straps. He doesn't know what to say. A man's voice from the kitchen: "Who's there? What does he want?" Chloe answers over her shoulder: "I don't know. They're begging their living again!" The voice: "Kick him out. Everything's getting cold!" Daphnis finally whispers through parched lips, "Do you really not recognize me?" Chloe: "No." Daphnis: "I'm your Daphnis!" Chloe: "Have you lost your mind? Daphnis is my intended. There he is sitting in the kitchen calling me in for supper. I searched a long time, my whole life, and finally found him. We're planning to get married—just as it was in the prophetic dream. Though in a completely different story." Daphnis: "But we're in that story! And I need to find a way to avert death by Friday. So I thought, maybe it's that ring? You remember, the one you told me about, something about an extended day." Chloe hides her hand behind her back and says, "That's all nonsense. Immortality starts between a woman's legs." And she closes the door. By the way, do you ever wonder why there is such an abundance of these unnecessary, fleeting people? It's a small story, not enough for everyone. Who's to argue? The principal mitts can't get along without all those waiters, newspaper sellers, receptionists, elevator boys, beach photographers, voices from kitchens, and police greatcoats. So they have to be left their "dinner is served"! What's the rest for? Take the photographer flashing his black and gold mouth. Who needs him? Why do we need to know about his long-held fear that suddenly the doorbell will ring and his fully grown daughter, whom he has never seen, will appear on his doorstep? He was always trying to calculate how old she must be now. Why do we need to know he once wanted to shoot apples, like with Man Ray, and nothing ever came of it? While he's making love to his wife, he pictures the woman who stayed at their dacha last summer, and once again, eyes shut, he sees her pulling down her panties, one leg then the other, and her firm buttocks tensing and squeezing so hard at his touch that the tip of his tongue couldn't get in, her pissing in front of him—and the stream flying out in bursts, wetting the sand, and hardening immediately. The photographer's wife has known for a long time that her husband cheats. Once at night she raised up on an elbow, sniffed him, and smelled someone else's perfume, yet she reconciled herself to the status of the wronged but wise woman. On the wall is a photograph of her younger brother—a soldier, a hero, he perished performing his official duties, but in fact he died choking on his own vomit in a ditch. Next to it is a photo of the triplets her sister had. From across the fence comes the conversation between their neighbor, an Azeri woman, and the mail carrier. Her Russian is bad. She meant to say "more than a month" but it came out "one moon and a little." In the summer they always let rooms to vacationers. One dacha visitor, an associate professor from Kursk, was compiling some dictionary. He cut himself on broken glass at the shore, took a bus to the hospital, and the bus got into an accident—and was stranded at a railroad crossing. Later, those pages with columns of words were on jam jars. Rather than twist-on lids, his wife covered the jars with the paper and tied it with string, the old-fashioned way. One time a sculptor rented the entire ground floor and was working in the garden when suddenly it began to rain. He shouted, "Help me, my bust. We have to carry my bust from the garden onto the terrace!" They dragged it together, he slipped—and it was all smashed. His son has a mathematical mind. A random number, like a license plate, is nineteen cubed for him. For some reason he recalled how his uncle, his mother's brother, came to visit them when he was a child. He never swam anywhere. He didn't even take off his jersey. But in the shower, through a crack, he saw that he had two pairs of nipples. He himself was stout, and the tops of his breasts were almost like a woman's, but below there were two more tiny spots. You could always see the sunset from the terrace. Once a cloud dipped a ray like an oar. The photographer bought the house from a Moscow veterinarian's widow. He had retired by the sea on his pension, rented out the lower rooms, and liked to talk to the vacationers in the evening about the animals he had worked with: before the war it was only horses, then hogs for cafeterias, and rabbits. During the war it was horses again. After the war, piglets, cows, goats, and hens. Animals were kept on both the Arbat and Gorky Street—in courtyards, attics, and bathrooms. In the rabies scare of 1952-53, dogs. For the festival of youth and students in 1957—doves, swans, and ducks on the ponds. Then more and more dogs and cats. Reading the newspapers, the old veterinarian rejoiced at disasters the way Blok did at the sinking of the *Titanic*—that the ocean did still exist. And no one needed any of this, neither the veterinarian who died in the Olympics, nor he himself roaming the shore with a yellow crocodile under his arm. The pebbles underfoot creaked and slid aside. Not his son the mathematician, who fell in love with a girl from a good family, an engineering student, smart but deaf. He whispers words of love into her ear, and she says, "What?" When she got her first hearing aid, the doctor said that if she wore long hair, no one would see the device. All that's beside the point. Especially since the war came later and the house burned down and the photographer and everyone else had already died or would. So why talk about them? From the very beginning we should have deleted this photographer and his beach, which shriveled so from morning on, and so quiet you could hear something indecipherable being shouted somewhere in the mountains, something like, "Thalassa! Thalassa!" Because of people like him, who appeared on two paths from this side and continued on the back, like a Moebius sky, the world would only ramify to infinity, grow like a ball of last year's snow, fending off the brigands' assault. That's why mum's the word about them in the prophetic dream. Although, truth be told, even prophetic dreams should be cut short. Because when something prophetic is dreamt, you hope you wake up in time. So nothing more happens. If only you could wake up at a mitt wedding. Chloe would break her heel—a bad omen—and cry incessantly when the priest at the lectern would insist that she rejoice, like Rebecca. The chorus would sing the Psalm of David: "You shall see your sons' sons! Peace shall be upon Israel!" And Daphnis, soaked in sweat in his uncomfortable new suit, with a nasty feeling on his fingers, which were sooty from the candle, would think, "What does Israel have to do with this?" And then the brigands would attack.

Question: When after a long faint Cyrus finally comes around, a few eunuchs who were nearby want to sit him on another horse and lead him to a place of safety. But he no longer has the strength to sit on a horse, and the eunuchs lead him, propping him up on both sides. His legs buckle, his head falls on his chest, but he is certain he has won, hearing the runners calling Cyrus the king and praying to be spared. Meanwhile a few beggars from Kaunos who follow the king's host, performing the lowliest and dirtiest jobs, happen to join up with Cyrus's escorts, taking them for their own. But as soon as they notice the red cloaks over their armor, they realize they're facing their enemies, since all the king's soldiers wore white cloaks. Then one of them, aiming a javelin at Cyrus from behind, severs the vein behind his knee. Crashing to the ground, Cyrus strikes his wounded temple on a rock and breathes his last. Learning of his brother's death, Artaxerxes, surrounded by courtiers and soldiers carrying torches, descends from the hill and approaches the dead Cyrus on foot. According to Persian custom, the head and right hand are severed from the corpse. The king orders he be given his brother's head. Grabbing it by the hair, thick and long and brightly lit by the flame from many torches, Artaxerxes shows it to all.

Answer: There was no time at all until Friday. Something had to be done and fast. We were sitting in the kitchen, holding each other's hands in silence. She was looking out the window. All of a sudden she said, "It's December and still no snow." And then . . . Oh, you're not listening to me anyway.

Question: After the battle, the king, wanting everyone to say and think that he killed his brother with his own hand, sent gifts to Mithridates, who had struck Cyrus in the temple with a javelin, and ordered him told, "The king is rewarding you with these gifts because you found and brought Cyrus's saddle-cloth," at which Mithridates said nothing and swallowed the insult. After all, to him belonged the honor of victory, and now some saddle-cloth! Here he was invited to the feast, and he arrived in expensive raiment and gold adornments granted him by the king. After the food and wine, the queen mother Parysatis's chief eunuch said, "What a beautiful raiment the king has given you, Mithridates. What jewelry and bracelets, and what a precious sabre! Explain to me, friend, is that in fact such a glorious deed, collecting and bringing a saddle-cloth that has fallen from a horse's back?" Unable to restrain himself, Mithridates, whose tongue had been loosened by wine, replied, "You can go on all you like about saddle-cloths, but I'm telling you: Cyrus was killed by this hand! I aimed for his eye but missed a little, but I struck right through his temple. He died from that wound." Everyone else, seeing Mithridates' misfortune and evil end, looked hard at the floor, and only the master of the house found what to say. "My friend Mithridates, why don't we drink and eat, bowing before our king's genius, and leave speeches that surpass our understanding alone." The eunuch turned the conversation over to Parysatis, and she to Artaxerxes. The king was beside himself with rage. That was when he ordered Mithridates tortured to death. They took two troughs precisely joined together, and in one of them they put the unlucky but loose-lipped daredevil upside down, and on top they covered him with the second trough, so that his head and legs remained outside but his entire torso was covered inside. Then they gave Mithridates something to eat and he refused, but they drove a needle through his eyes and so forced him to swallow. When he had eaten, they poured milk mixed with honey into his mouth and smeared this mixture over his entire face. They kept turning the trough in such a way that the sun was constantly shining into the tortured man's eyes, and uncountable flies clung to his face. And since he himself was doing everything a man who has eaten and drunk inevitably does, worms quickly infested the rotting filth, crawled into his entrails, and began eating away at his living body. Thus Mithridates was tortured for seventeen days because he is and can no longer be made nonexistent. And there is no way to intercept a javelin once it's been thrown.

Answer: That last night we loved each other so much, more than ever before. I forgot myself for an hour or two, but when I woke up it was dawning and outside everything was covered in snow. I arose quietly so as not to wake her. I dressed and put on my coat and hat. I peeked into the bedroom. She had kicked her leg out from under the blanket. She had a scar on her heel; as a child she'd jumped on a rake. I cautiously shut the front door behind me and went downstairs. I stuck my finger in the mailbox out of habit. The lobby door slammed behind me. The entire courtyard was white and the snow was still falling. Fresh, morning snow. Someone was using a yellow dustpan to dig out his car, which had turned into a snowdrift. The streetcars weren't running because of the drifts. People were walking single-file to the subway across the vacant lot; there was already a beaten path. Everything was hidden under the snow—the playground and the garbage both. And again it came down so hard that for a moment the street disappeared completely behind the snowfall. White. Mute. Winter.

I start attending the Bilinskaya School on Taganrogsky Avenue in the Khakhladzhev building. That building is still standing, known to all Rostovans as the House of Shoes.

At the entrance exam, after gabbling out the Our Father to the priest, I'm so nervous I make a curtsey instead of a full bow.

School begins, actually, with Iosif Pokorny's stationery store on Sadovaya. All you have to say is, "Bilinskaya, first year." They outfit me with a packet that has all my textbooks, notebooks, paints, brushes of the right sizes, pens, erasers, and pencil case. Wishing to demonstrate the squirrel's softness, the clerk runs the brush across my cheekbone.

In the morning, Mama combs my hair and braids my braid so tightly that it pulls my skin and I can't shut my mouth, and my eyes are as slanted as a Chinaman's. She sends me off to school with my sisters, kisses us, fixes the bows on our aprons, and slips each of us fifteen kopeks for dinner. On the way there we spend the money on treats—hard candies or a piece of halvah from the street vendors, who choose spots near schools especially.

The doorman at the entrance wears galloons. The old man helps the teachers with their coats and rings the bell at the beginning and end of class, keeping an eye on the big grandfather clock in the vestibule. In his free time he sits in his corner holding a book. People say he's a Tolstoyan and doesn't eat meat and that after he read "Strider" he bequeathed his skeleton to the school's anatomical collection.

You must not be late. At eight-thirty they close the cloakroom, and you cannot appear in class wearing your coat. I even remember my cloakroom number: 134. The same number was inside my galoshes, on the velvety crimson lining.

But why do I remember it? Who needs to know about a nonexistent number in a nonexistent cloakroom? After all, no one is going to hang my coat, the hand-me-down from my sisters, on that hook. And never again in winter after classes will I go down to the cloakroom and pull on the detested thick trousers under my school dress and tie my hood before setting off for home. My home doesn't even exist. Nothing I once had now exists. No one and nothing.

Or maybe it does. Here it is, before my eyes, the auditorium on the second floor where the windows' reflections can snake so over the parquet floor. Each morning begins with a general prayer.

Yuli Pavlovich Ferrari, the singing teacher, gives the notes on the piano, G and B, for two-part singing of "To the Heavenly King," "Save Your People, Lord," and "The Holy Virgin." Good, dear Yuli Pavlovich! On the very first day he notices my voice and asks me to stay after classes. I am going to perform at all the school matinees and concerts.

All the supplies purchased at the store turn out to be nowhere near enough. Fortunately, I have experienced sisters who teach me that, besides textbooks and notebooks, every self-respecting schoolgirl has to have an album for verse and drawings, that the pink blotter inserted in a notebook is a sign of poor taste and virtual poverty and one should buy blotting paper in other colors and fasten it to one's notebooks with ribbons in fancy bows. In class I have the absolute right to look askance at the girls with pathetic pink blotters. This is how I treat my desk mate, a girl with a duck nose and golden curls. One time she declaims Krylov's tale "The Two Dogs" with such expression—"Zhuzhu, the curly poodle"—that behind her back everyone starts calling her Zhuzhu because of her curls. I remember condescendingly giving her a piece of "proper" blotting paper and how bitterly she wept over that.

Now, after all that's happened, it seems marvelous, fantastic almost, that an idiotic blotter could poison someone's life like that!

Zhuzhu studies for free because she is poor. Everyone knows that her mama is raising her without a father because she has been a governess in various families since she was young.

I make friends with Mila, who everyone calls Mishka. I like her for her desperation. Mishka wants to be a ship's captain or an African explorer, and in church she only crosses herself for travelers at sea. I like everything about her, even her ink-spattered ruler. In the washroom, near the lavatory, high up near the ceiling on a bar, hangs a towel, long and secured at the ends, and you have to pull it to dry off. Mishka grabs it and swings, like on a giant stride. She must not have weighed anything because the bar didn't break off.

In the interval in the assembly hall I run after Mishka, and the parquet is as slippery as a skating rink. I slam into the piano in the corner, lose consciousness, and only come to in the office of the school principal, Zinaida Georgievna Shiryaeva. She is dabbing my temples with something disgusting that makes it impossible not to come around. Everyone is afraid of the principal. Her dry lips kiss me. She would die of cholera in 1920.

Relations in the classroom are complicated. I write a note to Natasha Martyanova, whom everyone loves and calls Tala: "Dear Talochka, Let's be friends." In response, amazement: Don't I know she is friends with Tusya? I hate Tusya. She's a coward and nasty on top of that. She has myopia and can't see anything from the front row. At this time eyeglasses are a rarity and she's afraid of ridicule. Only after insistent instructions from the school authorities does she appear in class in glasses, which make her even uglier.

I'm also friends with Lyalya. She is growing big brown eyes. She is the most beautiful girl in the class, and everyone envies her. Not only that, she is released from morning prayers and Scripture.

Each class has its own place in church—the youngest in front, the older ones behind, shifting back each time they move up to the next class. Near each classroom there are always several chairs where class ladies periodically seat the weak for a few minutes to rest during the service. The girls say that at a certain point in the service, after the priest says certain words, you can make a wish and it will come true. Everyone stands there and waits, for fear of missing the words so that they can wish for something cherished.

If only those secret wishes could be collected and fulfilled . . .

Scripture is taught by Father Konstantin Molchanov. The priest is a lover of, and expert at, beekeeping. During the lesson the clever girls start asking him artlessly about bees, hives, and larvae, and he starts telling them, gets carried away, and talks about apian wonders the entire hour. Later, hearing the bell, he checks himself and reassures himself that that's all right, bees are Scripture, too.

One day he tells us about the resurrection of the dead, and Mishka suddenly asks him a question that stuns us all. "How can we rise from the ashes if the worms are going to eat our bodies, the birds eat the worms, the birds fly all over the world, and someone eats them, too?"

Father Konstantin is silent for a few moments and then answers, "If a cobbler sews a boot and then rips it apart and throws one piece to Africa, another to America, and a third to Asia or the North Pole, and then he collects all the pieces, it will cost him nothing to sew those parts again and make the original boot. So it is after our death. Our body becomes both heaven and earth, trees and water, and God will collect all the parts into one."

The worms have long since eaten Father Konstantin, and the birds have long pecked those worms and flown over the world. Sky, earth, trees, and water have eaten those birds. May the Lord rest your soul, lover of bees!

Behind her back we call Natalia Pavlovna, the class matron, Nataleshka. No one likes her because she is mean and unforgiving, and she also has a large birthmark covering her cheek. She's stout, short, and to look taller she wears her hair piled high and high heels. She always speaks sharply and ringingly, as if she were cracking the words like nuts. Even her praise sounds like scolding. One day, while substituting for an ill teacher, Nataleshka gives us an assignment and herself spends the entire lesson writing something. The school principal Shiryaeva peeks in and calls her into the corridor for a few minutes. While they are talking behind the half-closed door, Mishka, who sits in the front row in front of the teacher's desk, cranes her neck and reads the unfinished lines of the letter out loud, in which Nataleshka is making someone a declaration of love: "My beloved Volodechka! I want to kiss your feet, yes, your feet!" When she returns, Nataleshka suddenly notices by the silence that something's wrong. She sees her abandoned letter on the desk, snatches and crumples it up, and looks at the class in fright. One girl is the first to giggle, and everyone starts choking with laughter. I, too, giggle because it is utterly impossible to imagine our Nataleshka, with her crimson patch, kissing the feet of some Volodechka. All of a sudden she breaks away, runs for the door, stops, evidently remembering that in the corridor she might bump into the principal, and burying herself in the corner, begins to weep. Our mean, hateful Nataleshka is sobbing softly and inconsolably. The laughter sticks in our throats, and everyone for some reason wants not to laugh now but to weep as well. At this, the bell rings. Nataleshka turns around and her face is tear-stained, and her good cheek is just as crimson as the bad one. She sniffles into her handkerchief and says, for the first time not cracking nuts, but softly, almost in a whisper, "Go."

The girls are sure that Volodechka is our drawing teacher, Vladimir Georgievich Shteinbukh. Before our lesson the porter throws a large piece of green cloth over our blackboard. We can hear Vladimir Georgievich in the corridor now. He is always muttering under his breath, always cursing someone. He comes in and nods without looking at us, straightens the folds, and places the geometric plaster figures. He is neither young nor handsome and has a wet, runny nose and a jutting lip. We have no idea how anyone might want to kiss those feet in their old lace-up shoes. People say that in his youth he even studied in Italy and was a successful artist, but he turned to drink over some princess who toyed with him and threw him over. The younger girls tell each other what they've heard from the older girls. Sometimes the drawing teacher forgets himself and right in the lesson, threatening some invisible someone outside with his fist, begins snarling in a suppressed voice, "Go paint your flogging in the district office—that will get them applauding! Here, take a bite of this!" And he cocks a snook at the window and his lip juts out even harder and turns inside out.

German is taught by Evgenia Karlovna Volchanetskaya: Evgeshka. She doesn't let the slightest extraneous sound be made in class. She even forbids pencil sharpening during the lesson. And all this in a voice that could cut glass. People fear her and don't like her. They say the parents gave her a box of chocolates and put twenty-five rubles in. Our hatred for Evgeshka carries over to her articles and participles, too. It pains me even more that when we eat Hercules oatmeal at home; Papa always jokes, "Why Herr Kules and not Frau Kules?" Maybe that's why before I went to school I thought German was supposed to be something cheerful.

On the other hand, we are all in love with our Frenchwoman, who the other teachers and class matrons cannot stand. Maria Iosifovna Marten is not like the rest of them, dressed in their navy and black. She wears colorful blouses, a red fox on her shoulders, and a red wig on her head. In class we sing "Sur le pont d'Avignon"[5] and dance, holding hands with her. She skips down the aisle between the desks as if we were in fact on that famous bridge in some unimaginable, impossible Avignon. One day Maria Iosifovna brings a photograph, and we are amazed that that bridge, the only one in the world on which all anyone does is sing and dance, breaks off somewhere in mid-river. After lessons an officer waits for our Frenchwoman at the school gates.

Worst of all for me is arithmetic and the exact sciences in general. At supper Papa tries to explain to me the mystery of the muzhik, the boat, the wolf, the goat, and the head of cabbage, about all those trips from bank to bank, and all I can see is the goat's eyes and I vividly imagine the wolf itself, and the cabbage, and the stream, and the muzhik angry at me because his wife and kiddies have probably been waiting for him at home for a long time.

The crushes begin for us. The disease of notes and sighs grips one girl after another. I, too, have a crush. The object of my admiration is Nina Rokotova from the senior, teacher training class, who has a thick long braid past her waist. To me, Nina is some higher being. During the interval the girls walk through the corridor arm in arm,

---

5. "On the bridge of Avignon." *(Fr.)*

and I try to walk so that I end up right behind her. Her braid, tied with a white silk ribbon, dangles in front of me. Nina and her friend are discussing a fight at the skating rink—the subject of the whole school's conversations. Eighth-formers at the boys' school arranged a duel over her, my Nina, and fought on skates! Mishka, who was at the rink then and saw everything, said that they started separating the duelers, but one of them managed to rip the other's cheek with his skate blade, there was a lot of blood, and the other boy, who lost consciousness, was taken to the hospital. And all this for love! For her, my Nina! I run up behind her, catch the tip of her heavy braid, and kiss it. Nina doesn't allow anyone to touch her braid—only me.

I think the whole world is in love. All the girls at school are in love. My sisters are in love. My sister Katya has fallen in love from photographs with the pilot Kuznetsov, who sails in the sky in his own Blériot, as light as a butterfly, as the newspapers wrote. My brother Sasha is against Kuznetsov and for Gaber-Volynsky in his Farman. Their preferences are defended desperately, to the point of tears. When Kuznetsov schedules flights in Rostov, pandemonium sets in. The whole town rushes to the field near the Balabanovskaya woods. There's no squeezing through down Skobelevskaya or Gimnazicheskaya. All the paid seats inside the fenced-off site are jammed, crowds of the curious stand in a solid, immobilized mass by the fence, and people hang on gates, perch on roofs, and spill onto balconies. The public has been warned that the flight will follow the rules of the All-Russia Aero Club and will be recognized as having taken place if the mechanism can stay in the air at least three minutes. Met by a frenzied ovation, Kuznetsov gets into his Blériot, which really does look like a butterfly. The plane taxis and lifts its wheels off the field for a moment, but alights immediately, tipping onto its right wing. To console the audience, they announce that the tickets are valid for another demonstration in a few days, when the propeller and wing are repaired. The flight doesn't work a week later either. After barely taking off, the aviator falls back to earth again, and he leaves town ignominiously, carting away the broken Blériot. Katya's love for Kuznetsov passes. Sasha, on the other hand, triumphs. Gaber-Volynsky comes to Rostov soon after and flies above the audience and woods in his Farman for much more than three minutes.

Masha has a romance, too. She is being courted by Boris Mueller, the son of the German teacher at the boy's school. I take the most active part in her romance: I help my sister pass along her "little secrets." I am gripped by an unfamiliar but marvelous sensation: I'm not just passing a note, I'm serving love! Masha questions me. How did he take her letter? What did he say and in what tone of voice when he read it? What was the expression on his face? When Boris calls on us, Masha sometimes shuts herself in her room with him, and I have to warn them by a previously agreed signal if Mama suddenly appears. Behind the door I hear muffled, agitated voices. It even seems as though they're arguing. Then silence. What could they be silent about for so long?

Boris is planning to become a naval officer. He writes notes, full of assurances of his love, in even handwriting that resembles a honeycomb.

Boris and Masha go to the picture show and take me along. I am struck by a color film about butterflies. Boris explains that this is done by hand. Women workers in a film factory paint the frames and ruin their eyes, and later go blind. This simple connection makes me uneasy. Someone has to go blind so that we can see pretty butterflies.

Boris is a Lutheran, and once on our way, strolling with Masha, we peek into the Protestant church. I'm amazed that people are praying there seated at school desks.

Masha is constantly looking at herself in the mirror, turning so that the knobs on her chest are visible. She worries that nothing is growing on her. On the other hand, they are on me, although it's still a little early.

I see my sister circling certain days on her secret calendar, and out of the blue I ask her about it right when Boris is visiting us. They were planning to go to his house to play music and were choosing sheet music. Once I've asked, I'm horrified that I've asked something I shouldn't. Masha blushes and so does Boris. My sister hits me over the head with the music as hard as she can and hides in her room. Boris knocks on her door. She won't open up. He leaves, saying, "Fool!" through clenched teeth. I still don't know whether he was talking about me or Masha.

That same ill-fated day, Masha stumbles while setting the table and splits her lip on the edge of the table. It takes a long time to stop the bleeding, and then she goes around for days with a bandage on her upper lip, or rather, refuses to leave her room at all. She's afraid someone will see her face looking like that. Every so often she has hysterics that she's ugly now and no one will ever love her. We try to reassure Masha, but she won't listen to anyone and she shouts at me: "Go away!" She thinks this is all my fault. I know it isn't, but at the same time I realize it is all my fault. In tears I tell Mama what happened and search for consolation from her. She answers, "Once a month nature reminds a woman that she can become a mother." For the first time Mama doesn't understand me. And there's nothing to be done. Masha will have that unattractive scar her whole life.

My brother Sasha laughs at our "Loves," but he has a romance, too, and an unlucky one. He is writing someone letters. Sometimes he starts speaking about women condescendingly, with contempt. I sense he knows something we don't. I'm afraid to question him. But I see that from time to time Papa gives him three rubles for something, in secret from Mama.

Nyusya is in love, too. She has a suitor already, but she has almost no time to see her Kolya because she spends hours playing the piano. Nyusya is the pride and hope of our family. After all, she may go study in Petersburg, to the conservatory, and she is definitely going to be a world-famous pianist. She alone doubts this, apparently.

I study music at home. I'm taught unsystematically, by either Mama or Nyusya. Nyusya opens up "The School of Hunten" and begins to explain the notation system to me, but she tires of playing teacher very quickly and abandons me to Mama, reducing me to tears with her insulting verdict that I cannot be a concert pianist because of my small hands—I can barely reach an octave. No one thinks about the proper placement of the hand, and I strain as much as I can to extract more sound with my weak fingers, and Mama praises my "attack." In fact, these lessons are ruining my hand, but I study willingly, and as soon as I understand the bass clef I begin to figure out little songs myself.

The queen comes to Rostov on tour. Not the Spanish queen but the real thing, Vyaltseva. Every conversation is about her. At school they assure each other that the buttons on Vyaltseva's tall, stylish boots are diamonds. My brother Sasha, lying in wait for her with his buddies at the entrance to her hotel on Taganrogsky Avenue, says that he barely crawled out alive from the scuffle when she tossed her signed photograph into the crowd. At supper my father says that every time she arrives in a town that has a university or other institutions of higher education, Vyaltseva always goes to see the chancellor and asks which of the students have borrowed money for their education and immediately writes out a check. At a reception arranged in her honor by the city fathers, she asks what there is in Rostov. "Nothing!" my father says, flying into a passion and even throwing his fork on the table. "Nothing! It's a hole!"

Mama scoffs at the "incomparable":

"A chambermaid!"

Everyone at the table is indignant, and I most of all. My sisters and I listen endlessly at home to gramophone records of Vyaltseva. I sing her entire repertoire.

Papa is going to see Vyaltseva at the Asmolov and can only take one of us. He has two tickets. We draw lots. The cherished slip from Sasha's cap goes to me! I can't sleep that night, then I'm in agony all day and can't wait until the evening. Finally we're in the chockfull theater. It's sold out. The hall bursts out in ovations, then falls still, holding its breath as it listens to the divine voice. The hall breathes love. We have good seats, but I can't get a good look at Vyaltseva's face because of the tears spurting from my eyes. I greedily seize upon each instant, each gesture and pose, how she bows, how she waits out the storm of applause. The air is saturated like a sponge with love for the incomparable queen. The queen magnanimously accepts this love. She allows them to love her. I look at Papa and his burning eyes. From that moment on I know everything about myself. Falling asleep, I imagine the day when I will see my name in boldface on a poster, and I drop off to sleep happy.

We live on Nikitskaya, and the back door lets out here on the Palermo, a summer concert hall built in a garden. The front door is around the corner. Here visiting queens of a somewhat lower rank perform. We make a hole in the fence and listen to Nina Tarasova, Maria Yudina, and Ekaterina Yurovskaya. I watch closely, trying to remember what at the time seemed to me the main thing—how to bow to the audience while accepting their ecstatic ovations. At home I rehearse every possible kind of bow in front of the mirror. One day I'm walking across Cathedral Square and all of a sudden I'm startled by a burst of applause—a passing britzka has startled a flock of pigeons. I am gripped by incredible happiness at my certainty that all this must come to pass: a stage drowning in flowers, ovations, bows. And I bow gratefully to the pigeons.

Papa buys records. My sisters and I, as if in a fever, forgetting everything, take turns cranking the gramophone handle and listen over and over to our favorite voices until Mama starts to complain of a headache. If the gramophone isn't singing, I start to. I simply cannot be silent when everything inside me is singing and mad to get out!

We try not to miss a single concert. In the afternoon there are lots of flies at the Palermo; in the evening, mosquitoes. The audience fans away the insects, and the conductor, too, seems to be waving away the persistent bloodsuckers with his baton. During the entr'acte the men leave the pavilion to smoke, and the ladies and children, accompanied by nurses and governesses, stand in line by the doors to the powder room. I look at them and think that they know nothing about me yet, really. But I already love them. Not just for their future love for me even, but just because. I love them, and that's that.

There is no past, but if it were to be told, the words could stretch out for days on end, or maybe just the opposite, and entire years could be crammed into a few letters.

I come home happy and proud of myself with a report card noting my promotion to the next grade.

And again a report about my promotion.

And again.

Memories have no date, time, or age. I remember my friend, the beautiful Lyalya, teaching me to kiss. Instead of doing my homework and solving problems about a merchant who for some reason cannot calculate without our help how much fabric he needs to cut, we kiss until our lips swell up. I keep trying to find out who taught Lyalya to kiss like that. She won't say. Then she admits it was her girl cousin at the Christmas vacation. And what's the difference when it was, how old I am, what grade I am, what century this is, what planet? All that matters is that I see everything as if it were right now: here is Lyalya on the sofa in front of me; she is a special, tinted orange in the slanting rays of the setting sun; she is wiping an ink spot on her palm with her handkerchief; and the handkerchief is orange, too, colored by the sunset, and now violet and inky as well. Lyalya wets it with spit, then rubs the spot again, wets it and rubs, and now both her lips and her tongue are stained with ink. And nothing will ever wipe that ink from her lips, neither time nor death.

At last I fall in love "for real," with a grown man. Or rather, with his photograph, which I've seen in *Ogonyok*, with the caption:

"Prince Yusupov, Count Sumarokov-Elston." He is wearing white trousers, is holding a tennis racket, and has a blinding smile. At first glance I feel that he is my chosen one, my knight. I have no doubt that fate will make sure we meet. How and when don't matter. Fate arranges everything itself, pushes us together, throws us into each other's arms. A drawing in my textbook: two teams of eight horses are pulling Magdeburg hemispheres in opposite directions. Nothing joins them; the air has just been pumped out of them. The driver lashes the horses with all his might, but these hemispheres press to each other with such force that nothing can tear them apart. I know that we will have that same kind of love. No force on earth will be able to tear us apart.

People fall in love with me, too, but how unlike Prince Yusupov, Count Sumarokov-Elston, my Rostov suitors are! The Nazarov twins—callow, obtuse, and violent—from the Stepanovskaya School are wooing me. They won't let anyone even come close to me. When one boy from their school skated around the rink with me, they gave him a beating in the cloakroom, under the coats.

Papa tells me about twins, that they are a mistake of nature, nothing terrible, but a mistake. Left to their own devices, there would definitely be a master and slave, and one would overshadow the other. I note the constant struggle for primacy between them. One winter, in the ravine in the Novoposelensky Garden, where everyone slides down the two slopes, the Nazarovs set up a test for themselves. They fly at each other to see who will swerve first, be frightened, lose his nerve. Everyone stops and watches them rush head to head, eye to eye. Who will be the first to blink and swerve? At the last second one of them turns onto a well-worn snowdrift and flies off to the side. Had it not been for that snowdrift, they would have killed each other.

In the beginning I can't tell them apart at all, and then, at a certain point, it seems to me that they're not at all alike, they're so different. But it is absolutely unthinkable to love either one. When we are invited to common friends' for a name-day party, one of them, Semyon, catches a moment to be alone with me in a room. We have to talk about something, but he's standing there sweaty and red.

In May, when the brothers walk under the windows of our school, identical, in their white calamanco tunics and buttoned collars, drawn to the windows where the schoolgirls are looking out, the other one, Petya, is looking so intently that he slams into a telegraph pole.

In the summer, during vacation, their parents take them to Germany. From the whole trip, when the twins are asked what they saw in Europe, all the Nazarovs remember is the fortress at Nuremberg and the *Folterkammer* in it, the torture chamber, with the Iron Maiden where they tortured unfortunates, and the instruments for various types of execution and torture, which struck them so: iron scissors for severing tongues, needles for gouging out eyes, the splinters that were driven under people's nails and lit, and everything of that sort. What made a special impression on them—and here they only whisper into the ear of other boys but we can hear everything—were the pincers for squeezing the sensitive parts of a man's body.

But the Nazarovs are our saviors when Mishka, Tusya, and some other friends from school and I take a hike to Nakhichevan. Drunken factory hands from Temernik accost us, and the Nazarovs, who had tagged along, bravely start a fight with them. After that we take our walks in Novoposelensky Garden, where there is no salvation from hooligans, with the twins, who carry knives and brass knuckles.

The world is oddly arranged. The twins Petya and Syoma are prepared to knife a man for me, but I don't love them; I love a photograph, a piece of paper, a fanciful mixture of black and white, and all this is so simple it's impossible to explain.

I started rereading what I'd written and suddenly remembered I hadn't said anything yet about Mama's younger sister, Aunt Olya, who visited sometimes from Petersburg.

Here she is clacking her heels, flying into our rooms, which have become small, dusty, and boring with her arrival, all impetuous, perfumed, and cosmopolitan. We swarm all over her on the sofa and smother her with kisses. She brings everyone presents—as frivolous as possible, as Mama shakes her head reproachfully. For some reason the frivolous things turn out to be the most remarkable: all these feathers, hairpins, cards, and fans. Aunt Olya says that one should live *zefiroso*. That's how she breathes, walks, eats, and laughs—*zefiroso*—lightly, airily. Sometimes she likes to ask disconcerting questions, like, "What do you prefer, good food from an ugly dish or bad from a pretty one?"

One evening after dinner I act all the parts in the fable I learned at school, "The Grasshopper and the Ant," not doubting that everyone is going to applaud me, thrilled over my acting talents, the moment I point a moralizing finger up and say, "Now go dance your dance!" But Aunt Olya jumps up without waiting for the end, interrupting me, and exclaims, "This is all wrong! Wrong, Bellochka!" Aunt Olya explains to me the right way to understand the fable's meaning. "The grasshopper is cheerful and sweet and lived the way one should live this life—making merry, singing, rejoicing at the sun and sky, both being good and relying on the kindness of others! She served beauty, do you see? But the ant is a scoundrel and greedy, like all the rich, a vulgar petty bourgeois!"

Aunt Olya brings us the diary of Bashkirtseva, to whom she practically prays, and in the evenings reads out loud from it: "People are embarrassed by their nakedness because they consider themselves imperfect. If they were certain there was not a single spot on their body, not a single badly formed muscle or disfigured leg, they would walk around without clothing and not be embarrassed . . . Can one really resist not showing something so truly beautiful, something one can be proud of?" Aunt Olya tells us about being in Switzerland at Lake Lugano and staying there for a few weeks at a colony where everyone went around naked, men and women both. She is also exasperated by the fact that even in art male genitalia are not depicted, supposedly this is indecent, but after all, this is the holy of holies, the mystery of being, and the meaning of the universe! Christ was crucified naked, she continues, the way condemned slaves are supposed to be, but afterward the priests destroyed all the real crucifixes and began clothing Christ!

Our old nurse listens to her through the open door and spits loudly: "It's a disgrace!" She doesn't like Aunt Olya and especially this kind of talk, which, she is convinced, only spoils us.

Mama doesn't like this talk either, but she can't leave or keep silent, and she tries to argue with her sister. "What are you saying, Olya! After all, there is natural shame, man has moral boundaries that separate down from up, and ultimately there are moral limits sanctified by millennia of human experience, laws, and religion!"

My aunt is agitated, she jumps up and starts dashing around the room, trying to prove that in every religion since the beginning of time all this was completely natural and stood at the center of worship. The ancient world venerated Priapus as a divinity, and only Christianity distorted everything—because it cannot stand all things living and in general is the religion of death and therefore is unviable and will soon die out of its own accord. It nearly has. "You have only to glance at the Bible," Aunt Olya says passionately. "There, too, people bowed to these as the most holy, picking up on just this place. When Abraham sends his servant for a wife for Isaac, he tells him, 'Put, I pray thee, thy hand under my thigh, And I will make thee swear by the Lord, the God of heaven, and the God of the earth.' Then the slave puts his hand on Abraham there and swears to everything! There!"

Aunt Olya is addressing my older sisters, but I am curled up in an armchair, listening and remembering. I admire her, but at the same time I feel sorry for her because, as my sisters say, she is alone, despite many romances. Aunt Olya was once married but her child died. Then she left her husband and she had no more family.

"And really, we missed the mark on being born," Aunt Olya continues, lighting a cheap cigarette and opening the hinged pane onto the frosty darkness so that drunken shouts and dogs' barking crept into the room. "We should have come into the world not here but somewhere by the warm sea and in another millennium altogether, in Ancient Greece, where they loved love and weren't afraid to love, where life was crude and natural, not crude and unnatural, like nowadays. Life in Hellas could hardly have been cruder than life in your Temernik!"

I love Aunt Olya because she always says bizarre things. I know that Christ told us to love everyone, but she is outraged by Christianity. "As if you could separate one from the other in man, the body from God," she says. "This is like saying that the roots and the flower are two different beings!"

Papa listens to Aunt Olya in silence and only interjects a few comments here and there. Once, when the conversation veers into the origin of religion, he says that at first there wasn't love at all, there was the hunt. Man had to kill the beast in order to survive. Hunters looked for a large, strong helper, one who would help them kill. "No," Aunt Olya objects. "God began with the woman whose child fell ill and no one else could help her. There was nothing left for her to do but raise her arms to the sky and pray."

I listen to Aunt Olya and think of the outskirts of Rostov and the area of the Vladikavkaz Railroad workshops: the stink from the beer stands, the "living corpses" lying everywhere in their own vomit and blood. Women's shrieks near the tavern doors and drunken, sullen fighting. Everything exuding despair, squalor, and senselessness—the cursing, the dirt, and the people. But Aunt Olya insists that we must live in peace, like newlyweds, and fall in love with this life every day because newlyweds are full of love and look on everything as if for the first time. "One should spend one's entire life on a honeymoon," Aunt Olya tells us, "and marry everything—the tree, the sky, books, and all the people in the world, the pretty flower, even this frosty air coming through the pane!"

Dear future former Nebuchadnezzasaurus!

Hurrah! I received your postcard! It's good, being in a faraway kingdom, in the capital of capitals, to look at your handwriting and learn that all is well with you. Naturally, the interpreter is quite upset that you don't feel like going to school. Judge for yourself, though. Who does? On the other hand, later, one day, you will have something to remember.

Even if you don't want to remember, you will. Trust me. It's always like that with the past.

For instance, take Galpetra, whom I mentioned in one of my previous letters. So many years have passed, and I don't even know whether she's alive, but she's still here the same as ever.

I don't know what discipline is like in your school, but in Galpetra's classes there was always perfect silence. At the same time there were drawings of her in the bathrooms—naked with a mustache and hefty tits. Innocent childish revenge. No one dared do more. No one liked her. Neither the children nor the teachers.

Galpetra's favorite hero was Janusz Korczak. We would cook up some kind of trouble and she would start shouting at us and sooner or later move on to Korczak. When she talked about him she became completely different. Even her voice changed: "How, how can anyone leave children alone in a sealed train car or gas chamber?" She always told the same story, using the same words. Everyone already knew what she would say by heart. Each time, tears would well up in her eyes when she reached the words, "And so, on the fifth of August of forty-two, Janusz Korczak took his orphans outside, they formed up in a column and, unfurling the green banner of King Mateusz, started on their last journey, and Korczak himself walked at their head, holding the hands of two children." And it always ended like this: "Do you understand who he suffered for? Who he gave his life for? For you! But you . . ." At this, when one well-read smart kid said that Korczak was really Goldszmidt, not Korczak, she took offense, saying he was no Jew! She began defending him and was indignant that if a decent person is born once in a blue moon, before you know it people are saying, look, he has a Jewish name!

The smart kid did not have that in mind at all, but he could no longer defend himself.

Galpetra taught botany and zoology, and she had every possible plant growing in pots on the class windowsills. She knew the Latin name of each one and was always repeating, "Plants are living, but they're named in a dead language. There, you see, in a southern climate these are weeds and grow anywhere, but here it's a houseplant. Without human love and warmth they won't survive our winter."

All that remained of her lessons was that there were flowering plants and cryptogamic ones.

There! I remembered. But why does an interpreter need to remember all that?

Once Galpetra was walking down the corridor with a piece of paper taped to her back. That very same pictogram. With the huge tits. Someone found a way to tape it to her, unnoticed, in the crush after class. For a second it occurred to the future interpreter to rush over and take the piece of paper off her or tell her to look around. But only for a second.

So too, dear future former Nebuchadnezzasaurus, you must go to school so that later you can remember all sorts of trivia, like cryptogamic plants and toilet drawings, because that's what it's all made up of.

I'm writing to you from the roof. Here, on the roof of the Istitutto Svizzero, there is a terrace with a view of the eternal city. As if all Rome were in the palm of my hand. Only my hand was very big.

Here is my postcard for you. On the right, above the Villa Borghese, a blue balloon has risen up again, decorated like an old Montgolfier. On the left, somewhere over the Piazza Venezia, a helicopter is buzzing, stuck to the sky like a fly to flypaper, buzzing and going nowhere. There are cupolas and roofs all the way to the Albano mountains. And straight ahead, over Saint Peter's, a dark, living spot is wheeling. A huge flock of birds. It contracts, darkening, growing denser, and stretches out, swells—kinking, spilling over. Like a huge black stocking flying across the sky while continuously turning inside out. Where did all these birds come from?

The interpreter sits here on this roof for half a day. And then descends. It's quiet in the enormous building; the statues view the pictures in silence. Everything is white marble: walls, stairs, and columns. As if made from granulated sugar. The villa was built by a Swiss sugar magnate who wanted to see Rome in the palm of his hand. Now it was the Swiss Institute. Fellows sat behind every door doing something for days on end. The first evening one artist invited the interpreter to his studio and spent a long time telling him about his project: a huge stomach digesting Bern. He even ran the animation on his computer. Another artist invited him to his studio, too, and showed him how he made a *Lampenbrote*.[6] He hollowed out large loaves through a hole, inserted a lamp, and hung it from the ceiling. The artist turned off the light and they sat in darkness while the loaf shone overhead. In a third studio, in a tower with an end-to-end view of Rome, the artist pulled hairs out of her head and glued them to a piece of soap to make a map of the world. She even gave the interpreter a world soap.

The interpreter leaves his laptop in his room and goes out onto via Ludovisi. The smells of a Roman street: gasoline, coffee through a bar's open doors, incense and candles from a church, perfume from

6. "Bread lamp" *(Ger.)*

a boutique, urine and wet grout from a dark corner. Commotion all around: pedestrians trying to explain something over their *telefonino*. A rabid dog bit a motor scooter, and now there's an epidemic in the city, the disease has spread to cars and buses, and they're speeding around like crazies. Even the manholes have gone bonkers, imagining they're God knows who: everywhere you step it's S.P.Q.R.— *Senatus Populus Que Romanus*.[7] Steam gushes from a manhole, thick and heavy, smearing the scooter-blocked street. A gap in the street landscape. A rent. Or has Rome finally been viewed to shreds?

Overhead is a guide's sign pole tied with a pink scarf. The interpreter follows her. She leads him to Barberini. On the square, Triton is blowing on a conch, huffing and puffing, each cheek the size of an orange. Streaming, with a straight part at his crown. Once upon a time they laid out dead bodies they'd found here for identification. The water cracks on the paving stone.

The smells, the sounds—they're Roman, but the color of the buildings is all Moscow. On Sivtsev Vrazhek this was the color of the shabby, half-crumbled plaster on the old private houses—warm and cozy.

Down via Sistina toward Gogol. The building numbers are bonkers, too. They've lined up in an order possible only in Rome. Here it is, no. 125. Names on the plate by the door. Some De Leone lives here now. The top-floor windows. Someone looking out from behind a curtain. A donkey stall downstairs. If you only knew the joy with which I abandoned Switzerland and flew to my sweetheart, my beauty, Italy. She's mine! No one in the world can take her away from me. I was born here. Russia, Petersburg, snow, scoundrels, the department, the school, the theater—I dreamt all that!

Should I ring? A little old man will open up. When he finds out a foreigner's come to see Gogol, he'll declare studiedly that Gogol's gone, he left and no one knows when he's coming back, and when

---

7. "The Senate and people of Rome" *(Lat.)*

he does arrive he'll more than likely take to his bed and refuse to see anyone.

A guide with a bamboo stick over her head guides the street toward Trinità dei Monti. The white rag tied in a bow flitters mothlike over the crowd.

The Spanish Steps are woven of bodies, arms, and legs—a living tapestry escaped from the Vatican museums. A black man accosts a couple with a bouquet of roses. Plastic wind-up soldiers creep underfoot, shout something in their plastic language, aim and fire at crumpled napkins and crushed cups. An old woman with a cane, doubled over on a marble slab, holds out her hand, mutters under her breath, but all I can hear is *prego* and *mangiare*. Her dirty fingers tap convulsively. She could have come straight out of the underground passage at the Elektrozavodskaya station, except she learned to say two words in Italian.

The interpreter sits down on the steps and watches the crowd below around the Fonta della Barcaccia, on via Condotti, which is filled to the brim with heads, like porridge. As if somewhere a little pot was preparing these heads for itself, cooking them up, and no one was going to tell it, "Don't cook them, little pot!" And now they'd spilled onto all the streets.

The interpreter looks at the winter-gray buildings and the dingy December clouds.

A few years ago the interpreter sat on these steps, but not alone.

Leucippa and Klitofontus. Pyramus and Thisbe. The interpreter and Isolde.

The interpreter was here with his Isolde. Their child had turned one, and they had left him with his grandmother and flown here for a few days. He had to get out of the apartment's baby smell and take Isolde away from that all that wind-up, imperceptibly demeaning domesticity, which was quietly driving him mad, all those scheduled feedings, diapers, laundry, baths, and sleepless nights. It was so important for the sleep-deprived, tormented parents to go back, if only for a few days, to being what they were before this: a man and a woman in love.

They arrived at the Spanish Steps late in the evening and saw the wedding there, the same bride and groom they'd seen before in the Lateran. The nighttime bride was still wearing her daytime wedding gown and sitting on the steps, playing the guitar, and singing "Yesterday." The groom was singing, too, and so were the guests. The entire Spanish Steps sang with them, too: "I believe in yesterday . . ."

Only a few years had passed, and Rome was different, even though everything was where it was supposed to be. The statues hadn't scattered. The same peeling palazzos pockmarked by pitted plaster. From far away the statues on them were like huge insects rearing on their hind legs—just like then. The same cats hiding under cars. The same street dirt, the same marble coat of arms covered in green moss over the door, and the same rusty gratings in the dark squares of the long-blind windows. The same gurgling of water in the baroque basin, mossy and ivy-entwined. And yet everything was different.

Because that first Rome had left a feeling of rain and sun. The soaked blouse adhering to her body—Isolde plucked the clinging fabric away. The sound of tires over the still rainy paving stones that were already shining in the sun—a totally special sound, with a smacking and a moist whistling. On the wet walls, leaves, and stones, a blinding liquid sun. Steam rising from it all—the sidewalk slabs, the wet linen hanging overhead, and the statues' backs. After the rain the air was sharp, fragrant, and fresh, but just for a few minutes, and then everything baked dry again and the car exhaust left nothing to breathe.

Museums, galleries, and churches from morning to night. Dark canvases, gilded altars, marble bodies.

The Rome of bodies. Bodies everywhere: stone but corporeal; male, female, half-animal. Muscles, breasts, nipples, navels, and buttocks on *dioscuri*, emperors, madonnas, tritons, gods, fauns, and saints. Hips, knees, ankles, heels, and toes spread wide.

That Rome had crumbled to bits.

Here a lizard rushed headlong across a wall on the diagonal and hid under a leaf, leaving behind just his tail, like a tiny crescent. Where was that? In some ruins made of slender bricks two fingers' wide.

Suddenly rain again, and splashes fly through the trattoria's open door. A true downpour: streams seething over sidewalks and pavement. A ginger cat peeks out from under a car—where it hides from the rain. The interpreter orders lasagna and *due bicchiri*. Isolde is teaching him to toast in Italian. You have to say, "Cento giorni come questo!"[8]

They drink so that these splashes flying as far as their bare legs, the downpour's sound, the ginger cat, and the Italian at the next table cradling his *telefonino* between ear and shoulder because that makes it easier to gesture—so that all this will be repeated a hundred times. That restaurant is very nearby, on via della Croce. They sat there a long time, exhausted, feet aching. The menu was only in Italian, and they pointed at the soiled cardboard while the waiter explained by pointing to himself: this is liver. And this? He slapped his haunch: a loin filet. And this? He held his elbows to his sides and flapped his wrists, like little wings: *piccione, piccione!*

Then, in Rome, for the first time in a year crammed with worries—how to find a job and an apartment, how to arrange a life with a small child—the interpreter saw how beautiful Isolde had become since giving birth. He saw this as they were walking down the hotel hallway. They had changed clothes and wanted to have dinner somewhere in the city. She was walking in front and saying something and he saw her hair, as if for the first time, the low neck of her dress, the way her hips swung, her tread on high heels. She

---

8. A hundred days just like this one! *(Ital.)*

was saying something, turning around in the low light of the narrow passage, and the overhead lamps changed her face every few steps—first her familiar, perfectly homey profile, then a strange, unfamiliar one that he wanted to touch with his fingers and kiss.

They had dinner that time at Ulpia, right above Trajan's forum, and sat on the open terrace. Pot-bellied candles in small glasses were burning on the tables; it was already growing dark. Deep under, eight or ten meters down, where time is measured in meters, lay ancient Rome, or rather, its debris: each ruin was illuminated. The columns lay about like gnawed marrowbones. In anticipation of the *carrè di agnello* they'd ordered, they drank wine and read the guide to each other, trying to figure out what was where two thousand years before them, but it was utterly impossible to sort out all those forums of Vespasian, Augustus, Caesar, and Nero, which kept blurring, and it also turned out that most of those forums had been reburied under Mussolini. The interpreter looked at Isolde and then, in the candle's light, noticed for the first time that the tip of her nose wiggled when she spoke or ate. He had never seen that before for some reason.

They tried to find something in the guidebook about the restaurant's name, who this Ulpia was: goddess, woman, city? But there was nothing in the book about her. From somewhere below came the shrieks of cats celebrating a cat wedding unseen in a huge, stealthily overgrown trench. It was hard to believe that once, right here, Cicero's severed hands had been set out for general viewing, nailed to the orator's tribune. There was a disconnect between those nailed hands and this big hole, so empty, so catty, and so overgrown with green, green grass.

Isolde removed her sandals and put her feet in the interpreter's lap under the table. He stroked her toes under the tablecloth and listened to her read about Traian's column, where Peter stood under a spotlight for some reason. It seemed as if it were snowing because, as night fell, piles of night moths rained down on the streets of Rome, as from a ripped pillow, blazing up under street-lamps, windows, traffic lights, and spotlights. The moths kept circling, trying to fall into the candle, and Isolde kept driving them from the fire with her book.

They were on their way back to the hotel, a little drunk after the Chianti and grappa. They stood examining the bas reliefs on the most famous column in the world: here were the Roman scouts returning with the severed heads of the Dacians, here were the Dacians surrendering and the women and children leaving their homes while the Romans moved in with their livestock, here was a Dacian impaling himself so as not to surrender to the Romans, there was a soldier kissing Traian's hand, the Dacian women a little higher up were torching the naked fallen Roman soldiers, above them were the heads of Romans on spears on the walls of Dacian fortifications, and even higher the Romans were chopping down trees—and someone's heads were on stakes again—and so on without end up the spiral, the symbol of movement and progress, and at the very top an old man had fallen still, afraid to budge, afraid of losing his balance, dumbfounded at winding up here, so high up. The main thing was not to look down or your head would spin.

An entire city in night moths. They circled street-lamps, lay dead on pavement, and still fluttered. Little boys set fire to them with a lighter. As a child the interpreter had lit piles of poplar seed tufts with matches. All Moscow had been adrift in the tufts, like snow. These were setting moth snow on fire.

It was hot even at night. When they went up to their hotel room, it was stuffy. Isolde turned on a forceful stream of cold water in the sink and ran her palms, wrists, and elbows under. The interpreter put his arms around her, picked her up, and carried her all the way across the room, letting her down on the bed, and she pulled him toward her with icy wet hands. The stream from the forgotten tap kept on noisily. Isolde whispered, "Go turn it off!"

But the interpreter replied, "It's raining outside."

That first day in Rome the interpreter kept looking at this woman, so familiar, ordinary, and strange simultaneously, and he thought that this was happiness: to hear her teeth click against the glass when she drank, to see a wet spot spread across her breast when she spilled water. To sniff her smells. That day she smelled of new sandals—the store, leather, glue, sweat, perfume. To lie on the hotel bed and see her in the mirror, through the crack in the door, walking around first without her skirt, then without her blouse. To watch her straighten her narrow bra. To feel with his cheeks and hands the sharp tiny needles—she had shaved her legs a few days before and now they had grown out a little and prickled. When Isolde climbed into the tub and turned on the shower, she seemed to be dressing in water.

Before falling asleep that night, they massaged each others' feet, weary after their day. They lay top to tail, propped on an elbow. The interpreter rubbed fragrant lavender cream into her heels and the scars on her feet, traces from the operations after her accident, and Isolde told him how when she was a child she and her parents were driving in the heat through the Iranian desert and she had asked, "Mama, bring me some cold!" Her mother had stuck her hand out the window, held it there for a minute, and then brought in a handful of air from the outside into the scorching hot car and rubbed her daughter's neck.

In her sleep, Isolde threw off the blanket, and in the light of the moon her skin, covered with perspiration, glistened. And once again the interpreter thought then how much you need to be happy: to be a little drunk on grappa, Rome, love, and the bright moon outside that hangs like a tail hidden behind a cloud, like a lizard behind a leaf, to fall asleep with this woman and know that it would be morning tomorrow and not just morning but morning in Rome, when you feel so keenly that there is so little time and you can't waste a moment but must plunge quickly into this city.

That night the interpreter woke up because mosquitoes were biting him. He couldn't sleep because of their buzzing and kept scratching the bites. He turned on the light and started smashing them on the walls with the guidebook, leaving bloody stains on the wallpaper. After that he couldn't fall sleep. He picked the blanket up off the floor, wrapped it around himself, and stretched out on the windowsill, sticking his head out into the brightening Roman street, still sleepy and empty, already cold. Toward dawn it began to rain again and everything twinkled—the reflections of street-lamps, advertisements, bar signs, and shop windows lit up in the wet pavement blocks. Everything smelled good, even the windowsill and building wall seemed to give off special Roman smells.

The interpreter thought about Tristan.

Before the interpreter, Isolde had had Tristan. They had loved each other and had also taken vacations in Italy.

One day they left for vacation and got into an accident. Some-where between Orvieto and Todi. They were driving along a wind-ing road above the Tiber. A truck flew straight at them from around a turn.

Tristan was driving. He died instantly. The steering wheel crushed him.

But Isolde survived. She had sixteen fractures.

A few years passed and she married the interpreter, and now they loved each other and took vacations in Italy.

Once the interpreter sat down at his computer to do some kind of translation. At the time they still shared a computer. Suddenly, when he glanced at recently opened files, the interpreter saw a strange name. Isolde had been working with that file the night before. The interpreter knew he shouldn't read other people's letters and files. But he opened it. It turned out to be the diary she was keeping.

At first the interpreter wanted to close the file without reading it.

Then he started reading.

It was an odd diary. Isolde didn't write entries every day or even every month. Only when she felt bad.

The interpreter started reading the entries to find out what she was writing, hiding from him, the man she was sharing her life with.

When everything was good with them, she didn't write anything, as if those days never happened. But when she couldn't stand it any longer, when she felt as if she were suffocating from the life she shared with the interpreter, she sat down at the computer, opened that file, and vented. Their arguments, which the interpreter had long since forgotten, lived on, recorded in hot, still aching, unforgiven pursuit.

It was also odd that she was writing this diary to Tristan.

In these pages the dead man got the love and the interpreter the hurt, the bitterness, and the bile.

She wrote down the words they had hurled at each other to hurt but not what they had whispered to each other afterward.

The interpreter decided not to say anything to Isolde and never again to read what was not meant for him.

For some reason, when they were ordering tickets for Rome and the hotel, Isolde wanted to stay at just this hotel, although there was nothing special about it. And then, when he stuck his head out the window and looked at the rainy nighttime street, the interpreter suddenly thought that this was the hotel where she and Tristan had stayed. And immediately he was amazed. How could something so foolish have occurred to him?

The interpreter went to bed but for a long time couldn't get to sleep—he kept thinking about Tristan, since Isolde had been with him in Rome. He ran over what had happened that day, and suddenly it occurred to him that it was she and Tristan who had toasted like that and said, "Cento giorni come questo!" Might they have sat in that very same trattoria as well? Why had she led him there specifically? It had been raining, too, and they too had waited for their lasagna and sipped Chianti, possibly served in the very same carafes.

Trifles, details came to him whose meaning was revealed only now. They had flown into Fiumicino, and they'd had to buy a train ticket to Rome. There were vending machines where you could pay with a credit card. Isolde had said, "Don't! It might swallow it! That happened to me before."

There was a long line at the ticket window, so the interpreter inserted his credit card anyway—and that's exactly what happened: no ticket, no card. *Benvenuto all'Italia!*[9] The interpreter waited by the vending machine while Isolde went to look for someone to help. She spoke a little Italian. The people at the windows couldn't help. The people who could weren't there. So they stood by the vending machine waiting for something. Isolde got nervous, and the interpreter tried to reassure her that this was nothing, it would all be fine, and he himself was about to call to block the card. Isolde kept repeating, "Gottverdälli!"[10]

Then some Italians came, opened the vending machine with a key, and the interpreter got his card back. They bought a ticket at the window and boarded the express to the Termini. Now, at night, it occurred to him that the vending machine had probably swallowed Tristan's card like that, too.

Before, Rome had met visitors at the front door, the Porta del Popolo, but now it received them through the back door. You dragged yourself to the station through the filthy suburbs. The interpreter kept looking out the window as they approached the Termini to see where Rome was, but what he was shown was back alleys, ugly and unwelcoming. The first thing he saw when he exited the station was a McDonald's. *Ecco Roma?*[11] Isolde reassured

---

9. Welcome to Italy! *(Ital.)*

10. ★★ *(Swiss German, vulg.)*

11. Here is Rome? *(Ital.)*

him that for Rome to begin you had to stop in at a bar and drink your first espresso standing. They stopped in at a long, narrow bar where a snorting coffee-making machine resided, as in a cave, and they drank their first espresso standing, as if it were some magic potion, and indeed, Rome began. Now the thought occurred to the interpreter that it was probably Tristan who had once told her, "For Rome to begin you have to stop in at a bar and drink your first espresso standing."

Suddenly, then, in Rome, after that night, the interpreter's eyes were opened to simple things he had never given a second thought. For instance, Isolde liked having nails pressed into her scalp in different places; it helped the pain, or helped wake her up if she needed to rise early. Blood probably flowed to her head and really did bring a special clarity, a sobriety. The interpreter, too, liked it when, in the morning, Isolde pressed her nails into his head, just barely at first and then harder and harder. And here they had waited a long time for the train in the Rome metro, stuffy and sweaty, and Isolde got a headache. She sat down on a bench and the interpreter started to massage her head like that, with his nails. She shut her eyes and began murmuring.

The interpreter asked, "Did he think this up?"

She stopped murmuring and opened her eyes.

"What are you talking about?"

Right then the train burst into the station, slathered in graffiti. At the time she didn't understand, or didn't want to understand, and the interpreter didn't ask any more questions.

They wandered through the Vatican museums and found themselves in a long deserted gallery: rows of white sculptures along the walls. Lifeless bodies. Arms, legs, heads, breasts, bellies—all this had been found in the earth and had now been set out for identification. Vases, sarcophagi, bas-reliefs. And bodies again: eyeless, armless, legless, castrated. Leaves where the genitals should be. If they couldn't be covered up—hammered off. At one muscular blind man Isolde looked over her shoulder—anyone looking?—and touched the spot where nothing was there anymore.

"What idiots! Why did they hate life so?"

At one time all these statues were gods or people, but now they've turned into pillars of salt and been carted off here. Marble corpses. Lined up like an honor guard at a reception in the kingdom of the dead. Isolde got the idea of bringing them to life, giving each one a story. "This one here, look, was superstitious and put his sandals on, left foot first and then right. The doctor prescribed ass's milk for his chest, and he would drink a big glass at six in the morning. He also had fur growing on his buttocks." And so she and the interpreter came up with something for each one. This one here, a Roman copy of a lost Greek original, liked to sing, and when he sang his nostrils flared. One day he was riding home content and singing and met a man who told him that here he was riding and didn't know his house had burned down and he had lost everything, including his wife. In his childhood his mama had taught him to use bur-dock and leaves when he went to the toilet, to tear them off on his way. This one here, also a Roman copy from a lost Greek original, loved a married man and was afraid to be happy with him, could not enjoy her happiness because she knew she would have to pay for her happiness, and when his child fell ill she immediately understood why. And this warrior here, again a Roman copy, returned home from war unharmed, and his wife rejoiced that he was alive and his children that he had brought presents. He had teeth that could bite through a tack. One day his nail got smashed; the nail grew back and the black spot crept outward. All of a sudden he guessed that when the spot reached the edge of the nail something good would happen. But the spot never got there, it didn't make it.

They walked around like this bringing the dead to life. Now the interpreter could not shake the idea that Isolde had already done all this with Tristan, that he had come up with this game then, and that they had walked around this endless gallery decorated with dead sculptures just like this, with their arms around each other, and had doled out bits of life to the marble fragments.

There was also a sarcophagus there: a husband and wife, shoulder to shoulder. Her hair was in tiny curls and he had a closely cropped beard. They were looking at each other and smiling, as though they had only just turned around and before this had been lying top to tail, propped up on their elbow. They had just massaged each other's feet, weary after their life, and now they would go to sleep and awaken together.

Nearly all the sculptures were copies of lost originals. Even the Apollo Belvedere. Though for the interpreter it was a copy of the Apollo that he had once thrown snowballs at in the Ostankino snow.

The interpreter told Isolde about Galpetra and the Ostankino Apollo and she laughed.

Every month Galpetra took her class to museums, usually the Pushkin on Volkhonka. When they walked past the David, the girls, peeking at his groin, whispered and giggled, and for some reason he felt uneasy because of the iron rod stuck into the hero's back to keep him from falling. There was some deception about it, and also the guide kept repeating that everything around them in this museum was a copy.

At the copy of Laocoön she said, "Look at how beautifully the ancient sculptor depicted the sufferings on the face of the father, both of whose sons are dying in front of him!"

About the original she said that it was in Italy, in the Vatican museum, and the interpreter recalled the way Galpetra sighed: "If only I could take one little peek there someday . . ."

To the question of whether there were questions, the future interpreter in his school uniform, which was shiny at the knees and elbows, asked, "Why do they show copies here? Everything in a museum should be genuine."

In reply the guide explained that everything genuine was in Italy and these sculptures were exact copies, that is, virtually exactly the same as the originals, and she led the group farther.

And now the interpreter was here in Rome, and again everything turned out to be a copy—the sculptures in the Vatican museums, the Bernini angel statues on the Ponte San Angelo,[12] Marcus Aurelius on the Capitoline Hill, the Egyptian obelisk in front of Santa Trinita dei Monti[13]—and you had to go somewhere and search again for what was genuine.

Even the Tiber was a poor copy of something else vanished and genuine. The interpreter and Isolde looked at the dead brown water from the bridge, at the low embankments coated with a layer of dried and cracked silt, and somehow he couldn't wrap his mind around the fact that this fidgety stream, bearing that dirty froth, was the same Tiber in which one sunny October day a cross helped Constantine drown the pagan Maxentius, as a result of which the world became Christian. In that muck?

Even the interpreter himself seemed like a copy of a lost original.

They read in the guidebook, in the chapter on the Lateran, about the holy staircase from the palace of Pontius Pilate and about the heads of Peter and Paul, which were kept in the papal basilica. They headed for the Lateran. They descended into the metro, where there was no air to breathe, and Isolde said she was tired and would rather just walk around some park. The night before they had been at the Villa Borghese and in one allée had found an empty bench, somewhere behind the stadium, and the interpreter had lain down on the boards and rested his head on her thighs and pressed his cheek into her soft belly. Isolde had raked her fingers through his hair. There was a wind, and the branches' shadows ran across her face and bare shoulders, the grass, the sandy path, and the statues' marble. The

---

12. Bridge of the Holy Angel *(Ital.)*.

13. Holy Trinity on the Hill *(Ital.)*

interpreter lay there and read aloud from the guidebook about some triumphal arch: one emperor had stolen statues and bas-reliefs for it from the arch of another emperor.

Isolde had said, "Look! There's the triumphal arch!"

Standing there were Italian umbrella pines, shoulder to shoulder, and they held the sky under their arms.

That was the day before, but now, in the metro, Isolde asked, "Do you really want to look at the stairs and those heads?"

"Yes."

"Do you think they're genuine?"

"That's what I want to find out."

They stepped into the graffiti-bedecked car, stuffy and stuffed to the gills.

On the way Isolde told him how in school they'd had religion lessons and everyone had hated all that. And the interpreter told Isolde that in school they'd had classes in anti-religious propaganda. Taught by the very same Galpetra. The interpreter had known since childhood that there wasn't a God, so for him, that schoolboy who agonized over his pimples, early hirsuteness, and dislike and fear of death, it was very important to find Him. Or something resembling Him. Here the class was dying of boredom and Galpetra was nattering on about how God had been thought up by clerics to make it easier to confuse naïve, uneducated people, that Judgment Day had been invented in order to permit people to sin themselves but forbid others, and everything she was supposed to say in those lessons. "Only old women can believe in God," Galpetra used to say. "Christianity is a religion of slaves and suicides. There is no after-life, nor could there be. Everything living dies, and resurrection is impossible. It's simple logic. If there is a God, then there is no death, and if there is death, then there is no God." Isolde laughed and said that in their religion classes, on the contrary, they'd tried to convince them that there was a God and they too had died of boredom.

Here the interpreter and Isolde were standing in front of a building on which was written "Sancta sanctorum."[14] They went in. There, below, to the left of the entrance, a model of Pontius Pilate's palace was exhibited under glass, and you could see exactly where the staircase was. It had been moved from Jerusalem to Rome, the steps had been covered with boards, and the places where drops of Christ's blood had fallen were covered in glass. Here the interpreter and Isolde were standing and watching people drop to their knees and scramble up. Each crawled in his own way. One slipped on by, one-two, overtaking the others. One stopped for a long time on each step, touched the polished, half-worn boards with his forehead, and kissed each one. One woman kept looking around and straightening her skirt. The memory of a very young disabled woman stuck with him; she was brought in in a wheelchair and helped to kneel on the lowest step. Then she climbed up, crab-wise. You could see how hard every movement was for her. Then came a group of schoolchildren, and they climbed up cheerfully and noisily, pushing and soiling each other with their sneakers and sandals—which obviously brought them special satisfaction. And right then, as he and Isolde were standing in front of this staircase and watching the schoolchildren overtake the disabled young woman, at that moment someone tapped the interpreter on the shoulder. At first he paid no mind; there were crowds of tourists everywhere and everyone was shoving everyone. Then someone touched him again. He turned around and saw Galpetra. She was wearing the same mohair cap and the same violet wool suit. Even her boots were half unzipped, and she was wearing museum shoe covers. The same little mustache, the same belly. She nodded toward the staircase: "What's the matter with you? Climb!"

And shaking her head reproachfully, she added, "And you didn't believe me then . . ."

---

14. Holy of Holies *(Lat.)*.

For some reason the interpreter thought it was important to tell Isolde about this, but she didn't understand. She asked, "You met someone you know?"

Galpetra had vanished.

They went to look at the heads.

While they were crossing the square, music thundered some-where, an Italian tune that kept repeating "amore, amore, amore,"[15] and it felt weird to the interpreter that they were just about to see the head—or at least a piece of bone, it didn't matter—of the same man who on the fourth night watch followed Him over the sea, who stepped out of the boat, over the side, and placed his foot on a wave.

The cathedral was packed with tourists, as everywhere, and the loudspeakers mumbled in Latin. They roamed through the crowd, and the interpreter just could not understand where the head was. The current washed them up at a kiosk by the entrance. Isolde asked the saleswoman in Italian. She poked at one of the postcards that showed an altar, all in gold and marble, like a turret—resembling an illustration for the Tale of the Golden Cockerel. The saleswoman tapped her long nail, which was green with star-sequins, on the postcard and pointed up, as if to say, go to the altar and look up.

The interpreter realized why they hadn't seen what they were looking for right away. They had entered the cathedral through a side door rather than the main portal. Now they cut through the crowd toward the altar, approaching from the main entrance. On the second story of the fairy-tale turret, behind a gold volute grat-ing, there were indeed two busts. The interpreter looked closely but only saw something greasy, rosy-cheeked, and black-maned. The loudspeakers switched to Italian and became noticeably more cheerful and lively, and every other word was *amore*. The red lamps over the confessionals would turn off and then on again. A group of

---

15. "Love, love, love" *(Ital.)*.

Japanese tourists squeezed through the crowd, following a ski pole with a green kerchief tied to the tip.

Isolde said, "Are you satisfied? Let's go!"

Before leaving, they stopped at a chapel to the left of the entrance where a wedding was under way. They watched through the gate. The bride and groom were sitting on chairs, and a priest wearing white and saying something was standing in front of them. It was entertaining how he waved his arms. Obviously, words had failed him, and he was trying, it was so Italian—gesticulating desperately— to convince the young people to love each other until death and after.

The interpreter and Isolde exited and took out the map they used for walking around Rome. The map was old, worn to holes at the folds, and had also been caught in the rain with them a few times— it had turned to tatters. But Isolde wouldn't buy a new one. She said she was used to it. The interpreter thought that this was probably the map she had used walking around Rome then, with Tristan.

Quite close by was the church of Saint Clement, where Cyril was buried, after whom the letters were named without which the interpreter would have nothing in life.

"Let's stop in!" the interpreter suggested, but Isolde said her feet hurt and she wasn't going anywhere else.

They sat down at a table at a street café.

"Were you there last time?"

"No."

The interpreter tried to convince her that it wasn't far at all, ten minutes in the direction of the Coliseum, and they could take the Metro from there to the hotel, but Isolde said her new sandals were rubbing. And she added, "And anyway I don't understand why we absolutely have to see all these fused chains, these chips picked up somewhere, and bones of no one knows who!"

The interpreter knew why he wanted to go there no matter what.

He had to take her away from Tristan—from their Rome to another.

The interpreter began telling her about Cyril. Or rather, he wanted to tell her something Tristan probably didn't know. All of a sudden the interpreter felt as though he were talking to him, not her. Here, Tristan, you don't know this, but I do. Listen! Ancient Chersoneses is now Sevastopol, and right here, Tristan, the world without you begins. Where they drowned the holy martyr Clement, the third Roman pope and Peter's disciple, they drowned officers in the Civil War. They tied old anchors, pieces of iron, and stones to them—some to the neck, some to the legs—and threw them in the water. In certain memoirs the interpreter had read that divers who had dived all the way to the bottom at that spot found themselves in a kind of forest: the dead bodies wanted to float, and tied down they stood in the deep, some upside down, some right side up, all leaning in the same direction, pushed by the underwater current, like trees by the wind; on one the remains of a shirt lifted up like wings. It was on that shore that Cyril walked, the Cyril who received the Cyrillic alphabet, the interpreter's letters, from the clouds. The recipient of the heavenly letters talked to the residents of Chersoneses about Clement's martyrdom; they knew nothing of this anymore and did not believe him. Then Cyril sailed to that place and began his searches in order to convince them. In the centuries that passed after Clement, the sea level had dropped. The sea receded, and a sandbar was formed. It was here that Cyril searched in the sand, but he did not find anything. The inhabitants laughed at him. Nonetheless, Cyril kept digging through the sand because, naturally, he was not looking for bones. Who needed bones? He wanted to find proof, not a rib or a skull. A rib whitened by sea and sand simply was supposed to shine in the sun. After all, something had to prove there was a God, and therefore no death. Only a miracle could prove that. And here in the sand something gleamed and shone in the sun: a rib. A bone blinding in its whiteness. They started digging further and found the head and all the rest. They were even more struck by the sweet smell. After all, smells are the language of God. And it was these sweet-smelling bones that Cyril brought to Rome. And he himself was buried in this church along with Clement. Probably because his bones smelled good, too.

"Bones again!" Isolde sighed. "Fine, let's go!"

They sat a little longer at the café, drank espresso from tiny cups, as if from an eggshell, and headed for San Clemente. Isolde said only that she absolutely had to stop in at a pharmacy along the way to buy a bandaid. But there was no pharmacy along the way.

Isolde was already limping when they got there. She was angry and close-mouthed. She sat on a bench in the church and said she wasn't climbing anywhere underground.

The interpreter descended alone.

He wandered under the dimly lit vaults and was angry at Isolde but even more at himself for dragging her here for some reason with her blistered foot when they could have come the next day or the day after that.

There were fragments lying all around. It was damp. The interpreter was overtaken by a group of tourists being led to a lower floor where people had worshipped Mithras in dank, dim cellars. The interpreter made his way there, too, but it was just the same: debris and damp.

In the half-gloom of the passages he finally found Cyril's tomb. Hidden away, off to the side. Paper flowers coated in a thick layer of dust lay on the stone slab. While the walls all around had memorial plaques where forgotten rulers who had issued decrees in Cyrillic letters had immortalized themselves.

Right then the interpreter saw Isolde. She had come down after all. She was holding the guidebook.

"Here's where you are!" Isolde said. "I was sitting reading. Listen, it turns out there are no relics of Cyril here. They were thrown out in 1798—there was an uprising and all the bones were tossed outside. And there wasn't any martyr Pope Clement either, or rather, there were two: some consul, who really was a martyr, but not a pope; and the other was a pope but not a martyr. Later, in the legend, they were merged into one person. It also says here that according to the latest research Peter was never in Rome at all!"

A group of Japanese walked by without stopping and were led into the mithraeum. In the half-dark they picked their feet up so they wouldn't stumble on the uneven earthen floor. The tourists vanished one by one in the narrow passage leading to the next underground space. The interpreter and Isolde went upstairs and outside, where after being underground even the gasoline-infused wind seemed like fresh air, and headed for the Coliseum, slowly, with frequent stops. She was limping and holding his arm.

The kiosks started again. They stopped at a stand where there were guidebooks to Rome in every language. The interpreter picked up the Russian edition to flip through. He showed Isolde, as if to say, look what nonsense they print, just photos and captions instead of publishing something decent. At this the Italian seller came running up to him and started babbling, probably talking it up, trying to convince him to buy, practically shoved the book in the interpreter's hands, pointed at the illustrations, as if to say, look what pretty pictures! The interpreter shoved the book back at him, but it was kind of clumsy and the book slipped from his hands and fell. Isolde rushed to pick it up and smiled at the seller. She whispered to the interpreter that he should smile and apologize.

"He's trying to stick me with this crap and I'm supposed to smile at him politely?"

"Yes," Isolde said. "You have to smile politely all the same."

"Why do I have to smile politely at him?"

"Because."

"I don't have to smile politely at anyone."

"Yes, you do."

When they had moved away from the stand Isolde blurted out, "You're rude."

Suddenly he exploded.

"Not like Tristan."

Isolde stopped. She looked into the interpreter's eyes. Her look held amazement, insult, and pain. She turned abruptly and quick-stepped away, limping on one foot. They were supposed to go to the Metro, but Isolde went in the exact opposite direction, back, toward the Lateran.

The interpreter wanted to run after her, grab her by the hand, and stop her, but instead he turned and headed for the Coliseum. As he walked he tried to convince himself that it was nothing. There was no getting away from each other in any case, for her or for him, and they'd see each other at the hotel that evening.

The sidewalk was littered with wrappers, slips of paper, and crushed plastic bottles. The interpreter was holding the tatters of the map. He tossed them aside.

29 September 1914. Monday

Today I had a nightmare! I'm ashamed to write. I was flying down the hallway of our school—naked, for some reason.

First thing in the morning, Tala and I went to the Ignatievs'. Again we cut gauze bandages and rolled them, but not by hand as before. They brought us little machines for cutting the bandages, and you can roll them with a special machine, too, so all that's left to do by hand is stack the packages. It's very convenient and you can get a lot more done!

The weather is cold—first sun, then rain.

I read what I wrote on this day a year ago. What a child I still was then!

30 September 1914. Tuesday

Masha had a letter from Boris and read it out loud to us. Not everything, she left out something, probably the most interesting part, because we only got to hear detailed descriptions of his classes at the institute, his daily schedule, what they were feeding him, and what the weather was like. He and his father had decided to change their last name. Now they were Melnikov, not Mueller. As soon as he was graduated as a warrant officer he would come for Masha and they would get married. When she read about that she blushed bright red! Such a marvelous evening, everyone sat there for a long time and talked, but that night Masha, all in tears, climbed into bed with me; she'd dreamt that Boris was on a ship and going to the bottom. I wanted to reassure her but burst into tears myself.

How could God take everything away before he had even given anything? He couldn't, of course.

I envy Masha very much. She loves her Boris so!

1 October 1914. Intercession

"L'amour est ce je ne sais quoi, qui vient de je ne sais où, et qui finit je ne sais comment." Madeleine de Scudéry.[16]

Tomorrow classes start at last. I've missed Mishka, Tusya, and all our friends so much, even our teachers! The Bilinskaya Classical School has been taken over for an infirmary, so we'll be going to the Petrovskoye Secondary School on Bolshaya Sadovaya, opposite the Bolshaya Moskovskaya Hotel. Classes will be in two shifts, girls in the morning, boys after the midday meal.

First thing it was still sunny, but now it's been nonstop rain.

3 October 1914. Friday

I found my initials carved into the bench with a knife. What foolishness!

The girls are corresponding with the boys and leaving notes in the desks. But Tala and I think this is silly! All the conversations are

---

16. Love is an unknown that comes from an unknown place and ends at an unknown time.

about nothing but the second shift and who is in love with whom. All the girls are out of their mind en masse over Terekhin. The peacock! A perfect fool! I don't even feel like writing about it.

Masha signed up for the Sisters of Mercy and matriculated in the two-month course. She definitely wants to go to the front, join the active army, and is upset that she might not get there, that the war will end while she is still studying. She is learning to bandage and accosts everyone in the house with her bandages. But not everyone is up for it. So she torments our poor nanny. Right now in the kitchen nanny is sitting meekly on the stool with a bandaged head waiting as Masha checks it against the book.

Yesterday Masha had her first day in the infirmary. When she came home she washed and washed endlessly and splashed herself with eau de cologne. She was trying to get rid of the hospital smell. She ate nothing at the table. She promised to take me and Tala with her to the hospital. They shall allow us to read and sing for the wounded.

6 October 1914. Monday

Today we received a letter from Nyusya in Petrograd. She writes about her studies at the conservatory and also that the war can be felt everywhere in the capital. At the Mariinsky, before each performance, they perform the anthems of the Allied powers. First the Russian, then the "Marseillaise," and then "God Save the King." How long do they have to stand? Wagner—the Germans in general—have been cut from the repertoire altogether. Signs have been hung in the big stores: "Please do not speak German." An announcement even appeared in the German section of the Public Library: "Bitte, kein Deutsch!"[17] On the streetcar Nyusya took to the conservatory, some old man trying to look younger gave a lady

---

17. "Please do not speak German!" (*Ger.*)

his seat and out of habit said, "Bitte, nehmen Sie Platz!"[18]—and he was thrown off the streetcar! Horrors!

8 October 1914. Wednesday

The world has gone mad! Just last week we read in the newspaper that a girl threw herself out a window in Petrograd holding an icon. Today in the pouring rain, under umbrellas, we buried Dmitry Poroshin from the men's Belovolskaya Classical School, the investigator's son. He shot himself with his father's revolver! Lyalya said he was in love with his father's lover. What foolish nonsense you hear from our young ladies!

10 October 1914. Friday

"L'amour est un traître qui nous égratigne lors même qu'on ne cherche qu'à jouer avec lui." Ninon de l'Enclôs.[19] Where does Tala find all this!

The Nazarov twins ran off to the front. They left a letter. And to whom? Tusya! She found it in her desk and was terribly proud, and before taking it to the principal, she read it out loud to everyone at the class change. The Nazarovs wrote that they would be buried under an oaken cross or return with the Cross of St. George.

Tusya was simply brimming with pride!

14 October 1914. Tuesday

During the class change the other girls and I looked out the window and saw Tala's brother, Zhenya Martyanov, in the yard doing calisthenics on the parallel bars. What if it was he who was scratching my initials everywhere? Foolishness! But then, at the window, I had gooseflesh up and down my arms and legs.

---

18. "Please, sit!" *(Ger.)*

19. "Love is a traitor that scratches us until we bleed, even if one simply wanted to play."

Zhenya hopped off so deftly, like a circus athlete, threw his arms back very handsomely, and looked proudly in our direction. The girls started to clap. I moved away from the window because I thought, what if his eyes were searching for mine? I opened my textbook and buried myself in the letters. It was about Cicero.

I spent half the evening looking at myself in the mirror. Everyone at home assures me I'm a beauty, but I have a potato for a nose, fat cheeks, a horrid chin, and a repulsive forehead! And my eyes! And eyelashes! My eyebrows! It's all so incomplete and pathetic! Could someone really love that? And here I have these idiotic lessons, too! Lord, what does Cicero have to do with any of this? What is this Forum? What does Rome have to do with me? Why do I need some Numa Pompilius?

19 October 1914. Sunday

We were at mass. I saw the Nazarovs' mother in church. She was kneeling on the floor. Afterward she couldn't get up until she was helped. I feel so sorry for her! No news from the twins.

22 October 1914. Wednesday

There was a church service at school to celebrate the Virgin of Kazan. We prayed for Russia's liberation from the Germans, as we had then from the Poles. I didn't like the fact that our girls kept whispering about God knows what the entire time! All the girls are head over heels and showing each other their diaries under an oath of silence. "Today I stopped being in love with N. and fell in love with Kh.," with a note of the hour as well as the date! What children they all still are!

I don't show anything to anyone. This diary is for me alone. No one else. Maybe I'll show it to the person I come to love truly. After all, for Tala, Lyalya, and the others none of this is real! The real thing is never like this!

I've just taken Maria Bashkirtseva off the shelf again, opened it in the middle, and there one of my sisters has noted in pencil: "I am like a patient, indefatigable chemist spending my nights over my crucibles so as not to miss the anticipated, desired moment. It seems that this might happen any day, so I think and wait . . . I ask anxiously, Might this be it?"

And so I, too, am constantly listening to myself—might this be it?

I guess not . . . No. No!

Written in the margins of the book: "Love is the greatest happiness, even unhappy love." Masha's handwriting. Is it she who has the unhappy love with Boris? I would like a little bit of that love! How I envy her!

29 October 1914. Wednesday

Everyone at school has started giving themselves manicures. They're trimming their cuticles, letting their nails grow long, and filing them so they'll have a pretty shape.

I have such ugly hands!

Yesterday in class the light was damaged, so the electrician came. He brought a long extension ladder. He climbed up to the ceiling and was rummaging around there—and all of a sudden I noticed the girls putting on airs for him and flirting. I despise them! And all because a young man walked into the classroom!

31 October 1914. Friday

Evgeshka has fallen ill, seriously probably, because now Boris's father is teaching us German in her place. I saw him when Masha and I went to visit them. At the time Nikolai Viktorovich was very pleasant and cheerful and kept offering us Landrin chocolates. In front of the class he is completely different, gloomy and unapproachable. Everyone hates German so much because of Evgeshka and the war, and now no one can forgive him for changing his name. He was Mueller and he became Melnikov. Everyone sees nothing but cowardice and careerism in that. After classes, in the coatroom, the girls started saying terrible things about him and mimicking the way Nikolai Viktorovich teaches pronunciation. He does have bad, crooked teeth, but why do they have to mock the man over that? All of a sudden I felt such fury inside me! What kind of friends are they! Just a malicious herd! I spoke loudly and distinctly: "He changed his name not because he is a coward but because he is ashamed of his nation!" It got quiet. Everyone looked at me. I turned and left. On my way I started feeling very very bad. I was afraid they would start boycotting me now. And when I got home another fear came over me: the fear of fear. Was I really so faint-hearted that I was afraid of being left alone? I am terribly ashamed. I'm just like them. No better. No, worse. Because they were laughing at Nikolai Viktorovich sincerely, while I stood up for him and then took fright at my own intercession.

I also reread my entry for Wednesday. How could I write about others like that and despise them if I am in no way better? Just think, they flirted in front of some electrician! It is not a matter of the electrician! They just want everyone to like them, everyone in general, and for the whole world to fall in love with them, down to the last electrician! And I am the same.

How horrid!

4 November 1914. Tuesday

Today was a fine, sunny day. I dropped by Tala's to go for a walk. She went to change clothes and, as usual, dawdled for nearly a solid hour. While I was waiting for her, Zhenya peeked out of his room and invited me in. I went into his room and he showed me crystals of copper sulfate he'd been growing for two months on his windowsill. Just like real emeralds! I'd never seen anything like it before! Zhenya is wonderful! Then Tala came down and we left.

Now I've gone to bed but I can't sleep; I keep thinking about him. I see his eyes, his strong, muscular arms, and his slender legs in gaiters. He has handsome hands, even though they've been scalded by reagents. And he has a scar on his temple from fighting in the Novoposelensky Garden with hooligans from Temernik, one of whom injured him with brass knuckles. How strong and fearless he is!

Is this still not it? Is he not the one? No, no, no.

This morning on the way to school, I saw the old madwoman in the cap on the corner of Taganrogsky again. What a nightmare: she's incontinent. She's standing there with a puddle beneath her. Suddenly she asks me in a dead voice, "Did you learn your lessons?" Her voice is still in my ears. How horrid all this is: old age!

11 November 1914. Tuesday

I haven't written anything all week because nothing happened.

What our Zhuzhu got up to today!

After classes, in the chemistry room, she swallowed a large crystal of carbolic acid! Who would ever have expected such a thing from our little gray mouse? In actuality, romantic suicide looks anything but romantic. Poor Zhuzhu was doubled over vomiting and completely smeared—dress, boots, stockings, even the ribbons in her hair. You could see she'd eaten noodles. Disgusting! She was taken to Papa's hospital for sluicing.

Everyone tried to guess who he was. Zhuzhu is so secretive!

"There are three types of women: cooks, governesses, and princesses."

12 November 1914. Wednesday

Even today, you could smell Zhuzhu in the classroom, though it had been airing out all night. She's completely fine. For sure everyone is going to laugh at her when she shows up again! Poor thing. And she's fallen in love, it turns out, with Zhenya Martyanov!

My Zhenya! I don't know whether to believe it or not. That's what Lyalya says, but maybe just to get my goat. What's to become of her? And this is what's called my best friend!

My Zhenya? Why mine?

In class I looked at the stuffed animals on the shelves, the jars with frogs preserved in alcohol, and the idiotic papier-mâché busts of representatives of different races—Chinese, Indian, Negro—and all of a sudden I thought, it's all simple. I must be a monster. I probably don't know how to love. I just don't know how. Everyone but me does. I should be stuffed like one of those animals and put on display. Can anyone ever love someone like that? Of course not.

17 November 1914. Monday. Advent

The first snow. And what a snow! All Rostov is buried.

I had to get into my winter coat, which has gotten tight since last year.

Today I stayed behind after classes. Our girls had all left already when I came out into the yard, and the boys were throwing snowballs and I had to walk past them. Frightening alone! But I did it anyway. Then a snowball hit me in the shoulder! And a vile guffaw. I thought, I won't turn around! I clenched my teeth and walked on. I heard stamping behind me. He ran up. Kozlyaninov, from the top class. He ran up and mumbled, "Sorry!" I was so surprised I didn't know what to say. And then I suddenly felt so gay! I flew home and went straight to the mirror without taking off my coat. Rosy cheeks, blazing eyes. What marvelous eyes I have! Yes, I am pretty!

My nanny started muttering that I'd brought in snow, but I kissed her.

22 November 1914. Saturday

Everyone says there have never been such early frosts.

Zhenya and I went to the ice rink. He carried my skates and then laced my boots for me. How nice that was! We skated arm in arm.

Everyone was looking at us. We skated by Zhuzhu a few times. Each time she pretended not to see us! Then we sat on a bench. Zhenya told me very funny stories about his classmates. I laughed so hard!

What is this? What's happening to me? Do I love him?

I wrote that and those three words frightened me: I love him.

23 November 1914. Sunday

I think it's come. I love him. I waited so long and now I'm afraid to believe it. Could this really be true? No, better not to deceive myself. None of this is genuine. No!

Today I saw Zhenya just from a distance. He looked at me. He smiled. Of course, I love him! I do! Zhenya is special! He's nothing like the others!

Viktor stopped by this evening. He's been gripped by the general impulse, too! Viktor wasn't called up, as the only son, but he's burning with patriotism and has enlisted in the home guard as a first-echelon soldier. It's utterly impossible to imagine him—myopic and clumsy—going on the attack. He's come in his uniform: tunic, riding breeches, boots, peakless cap, and overcoat. The soldier's attire has suddenly made him resemble the men leaving in draft companies. He said his mother is in despair because he is going in at a lower rank and will be in the soldiers' barracks.

25 November 1914. Tuesday

I hear a whisper behind the door: Mama is telling my father that something is wrong with me, that I've been reading the Bible for three days straight. My father, irritably: "If someone reads the Bible, that does not mean he is ill!" Mama hushed him and came in to see me, sat down, pressed her lips to my brow, and began saying I shouldn't stay home all the time, I must go for a walk and get some air. But I just shake my head and wait for her to leave—so that I can read the same thing for the hundredth time. How can I tear myself away from these lines? "I sleep, but my heart waketh: it is the voice of my beloved that knocketh, saying, Open to me, my sister, my love, my dove, my undefiled: for my head is filled with dew, and my locks with the drops of the night."

27 November 1914. Thursday

Today I sang for the wounded. After classes, Lyalya, Tala, and I went to the hospital, which is in our old school. We went from classroom to classroom, which have been turned into wards, and asked who wanted us to write letters home. Some soldiers were glad and asked us to sit for a while, wouldn't let us go. Others, on the contrary, were shy and avoided us. One is wounded in the bladder and barely gets around with his bottle. I saw him with a full bottle and wanted to take it to the lavatory, but he blushed and wouldn't let me. I myself was terribly embarrassed, too. It's just silly. There is nothing to be ashamed of here!

In every ward they asked me to sing. They said my voice heals wounds better than any medicine!

One redhead had lost both hands. Such a likable jokester, he kept everyone laughing the whole time. He spoke with pride about routing the Austrian army and how Slavic soldiers don't like to fight and how entire companies let themselves be captured. He couldn't eat by himself, so we spoon-fed him.

He also talked about how big the sheatfish they caught at home were and spread his stumps wide. At the time I restrained myself, but now I can't. I'm writing and sobbing.

I didn't see Zhenya today. What if he doesn't love me anymore? What if I only dreamed all this?

2 December 1914. Tuesday

Today! It happened today!

He kissed me!

I dropped by Tala's, as usual, to go to the infirmary. A little early. Not at all intentionally, it just happened! Only Zhenya was home.

He asked if I'd like to see his crystals. I walked over to the window and he put his arms around me from behind. He kissed my neck, ear, and cheek!

I'm so angry at myself! I just looked at him stupidly and couldn't get a word out. I was petrified! I couldn't move a hand or foot. It was as though my eyes had stuck to this idiotic copper sulfate! All I could think was, Lord, he's kissing me, and I'm completely like a stuffed animal! I so wanted to turn around, entwine my arms around his neck, and kiss him, too! On the lips! And I so want to kiss the scar on his cheek, I don't know why—and I couldn't!

Then we heard the front door! Tala had come! I tore myself away and quickly left the room before she could notice anything.

We went to the infirmary, and Tala was chattering on, but I heard nothing and saw nothing! Inside, everything was singing, I was simply bursting with happiness! I could feel what a silly smile I had on.

And now I feel so bad. What did he think of me?

They had just brought a boy to the infirmary who had picked up a detonating cartridge on the street and lit it, and it had blown up in his hands and burned his face. While the doctor was removing the burnt skin and applying a bandage, the child's father suddenly burst out weeping and started sniffing and could not find his handkerchief. I handed him a towel, put my arms around this stranger, kissed him on the cheek and temple, and whispered something reassuring.

This, too, is a kiss, after all, this, too, is an embrace, and why here, with a stranger, is it all so easy, while there, with my beloved, it is all so hard?

My beloved? My God, how fine: my beloved . . .

3 December 1914. Wednesday

Lord, how I love him!

Yes, I'm certain. This is what I was waiting for. This is real. How happy I am!

I think about him constantly, my Zhenya. He is so special. He is going to be a great chemist. Today at the rink I was tired and sat down right in the snow, and he performed pirouettes for me. He skates so remarkably! How I hate that hooligan from Temernik. Had he struck Zhenya a little higher he would have hit him in the temple!

Zhuzhu won't talk to me. So be it. This is my love! This is my happiness, not hers! Not everyone can be happy.

All my girlfriends have romances, only Mishka is alone. But she isn't suffering over this at all or is pretending she's not. She listens disdainfully to our friends' conversations and skates down the icy hills standing. Most of the boys wouldn't even do that. It's frightening! She could get a bloody nose!

The snow-blanketed coachmen are like Father Frosts. Everyone says that Christmas will be snowy and stormy.

6 December 1914. Saturday

God grant health and happiness to every Nikolai, and the most important one is the one on whom the Russian victory depends!

Viktor has returned. He didn't last long. He told the commission he couldn't see anything and they let him go. He came back angry and started saying he couldn't bear the drilling, the savage manners, and the stench. He said very gravely, "I went to defend the homeland, but all I learned was how to greet generals." This sounded so funny when he said it that everyone burst out laughing. At first Viktor was offended, but then he began showing us hilariously how you're supposed to stand at attention and salute at the sight of a general. He popped his eyes out so, you could explode laughing!

And Katya is happy. All evening she held Viktor's hand, as if she was afraid he would run away again. What does she find in him? He's a clown!

How different Zhenya is! Not like that at all! Smart, deep, genuine! What interesting things he told me today about the chemist

Lavoisier! When his head was chopped off in the guillotine, Robespierre said, Revolutions don't need chemists.

What a fool that Robespierre!

11 December 1914. Thursday

Why, oh, why does that Zabugsky hate me so? Because I can't make heads or tails of his geometry? No one understands anything about it! Not Lyalya. Not Tala. Even Mishka! And they're stupider than me! Zabugsky curses, saying we're dividing without a remainder, but it's just that he can't explain anything properly!

Today Zabugsky broke a large compass and began making a circle on the board using a rag, pressing one end to the board and holding a piece of chalk in the other. We all started laughing. He became furious, wrote down some formula, and put a period on the board so hard that the piece of chalk shattered to bits. Everyone laughed! But he called me to the board! Again he brought me to tears. He knows how to do that! He calls me up and silently examines me with a contemptuous gaze. I wish the earth would swallow me up!

On top of everything else, he has an ugly mole growing next to his nose. It's like a magnetized mole because it's constantly drawing my eyes to it. You don't want to look but you do.

Papa is working at the town council now, working with evacuees, racing around town the entire day. I was with him today at the hospital for lunatics. He was chewing someone out, and I was watching a nurse scrub the floor, there was a nasty smell of chlorine, and next to her stood a patient but with a normal, intelligent face. All of a sudden he grabbed her hands, dirty from the rag, and kissed them. That struck me.

Now I remember that kiss and feel uneasy. How awful it must be to lose yourself like that. Lose yourself. God forbid I ever start a diary entry with "the teenth of Martober."[20]

---

20. A reference to Gogol's "Diary of a Madman."

12 December 1914. Friday

Today something horrible happened at the hospital. I was writing a letter for Evryuzhikhin, who's been blinded and has a thick bandage over his eyes, to his village, his parents, and fiancée. We were sitting in the corridor by the window. He asked to touch my hand and began stroking it with his rough, earthy fingers. Then his fingers crept upward and he grabbed my breast. I took fright and panicked, and he tried to put his arms around me and squeeze me. I wanted to cry out but restrained myself. I threw off his hand, jumped up, and ran out. Outside I suddenly felt ashamed. I wanted to tell Zhenya but couldn't. All of a sudden I realized there were things you couldn't tell anyone.

13 December 1914. Saturday

I got a note from Zhenya saying that no one would be home after four. I barely held out until three-thirty! I raced there. I walked up to their building dying for fear of running into Tala and her parents.

We sat on the sofa in the parlor without turning on the light and kissed!

We kissed!

What an amazing feeling! No, this is utterly impossible to describe! I'm happy! How well he kisses!

I've written this and now I haven't slept half the night, I keep thinking, Who taught him to kiss like that?

16 December 1914. Tuesday

At school we assembled presents for the front, tobacco pouches and handkerchiefs. Then it occurred to me that the person who received my handkerchief might be the very same fellow from Temernik who fought with Zhenya.

At the hospital, one injured man whose leg they amputated has lost his mind. When Masha brought him a crutch, he flung the piece of wood at her with all his might. Masha has a big bruise on her leg now.

27 December 1914

For the first time, a sad Christmas. I feel so bad! The Martyanovs went away on vacation. I won't see Zhenya for two weeks!

My girlfriends and I went to the Alexander Garden in Nakhiche-van, where people go to stroll and there's music. We rode little cars down the hill. Throngs of people.

I'm walking and thinking, what is all this to me without him by my side?

That evening we told our fortunes. We stuck slips of paper with our wishes to the edge of a basin of water with chewed bread. We lowered the lit end of a slender church candle in a nutshell onto the water, like a boat. You had to blow so that the candle, when it reached your paper, would set it on fire. Whoever did that would have her wish come true. You had to blow carefully so as not to put out the flame. That is bad luck. I wrote one word, I can't say which one or else it won't come true. I wondered whether I could write it in my diary and then decided it was better not to risk it, so I won't. We agreed to blow lightly, just barely, and started blowing for all we were worth and the shell was upset. Our little boat drowned! Everyone started laughing and splashing water from the basin. I looked and Masha had gone to the corner and was sitting alone, her eyes filled with tears. Of course, she immediately decided this was a bad omen for her Boris. He's supposed to put to sea soon. I felt so sorry for her! I walked over, sat down next to her, took her hand, and started stroking it. "Little sister, Mashenka, don't, you mustn't. Everything will be fine!"

How am I supposed to know that everything will be fine? How am I supposed to know what will be in general? I know nothing about myself.

Zhenya, where are you? What's happening to you? Are you thinking of me?

1 January 1915

The new year. At first we were at home, then we all went our separate ways. Papa and Mama to sleep, Sasha to some gathering of hers, and my sisters to theirs. I was invited but declined. Here I am sitting alone now on New Year's night and pining away. For the first time in my life I drank a glass of Champagne. I so wanted to clink glasses with Zhenya and Tala, but they're far away. Their uncle has an estate in Ekaterinoslav Province. They always spend their vacations there, in somewhere called Sokolovka.

I spent a long time getting ready, put on my blue dress, pinned on a broach, and made a pretty bow. But all I could think was, Why? He won't see it, after all. We told our fortunes: when the clock struck twelve, each one lit her note with her wish and swallowed the ashes, otherwise it wouldn't come true. We even made Mama and Papa swallow theirs. But somehow it wasn't funny. Once again I wrote the same single word. I started singing with my cinder-black lips. And all of a sudden I couldn't bear it again. Without Zhenya everything is boring, foolish, and pointless. I went to my room and everyone dispersed quickly. I think something is wrong in our family. Lately Papa has changed completely. He and Mama barely speak to each other.

I love him! I love him! I love him!

If only I could be at that marvelous Sokolovka right now!

2 January 1915

My nanny's godson came to see her. A handsome young fellow— missing an arm. He's a clerk, and he had his right arm blown off at the front. Now he's learning to write with his left.

I'm rereading Maria Bashkirtseva. My God, I read this just a year ago and understood nothing! "I think I was created for happiness.

My God, make me happy!" This is all about me! "I was created for triumphs and strong sensations, therefore the best thing I can do is to become a singer." I'm beginning to think that she and I are the same person, that she never died. I am alive, after all. It is not she but I who loves most in the world "art, music, painting, books, society, dresses, luxury, noise, silence, laughter, sorrow, longing, jokes, love, cold, sun, all the seasons and every kind of weather, Russia's peaceful plains and the mountains around Naples, snow in the winter, rain in the fall, spring with its apprehension, peaceful summer days and its beautiful nights shimmering with stars." And also Zhenya. She didn't know my Zhenya.

3 January 1915

In *Niva*, at the back of the issue, they are printing notices of officers who have perished at the front. In front of each name is a cross like an ace of clubs.

A terrible war is under way, and we're copying down a questionnaire about love from each other. How horribly the world is made. This question on the questionnaire has suddenly become more important than all the wars in the world: "The tsar had a daughter who loved a commoner. When the tsar learned of this he lost his temper and wanted to punish him. The princess wept and begged her father, and he decided the following. He would build two doors at the circus arena: behind one would be a terrible, hungry tiger; behind the other, a beautiful woman. Her beloved would be led out into the arena, and he would have to open one of the doors at random. If he opened the door with the tiger—death. The other door—they would give him the beauty for his wife and a great deal of money and send him on a ship to a distant, beautiful land. The princess knew where the tiger and woman were. People gathered at the circus, and the condemned man looked imploringly at the princess: Help me! The enamored girl was in agony. She blushed, then turned pale, then pointed to a door. What was behind it?"

I sincerely answered that of course it was the woman, because love cannot be venal and wish evil. That sleepless night I thought of how the three of us—Tala, Lyalya, and I—had sat at Tala's house, and Lyalya had asked Zhenya to explain some problem for her, and they had shut themselves up in his room, and I realized: the tiger.

My good Nebuchadnezzasaurus!

Nothing from you. Except that postcard. While I send you Roman cards every other day. That's all right, pay no attention, it's all fine.

By the way, your postcard flew here in jig time. Wonders!

And I wonder when you'll get this message of mine?

Letters like this travel slowly, especially if they're not sent.

Unsent letters travel more surely.

Unsent letters can skew time. No stamps or postmarks and—hop—they're already in your hands. Many moons from now we can chat about the weather; right now I'm here, and right now you're here, too. What's going on with you? Has the universe expanded? What day of the week is it? What's that hemisphere outside?

Maybe you have a family, a child, already. A son?

I don't doubt that one day you'll show him the trick I showed you, and my former submariner showed me. I can see it as if it were now. We're on our way to get haircuts on Sunday and I'm whining because I'm afraid of the shears and hate the barber's, and he's dragging me by the arm, and then all of a sudden he says, Look, a trick! And a miracle happens. In the wink of an eye my father gets big and becomes a giant. He takes the streetcar from the stop and holds it out to me.

Not much of a trick, of course, but I think one day your son will show it to his child. He'll become a giant and hold out a streetcar, or a house, or a mountain to him in the palm of his hand.

Maybe that is the whole trick.

Weeks passed, months, and occasionally the interpreter would suddenly turn on Isolde's computer when she was out—they each had their own laptop—and read her new entries.

At the same time the interpreter felt as though he were stealing. And he was.

Occasionally she would record just excerpts from that life, before the interpreter. About their vacation in Italy.

"And do you remember when we fought that time in Pisa? I jumped out of the car and slammed the door. Slammed it so hard I broke it. You drove off, furious, angry, and abandoned me. They were mowing the grass there, and it smelled of freshly mown grass and gasoline. Everywhere on the square there were tourists with their arms held out as if they were leaning on the air. They were posing for a photograph: holding up the falling tower. I went into the cathedral and sat down on a bench since I didn't have anywhere to go anyway. It was cool there, and outside it was so hot. I shut my eyes and the mowers' chirring came through the open doors, and even in the cathedral there was the sharp, fresh smell of mown grass. I sat and thought about you and how I loved you. And that I would sit here and wait for you. I knew you'd come back and find me."

The interpreter only read her diary when they'd quarreled. And now they were quarreling more and more often.

The interpreter knew that Isolde could check when the file was last opened, but he was afraid to ask his friend the programmer how to make it so that she couldn't tell.

It was also strange to read that Isolde was with the interpreter at night but imagined it was Tristan holding her in the dark.

It was Tristan, not the interpreter, kissing her and entering her night after night.

Once Isolde came home when the thief was sitting at her computer, but he managed to turn everything off in time because she went straight to the bathroom.

Once the interpreter had read a new entry about how their son looked like Tristan in his childhood photos.

The interpreter started rummaging through the folders, albums, and boxes on Isolde's shelves. He wanted to find photographs of Tristan. She had shown him them once, but he hadn't paid attention and didn't remember them. Now he stared at each photo. Was there really a resemblance?

Each year friends of Isolde and Tristan gathered at their house, on the day of his death.

As it turned out, the night before their next gathering the interpreter and Isolde fought over something trivial again. There was even plate smashing. When Isolde left for work, the interpreter turned on her computer, opened that file, and read:

"Today I went to sleep in the nursery. I heard the child breathing heavily in his sleep, and I so wanted for him to be your son. He is your son. Yours, not his."

When Isolde came home from work, the interpreter went up and put his arms around her the way he did after their arguments, to make peace. He said, the way they said to each other, "Peace?"

She smiled and pressed her face to his chest.

"Thank you! I was so afraid things would be bad for us again today."

The interpreter smiled.

"Everything's going to be fine!"

The guests arrived. Isolde made a raclette. There was warmth and lots of good talk.

The interpreter went to put their son to bed and read to him about Urfin Jus and his wooden soldiers. The child should have been asleep long before, but he kept asking him to read more, so the interpreter read and read.

He didn't feel like rejoining them.

At last his son fell asleep, the interpreter turned off the light, lay in the darkness, and listened to the child's heavy breathing.

He emerged in time for dessert. The conversation had moved on to Russia and Chechnya. The dental tech, pinching off grapes, asked the interpreter what someone experiences who belongs not to a small nation, like the Swiss or Chechens, but to a major nation— and here he stumbled—not of conquerors or oppressors, but how to put it—he rolled a grape in his fingers and still couldn't find the right word and looked at the interpreter with a smile, as if expecting help.

The interpreter suggested, "If he belongs to the Russians."

The tech laughed, popped the grape in his mouth, started chewing, and nipped off another: "You did understand what I meant!"

"Of course, I did."

The interpreter poured the rest of the wine from the bottle, went to the kitchen for another, and when he returned to their guests, he started talking about a video the Chechens had shot. Someone had seen brief clips on television. The interpreter said that some journalists he knew from Moscow had sent him the cassette. Isolde interrupted him.

"Don't!"

The interpreter pulled her to him and kissed her on the neck.

"Of course, I won't."

Their guests started insisting.

"Show us!"

The interpreter started pleading that it was really better not to because these frames had not been shown on television anywhere, even in Russia.

"All the more reason! Show us!"

The person who especially wanted to see what he shouldn't was the dental tech.

The interpreter carried the plates to the kitchen and Isolde followed him and said quietly, so that no one in the room would hear, "Why do you want to spoil this evening for me?"

The interpreter replied, "Why do you think I do?"

Finally, the tape in the VCR, everyone took a seat and the interpreter turned it on.

First someone is asking that a ransom be paid for him. He's still just a boy, gaunt, dirty, probably a captured soldier. They cut off his finger and he begins to whimper softly. They twirl the finger in front of the lens.

Then some foreigner—he speaks English—holds out to the camera a jar of cloudy liquid, his bloody urine, and complains that they beat him in the kidneys, and at that they beat him from behind with a steel rod, he twitches, and he shouts.

From the very beginning Isolde refused to watch and went out on the balcony to smoke.

After the first frames one of the guests stood up and followed her.

They were about to slit the captive soldier's throat. He struggles and says hoarsely, "Stop! Stop!" He goes somewhere below the frame. They lift him back up, a black hand with crooked fingers on a red face.

Another one of the guests got up and silently left the room.

An old man calmly crossed himself for the camera and said, "They're going to kill me now, and I want to say that I love you very much, Zhenechka, and you, Alyosha, and you, Vitenka!" They cut off his head. The camera in the first second showed not his head but his neck—zoomed in—it's thick, probably a 45, and suddenly it reduces to a fist and from it his throat juts out and black blood gushes.

The two of them—the interpreter and the dental tech—were left alone in front of the television. They sat and watched a woman being raped; she kept shouting, "Just don't touch the child!" They set the hair between her legs on fire with a lighter, then thrust a light bulb inside her and smashed the glass. The woman moaned, gasped, and doubled up on the ground. Blood flowed. A bearded man in sunglasses, smirking, thrust the barrel of his gun into her anus and cocked the trigger.

"Enough," the dental tech said. "Turn it off!"

The interpreter turned off the television and went to the kitchen to make tea. The guests dispersed quickly.

That night Isolde went to sleep in the nursery again. Instead of "goodnight" she said, "I hate you."

26 August 1915. Wednesday

Today at the rollerskating rink my brother introduced me to his new friend Alexei Kolobov, a student who was evacuated from Warsaw with his university. I was skating with Lyalya and from a distance saw someone waving to me from one of the tables around the track. I skated up to the barrier. Sasha introduced us. The band was playing so loudly we had to shout. He has amazing blue eyes and a handsome slender hand, and he blushed very amusingly when he said hello to me. I suggested we skate, but he refused. He doesn't know how. I felt awkward with them and a little bored. There was nothing to talk about. Or rather, not bored but anxious in a way. I felt like running away and hiding. I sped back to the middle of the track, into the throng.

Now I'm writing and wondering what it was that affected me so? Maybe, maybe . . .

27 August 1915. Thursday

The Martyanovs are back. I saw Zhenya today. I was amazed. What did I ever see in him?

Papa came with a map and everyone started examining it. Matters keep getting worse at the front. We've surrendered Poland and all of Lithuania and Belorussia. Sasha and Papa follow the retreat every day on the map. Refugees have flooded into Rostov from everywhere.

That night I thought about Zhenya and once again remembered him showing me his experiment then, how a magnet behind a sheet of paper creates a symmetrical drawing with the iron shavings and

I said I didn't love him anymore—and how after I said that he was so pitiful, hangdog, and helpless with the magnet and paper in his hands.

I am probably very bad. But I don't feel at all sorry for him. Or rather, I do, of course, but this pity makes him even more pitiful somehow.

I haven't fallen in love with Alexei. Yes, I can feel it. I know.

29 August 1915. Saturday

After the vacation everyone gets together and tells each other about their summer romances—invented for the most part, I think.

Mishka astonished everyone. That summer she met a young lawyer; his mother had rented the dacha next door. He said he loved her, and next year he would graduate from university and marry her. The next day his mother arrived, grand and proud, and got down on her knees before her—before Mishka!—and began imploring her to refuse her son. She assured her that they were both young and not a good match, that Mishka would feel awkward in their circle. He would be ashamed of her and he would be unhappy. Later she informed her that they were up to their ears in debt and that he had a fiancée, a beauty, a rich girl, a society lady, and that if she truly loved her son, Mishka should refuse him, for his happiness. Mishka sent him a farewell letter where she wrote that they would never see each other again and he was free, but she would love him always.

I don't know whether to believe it or not. Although Mishka has never lied before.

I went to the hospital.

Clouds as gray as the hospital gowns.

I was sick at heart. I keep thinking about Alexei. He is Sasha's friend and sometimes stops by to see us, but he pays no attention to me whatsoever. Nor I him. He is either shy or boring. More likely the latter.

31 August 1915. Monday

Petya Nazarov showed up. He's changed a lot, matured. At first they said Syoma had been killed, but a card came through the Red Cross. He's in German captivity.

4 September 1915. Friday

Today Alexei was here again. I wish he wouldn't come! He walked in and I had just come from school. I still hadn't changed and was wearing my horrid brown dress and black apron—and there was an ink stain on my hand! We bumped into each other in the vestibule. I was coming out of the lavatory and was so horrified that he would see me and hear the noise of the water in the WC that I froze, my palms started sweating, and I blinked. I couldn't get a word out. He and my brother started talking in front of me—and about what? At the university they have a post box on the staircase that says "Sex questionnaire." They have to submit anonymous information there about their sex life. I'm standing there red-faced, like a little idiot. Tears spurted out. I ran off like a shot.

I hate myself!

8 September 1915. Nativity of the Holy Virgin

My brother is quite grown—he's shaving.

Everyone's quite grown—Katya and Masha, too.

And I? I'm in the graduating class at school! And what have I suddenly noticed? Now I am the object of worship! I have an admirer from a lower class, Musya Svetlitskaya, who is burning with love for me and does everything she can to show her admiration. She runs after me at class break, like a dog, clings to me, kisses my hands! At first I liked it, but it's become tiresome. Most of all, I can't shake her! In the morning on the way to school I bought her a cream-filled chocolate, the same one, my favorite since I was a child, in a colored wrapper with two tabs. Only now when you pull on one a picture of Wilhelm's malicious face pops out, and if you jerk at the other the forelocked head of the ubiquitous Cossack Kozma Kryuchkov appears. I gave it to Musya and she nearly wept for joy.

Lord, how I want to love someone like that!

10 September 1915. Thursday
Repulsive weather.

Alexei was here again. He doesn't notice me at all. The same goes for me. I dislike him more and more. What is this? Arrogance? Disdain? He thinks I have yet to mature to their high-brow conversations?

No need!

12 September 1915. Saturday
That's it. I've fallen in love! And how! Moreover, I fell in love from the very first moment, there, at the rink. I'd just been hiding it from myself, for fear of getting hurt, of causing myself pain. What I had with Zhenya was nonsense. Kid's stuff. Zhenya is a baby, a little boy. I just didn't know what love was yet!

Alexei! Alyosha! What a wonderful name!

And what a marvelous day!

13 September 1915. Sunday
Today Alyosha and I went to the Renaissance picture show to see *Stenka Razin*. I sat there and saw nothing, I only felt his closeness, his hand on my hand.

How good he is at kissing me! Only with him, with my Alyosha, have I learned what a man's kiss is! There is nothing to compare with it! I've been in a fever for almost two days.

And something else very important: on the way home Alyosha told me that the students have organized a theatrical circle and are preparing a charity performance. He doesn't act himself, but he's responsible for the lighting. He asked me if I'd like to act. Lord!

Me? Act? And work on a performance with Alyosha? I shall die of happiness! I asked what they were planning to put on. They haven't decided yet. The performance is going to be directed by Kostrov, who studied at the Moscow Art Theater Studio!

Oh my! I'm a hair's breadth from being an actress!

I should probably be ashamed, but I want to be on stage, I want to be the center of attention, I want applause, I want waves of admiration and love flooding me from the audience! This is bad, no doubt, but there's nothing I can do about myself.

The Women's Medical Institute evacuated from Warsaw along with the Women's Higher Courses. Tala and Lyalya want to enroll there. They're inviting me to go with them.

No, I know my path. I'm going to sing. I want to sing, and nothing can prevent me—not war, not an earthquake, not a world flood! All these years I've been waiting for this moment, to appear in that world! And what? Deny myself? No, I'm going to sing in this life and don't plan to wait for another!

Or the theater.

How happy I am! My dear Alyosha!

17 September 1915. Thursday

Today in zoology class R.R. brought in a skeleton. Our young ladies were terrified and started squealing, but he found a way to calm them, saying that this was the skeleton of our old Bilinskaya porter, the Tolstoyan, who bequeathed his body to science and enlightenment. I didn't even know he'd died. The old man had disappeared somewhere after the school moved. People said he'd gone to his sister's in Novocherkassk.

God rest his soul! The body did not get its rest.

In profile R.R. reminds me of some kind of rodent. Repulsive. Even uglier than Zabugsky, and he too considers us all dullards a priori. At the first lesson he started showing us an experiment. He said it wasn't God who created the solar system. Look. He started stirring a drop of grease in a glass with a spoon. The fast movement made the large drop burst and separate into several small ones—a graphic picture of the origin of the solar system and planets. "Understand?" "Yes." "Any questions?" "No." He became angry. "You were supposed to ask who was stirring the spoon then! Smarties!"

He says "smarties" so as not to call us fools.

People say the principal is in love with him.

Zhenya is still an utter child. He ran into me on the street, walked up, and wanted to say something, but he was tongue-tied and twirled his school cap in his hands helplessly.

Whereas Alexei is mature, intelligent, genuine. He's so interesting to be with! So well read and knows so much of everything! It turns out that it was the French who came up with the idea of acting, whereas the Greeks' theater is *ago*, i.e., I act, I live. Hence the word "agony."

That is it precisely. For me the theater isn't acting but life and death itself.

I can't fall asleep. I bury my face in my pillow and see him, the way he smiles, the way he kisses me. Today an eyelash got in his eye and I licked it out with my tongue.

19 September 1915. Saturday

So it's decided. We're putting on *The Inspector General*! I'm to play Maria Antonovna.

Kostrov really is an incredible know-it-all. He's got it in his head that he's practically Stanislavsky and is demanding that everyone obey him like a god, as if we were in fact the Art Theater Studio. On the other hand, he is clever and a real talent. And I like that we're taking everything seriously.

And he is a genuine artist. He knows everything about the theater. A page accidentally flew out of his script onto the floor and he quickly sat on it. He explained that this was a long-time actors' superstition. If you don't sit down on a dropped script, it will be a failure.

Tala is insulted that I don't have time to go to the hospital with her anymore. Or is it because of Zhenya? She loves her brother so!

What I'm doing is probably bad; between helping the wounded and the theater, I chose the theater. But art, isn't that helping people, too? I don't know. I'll have to think some more about that. But there, at rehearsals, it's so interesting! While at the hospital it's always the same thing!

I reread that and thought, what an egoist I am! I felt ashamed before Tala.

Today after rehearsal, when everyone was dispersing, Kostrov told a very funny story about how the local residents came with petitions and complaints at the shooting of *The Defense of Sevastopol*. They had seen an entire suite with embroidered greatcoats and decided this was some kind of brass. Some old woman latched onto Kostrov, who was wearing a general's uniform, wept, and asked him for something. She just couldn't believe that he was no general. So as not to interrupt the shooting, they had to ask the police to drive the peasants out.

At supper I was talking about the rehearsal, but Papa asked, "Do you know what the main point is in *The Inspector General*?" "The denunciation?" "No." "The famous final scene?" "No." "Then what?" "The main point is the way Bobchinsky asks that the tsar be told there is a Peter Ivanovich Bobchinsky." "Why?" "I can't explain it. You just have to understand it."

Sometimes Papa knows how to be simply amazingly repulsive!

I kiss you, Alyosha! Goodnight!

3 October 1915. Saturday

It's been so long since I wrote anything! There is absolutely no time. I'm with Alyosha and at the theater all the time. I do almost nothing for school. I absolutely must hang in there, and it would be shameful to get bad marks!

I'm getting the feel of my role. At home I change clothes and walk around in makeup. When my nanny saw me she burst out laughing. I got furious at her and slammed the door. She's an old and foolish woman!

I'm trying to get into my role, to delve into my character's personality. Here I am in love with Khlestakov. But how can that be? Why? After all, he's a nobody, a clown, a drunk! Ultimately, a fool! That doesn't happen! Here I love Alyosha. That I can understand. He's not like that at all. Smart, charming, gentle, tactful. Handsome, courageous. And he has such a handsome mouth, and nose, and forehead. And his hands! You could fall in love with his hands alone!

But all of this leads nowhere in my work on my role. I have to find points of contact, something understandable and close to me, something I too could fall in love with.

Once again I picture the foolish face of our lop-eared Petrov, our Khlestakov. No, nothing works.

And it doesn't work because I'm constantly thinking about Alyosha. Today he's going to have supper with us. I'm sitting by the window looking out. At the fall, the cold, the rain, the puddles.

All of a sudden I had the idiotic thought that I was just about to die and this pavement and this half-dead tree, the wet dog running by, and this rainy sky over Rostov was all there was. This was my whole life. What a nightmare!

He's coming!

I'll finish this tonight.

Alyosha told a very interesting story about how at the beginning of the war he and his parents and younger brother were in Germany and like all Russians headed for Switzerland. People who had lived there for years were given twenty-four hours to collect their things!

They took a ship across Lake Bodensee with Kachalov himself! They returned via Italy and by sea to Greece.

Just where hasn't he been? While I've seen nothing but this accursed Rostov. It turns out, Leonardo's *Last Supper*, painted on the wall of a monastery's refectory in Milan, is perishing! He painted it in oils, and the layer of paint is curling up in fine petals and detaching from the wall. I couldn't help myself and exclaimed, "What a horror!" And Sasha, the fool, said, "Thousands of people are dying in the trenches, and we have paints!" Here's what I said to him: "Fool!" My brother and I started arguing, and Alyosha—my clever one—made peace between us again so tactfully!

They were taken by train from Salonika to Serbia. Taken for free, moreover, because Russian blood was being spilled over Serbia. Instead of tickets, the conductor checked their passports. Alyosha told us that the Serb looked at the Russians sympathetically, but this was painfully unmerited. "Had we spilled our blood?" Alyosha said. "We were just fleeing, muttering about the inconveniences and lack of money, and fighting over an extra seat!"

Then they got to Bulgaria and from there to Romania—and there by ship down the Dunai to the Black Sea. Alyosha said that it looked like the lower reaches of the Volga. Papa asked, "And Izmail? You must have sailed past Izmail!" Alyosha began to laugh and said that he saw Izmail quite by accident—he had stepped out to smoke. "But all Izmail is rather like our Don floating docks." "And that's all?" "That's all."

I'm tired. I haven't the time or strength to write.

Dear Alyosha! I love you and kiss you! I shall see you tomorrow!

5 October 1915. Monday

Again this Zabugsky! He will drive me to the noose! Today during the test he was walking around the classroom to make sure no one was copying. Each time, as he walked past, he stopped behind me, glanced over my shoulder at my empty notebook, and hissed, "Such style! Such style!" I nearly burst into sobs. He leaned over so closely I could feel his breathing—disgusting. One time I even thought he'd touched my hair. He probably could barely stop himself from grabbing my braid and ripping it off. And he's always scratching his mole!

I'll finish writing after supper. All I told them was about my tormenter, and Papa said that last year Zabugsky buried his wife, who died in childbirth along with their baby. I hadn't known. Why are people so mean? Why am I so mean?

9 October 1915. Friday

Today I was at Alyosha's. He wanted to introduce me to his parents. It was rather terrifying. Later Alyosha told me they liked me! Very nice people. They've seen the whole world and lived in different countries. His father was telling me how in 1894 he came to live through the terrible earthquake in Constantinople, when two thousand people perished in two minutes. He also said he had seen high on the wall of Hagia Sophia the bloody handprint of the sultan, which he had left when he rode into the church on horseback over piles of corpses after the siege of the city.

So why haven't I been anywhere? Lord, I want so badly to see the world!

Alexei's parents spoke a lot about Warsaw, where they lived for so many years. They said that the Poles did not always like Russians, and even clerks in stores, when they heard Russian, immediately began with their *nie rozumieć rosyjskim,* and passersby, if you asked them the way, would send the *moscowals* in the wrong direction. I had been keeping quiet and suddenly stated that we Russians were incapable of bearing malice and always forgave everything, and I told them how Nyusya had written in a letter that because of our sympathy for Poland in *Life for the Tsar,* now our national hero was dying of the cold, not Polish sabers. Everyone burst out laughing and I was terribly embarrassed, but Alyosha looked at me so nicely that I felt easier, too, and I laughed along with everyone else.

Alexei's younger brother is a very nice boy but an awful pest. He ran into his brother's room and simply would not go to his own. Alyosha promised to show him a trick, and only for that bribe did Timoshka agree to leave. Alyosha poured water into a child's bucket and in the courtyard began twirling it so that the water didn't pour out when the bucket was upside-down.

We kissed and then talked about the theater, and then he asked about the hospital I've been going to. But I haven't been there in a long time and I was ashamed. Alyosha started talking about how it bothers him that others have to fight while he sits it out in the rear. He's not subject to the draft. He also said that his maternal grandfather was a German.

I simply hadn't known what strong genuine feeling was! Now I love him. Now I know this is genuine.

12 October 1915. Monday

Zhenya is demonstratively courting Lyalya—to get back at me. Let him. I actually think it's amusing.

13 October 1915. Tuesday

Today Alyosha said he wants to go to the front. That frightened me. He wants to volunteer. "I have no right to stay nice and clean amid the universal mud."

I'm frightened.

15 October 1915. Thursday

Today I finally told Mama that I want to become an actress and after graduation I'm going to Moscow to attend drama courses. At first she was silent, then it was as if she'd exploded. She began shouting that she would never let me go anywhere because I was drawn by the "slough of bohemian life," as she put it. But I told her that I definitely considered the peaceful bourgeois life, with its total deception and boredom, much worse—and I wanted to dedicate myself to art. She rushed to the sideboard for her drops. "And what do you understand about the theater? Everyone dreams of being a Ermolova or a Savina, but they become the mistresses of rich scoundrels and portray poor countrywomen in thousand-ruble earrings or become theater hags for forty rubles' pay!" I'd known she would be against it and had been prepared to hear something in this vein. But then she did something I cannot forgive! I was already leaving and she shouted after me, "Look at yourself in the mirror! How can anyone who looks like that dream of being an actress?"

I am a horrid, vile person. I hate my own mother.

Dear Alyosha, how I need you right now!

17 October 1915. Saturday

Papa is golden! My dear, good, smart Papa! He and I talked half the night, and he said he would pay for me to have lessons with Koltsova-Selyanskaya! Only I mustn't say anything to my mother. Papochka, my wonderful Papochka, how I love you!

My first lesson is on Tuesday.

18 October 1915. Sunday

Today I was running late for rehearsal, rushing as fast as my legs would carry me, tripped, and my notebook with my script fell out on the ground! What a nightmare! I sat on it immediately—right on the dirty sidewalk. Everyone looked around as if I were a madwoman. But I sat there, caught my breath, and ran on. I was barely late!

Alyosha looked very bad today. He has caught a chill and was sneezing. I wanted to take him home, but he sat through the entire rehearsal.

Katya's Viktor is playing Dobchinsky and Bobchinsky—our director's innovation, that one actor is playing both. Viktor doesn't have to do any particular acting. As it is he is Bobchinsky and Dobchinsky rolled into one.

Ogloblina is head over heels in love with Kostrov—and again blushed endlessly and got her lines wrong. Finally Kostrov couldn't take it, he blew up, and he started running around the stage and shouting at her. "You come out on stage—from where? What life? What happened in the wings? What were you doing there? Sleeping? Here you show up sleepy, shuffling your slippers, and dragging your skirt! You've lived in the wings, now bring that life here!" She was in tears, of course. He had to beg her forgiveness. He even got down on his knees when she decided to leave for good. It's a madhouse!

19 October 1915. Monday

Alyosha and I went to the Renaissance. The film was interesting to watch but basically nonsense to retell. Mario the sculptor has a fiancée, but he meets with his former beloved Stella. The wedding does not take place, and in despair Mario goes into a monastery. There he works on a statue. Then a merry company comes to the monastery, and Stella is with them. She recognizes Mario and tries to seduce him. "You can't forget me! The statue's features are mine!" At that he picks up his hammer, smashes the sculpture, then kills Stella, and throws himself from a cliff.

We went out and were walking in the rain. All Rostov was carrying umbrellas and wearing galoshes. I leaned toward Alyosha and thought, That's no kind of love, that's silly. This is love, right here. He and I.

Does Alyosha really want to go to war? How can he go and leave me like that?

20 October 1915. Tuesday

I've just returned from Nina Nikolaevna's. How delightful she is! Old but beautiful, gracious, and intelligent! She knew everyone!

And how unfairly the world is arranged after all! No one needs all this anymore. All her life, all her experience, all her beauty, all her words, knowledge, memory of people, and history, all that will be gone with her!

On Kadmina, the famous singer, with whom she was friendly in her younger years: "Silly girl! She poisoned herself with matches on stage over unrequited love!"

About herself: she left the theater because did not want to end up a comic old lady.

On her partner: "He could not have sweaty hands."

On her stage name: when she became an actress, her mother's family forced her to change her last name so as not to disgrace the family. "What mattered was that the initials be the same, because of the monogram on my linen and spoons."

She also told me, "You have talent, child! But that is not enough. Nor is diligence. Nor is love of the theater. Nothing is enough! Grief has to knock at your door—you have to suffer through and learn everything, including what you should not know."

Why should I know grief? I don't want any grief!

There is nothing in the large pot on her windowsill but dirt. I asked, "Nina Nikolaevna, what is this?" "I planted a lemon seed and thought that if a sapling grew I would live a long time. An old woman's foolishness!"

On her chest of drawers is a photograph of her second husband, the actor Selyansky, a very handsome man. She saw me examining him and burst into laughter. She started telling me what a drunkard he was. He'd been up to something and landed in court, and before the case was heard his attorney said to him, "Not a word of your own! Here, I wrote your script. Memorize it and play it!" He was acquitted. "His finest role!"

And she explained to me all about Khlestakov. It's all very simple! I hadn't fallen in love with any Khlestakov but with Petersburg, that far-off, genuine life! Not even Petersburg, really, but simply with my love. I was in love with love! How clear everything was suddenly!

She remembered Sarah Bernhardt's visit to Odessa. They tried to block the French celebrity's visit due to her Jewish origins, and on Deribasovskaya someone even threw a stone at her carriage. At that time, Bernhardt was skinny and red-haired. Everyone talked about her eccentricity, that she slept in a coffin and walked around at home in a Pierrot costume. "But in fact, she was simply an affected woman. And her lauded voice did not hold a candle to Ermolova's!"

I listened and thought, Could this really be just the envy of an old failure? One gets everything—world fame and success—and the other drags out her old age in Rostov. But she may have had as much talent as the famous Sarah Bernhardt. So what does this mean? Why does fate take pity on some and punish others?

My fate! Be kind to me! Please! Is that too much to ask? Give me everything!

24 October 1915. Saturday

I woke up this morning and the first thing I saw were dust mites in a hill of light. It was like a hill straight across the room, made of sun and dust, solid, firm—I wished I could slide down it!

How wonderful it is to wake up like this, to return to yourself from somewhere—hands, put yourselves back on; feet, put yourselves back on!—and to know that love is already waiting for you!

Dear Alyosha! Light of my life! How I love you! How did I ever live without you? Without your blue eyes! And how they know how to change color! How I love to watch them shine blue, then turn gray, and then quite black when your pupil dilates.

It was all so difficult with Zhenya—cuddling, kissing—but with Alyosha it's so nice, so easy! It's just awful that I don't know how to show him all my tenderness, love, and devotion.

How fine to wake up and know I'll see him today!

4 November 1915. Wednesday

Nina Nikolaevna's homework assignments: I've been left alone at home. I'm supposed to tidy up, but I've begun to imagine I'm serving some shrewish mistress and she follows me around muttering that I'm doing everything wrong. Go mop up there yourself then! I talk to myself.

Then I started thinking about him again. And here I've sat down simply to write that I love him.

5 November 1915. Thursday

I don't know whether to laugh or cry! For the play I'm supposed to fall flat on my face, so in the evening I'm rehearsing in my room, working on my fall—and my frightened mama runs in. "What happened?"

7 November 1915. Saturday

Alyosha's mama turns out to be an epileptic. We were sitting in his room when his brother called for him. We ran in and she was lying on the floor having a seizure, arching her back, as if she were being drawn like a string across an invisible bow. Foam was coming from her mouth. I wiped it with a handkerchief and Alyosha held her head. Her eyes rolled back, she wet herself, and then, after the seizure, she lay there like a corpse.

Poor Alyosha! He suffered so!

14 November 1915. Saturday

Something horrible happened today. I don't think I've even comprehended the full horror yet. But it feels as though inside, in my soul, everything has been contaminated by it.

As always, rehearsal began with exercises. We had to act as if our character had just murdered his lover. Murdered her in the next room and has now come out to us. We were falling about laughing, especially when Viktor played the murderer. He pretended he'd dismembered and eaten her. Then Kostrov told me to play the same thing: I had just murdered my lover behind the door. So I went out into the corridor, and all of a sudden I felt I'd been paralyzed. Me murder? My lover? What lover? How could that be—murder? How could that be—a lover? Is Alexei my lover? They're calling me in but I'm still standing there. I realize I could never act anything of the kind. I couldn't, and most of all I don't want to. Kostrov says with displeasure, "Well, where are you?" I made a joke and shouted to him, "I poisoned him and then I poisoned myself and I'm lying next to him dead."

Everyone laughed, and suddenly I felt frightened.

Lord, am I really not an actress?

17 November 1915. Tuesday

I reread this and was horrified at myself, at the nonsense I write! Today Alyosha said he was leaving for the front. It's all been decided. He didn't tell me until the last moment; he didn't want to upset me.

I was at Nina Nikolaevna's and just could not collect myself. She immediately noticed that something was wrong with me and was very dissatisfied.

"Every actress wants to play a genuine woman, in love and unhappy." I don't understand. That's not true. It shouldn't be like that. Why must a genuine woman be in love and unhappy rather than not in love and happy?

She showed me something in front of the mirror. In her parlor she has a large, three-leaf mirror where you can see yourself at full height and facing every way. I looked at her and thought how old she was and how no one needed her. God forbid I live to that point. All of a sudden she seemed to read my mind and said, "I was like you, young and pretty and afraid of old age. Now God has punished me." And she added, "Better old than dead. But you can't understand that yet."

As I was reading the monologue I suddenly broke down sobbing—over Alyosha. Nina Nikolaevna shouted at me and slapped her hand on the table. "You mustn't cry real tears! Let the audience think you're crying, but you yourself must not cry!" I couldn't go on with the lesson. I didn't try to explain anything to her, just excused myself, saying I felt unwell, and left.

18 November 1915. Wednesday

In a week he will be gone.

Alyosha is my fiancé. I am his fiancée. Today we told his parents. His mother wept. She's horrified that Alyosha is leaving for the front, but his father kissed me and said some very fine, important words. He called me his daughter. He blessed me with the icon but picked it up upside down. Timoshka noticed and burst out laughing, and laughter overcame all of us. It was so easy, so nice!

We'll get married when I graduate from this idiotic school.

I don't want to tell mama and father anything. Later, not now. I know it will all end in a row and valerian drops again. I don't want that.

Alyosha saw me home and we stopped in at the Alexander Nevsky Cathedral. There were many new arrivals in the cathedral. The city is overflowing with refugees in general. People are fleeing to Rostov from everywhere—Armenians from the south fleeing the Turks; Galicians from the southwest; Poles, Ukrainians, and Jews—they've been permitted to live outside the Pale of Settlement—from the West; and Balts from the northwest.

We stood there holding candles, and I imagined us getting married here. I looked at it all and in a way made my own covenant with the candles, and the Vasnetsov paintings, and the mosaic on the floor, and the marble icon screens and altars, and the Canadian poplars in the windows, and the booming vault, and the smell of the incense and melted wax—for these to wait for us and we would certainly be back.

Alyosha leaned over and said into my ear that I should take a look at the priest hitting the old ladies on the lips when

My cell rang mid-sentence.

"Baumann, Direktion für Soziales und Sicherheit."[21]

It's understood—they're looking for interpreters.

"Grüzi, Herr Baumann! Kann ich Ihnen helfen?"

"Wir haben einen Dringlichkeitsfall, hätten Sie jetzt Zeit zu kommen?"

"Nein, Herr Baumann, es tut mir leid, aber ich kann nicht."

"Schade. Es ist eben sehr dringend. Und ich kann niemand finden. Vielleicht könnten Sie sehr kurz bei uns vorbeikommen? Ich habe da einen jungen Mann bei mir, ich muss ihm etwas mitteilen. Aber er versteht nichts, weder Deutsch noch Englisch."

"Es geht wirklich nicht, Herr Baumann. Ich bin jetzt in Rom."

"In Rom? Schön! Wissen Sie was, vielleicht könnten Sie ihm etwas per Telefon ausrichten? Nur ein paar Worte. Der junge Mann steht hier neben mir, ich gebe ihm den Hörer, und Sie sprechen kurz mit ihm."

"Gut. Was soll ich ihm sagen?"

"Also, er heisst Andrej. Es geht um zwei Brüder, Asylsuchende aus Weißrussland, aus Minsk. Sagen Sie ihm, dass sein Bruder Viktor gestern um 18 Uhr vor dem Durchgangszentrum in Glatt bewusstlos aufgefunden wurde. Er lebte noch, aber starb auf dem Weg ins Spital. Es ist nicht klar, was passiert ist. Entweder hat ihn jemand aus dem Fenster gestoßen oder es war ein Selbstmord oder ein Unfall, die Ermittlungen laufen noch. Alles zeugt davon, dass er betrunken

---

21. Baumann, social issues and security administration *(Ger.)*.

war. Er ist vom dritten Stock mit dem Hinterkopf auf den Asphalt gefallen. Wir haben versucht, Andrej das zu erklären, aber er hat nichts verstanden. Das ist alles."

"Gut, Herr Baumann, geben Sie ihm den Hörer."[22]

The receiver said in a small boy's frightened voice, "Hello?"

"Andrei, something's happened. Your brother Viktor—"

"Did something happen to him?" The voice in the receiver got very quiet.

I told him everything I was supposed to.

For a while the receiver was silent. Then I heard an odd noise like hiccupping.

"Hello, Andrei, can you hear me?"

Subdued, between hiccups: "Yes."

"Hand the phone to Mr. Baumann."

---

22. "Hello, Mr. Baumann. How can I help you?"

"We have an urgent matter. Could you come right now?"

"No, Mr. Baumann. I'm sorry, but I can't."

"Too bad. The matter is really very urgent. I can't find anyone. Could you come by here just briefly? I have a young man with me and I have to tell him something. But he doesn't understand any German or English."

"It's impossible, Mr. Baumann. I'm in Rome right now."

"Rome? Great! You know, could you tell him something over the phone? Just a few words. The young man is standing next to me now. I'll give him the receiver and you can speak to him briefly."

"Fine. What should I tell him?"

"So, his name is Andrei. We're talking about two brothers who came from Belarus, Minsk, to request asylum. Tell him his brother Viktor was found yesterday at 18:00, unconscious in front of the refugee shelter in Glatt. He was still alive, but he died on the way to the hospital. It's not clear what happened. Either someone pushed him out a window, or this was suicide, or an accident. The investigation is still under way. Everything attests to him being drunk. He fell from the third floor and struck the back of his head on the asphalt. We tried to explain this to Andrei, but he didn't understand anything. That's all."

"Fine, Mr. Baumann. Hand him the phone." (*Ger. with elements of Swiss-Ger.*)

The brisk police voice again: "Baumann."

"Ich habe es ihm gesagt, Herr Baumann."

"Merci vielmal! Und schönen Tag noch!"

"Ihnen auch!"[23]

Alyosha leaned over and said into my ear that I should take a look at the priest—he was hitting the old ladies on the lips when they went to press them to the cross, but holding the cross out gently to the young women.

At first I was angry at him, but then I was suddenly ashamed that I could be angry at him over something so trivial! Lord, what if he's killed! How will I go on living? And once again I was so frightened my legs buckled and I grabbed onto Alyosha to keep from falling.

20 November 1915. Friday

Name-day party at Anya Trofimova's. Dancing, laughter. I ran to the lavatory, locked myself in, and burst into sobs. How can I have fun if he's leaving in three days—maybe forever.

22 November 1915. Sunday

Tomorrow Alyosha leaves for the front.

We walked the streets, we were freezing, we stopped into a picture show. I didn't see anything, just a blind beam of light stirring in the dark. It was strange and impossible. Tomorrow he's leaving for the front, and here we were sitting and watching this nonsense. I tugged on his arm. "Let's go!" We left before it was over.

I don't know whether to write about this or not.

I will.

---

23. "Baumann."
   "I told him everything, Mr. Baumann."
   "Many thanks! Have a good day!"
   "You, too!" *(Ger. with elements of Swiss-Ger.)*

We got to my house. We went up to my room. I locked the door from the inside. Turned off the light. Embraced him. Said, "Take me, Alyosha!" We stood there like that, embracing in the middle of the room. He started to say he couldn't like that, but I said, "I want to so much!" We were both afraid and shy. No, I won't write anything.

I don't understand anything about what happened. All I know is I did everything wrong!

I am truly sick at heart. It was all painful and embarrassing. Nothing worked. He left without explaining anything to me. What? What did I do wrong?

Alyosha, I love you so much, and I feel so awful and afraid!

23 November 1915. Monday

Today I saw Alyosha off. We all went to the train station. There were many different people he knew. The train was on the tracks past where the platforms stopped, and we walked for a long time over the ties. I kept waiting for Alyosha to come over to me, but he was surrounded by friends or else was standing with his parents. After what happened yesterday I felt so awkward, so bad, I didn't dare approach him. Then he finally came over and we embraced. I couldn't look him in the eye. All the women around us who were seeing their sons, brothers, and fiancés off were weeping, but I felt stunned. I could only press close to his greatcoat and watch, in a stupor, as the soldiers ran to the train car over the boards—and the boards bowing under them.

When we moved apart, out of the corner of my ear I heard someone whisper to someone about me. "He might not come back, and she hasn't shed a tear." I even know who said that.

When I got home, I burst out sobbing.

Dear Alyosha, how am I going to live without you now?

He gave me his watch to remember him by, with a lock of his hair in the lid.

24 November 1915. Tuesday

My first day without Alyosha.

Saint Ekaterina's Day. During the day, a literary and musical matinee for the lower classes; in the evening, a concert and ball for the older ones. I didn't go.

I've just returned from Nina Nikolaevna's. I was reciting a monologue, "I am alone . . ." and I kept breaking off. I started over a few times: "I am alone . . ." And I'm thinking, What the devil? I'm not alone at all, and I'm not where I'm supposed to be according to the play's action. I'm in this room which smells like an old woman's body. And here in front of me, on the table, is a pitcher of water that is supposed to settle and be purified with the help of the silver spoon thrown in there, otherwise the old woman, who calls me child, won't drink it. All of a sudden, all the words I was supposed to say on stage felt like lies and rubbish. I try to start over again: "I am alone . . ."

And right then I realized that I wasn't learning an art. I was learning to lie. It was repulsive and tedious. I rattled it off any old way and fled as quickly as possible.

I sat down to write Alyosha a letter. But I didn't know what to write. I wanted to write how much I loved him, but I couldn't. I'm going out of my mind. What did I do wrong? I was the one who spoiled everything that evening! What does he think of me now?

I wanted to kiss him, caress him. I wanted him to be happy with me! Why did it all come out so horribly? And so shamefully! So shamefully, and painfully, and bad!

Nothing from Alyosha.

27 November 1915. Friday

Nothing from Alyosha.

When I recall that evening again, how I started unbuttoning my blouse, how I took his hand and pulled it toward me, I feel so unbearably ashamed again! He was so embarrassed, in such agony, that nothing worked for him! And how we got dressed afterward, afraid to look each other in the eye!

Forgive me, Alyosha. It's all my fault!

1 December 1915. Tuesday

Today Nina Nikolaevna told me about the famous Meininger theater's Moscow tours and how the mere image of the forest on the stage made you smell the pines.

I decided I would not go to see her anymore.

Nothing from Alyosha. After what happened, he probably won't write to me anymore.

4 December 1915. Friday

At last! A letter from Alyosha!

I waited and waited, and here it's come and I can't open the envelope. I reread the address several times—his hand, his writing.

"My dearest! My beloved! My distant one!"

I swallowed and scanned the lines—three pages—searching for the main thing, but the main thing was at the very end. "Now that we've parted, only now do I genuinely understand how much you mean to me in this life and how powerful my love for you is and how insignificant, compared with my love, the fear of dying and this whole war are!"

I copy out the lines from his letter, and Alyosha seems closer, as if he were somewhere very near, over my shoulder. As if he and I were uniting this way: through these words and letters!

"I sent you a letter from the road, but I don't know whether you received it. All's well with me." I received nothing, Alyosha! Nothing!

"I'm sitting in a trench fashioned from the cellar of a destroyed house. On the table is a bottle of, alas, milk, bread, and a candle.

Today we only fired in the morning. I'm alone at the battery. The officers have all gone to the village.

"I'm busy all day now. Being an aide-de-camp is not that burdensome, but on the other hand I can't step away from the telephone. You fall asleep and it jingles under your ear, so you wake up quickly and listen and then run to report to the commander.

"Yesterday at ten at night they reported that a dirigible was on its way. I immediately ordered all lights extinguished, and a few minutes later a terrible cannonade began. A blinking red star flickered in the starry sky, and near it, around it, shells exploded. Soon the dirigible was directly overhead. There was a terrible chirring and whistling from the shells in the air. Fragments and bullets rained down, producing a sound like what milk makes during milking, only more prolonged. Shells exploded very close and often, lighting up the body of the dirigible—cigar-shaped and dark."

And another three pages. I reread them a hundred times. Lord, save him and protect him!

Only now, only since he's gone where death threatens him, every day, every hour, have I begun to understand what love is and how I was unable to love and show him my tenderness, everything I feel for him, and couldn't even simply tell him of my love! Suddenly it became clear that I was immeasurably beneath and unworthy of him and how much to blame I was for giving him so little love!

Today when I came home from the infirmary it was already dark, chill. One wounded man there had died—and I imagined with horror that Alyosha had already been wounded, God forbid, and that he was dying right now somewhere in an infirmity or simply in the dark, in a ditch, or simply in the snow, and calling for me, and all of a sudden my heart seized up: he's not coming back! He's not coming back! And it will be my fault. After all, it was my love that was supposed to save him, and he got so little of it from me, not enough, not enough to save him.

It's my fault for not being able to love him the way he deserved.

8 December 1915. Tuesday

"It's night. I'm sitting in a trench by the telephone that I, as division adjutant, cannot step away from. From time to time it rings.

"War is not at all like what you imagine. Shells do fly, but not that thickly, and not that many people die. War right now isn't horror anymore, and really, are there horrors in this world? Ultimately, you can make a horror out of the least little thing. A shell flies, and if you think it's going to kill you then you're going to moan and crawl—and you will in fact be scared. If you look at things calmly, you reason like this: It might kill me, that's true, but what can I do? Stew in my own fear? Agonize without agony? As long as you're alive, breathe.

"I don't want to boast, but I'm not afraid anymore—at least hardly afraid. If I were in the infantry, I would get used to infantry fears, too, and there are more of those. The only thing I could concede to my mother's fear was that I went into the artillery and not the infantry. One officer in our battery commented that an artilleryman pays no attention to shells but is afraid of bullets, and infantry is the opposite. You see what silly fears we have here.

"I think about you all the time, my dearest, and feel each day my love for you growing stronger and stronger. How are you there?"

11 December 1915. Friday

Today was the literary trial against Rudin. Mishka got so worked up, saying that Rudin didn't know how to love and didn't want to, that he was afraid of a genuine great love, and she flew into such a rage that she suddenly declared that Rudin should be shot. That's what she blurted out: shot! Everyone laughed!

I woke up in the middle of the night and couldn't get back to sleep. I was thinking about Alyosha.

12 December 1915. Saturday

"Yesterday for the first time it was truly dangerous. A shell fell two paces away. God saved me. It was a camouflet. A camouflet is a shell that falls plumb, almost vertically, and burrows deep in the ground. The blast doesn't have the power to lift the earth, and there is just some smoke. Camouflets are rare. I was lucky.

"You write that you went to our church to pray for me. You see? It helped.

"And you know the most amusing part? That was what I was thinking at the last moment, when the shell flew at me. You probably think your hero, looking at the sky, imagined himself a kind of Andrei Bolkonsky on the field at Austerlitz—or something like that? Nothing of the kind. My thoughts were turning around the fact that they had come up with the idea of small hand warmers to keep in our pockets—coals smoldering in a velvet-covered metal case. There, you see how good it is I didn't die then? It would be insulting to die with that kind of nonsense in my head.

"Sausages hang on the horizon all day, correcting the firing. Today I looked out from the observation point. We have a magnificent Zeiss scope.

"The hardest part is the enforced idleness. It's so important to keep your mind busy! This afternoon I felt like reading a little and looking at some mathematics, and I wished I'd taken along Granville's *Elements of the Differential and Integral Calculus.* I've already asked Mama to send me the book. But for now I have to read what comes along, in snatches. Sometimes I'm lucky. Luck has smiled on me now: from one officer in the second battery I borrowed a popular book about the wireless telegraph, and I sat over it until night fell. In the morning, I paid for my joy. I had bad luck lighting up. A 'safety match' flicked right into my eye and burned the cornea. A white blister formed and I have a hard time closing the eye. The local railroad doctor looked and told me I got off easy, since, according to him, in these instances it usually burns right through. Moreover, it's amazing that on the same day misfortune lay in wait for my friend Kovalyov. Lately he and I have become very close. At first he seemed rather dim and pretentious, but in fact he's a good and simple soul. So you see, when they were diluting the alcohol, Kovalyov, wanting to test the vodka's strength, tried lighting it with a match. The alcohol burst into flames and scorched his hands, neck, and lips, so that he has blisters everywhere. See how people maim themselves without any war whatsoever?"

13 December 1915. Sunday

I've nearly stopped writing in my diary because I'm spending all my free time on letters to Alyosha.

On the other hand, I've slipped his letters in here, so this is becoming my and Alyosha's shared diary. Lord, a year ago I was putting flowers between the pages—now it's Alyosha's letters.

It snowed all night, and the city is beautiful, festive, fresh. And right then I think, but what is it like for him there, in their positions? He must be freezing. I look at the snow now and feel no joy whatsoever.

Or at school. All of a sudden I started thinking about Alyosha, and it was as if I'd woken up in some other age—the ancient Greeks. What does any Hellas have to do with this? Why did Homer write so many pages about someplace called Troy? None of that is worth a single one of Alyosha's lines! What agony to go to school and sit through these pointless, silly lessons! What is this for, if I want to hold him and can't?

I wrote one letter that was very special. About something I haven't told anyone yet. And decided not to send it. I imagined Alyosha returning and us reading it together, lying on his sofa, shoulder to shoulder, temple to temple.

14 December 1915. Monday

"They gave me leave to go to town. We rode through a few villages. Utter devastation everywhere. Expensive furniture abandoned, broken sewing machines, gramophones lying in the streets and courtyards.

"I stepped outside headquarters and on the main square heard martial music—a funeral. Some general being transported on a gun carriage. All of a sudden I wondered how a coffin gets attached to a weapon. Since I was an artilleryman, they might bury me that way, too. I found a spot where I could see. There, my distant one, you see the kinds of foolishness that interest me. Then I stopped by a church. A deacon there was calling on God, asking him to grant 'victory to our Christ-loving host.' They're not Christ-loving over there? All of a sudden I thought of my German grandfather. He taught me the *Vater unser.*[24]

"And now, at this moment, in the German trenches on the other side of the woods, someone is saying a prayer and asking God to grant victory to their Christ-loving host. If one beats the other, does that mean he loves Christ more?

"It's only with you that I can talk about anything in the world, but here, in the trenches, people never talk out loud about the main thing. People smoke, drink, eat, and talk about trivial things, boots, for instance. You can't even imagine how educated people can talk for hours on end on that topic! Death may be listening in on their conversations, but they're going to remember how before the war there were boots you couldn't get off without a batman, so narrow you couldn't slip a finger in. And argue over which was better to use, talc or rosin. And talk about who had a board with a heel cutout in case there was no one to help him. And laugh amiably, happily, when someone would talk about sewing their boots on for a parade and then ripping out the seams. You know what's coming into

_____
24. Our Father. *(Ger.)*

251

fashion now? The latest craze is boots with leggings, the kind officers in aviation and armored troops wear. But these are all dreams. Here we're wearing felt boots and burkas, which are a kind of warm Caucasian boot made of black felt.

"Last night, as I was going to sleep, I thought of Gogol's lieutenant from Ryazan who simply could not fall asleep because he was admiring his new boots. And I thought, now all of us who were talking about boots today are going to disappear, but that lieutenant will remain. He'll go on admiring his marvelously stitched on heel.

"I went to bed and recited my nighttime prayer, but I still couldn't sleep, so I lit the light again and am writing to you. I so want to say everything. But what else I should write you, my dove, I don't know.

"One soldier taught me a prayer that he says nine times every day, in the certainty that then nothing can happen to him. Here it is: 'God the father is in front, the Mother of God is in the middle, and I am in the rear. What happens to the Gods, happens to me.'

"Now every morning I repeat it nine times. I predict that if you and I see each other again, that means the soldier's prayer helped!"

16 December 1915. Wednesday

In class at school Zabugsky looked me up and down again repulsively. And he kept squeezing his mole. And all of a sudden it was so awful! I don't want to write Alyosha about it.

I was sitting in class and suddenly it struck me. What am I doing here? Why am I here? I asked permission to leave. It was quiet on the floors, lessons everywhere. I went downstairs and heard the porter talking on the telephone. I didn't want to eavesdrop, but he didn't see me and, thinking he was alone, he had made a telephone call to some housemaid passion of his and was joking crudely, agreeing on a meeting.

How incredibly base, and wretched, and sickening it all is.

Dear Alyosha mine, where are you? When will we see each other? After school I went to the Cathedral of the Nativity of the Virgin on Staropochtovaya Street. I stop in every day to pray for Alyosha in different churches. Mothers, wives, sisters, and fiancées all around. Here we all are standing and asking for the same thing: preserve and protect!

18 December 1915. Friday

"The day before yesterday a bomb fell on the third battery's shell depot, but it didn't detonate the way they should have. They got thrown around like skittles. Everyone's talking about spies in the rear. But paradoxically, these spies have saved the life of many. How God mixed everything up in this world!

"Lieutenant Kovalyov—I think I wrote to you about him— brought me boots from the Caucasus. They cost just twelve rubles, but they're tall and very soft and light as a feather.

"Soon I'll send you a photograph of me on horseback.

"I reread your letters all the time. I kiss the words on the crumpled paper and kiss your hand, which wrote these words. Kiss and wait. When will we see each other? It couldn't possibly be that we never see each other again, right?"

20 December 1915. Sunday

I went to see Alyosha's parents. I wanted to sit in his room, but Timoshka has taken it over. He started showing me a trick. He rubbed sealing wax on a rag so finely cut pieces of paper would jump up and stick to it. Timosha cuts out paper people and soldiers. They don't come out too well for him, they're uneven, and sometime he cuts off a leg or a cap and ear. I started helping him.

Then I walked home, but with the war the streets have filled with cripples, as if someone had also cut them out clumsily, cutting off an arm here, a leg to the knee there.

Lord, please let Alyosha return to me whole and unharmed!

21 December 1915. Monday

"Here I've been on the front lines for so long and only yesterday did I have my first real battle. Everything I saw and experienced here up until this, and wrote about to you as if it were important, is in fact trivial.

"We moved up to the position of the adjacent regiment for reinforcement, waited for the attack, and suddenly found ourselves nose to nose with the Germans. I fired a rifle at someone for the first time. Being unused to it, at the very first shot the recoil struck me in the cheek. We occupied the trenches, and immediately they carried an injured man toward me, the same soldier, Vasilenko, who taught me the prayer. Remember I wrote you about him? I had to press up against the wall to let them pass. Though I've been at the front more than a month, this was the first time I'd seen a human body splayed out. I was nauseated and wanted to go home. For the first time the thought flashed through my mind that they could kill me just this way, so that first I would suffer for a long time and to no purpose.

"The Germans went on the attack and we ended up in hand-to-hand combat. I didn't kill anyone. Or I did, I don't know. All I know is that I nearly died, but Kovalyov saved me. A German lunged toward me and was about to bayonet me, but Kovalyov managed to shoot him with his gun. He fell. The bullet stuck somewhere in his mouth. He covered his unfolded cheek with his hands. Blood spewed from his mouth. He lay there looking at us. Kovalyov walked over and shot him in the eye. He was still alive for a few instants and looked at us with his left eye; his eyelid twitched. I remember the bloodied teeth fragments.

"My dearest, my beloved, what am I doing? Why am I writing you all this? Forgive me!"

25 December 1915

Christmas. Horrible. Repulsive. It's utterly impossible to be at home. Everyone has fought and argued with everyone. And I can't write Alyosha about it.

Papa argued with Mama and went there, to be with his other family.

There we were sitting at the table without him, and everyone was silent. Nothing would go down—not the barley porridge without milk and butter, not the fruit compote. We waited for a star, but there was a heavy snowfall.

Just to say something, Sasha started insisting that the star of Bethlehem was Venus, and at this, out of nowhere, we all started fighting and shouting at each other. I burst into tears and ran to my room.

Christmas is a holiday for people who love each other, for a family, but we haven't had a family for a long time.

And Papa is there now, with his other child. They're probably unwrapping gifts.

Alyosha, I can't go on without you! Life just doesn't work without you.

29 December 1915. Tuesday

"Hurrah! Today I received a package from home and—hurrah again!—I took out the scarf you knit, unwrapped it, and suddenly smelled your perfume hidden in the wool's pores. Your smell! The smell of my beloved from a scarf come to life! Who would have known how much I wanted to hold you, press my face to your hair and sniff it, kiss it, breathe it!

"We're going to have to spend Christmas at front-line positions. I'm very sorry I won't be able to slip off to vespers.

"I started paging through the Gospels Mama gave me to take along. I began reading the revelation of St. John, and suddenly thought that the Apocalypse is from fear of personal death. Universal death is a reassuring justice. It's frightening to die because no one wants to be left behind. The others will go on and see what will remain forever concealed to you beyond the next turn. The worst thing about the Apocalypse, then, is that there won't be one.

"I tried to fall asleep and again could not. Now I've sat down to scribble the thoughts that won't give my mind a night's rest. This is the Apocalypse, in fact, here, very ordinary, cold, with drifting snow, just smeared across time. Everyone dies, just not simultaneously. But what's the difference, in essence? One way or another they leave by the world, the generation, the empire. Where is Byzantium? Where are the Romans? Where are the Hellenes? Zilch. Nothing. Nothing and no one, neither victors nor vanquished. Everything has vanished, just not as theatrically as 'and the heaven as a scroll when it is rolled together' but mundanely. People always want to make a tragedy out of everything, and invariably en masse, for greater effect. Read John, and it's pure Khanzhonkov! But I run on. Sleep, my darling! Sleep! Goodnight! I kiss you now, across all these versts, on this night, and that means I am with you!"

10 January 1916. Sunday

There have been no letters from Alyosha for almost two weeks and I'm simply going out of my mind, and tonight I had a terrible dream. I woke up all wet with tears. We were riding somewhere in a troika on a frosty night. And I felt him so close, his breathing, his lips. Such a strong desire suddenly gripped me to live fully, with all my being, I wanted to go on hearing the sounds of the bells and the runners' pleasant creak forever. Then all that vanished and I was alone. And I was being taken somewhere, as in my childhood, my cheeks rubbed with goose fat—my whole face. Sticky and nasty. The grease warmed up and ran. In front of me were the horses' croups and hoar-frosted tails. I saw them directly, smelled the bearskins I was sitting on, and the horse's sweat and the gasses animals always pass. All of a sudden I awoke and sensed that he was dead.

My heart nearly burst.

11 January 1916. Monday

A letter from him! He's alive! Alive! Alive!

"I had to spend Christmas at a front-line position. The Germans didn't bother us at all, not on Twelfth Night and not on the holiday itself. On Twelfth Night a tree set up in front of our dugouts was lit up at the battery. It was a quiet night and the candles didn't flicker. My thoughts flew of their own accord to you in Rostov. I vividly imagined the evening: first the bustle on the streets, then the street bustling coming to an end, and finally, the bells ringing out in the churches, solemn and festive, the beginning of the service with the great compline, and finally, the all-night vigil. When it's over, the people spilling out of the churches and dispersing in a joyous, holiday mood. It was totally quiet, both here and on the Germans' side. The night was starry, and this silence especially brought on the sadness, and I felt the separation from you even more strongly. I thought of home, my childhood, how we laid hay under the tablecloth in memory of Christ's birth and how delicious it smelled in the room, mixed with the scent of the needles. Christmas was a Lenten day for us, and no one ate anything from morning until the first star appeared. I would get hungry before nightfall and watch for the star—and then sit down at the table. We ate special Christmas pies: the white king, with rice; the yellow king, with beans; and the black king, with plums. I'm writing, and all of a sudden I wish I could taste those pies again! I would stuff my belly to bursting with them!

"I embrace you! Goodnight! I'll finish writing tomorrow.

"I'll finish the letter I began the day before yesterday and rush to find someone to send it with.

"No, I won't be able to finish in time. I'll send it as it is. Outside it's sunny and cold, the snow is sparkling, and the sparrows, with their piercing chirps, have swooped down on the fresh horse manure. Sparrow happiness!"

Question: Describe the route you took.

Answer: I went out and started walking without any idea of where I was going and I walked for forty days.

Question: What countries did you pass through?

Answer: I came to a land where people with dog's heads live. And they—the dogheads—watched me and did me no harm. In every place they live with their children, building nests between rocks. It took me a hundred days to walk across their land, and then I came to the land of the pygmies. I ran across many men, women, and children. When I saw them I took fright, thinking they were going to eat me. And I decided I would tousle my hair and give them hard looks. But if I ran, they would eat me. That is what I did and they fled, grabbing their children and gnashing their teeth. I climbed a high mountain where the sun does not shine and there is not one tree and the grass does not grow, and there are only vipers and snakes hissing and gnashing their teeth. The cobras, the anteaters, and the adders gnashed their teeth. I saw other snakes as well, but for many I did not know their names. I walked like that for four days, hearing their hissing. I sealed my ears with wax, unable to bear the snake whistling.

Question: Are you telling the truth?

Answer: Look, there's still wax in my ears. Then I walked on for another fifty days, not knowing my way, and I found an ice floe as high as my elbow, and I crossed that land gnawing on it.

Question: Where, when, and how did you cross the border?

Answer: I reached a big river and drank from it my fill of water, and my lips stuck together from its sweetness, which surpassed the sweetness of honey and its comb. And when the ninth hour struck, a light spread over the river that was seven times brighter than daylight. And there were winds in that land: the western wind was green; but from the sunrise came a reddish wind, and from the north a wind the color of fresh blood, but from the southerly direction the wind was white as snow.

Question: Are you really telling the truth?

Answer: The breadth of that river was like the sky reflected in the water and the depth, like the flash of an instant, had no bottom. And then, when I felt the urge to cross it, the river cried out and said, "You may not cross me, for man cannot cross my waters. Behold what is above my waters." I looked and saw a wall of clouds rising from the water to the skies. And a cloud said to me, "Neither a bird of this world, nor the blowing of the wind, nor can anyone else go through me."

Question: So how did you cross the border?

Answer: I prayed to the Lord God, and two trees grew from the earth, beautiful and much adorned, abundant with sweet-smelling fruits. One tree, which stood on this side of the river, bowed, gathered me in its crown, and lifting me high up bowed to the middle of the river. And it was met by the other tree, which gathered me in its crown, bowed, and placed me on the ground. And so the trees rose up and carried me across the river.

Question: Fine. Let's say that's true. But how old are you? Here you've written that you're nineteen, but in fact?

Answer: At that time, when I turned one hundred sixty-five, I begat my son Methuselah. After this too I lived two hundred years and lived out all the years of my life, three hundred and sixty-five years.

Question: What happened then?

Answer: On the first day of the month of Nisan I slept. And while I slept, great distress came into my heart. And I said, weeping, for I could not understand the reason for my distress, What will happen to me? I awoke and lay there for a long time unable to sleep. Drenched in sweat. I could not for the life of me understand where I had woken up. Then I remembered. I'd wanted to run away somewhere, as if I'd woken up someone else, not myself. Heavy breathing, snoring, all around. Water dripping somewhere. A truck passing in the distance. Suddenly I could hear a clock. Everything inside it was alive. Then I put on my cap, threw my pea jacket over my shoulders, and went out. I broke the ice on the puddle—and cracks fanned out.

Question: Was it then, that wintry night in April, though still with a March putrefaction, that it all began?

Answer: I don't know. I took off my cap and the moisture quickly dried. Someone stirred in the dark near the post. He shouted to me, "Enoch, is that you?" I answered, "Yes." He: "Come here! I have boiled condensed milk!" I walked over, only I didn't recognize him. He opened the can with his bayonet. We started eating it with our fingers. You dip your finger and lick it.

Question: But why Enoch?

Answer: That's what they always called me in kindergarten, in school, and in the army. My last name is Enokhin. So everyone called me Enoch.

Question: They called you that without any notion of the repositories of clouds or the repositories of dew, to say nothing of what lies between the corrupt and incorrupt?

Answer: What are you talking about? I don't understand.

Question: Fine. Only we don't have a lot of time. They're already striking the bells on all the ships, sunken and sailing. Here's what. Tell me quickly about how his boxer elastic snapped against his bare belly or we won't manage.

Answer: The first few days in the unit they beat us.

Question: Well, isn't that what's supposed to happen?

Answer: We didn't even resist. We knew that after the oath they would beat us harder, in the face, too, but for now, until the oath, they wouldn't beat us in the face.

Question: Tell me, what kind of unit was it and where was it deployed?

Answer: Just a unit. Nothing special. There, at the entrance, there were two pines, like sentries, whereas before there'd been a pine battalion. This isn't even that important. What is important is that I'm sitting in the common room on Sunday, watching television, and right then Gray comes in. "Get up! The barracks are a mess! On the double!" I run over and the soldiers there are lying on their beds and mine is all messed up. I straighten it, but Gray messes it up again. And so it went for a whole hour. And everyone's having a good time. I also take kicks from the ones who are lying around. And Gray keeps snapping his boxer elastic on his belly. We arrived, a few of us, young soldiers from the training unit, and the first night they arranged a welcome for us, as usual. They made us "drive out winter" from the barracks with towels. One refused and they hit him over the head with a stool. And there was also this instance . . .

Question: Yes, I know, I know all your instances! Now you'll start telling me how in the morning you were supposed to clean the "landing strip" in the barracks with a toothbrush.

Answer: What, you, too?

Question: Did you think you were the only one? You mean the others didn't make up the cots for the lifers and mend their collars? Remember the hut? Shaven-headed recruits launder and iron the short-timers' tunics. And Gray'd had his tunic taken in to the max, lifer-style. And all of a sudden you see yourself in the cracked, sweating mirror, and the only thing in your eyes is fear of damaging it, burning through it.

Answer: Did you have a Gray, too? And did he like to snap the elastic on his navy boxers?

Question: One time I was sewing an undercollar to his tunic and pricked my finger, and so badly that I ruined the undercollar: a drop of blood. Gray was furious!

Answer: That happened to me, too! First a fist to the belly—and he watches me double over, gasp for breath, covered in snot—then an elbow to the back and I collapsed to the floor. Then with his boot—not just any old way but so he wouldn't break anything. He also liked to twist my hands behind my back and cover my nose and mouth with the palm of his hand, so I couldn't breathe, and then wait. As soon as you start passing out, he lifts his hand a little so you can swallow some air and then cuts off your breathing again. Then he lets me go and wipes his palm on my bristly head.

Question: And do you remember them seeing your pee-pee in the baths—small, very white, without any signs of growth—and how they were beside themselves with laughter and couldn't stop? But you didn't get angry at them? Judge for yourself. Two years in the barracks, and only on bath day, when they take you through town, could you look at civilians, most of them officers in civvies, and the women are all officers' wives, and the bathhouse was just a block away from the barracks. The boots and the leaves, even they twirl around each other making hanky-panky on the parade ground. And the guys are all alive, in the sense that they're not dead yet, and what's there to talk about with them if not women, you know their whole political education is only about which hole who would stick it in if he could. And the deputy political officer put on his cassock and droned on in the red room about the feeble old Spartan who joined the service to go to war and gets asked, Where are you going like that? And he answered, twisting his lips in a smile, If I can't be of any other use, let the enemy at least dull his sword on me. How can you leave so many men alone without women? And for so long! It's a dirty trick! There you are lying at night and you hide your head under the blanket—and you so want to kiss, and squeeze, and stick it in! And you imagine God knows what. And drops of life, sudden and hot, die in the sheet. And afterward sleeping is wet and cold.

Answer: Yes, everyone has just one thing on their mind. Also drinking. When they gave us leave the first time, Gray tells me, Bring back a bottle, otherwise I'll line the company up one night and let you have it in front of everyone. Get your hole ready!

Question: Did you bring it?

Answer: What choice did I have?

Question: Didn't they search you at the checkpoint?

Answer: Gray came out himself. He may be the devil himself, but he's no beast. Mostly he tries to scare you. You can live anywhere really. Though it's very hard. As soon as you fall asleep, a drunk Gray flops down and you get up to take off his boots. He belches and you smell the half-sours and sauerkraut. "Bow!" he shouts, and makes you bow. You bow, and again, "Even lower, you shitty bugger. Lower!" You frown and bow, Gray grabs you by the neck and pulls your face right up to his ass in the blue boxers. He waits a few moments, concentrates, and farts.

"How about that?" he asks. "Get a good whiff?" Then he lets you go. "Well, go on, go to sleep!" So you crawl back into the double bunk and try to think of something good before you fall asleep. Your mama, for instance. If only I could wake up at home and she would make oladushki and it would all be on the table. But it's already dawn and they wake you up with a floor brush in the face.

Question: Couldn't you have gotten out of it?

Answer: One of ours did. He hung himself with his belt, but so he wouldn't strangle. That's how much he wanted to get an Article 7-b. Nothing came of it. Gray forced him to dig himself in behind the barracks and everyone pissed on him.

Question: You too?

Answer: Me too.

Question: Why?

Answer: Do you really not understand?

Question: I do.

Answer: Then why ask?

Question: What happened then?

Answer: I got a submachine gun in the depot and put my signature in the log. All of a sudden, joy. Freedom. Now I could just go and empty a round into everyone around me. Mainly Gray. And no one and nothing could stop me. I took my Kalash and went for a walk along the barbed wire. I'm walking and staring into the dark. Snow had fallen already, and everything was shining a little from the snow. It was chilly. And there was a crunching underfoot. And I so wanted a green apple to crunch just like that in my teeth. I'm walking and looking at the stars, trying to make out the constellations, and I don't know a single one, in fact, except for the Bears.

I found two stars, like a colon, and I thought, let that be my constellation, the Colon constellation. And I also thought about how Gray had explained how the world was made, that all the planets were atoms of some other, higher world. And our atoms were someone's planets, too. "Now I'm going to spit," Gray would say, "and in those worlds thousands of galaxies like our Milky Way fizzle out!" Maybe Gray's right. Maybe that's how it is. I'm walking, thinking about God knows what, and at any moment a guard commander or sentry might turn up. Then, you know this, according to the manual I'm supposed to shout, "Halt! Who goes there?" If he doesn't answer the right way, fire in the air. That's the first shot. If he doesn't stop at the warning shot, then the next bullet goes into the person approaching.

Question: So? Where's the problem?

Answer: That's the whole point, to fire first at the person approaching and only then in the air. The question is, can it then be determined which bullet was first and which second?

Question: This is all theory. Tell me how you squatted and stuck the submachine gun's barrel into yourself with the bolt cocked and the safety released.

Answer: At the time I felt like I was sitting over a hole. And this life was that shitty hole, and that's where the stink came from. And I was just about to fall into that pit. And afterward they were going to laugh at me, even after this. They think everything's funny.

Question: Was that the moment you heard thunder?

Answer: Yes, somewhere in the distance it started thundering, a booming cascade, like someone running over garage roofs. Where we lived, out our window there were the gates to some factory to the right and garages to the left. I ran over the roofs with the other boys. The roofs bowed; the iron was rusty, and it was rotted out. I liked the way our footfalls clattered. As if we were making the distant thunder. But the garage owners yelled at us and chased us. Once, they organized a roundup. We were jumping from one garage to the next and I missed and fell to the ground. They dragged me off and started beating me. My mother saw out the window and came running. If it hadn't been for her, they would've beaten me to death.

Question: So there, in the sky, there was thunder, like someone running over garage roofs—and what?

Answer: And I asked, "Lord, how could you have arranged all this?"

Question: So you were called in to see Gray and he was sitting in a gynecological chair. Right?

Answer: Yes, we'd had to drag out all kinds of junk from the basement of the old hospital. In the courtyard there was a weird, rusted out chair. This very one. Gray sat in it and spread his feet in their boots, snapping his boxer elastic. That's all he was wearing, his navy boxers.

Question: And it didn't bother you that you were crunching over the snow, breathing the light night frost, and he was just wearing boxers?

Answer: At the time I didn't give it a moment's thought. They called me over to Gray and I went. What was there to ask? They were beating a Gagauz right then. This skinny guy from Moldova. I don't even know how he ended up with us. Gray said Gagauzes weren't even a people but the descendants of some stranded Turkish army, and when you translated *gagauz* from Turkish it meant "traitor." Everyone had to go up to him and do something to him. I kicked him in the knee, and he even jumped up and grabbed his leg in pain. A traitor's a traitor. What's

there to pity? It doesn't even matter whether he's a Gagauz or not.

Question: What about the Gagauz?

Answer: Nothing. He whimpered in a corner for a while and
started dragging hospital beds into the courtyard along
with everyone else.

Question: And then?

Answer: And then I asked, "How did you make this world,
Gray?"

Question: What did he say?

Answer: He said, snapping the boxer elastic on his belly, "A universe lets fly every time I spit. It just looks like the watch
isn't moving and the sun's setting, whereas everyone
since Copernicus has known that the sun stays in one
place and the world is going to hell. First there was man,
then his spit. In order to send a universe flying, I had to
create a man. And I created his flesh from the butt-sown
ground, and his blood from the rusty tap water, his eyes
from green bottle glass, his bones from cot legs, his mind
from the clouds, his sinews and hair from withered grass,
his pulse from a draft, his breath from the wind, and his
dandruff from dry drifting snow. And I ordered him to
roam the world in search of God, meat, and bitches. To
leave his foot but no tracks on the road. And to say that a
dog passed away but a man crapped out."

Question: But you realized how hard it was to be master of the
world! Nails want to live, and it's not their fault if you
chew them. A tortoise wants to find out what's going to
happen at the end, but a child smashes it on the asphalt
to find out what was at the beginning. A plowman asks
for rain, a sailor for a fair wind and clear weather, a general for war, but a soldier dreams of coming home and
throwing his epaulets out the window.

Answer: What are you talking about?

Question: About the fact that if we really are just an atom in Gray's expectoration and are going to hell, then in that spit universe, nonetheless, there is a cat sitting in a window trying to catch a snowflake with its paw. And in that universe there is also a Talmud that tells the story of a calf running to a wise man, lamenting that they want to slit its throat, and the wise man telling it, "Go where they lead you. For this were you created."

Answer: What cat? What does all this mean?

Question: It means that in the beginning I've already been here a year and you're the rookie, but later, it's the reverse, and you've got the status and I'm the rookie. Someone has to teach us rookies, after all! You just have to understand destiny's language and its cooing. We're blind from birth. We don't see anything and don't pick up on the connection between events, the oneness of things, like a mole digging its tunnel and bumping into thick roots, and for the mole these are just insurmountable obstacles and he can't imagine the crown these roots nourish. It's like a platoon in full marching order going down a forest road in the middle of a snowless winter, when the trees' bare branches have climbed out of the morning fog but the platoon can't comprehend that crown either—its color in fall, the wind, the rustle of its leaves, and the fact that it resembles someone's lungs. Vertebrates and invertebrates react differently to their surroundings. The former raise their temperature when temperatures fall and they still freeze; but the others always live in harmony with their environment, and if winter comes they turn to ice and then, after waiting it out, they thaw. You have to wait it out, endure, and then we'll be recruits, and we'll be released from the beatings, and then we'll be old-timers and they'll launder our tunics for us, mend our collars, clean our boots, scratch our heels, and in the dining hall we'll heap our plates, and what we can't eat we'll leave on the plate, first spitting in it so the hungry youths who know so little about love and so much about hate can't finish it. And if any of the rookies sits down on the only stool in the hut in our presence, we'll snap the elastic on our belly and say that there's been an insult here to an old-timer and therefore each of us is going to go up and spit into the blunderer's ugly face. And no one will dare contradict us. Each one will go up and spit. That's what makes the universe in the flying ball of spit go round. Otherwise the world would fall apart, collapse, scatter like a stack of used paper over a parquet floor.

Answer: Is this really necessary?

Question: It's an initiation. The miracle of transforming a pimply caterpillar into a mother-of-pearl butterfly! Contact with the puzzling and amazing world of adults! A ritual of courage. Once you go through it you carry this mystery throughout your homeland, to every garage and bed. Imagine! Spitting, shitting, farting. Every culture has come up with something for becoming a man. You aren't the first and you won't be the last. Tacitus again tells us that among the Hittites, a rookie didn't shave his beard or mustache until he had killed an enemy. Among the Taifali and Heruli you didn't touch a woman until you'd killed a wild boar, unarmed! You can be thankful that they don't cut off anything between your legs, the way some do. In Sumatra they don't circumcise young men, they undercut, exposing the lower section of the urethra, after which the men can only urinate sitting down, like women. It's all very simple. Youths, young warriors, have to lose their human essence and acquire a higher essence, become wolves, or bears, or wild dogs. So it's nothing terrible. People have always suffered. That's not the point.

Answer: What is?

Question: Beauty.

Answer: What's beautiful here—the sound of boxer elastic slapping a belly?

Question: Remember the soldiers playing soccer in the hospital yard with a holey rubber ball, and after each kick some stuffing came out and slowly healed over, as if the ball were catching its breath, pulling in air through the little hole. Then Gray jumped out of his chair and kicked it so hard the ball looked more like a rubber cap. Can't you sense the beauty in that? Authentic, living beauty, not the kind on the glossy cover at the newsstand. I'm not talking about the fact that these men, in blue boxers and boots, running after a ball-cap in a hospital yard strewn with broken glass, made a vow and are prepared to sacrifice themselves, their cloud-brains, their draft-pulse, their wind-breath, for others, for the fatherland. Isn't there beauty in that? Isn't there beauty in the pair climbing the mountain with a bundle of firewood for the sacrifice, the old man and the boy, and the boy asking, "But where's the lamb, father?" And the old man replying, "Just wait, you'll see!" So it is here. Here they all are running together, a sweaty, sunburnt troop, tromping their heavy boots, sliding over the asphalt on the glass shards, and they think they're running after the ball to kick it into his belly so it hurts, but that's just what they think. They're running after a ball that has breathed its last, from the hospital yard onto a rundown dirt road, and onward through a rusty field, and then a birch forest.

Sometimes they stop to catch their breath when someone kicks the ball onto a garage roof, and then, while someone's boots are clattering over the iron roof, they all suddenly realize something and ask, "Gray, where's the sacrifice? Where's the lamb?" "Just wait, you'll find out!" he replies, and once again the ball is thrown from the roof and everyone runs on, a merry troop. They tromp their boots over the rusty field and through the birch forest. And there will always be war for tomorrow.

Answer:	How quickly night is falling.
Question:	That's all right, let's enjoy the dusk.
Answer:	It's quiet here with you. Bells. Cows grazing in the fog.
Question:	Yes, it is quiet here.
Answer:	Tell me, why do you write down what I say if nothing's going to come of it anyway? They're going to say, you heard the bells, now clear out! I know that's what they tell everyone.
Question:	So at least something remains of you.
Answer:	You mean what you write about me will remain after I'm gone?
Question:	Yes.
Answer:	And what you don't will disappear with me? And nothing will remain?
Question:	No. Nothing.
Answer:	And I can tell you about absolutely everything?
Question:	You can, but we don't have much time. Tell me about those you love.
Answer:	May I talk about my mama?
Question:	You may.
Answer:	Just a minute. Let me focus. I need to remember something important, after all. I remember how once in my childhood I fell asleep, but through my sleep I heard her

	come in, probably in her fur coat because it got cold in the room. Write that down?
Question:	Yes. Is that it?
Answer:	Wait a sec, don't rush me. I lost my thread.
Question:	Maybe about the boxes of candy and the ice cream?
Answer:	Yes, of course. Mama worked in a store and would bring home boxes of expired candies. That is, the ones she brought home were perfectly good. She sold the old ones. She was pretty much good-for-nothing. Later she got a job selling ice cream from a stall, and the very first night she got drunk and handed it all out for free and fell asleep right there by her spot. But none of that matters at all! You're mixing me up.
Question:	What else?
Answer:	I also remember lying in the hospital and them not letting my parents into the ward because of the quarantine. My mama came and stood below the window and shouted something to me, but I couldn't hear anything. They'd even sealed the vent pane. We wrote on paper in huge letters what they should bring for us and held it up to the glass. But that day the windows had frosted over.
Question:	Do you know why she gave you your father's name?
Answer:	No.
Question:	She pictured you growing up and running around with other little boys and she would shout joyfully, call for you, as if you were him—just so you'd turn around. Do you know anything about your father?
Question:	Nothing. Not that I ever wanted to. He's a creep. He abandoned us before I was born. He died. I remember he died in the winter in another town, where he lived, and in the spring Mama and I went to see him. Riding in the compartment with us was this strange old guy who was tattooed all over. Looking out at the tracks, suddenly he

said there was a dead man under each tie. We got to the cemetery, the snow was gone, the ground had thawed, and instead of a mound, there was a depression on the grave. Pressing me close, as we stood there in front of the clay that had subsided into my father, my mama said, "Well, now you don't have a papa anymore." As if up until that moment I had. Why is it you can never remember anything when you should? So many things happened, but I don't know what's important to tell.

Question: Tell me about something else. Did you like to read?

Answer: Yes. One book had pictures of what man is made of: five small nails showed how much iron was in each organism. A cup of salt showed how much salt we have in us. And so on: a spoon, a beaker, a paper bag. I also liked all kinds of sea adventures, and I liked the bells being struck on ships. But my favorite book was about history, about Prince Vasilko. One brother blinded his brother with a knife. I kept reading and thinking how savage those times were. The people were so fierce and crude.

Question: What happened there at the dacha with the ping-pong ball?

Answer: Oh, nothing special. I stole a magnifying glass from the neighbor woman and set ants on fire. I even remember thinking right then, Here comes an ant and it doesn't suspect a thing, but I already know its time's up! And then I focus the sun on it. Or on another one, and pardon this one. I punish and pardon. Some I punish, others I pardon. And nothing depends on them. And none of it's their fault. It's just that I am the master of the ant destiny! Right then someone whistled. I looked around. She was standing by the fence. The neighbor girl Lenka. Holding a badminton racket in one hand and a ping-pong ball in the other. She was inviting me to play.

273

That was it. Nothing came of the badminton, and we headed for the river, to spit in the water from the bridge. What's there to tell? It was summer vacation in Bykovo, we were at war with the boarding school, firing pine cones at each other over the fence. Hitting the cones with badminton rackets worked well. They flew like bullets. Lenka and I would hide in the bushes, collecting piles of cones in a T-shirt, our ammunition, and fire on the patients—it was a school in the country for TB patients. And they at us. Then Lenka threw gravel. And they started firing gravel at us: they were asphalting the paths and there were piles of gravel lying around. War is war. I hit someone's head so that it bled.

Question: Do you know you have a son?

Answer: I do. But I know nothing about him. I've never even seen him.

Question: Tell me about the child's mother.

Answer: I just dreamed of Lika. Picture this. I'm at my post, and all of a sudden she walks up. I shout to her, "Halt or I'll shoot!" And I whisper, "What are you doing here?" She walks up, kisses me on the lips, puts her hands on my shoulders, and her fingers felt like badges on my shoulder straps. Ridiculous. I used to climb a rope and crawl right through her dorm window. Lika laughed that it was her braid. She worked as a nurse and was taking correspondence courses. Sometimes I couldn't get to sleep at night because I wanted to touch her so badly, to sniff her hair. And all of a sudden you see, as if you were awake, her pink knees showing through her black stockings and her strong thighs swelling her short skirt. Once I had a broken nail and she was worried about her stockings. She said, "Wait a sec!" She took out her curved nail scissors and pared my nail.

Question: What did she tell you? Anything important?

Answer: Once, when I lay my head on her belly, she suddenly said, "In some past life I was your mama."

Question: Anything about chocolate coins?

Answer: Yes, as a child she was given a handsome velvet pouch on a gold chain and it was full of chocolate coins in silver and gold wrappers. They were riding somewhere on the train, and she wanted to keep the pouch in bed with her, but they told her the chocolate would melt and the coins would get crushed. But that night they were robbed and everything was stolen, including the pouch.

Question: What else?

Answer: I also remember the way she wiped her boots with a rag and said it was impossible to live in a city where salt got on your boots every day.

Question: But how did she explain to you that you weren't the only one?

Answer: She said her love was so big, it couldn't exist on its own. It was like an orange—whole but consisting of individual sections. You have to love this one, and the next, and the next for that great love to come out whole. It's just that the people you love are a lot smaller than your love and it doesn't fit in them. Lika had a notebook where she wrote down different thoughts. Not her own, of course. She read somewhere, and wrote it down, that a tree throws out more seeds than the earth can grow, a mountain river keeps in reserve a huge riverbed for the spring floods, and the soul has more folds than everyday life requires. And now the time had come for the soul to start opening those folds. I know it wasn't love. And if it was love, then an unloving kind of love.

Question: You don't know anything.

Answer: Let's talk about something else.

Question:	If you like. But now do you understand why she gave her son your name?
Answer:	You keep mixing me up. What were we talking about? Wasn't I telling you about my training unit? Right? Then they sent us to Mozdok. The dust there hung like a cave.
Question:	How's that?
Answer:	So much dust that you're riding in an APC and it rises all around you to the sky and forms a cloud over your head. Like in a cave. Then it all returns from sky to ground. On your hair, clothes, and food. And everyone starts looking like everyone else. In the first few days my face got so much dust and sun that while I was washing I couldn't run my hand over my face because the slightest touch produced searing pain. Our faces were a solid dark mask and only the whites of the eyes shone. We didn't wash for weeks on end, and when the water truck arrived, we stripped naked and swarmed under the hose. We washed our clothes and put them back on wet. Will you make it in time?
Question:	Yes.
Answer:	In a minute of rain the dust turns into impassable mud. Everything gets covered in a paste that eats up everything, all tracks. There's slime and wet everywhere. After it's driven over by tanks the greasy mud sticks to your boots in heavy clumps. You scrape your boots by the tent entrance with digging tools, but the clay still gets slapped all over the cots and blankets, eats into your felt boots, and gets crammed into submachine gun barrels. It's impossible to clean. You wash your hands, but no matter what you touch they're covered in sticky mud again. You get stupid, you're covered with a mud crust, you try to hide away in your warm pea jacket and retain

your warmth. Your hands are covered in unwashable mud, like gloves. You pour diesel fuel over the damp firewood in the tent—splash it from the can into the little stove, and an acrid, sooty smoke spreads through the dank tent.

Question: What do you remember from your first days there?

Answer: The way we walked past the children. A pack of boys and girls spilled out on the road. We smiled at them and tried to make them laugh, made faces—and none of the children smiled. Starving dogs on chains howled by abandoned, burned out houses. Whereas in Grozny the dogs were fat, having eaten their fill of carrion.

Question: I've got that. Go on.

Answer: One time we set up a tent inside a dilapidated house without a roof. The windows were bricked up and there was a children's bucket lying around where water had collected and frozen, and later I turned it over and an ice cake fell out.

Question: Go on.

Answer: We were so thirsty that no one used the water decontamination tablets they put in our rations because you had to wait four hours. You could die waiting. And we were thirsty. So you drink, scooping it straight from the river, and it's cloudy, cement color.

Question: What did that water taste like?

Answer: Why do you need all this? The water smelled like rotten eggs. Someone said sulfur was good for the kidneys. And each time we repeated that sulfur was good for the kidneys. But why did the water need to leave a smell?

Question: Keep talking.

Answer: I also remembered women in worn slippers and flowery dresses. The refugees in Chechnya have on something bright. They wrap their head in colorful, handsome

277

kerchiefs. For mourning we wear something black, but they tie on their most colorful kerchief. One of them, I remember, walked up to what was left of her house and stood there silently. She stared at it for a long time. Then she looked at me and walked away, also silently.

Question: What else?

Answer: I also remember how Gray was killed.

Question: Where was that?

Answer: Outside Bamut. He'd just lit up in his sleeve, hiding the fag deep in his pea jacket, when he shouted out, "Enoch, stop there!" and he jumped around the corner of the shed, wrapping his ammo belt around his wrist. Then there were shots—and he crawled back with a ripped open belly, his guts hanging out—in the straw and shit. That's where he died. I'm sitting next to him and watching the blood mix with the puddle of water underneath him. I also remember the ribbed sky and the feather clouds at sunset.

Question: What did you feel after all he'd done to you?

Answer: Gray was a good guy. Without him things would have been really bad there. In the end everyone there turned vicious, but he held on. Once after a battle we came across a wounded man. Before that we'd had our fill of watching what they did to our wounded. That was the first time I saw two guys get their eyes gouged out, ears cut off, and all their limbs turned around backward. We got mad, tied him to the APC, and dragged him over the dried mud to our heart's content. Then we tossed him on some vacant land. We wanted to leave him there to croak in the sun. But Gray went over and shot him. He took pity. Everyone was mad, but you couldn't say anything against Gray. But he died stupidly. Not that people die intelligently. Once I shot an RPG and swiveled wrong. A stream of exhaust hit Gray right in the ear. Things looked bad. He squeezed his nose and started blasting his ears and swallowing. I thought he'd kill me, but he was okay. He just cussed me out. There, at war, Gray was like a brother to me. We shared our grub, and in the winter, at night, wrapped ourselves in the same rug. Either you're sleeping outside or on a luxurious bed, but without undressing, in our filthy pea jackets. I feel sorry for Gray. When we drank he would always knock it back, consider for a moment, and say, "Oh yeah, it's like God walking barefoot over your veins." So much time has passed but I woke up one night recently, all of a sudden, because I thought he was snapping the elastic on his belly. I woke up and asked the darkness, "Gray, is that you?"

Question: That's it? Or is there something else?

Answer: Graffiti on the walls everywhere, on the destroyed buildings: Russian pigs.

Question: Did you kill civilians?

Answer: In the daytime, sure, at the bazaar, they're civilians, but at night they take their grenade launcher hunting for trucks with the wounded. We caught one of their guys firing at guys from our company. We tied the grenade launcher to him with wire, doused him with gasoline, and set him on fire. The men in the truck had burned, so let him burn now. At first he was silent. He despised us so. Then, when he caught fire, he started screaming.

Question: Did you fire at children?

Answer: Why do you care?

Question: To forgive. Someone has to know everything and forgive.

Answer: Who do you think you are to forgive?

Question: I'm just writing it down. Question-answer. So at least something remains of you. What I write down is all there'll be left of you.

Answer: There's no forgiving this. There he was standing wiping his snotty nose; his coat sleeve shiny to the elbow from snot. Just a kid still, but he knew it was us, the Russians, who'd killed his father. He'd grow up and take revenge. He wasn't going to forgive us. He had nowhere to go. He had no choice. So we grabbed him, and in his pockets we found ten cartridges—all the bullets had filed tips. When a bullet like that hits a body, it acts like an explosive. This kid with the snot-shiny sleeves wasn't going to grow up and fire at my son.

Question: Go on.

Answer: No one can forgive me because no one would dare accuse me of anything. Is that clear?

Question: What happened then?

Answer: Don't rush me.

Question: We have very little time left. Think of something else, only just what's most important.

Answer: What?

Question: How a child was playing outside and all of a sudden his head split apart in fragments—a Russian sniper. Or about the bombing at Shali, how a three-year-old girl was playing on the road near her house and a plane flew over and she was gone—literally. Instead of a child they buried her winter coat. In Chechen, "child" is *malik du.* Literally, it means "there is an angel."

Answer: What are you talking about? You've got something confused. That didn't happen to me.

Question: What's the difference? Tell me about how your mother went to Chechnya to look for you.

Answer: I don't know anything about that.

Question: They paid her a visit from the enlistment office and did a search. They showed her the paperwork: "Return your son voluntarily." That was how she found out her son was AWOL. She was walking down your Gastello and thinking, Lord, let him be alive and well, and if You can't, if he's been killed, then let him have been killed straightaway and not tortured. She asked for leave from work and for money to go looking for her son, and they told her, first get the certificate from his unit that he's missing. She gathered her things and went all the way across the country to Vladikavkaz and from there to your unit headquarters, where they told her, You go find him and bring him to us. She started traveling around looking for the body—the burned corpses were kept in huge refrigerators, and they were all identical. The major who went in with her advised her, "Mother, identify someone." She didn't understand, but how could he explain? A few other women like her had gathered there. They lived together and searched for their sons. They told themselves they wouldn't leave Chechnya until they'd found their children, alive or dead. In the evening they sat around telling fortunes. They pulled hairs out of their head, threaded them through a ring, and held them over a photograph. If the ring hung motionless the son was dead; if it moved, alive. During the day they wandered from village to village. A Chechen woman is sitting by a washtub in front of her destroyed home, and the Russian goes up to her with the photo. "You haven't seen my child, mother, have you?" But in those photos they all look the same. "Yes," she replies. "He's the one who killed my son."

Answer: Wait a minute . . .

Question: Did you run away without doing what you were supposed to?

Answer: Wait a minute! I just wanted to fall asleep and wake up
somebody else. Stop being me. Get back inside my skin
in some other place and time. So I dreamed I was at
my post and suddenly she's walking up. I shout to her,
"Halt or I'll shoot!" And I whisper, "What are you
doing here?" She walks up, kisses me on the lips, and
puts her hands on my shoulders, and her fingers feel
like badges on my shoulder straps. I woke up and just
could not understand where I was. I was on some ship,
a strange ship, like out of a museum. Around me were
these strange men, seafarers. Someone pushed me, and
it turned out to be the ship's captain, one eye gray, the
other brown, a lush and a killer, and he started yelling:
"What're you sleeping for when God's brought a strong
wind up at sea and a great storm is in the making and the
ship is about to smash up!"

Question: What ship was that? What seafarers? Where were you
sailing?

Answer: Some ship that was going from Joppa to Tharsis and
that's sunk long since, and the seafarers died long since, if
they ever lived. On the ship they rang the bells, and the
captain shouted at me that the sailors were terrified and
each was calling on his own god and starting to throw
their load overboard into the sea. "And here you are dozing in the hold!" he shouted. "Get up and call on your
god! Maybe your god will remember us and we won't
perish!" And the sailors told each other, "Let's cast lots
to find out who this disaster is going to hit." Everyone
cast lots, and the lot fell on me. Then they asked, "Tell
us why this disaster befell you? What's your business

and where do you come from? Where is your country and what nation are you from?" And I told them, "I'm AWOL. My nation is wearing navy boxers and kersey boots and playing soccer with a deflated ball. Last night I went out into the yard. Someone stirred in the dark near the post. He shouted to me, 'Come here! I've got boiled condensed milk!' I walked up but I didn't recognize him. He opened the can with his bayonet. We started eating with our fingers. Dip a finger in and lick it. Then he said the next day I had to go to somewhere called Nineveh near Katyr-Yurt for a mop-up operation. That scared me because I realized I'd woken up someone else, not me." And the seafarers were terrified because they realized who I was running away from. "Go," the sailors cried out. "Go quickly to Nineveh! You're running away from the face of the Lord!" I asked them, "But who is that?" They were even more astonished. "God is that without which life is impossible." I said to them, "Now hold on there! They told us something about a primordial clot of something, and then that cluster exploded, I think, and ever since it's been growing and growing—the universe is expanding. Is that right, seafarers?" They said to me, "Something like that. In the beginning there was love. This clot of love. Or rather, not even love yet, but the need for it, because there wasn't anyone to do the loving. God was lonely and cold. And this love here demanded an outlet, an object, it wanted warmth, to hold someone dear close, to sniff the delicious nape of a child, its own, flesh of its flesh, so God created himself a child to love. Nineveh. He took a dead soldier outside Bamut. You know him, it was Gray. And from his body He made the land. From the blood that flowed from his wound, we got the rivers and sea. The mountains are from his bones. The boulders and rocks are his front and molar teeth. The firmament is from his skull. The clouds his brain, the draft his pulse, the wind his breath, the snow his dandruff. But he told you all that himself. His hair became the withered grass. And that was how Nineveh began. For us this is unimaginable, but for Him it's an easy spit. Maybe we're just His spit. Who cares whether you woke up on this ship yourself or not?" I was frightened. "What's going to happen now?" "We're going to throw you overboard and the Lord will order a great whale to swallow you, but this is a mistake in translation, because you're not plankton, but it doesn't matter. What matters is that this fish will have a ribbed gullet." "And then? How will I end up in Nineveh?" "That we don't know. Seafaring's our business—striking the bells. Now you'll arrive in Nineveh and do everything you're supposed to. There's going to be something else there with a tree. We don't remember exactly. Either it's going to dry up suddenly or a dry one's going to bloom. In short, the Lord will be saddened and say, 'Should I not take pity on Nineveh, the great city, where live one hundred twenty thousand people who cannot tell their right hand from their left, and numerous cattle?' He takes pity and destroys Nineveh so its people and animals will suffer no more."

Question: It's late. Look, it's very dark.

Answer: I told them, "Take me and throw me overboard—and the sea will grow calm for you." And they struck the bells again and replied, "Haven't you figured out that we're already in the belly of the whale, since it has the same ribbed throat as the sky over Bamut? As it is, we've been swallowed by the sky. As it is, we are inside that fish. We settled in and are taking things as they come.

Every day we see the ribbed vault of its throat—and it's fine, we're used to it. Because inside the fish everything is balanced and harmonious. There are an equal number of deaths and births, and an equal number of births and deaths—not one more, not one less—and in this book-keeping everything does and will always tally." And I asked, "So where am I to go?" They replied, "It's all the same. All roads will take you to Nineveh. Go where you want." So I went. I turned the corner and found myself in twilight. In the half-dark I saw a stork on the roof. Because I couldn't see its legs, it seemed to be hanging in the air. The boules de neige had finished blooming and the honeysuckle had closed up for the night. The distant sound of a bell reached me, as if a ladle were scraping a huge vat in the kitchen. A train in the distance, like a schoolboy's ruler. I walked down the highway for a long time, blocking the high beams with my hand. Then I stood at a crossing and watched vehicles go by on carriers in indecent poses: one truck humping another. The sunset was still a little warm, and in the still water of the pond the clouds did not sail like a film across the surface but rather glowed from the depths. I looked more closely: it was the same feathery clouds reflected, like a heavenly throat. A belated ladybird landed on my arm and crawled toward my elbow, tumbling over the hairs, or rather, lifted up by the hairs, like waves. I thought that this must be Nineveh, where the hot day begins with a pouring prayer, but when winter comes then everything is again drawn in black on white, where, apart from common sense, there is also another, uncommon one that is stronger, where even the snow is love and man is where his body is.

Question: I'm tired.

Answer: Wait a minute, there's only a little left. I was in Nineveh.
I was amazed that everything was exactly like here. A
cat caught snowflakes with its paw, they struck the bells
on shipboard, Prince Vasilko blinded his brother with
a knife, my mama handed out ice cream for free and
curled up in a ball to sleep. I was named after my father,
and my son was named after me. Booming thunder-
claps—either a storm approaching or someone running
over garage roofs. My broken nail caught on her skirt
and stockings. In the hut rookies sewed under-collars for
the old-timers. Dogs belched after gorging on carrion.
In the mirror the lopsided clock was reflected the wrong
way 'round. Grenades were thrown into cellars. Mothers
showed photos in plastic bags to everyone at the market. A sniper knocked red dust out of a head. When the
old-timers didn't finish the kasha in their plate, they spat
into it. Instead of the child, they buried the child's clothing. Pine cones and gravel flew over the fence. They
shot them out of compassion. They played soccer with
a deflated ball in the hospital yard wearing boxers and
boots. The ball was hoarse and couldn't catch its breath
when they knocked the wind out of it. No one wanted
to take pity and stop the torture. Out of compassion.
God did promise to spare Nineveh, after all, but it was
all left just as before, the way it was. Then I saw Gray
sitting in the rusty gynecological chair. He was beckon-
ing me with his finger. I walked over, my boots slipping
over the broken glass on the asphalt. "Gray, is that you?
Weren't you killed outside Bamut?" He spat through his
teeth onto the asphalt, put his hands behind his head, and
grinned. "How could I have been killed if you're talking
to me?" Then I asked, "Gray, what are you, God?" He

spat again, scratched his armpit, and said, "You need to believe or know."

Question: But after all, belief and knowledge are the same thing.

Answer: That's what I told him. I also asked, "Lord, why won't You take pity on Nineveh?"

Question: What did he say?

Answer: He grinned. "Fool, haven't you realized yet that there is no God?" And he snapped his boxer elastic. Right then someone whistled. I looked around. She was standing past the fence under the acacia—holding a badminton racket in one hand and a ping-pong ball in the other. She jutted out her lower lip and puffed away the bangs falling in her eyes. She held out the ball to me, smiled, and called out, "Come here!"

Candlemas

I haven't touched my diary all this time. It's been a month since Alyosha was killed. I was at the Church of Alexander Nevsky. I lit a candle for him. I stood in the same place where he and I stood then. I looked at everything again, the way I did then with him: the Vasnetsov paintings, the mosaics, the icon screens. All as it was then. Even the same priest. Only you couldn't see the poplars in the snowed-over windows and Alyosha was gone.

Then I went to his house. Sergei Petrovich wasn't there. Tatiana Karlovna was lying in her room. I sat with her a little and then stopped by to see Timosha. He likes the funny little fat fellow who is made completely of tires and wears an automobile helmet and goggles—from the Michelin tire advertisement. He would find it in the newspaper and decorate it with colored pencils. I sat down with him and we colored them together. Tima can laugh in a carefree, happy way now. For him, his brother is gone.

He is so like Alyosha!

That night I felt it all—he was gone—and I woke up. But in the morning, a letter. I read it and rejoiced that he was alive, but Alyosha was already gone. I pictured the sun and frost outside his window so vividly, the sparkling snow, the sparrow happiness, but he had already been killed.

On my way back I ran into Nina Nikolaevna on Nikitinskaya. We hadn't seen each other since that day. She knew nothing. She said to me, "How can you go around like such a ditherer? In public you have to have your game face on, not be turned inside out, for all the world to see! Let everyone think that you could not possibly have any troubles and that you are used to everyone obeying you—men and circumstances both!" I burst into tears and told her Alyosha had been killed. She gasped. "Child!" She put her arms around me and wept with me. There was a bench and we sat down. She began telling me about how in her youth a man she had loved perished. He had been with Skobelev in Bulgaria. This touched me so. Here, this wise old woman knew what it meant to lose someone dear to you! How she knew how to find something important and genuine to say in that moment! And all of a sudden she added that my hat had obviously been put on without a mirror's participation. In parting she said, "If you want to become a great actress, you need to know everything about love and know how to live without it." Lord, even now she was not consoling me but rather playing the part of a comforting angel!

I don't want to become a great actress. I want my Alyosha back!

I wanted to put down the date and got confused. I know it's Saturday.

Even now I sometimes make a mess of things and get lost. Today I was wandering through the apartment and looked out the window. The dahlias hadn't been cut back in the fall and they'd been covered in snow, and so had stood there until the thaw, and now they were slimy brown clods. Right then Mama came back and silently took the pot out of my hands. It turns out I'd been wandering through the apartment all this time with the pot. I lie down and can't get up. Why get up and go somewhere, eat, talk? My eyes take to recounting the stripes on the rug. One, two, three, four, five. Thirty-seven, thirty-eight. One, two, three, four, five. My throat is so dry, it's as if I'd drunk a glass of sand, not water. I'm lying here and some monologues I memorized with Nina Nikolaevna are running through my head. "I am alone . . ." At the time I didn't understand what this was about. "I am alone . . ."

8 February 1916. Monday

At class change today I stayed in the empty room. The windows were open, they were airing the room out. Everything seemed so unfamiliar and strange. What is this around me? Where am I? What is it for? Right then Musya peeked in the door—my Musya, whom I again forgot to buy a candy for. She ran up, kissed me, and petted me. I squeezed her and held her very very tight.

Heavy snow fell.

9 February 1916. Tuesday

Today something very bad happened. Kostrov was looking for me. The moment I saw him I immediately guessed, felt, what this would be about, and from the very beginning I knew I would refuse. He said Ogloblina had fallen ill and the premiere was in three days. L. himself, who was on tour in Rostov right now, had been invited. He began imploring me to replace her, rescue him, save him and everyone. I answered, "No." Kostrov was so upset that all of a sudden I felt very sorry for him. I said, "Fine!" Kostrov flew off elated, but I'm beside myself. What have I done? What for?

This is betrayal.

Alyosha, my beloved, I will go tomorrow and refuse.

13 February 1916

Today was the premiere.

How odd it all is! How mixed up it has all been! Before the performance I was sitting having my hair combed by a makeup artist invited from the Asmolov Theater, and I nearly leapt up and ran away, but he sat me back down firmly. Everyone was running around like madmen, muttering their lines. Kostrov shook everyone's hand and repeated, Break a leg! Everyone told him to go to hell. All of a sudden I wondered what I was doing here among these madmen with glued on whiskers and mustaches wearing these carnival costumes? What was the point? Kostrov came up to me. "Well, how are you doing, Belochka? Everything all right?" I forced myself to nod. I closed my eyes and repeated to myself, You must focus, concentrate. Now only the lines are important, only the role. I'll think about all the rest tomorrow. I am sound, word, and gesture. Just as Nina Nikolaevna taught me. I heard her voice in my head: If you don't control your body, it controls you.

After that it was all a fog. I stopped being myself and turned into a completely different woman. I kept watching myself as if I were standing off to one side. My voice sounded completely different. I went out on stage and played my part. Was this really still me?

When we went out for the curtain call, a thought raced through my mind: What if Alyosha hadn't been killed at all and he suddenly came back without writing anything to anyone and now, learning I was here, he had come and was sitting somewhere in the last row, watching me, overjoyed, clapping? I burst into tears and everyone thought it was from happiness. But it was. Though I have no way to explain it.

After the performance, L. came backstage and Kostrov introduced everyone to him. Zoya Subbotina started to curtsey and landed on the piano keyboard! Everyone nearly died laughing! L. pressed my hand and whispered something in my ear. Still in makeup and deafened, I didn't understand a thing. I didn't hear what he'd said and was embarrassed to ask him to repeat it.

L. stayed to have supper with us. Everyone was over the moon about him. He told very funny stories about starting his career at a ballet school, performing as the hind legs of a lion in *The Pharaoh's Daughter*. He liked being the center of attention and knew how. He called Petya over, Kostrov's nephew, and pulled a coin out from behind one ear and a candy from the other. It's so simple and easy for him to bestow a smile and joy on the people around him. Kostrov raised a toast to L., and he to us. He said, "You are the Russian theater of tomorrow!" He looked at me all evening! I was probably just imagining it. He doesn't look at all like his photos. Much older. But even handsomer in real life. Tall and stately. He uses a cane of Spanish reed with a knob made from a human tibia. He joked that these were the relics of Yorick himself.

Now I can't sleep. What could he have whispered to me? What if he'd said I'd acted remarkably well and have talent?

Dear Alyosha! I acted for you today!

16 February 1916. Tuesday

Today Leonid Mikhailovich read for the wounded in our infirmary. He saw me, and when he was saying goodbye walked up simply, as if we were old acquaintances. He said he had two hours before the performance and he would like to take a walk and breathe the air. He asked whether I would not refuse him my company. Refuse? My God! Refuse? Him? We went to the Commercial Garden, where everything was still covered in snow and the paths had been cleared in some places and trampled in others.

He told me how he had come up with the wings for Stanislavsky in the famous scene in Hauptmann's *Hannele* when the angel of death appears and spreads its wings, which fill the whole stage.

He also told me he had been to see the ailing Chekhov. Next to his bed lay many cups fashioned from paper. He would spit into the cups and throw them in the wastebasket.

I'm walking and listening and there's a rapping in my head: Might all this be a dream? Lord have mercy! Look who is walking with me through our Commercial! He is so simple and so otherworldly at once.

Then he suddenly began saying that he had many people around him but it was impossible to find a true friend. Leonid Mikhailovich said, "Married men live their whole life like a dog but die a lord, whereas a bachelor lives his whole life a lord and dies a dog."

In parting he kissed my hand. When he removed his gloves, it smelled so marvelous! It was a good thing I was wearing gloves or he would have seen my gnawed fingers. Every time I promise myself not to gnaw my hangnails, but then I forget and all my fingers are bitten off!

He invited me to all the remaining performances. He's leaving for Moscow in a week.

He is dear, kind, and good. And so unhappy. Very lonely. I could sense that.

17 February 1916. Wednesday

I didn't recognize him when he came out on stage! How he was transformed! It wasn't him, it was Brand himself! That is how to convey the depth of emotions of someone who is prepared to sacrifice his personal happiness, his only son, and his ardently loved wife! Not for the sake of the fatherland on the battlefield but for the sake of something immeasurably more important! How brilliantly he acted the ending—lonely, abandoned, cursed! But not vanquished! Is there really something for the sake of which you can sacrifice everything, even love?

After the performance I waited for him at the exit. There was a whole crowd there! He saw me, waved, I pushed through, and he invited me to dine with the actors. We went to the Belvoir on Sadovaya, where they had taken a large room. How good and merry it was! Gogolev and Varinskaya clowned around and wouldn't let anyone get a word in edgewise. Leonid Mikhailovich looked very tired and was silent nearly the entire time. Gogolev was telling stories about reanimating the dead! I don't know whether it's the truth or if he dreamed it all up just to entertain. It turns out, there had already been attempts to reanimate people with galvanism. Some scientist named Bichat, during the French Revolution, conducted experiments with the bodies of people who had been guillotined and wrote an entire scientific treatise on how he was able to cause their muscles to move thanks to galvanism. Galvani himself, who invented galvanism, performed public experiments in anatomical theaters in London and Oxford; he would electrify the corpse so that the head opened its eyes and wiggled its tongue. Such conversations so late at night! Someone began reassuring us that it was all childish prattle and that modern medicine was taking such steps forward that in the near future it would be able to extend a person's life practically to infinity. Varinskaya was horrified. "To live an eternity as an old lady!" Everyone laughed! But Leonid Mikhailovich sat silently on the sofa, and I sat down next to him and asked, "What do you think?" "I think that Scriabin died of a boil, and that he was awarded his blood infection at the hairdresser's and he never managed to accomplish what he'd wanted to." "So what, now you shouldn't go to the hairdresser's for a haircut?" "No, you have to accomplish what you want to faster."

What do I want to accomplish? I want to perform on stage and to love.

Mama is unhappy that I'm returning so late every day. She grumbles that I'm impossible to wake in the morning. This has nothing to do with school. She just doesn't like my friendship with actors!

18 February 1916. Thursday

Today after dinner I went for another walk with Leonid Mikhailovich. He is very interesting to talk to. He's very smart and has read so much! He knows all kinds of things!

He spoke very interestingly about time and art. Time is like a machine of destruction. "A little desk guillotine, if you like. Sort of like a bread cutter. A head cut off for every second. It shows up and—swish! The artist's business is to halt the hand that cranks the machine. To put his hand on the other."

He kept talking about death and immortality. He said he was reading a lot of the ancient authors, the Greeks. Right now he was reading Xenophon. I said I'd tried to read him but he was terribly boring, the endless crossings, the parasangs, everyone killing everyone else. I asked him what he found interesting there. "You're right. These people aren't interesting. Mercenaries come to a foreign country to kill and replace one tyrant with another, and then they spend the whole book trying to find the sea and head home. There's nothing beautiful or noble in it. But it's not about them. They're no better or worse than today's soldiers, who are shooting at someone right now, this very minute." "If not them, then who?" "The author, Xenophon. Imagine, how many people have slipped by (that's what he said, slipped by, it has an unpleasant ring!), and these Greeks held on because he wrote them down. And now for the third millennia, each time they see the sea he has led them to they rush to embrace one another and shout, Thalassa! Thalassa! Because he brought them to a very special sea. Thalassa is the sea of immortality."

The seething sea ceaseth . . .

Lord, why does anyone need an entire sea of immortality?

We started talking about ancient Egypt. He explained why they considered the dung beetle a sacred creature. It turns out, the Egyptians mixed their dough with their feet and clay with their hands and smeared their hands with dung because the cow was a sacred animal, so its dung was sacred, too. And in general, everything that came from life was sacred, the greatest and smallest both. And what could be smaller than a dung beetle? That meant it was the most sacred.

How does he know all this? Could he be making it up? Maybe in fact it's all much simpler. In our climate dung remains a smelly wet patty for a long time, whereas in Egypt it's all dry in a few minutes? My God, how boring my dung philosophy is and what a marvelous world he lives in!

19 February 1916. Friday

Yesterday I saw him in Andreyev's *Thought*. His acting is amazing and cannot be compared to anything!

Today he and I walked again for an entire hour. We talked about very important things. I didn't understand everything.

All our Russian disasters come from our contempt for the flesh. Everything's been turned upside down; what is most sacred is reviled. "They will be saved who have not been defiled with women, for virgins they are." Among the ancient Babylonians, the man would burn incense after relations with a woman, while elsewhere in the house the woman he had been with would do the same thing.

In Babylon there was a custom that each woman was required to have relations with a foreigner once in her life in the temple of Melitta; this held true for everyone, rich and poor, nobles and common peasants. She would sit down in the temple with a crown of rope on her head until a foreigner, or any wanderer, or cripple, or freak tossed a coin in her lap and said, "I summon you in the name of the goddess Melitta." No matter how small the coin, the woman did not have the right to reject him and went with the man, no matter who he was. This is true love for one's neighbor. In this way decent women showed compassion for those who did not have love, kindness, and warmth, what each person needs and without which cannot live. Herein lies the highest chastity, purity, sanctity, and love. You may be a cripple, an outcast, a freak, or an unfortunate, homeless foreigner, but you are still a human being and worthy of love. This is true charity for one's neighbor, not our kopeks.

I can't agree with him, but I sense there is some truth in what he says.

Spring is in the air. Everything is melting. Nighttime dripping.

20 February 1916. Saturday

Yesterday was the final performance. Tomorrow Leonid Mikhailovich is leaving. He and I met to say goodbye, and we felt like going for one last walk through our municipal garden. It is the thaw, and everything was flooded. There was no taking the paths. We walked on the sidewalk by the fence, up and down. We said goodbye a few times and then started walking again. Leonid Mikhailovich invited me to have supper with him at the Bolshaya Moskovskaya. I opened my mouth to refuse and out of nowhere agreed! Then I grew shy at the front door. I was afraid people I knew would see me. Also, I was dressed quite unsuitably. Leonid Mikhailovich spoke with the staff, and we were led past the doors of the main hall into a private room. Silver service, crystal goblets, starched napkins, and a palm by the mirror. Beauty! And frightening! We sat down on a velvet sofa by the fireplace. He took my hand and was about to kiss it but I jerked it away. I was embarrassed by my gnawed fingers. He asked, "What will you tell them at home?" "I'll tell them I was at a girlfriend's." I act as if I went to restaurants every day! But inside I was shaking violently! I don't know who I feared more, him or myself! L. ordered all kinds of things. They brought champagne in a bucket with ice. We toasted: "To your future!" "To my future!" I just took a sip—and such a marvelous wave passed through my whole body! Leonid Mikhailovich told me about his wife and children, but all I could think was, "Where am I? What is happening to me? Is this all for real?"

This was his second marriage, and it too was unhappy. He and his wife had long been pretending to be a family. He had two children from his first marriage. The older, a daughter, had also gone on stage, but the younger, a son, had been blind since childhood. What a nightmare! How I wanted to show compassion! But I could find nothing smarter than to ask, "And you mean there's nothing to be done?" He smiled bitterly and said, "Forgive me! Why talk about that? Let's talk about you!"

He said I had an astonishing voice and enormous talent. He asked me to sing something. A guitar appeared from somewhere. He plays wonderfully! I sang a few ballads, my favorites. He said all kinds of nice things, not just to be polite. He liked it very much, I know that for certain! He also said that my love, the kind I will have, will depend on me alone. Just as thousands of actors play Shakespeare and it depends only on them what Shakespeare yields, so too love can yield a great deal, or nothing but disgust, and you need to have a special talent to love, to be gifted in love. That is so right! I've felt that, too, only I couldn't find those words.

I must have been drunk. I felt so good, so cozy! Wonderful music filtered in from the main room. And suddenly I lost all fear. It vanished. Only my hangnails hurt when I rinsed my hands in water with lemon after the shrimp, but I was no longer at all shy. They still hurt! I so wanted him to take my hands and kiss them! But now he was afraid since I had jerked them back so roughly. Or was it because of the shrimp?

Leonid Mikhailovich went out, and I so wanted a little champagne, I decided to drink a little straight from the bottle, but there was nothing there, just a sour smell. I didn't even notice that we had drunk the whole bottle. I had only drunk one glass. Or was it two? He came back and said he would drive me home, but I refused and said I wanted to go on foot. He accompanied me. Tomorrow is his train in the morning. We said goodbye quite ineptly. How foolish all words are! He wished me success. I so wanted to kiss him in parting, but I couldn't summon the nerve. He turned and walked away. It was starting to rain, and he had no umbrella.

I came home and Mama pounced on me right away. I locked myself in my room and am now writing it all down.

Lord, how decent, kind, and good he is! So sensitive and tactful! And how unhappy!

21 February 1916

I just had a note from L. He writes that he missed his train—for my sake. He asks for a meeting. I wrote him a single word: "No."

1 March 1916

A week has passed, and I still feel dirty. Yes, I am a dirty, awful creature. I disgust myself. I've decided I have to tell everything, just as it was, with all the details, the vilest, most demeaning details. Let it be even more demeaning, more shameful. I deserved it!

I wrote "no" and ran off. I raced to forestall the note. He was in his room. He was silent and so was I. All I could think was, "What am I doing? What am I doing?" He didn't embrace me, didn't kiss me, didn't touch me. He walked to the window. "I am going to recite a great poem for you now. On your knees!" My temples started pounding. "Me, on my knees?" But he gave me such a look that I completely lost my will. "On your knees!" My legs buckled of their own accord. He read like a god. I don't know how long. Two minutes? Two hours? Two years? Then he lifted me up and sat me at the table. I had completely missed the fact that the table was laid. I didn't eat anything. Neither did he. He asked me whether I regretted having come. "No." At that he stepped out from around the table and dropped to his knees before me. That's all. I can't write anything more.

I am a vile, degenerate creature.

That evening I came home very late. I stole into the kitchen and poured myself a glass of vodka. I drank vodka for the first time in my life. I sprinkled in two spoonfuls of sugar and drank it down. Then Mama came out into the kitchen. She started shouting at me. I was silent. She started demanding that I tell her the truth about where I had been. At first I wanted to lie to her that I was at Tala's, and then all of a sudden I felt like hurting her! I asked her, "Do you really want to know the truth?" "Yes!" "I was at the Bolshaya Moskovskaya with Leonid Mikhailovich." I said it and went to my room. I heard my mama sitting in the kitchen and weeping, but I didn't return to her.

Alyosha, I betrayed you.

Remember how nothing worked for you and me? Neither you nor I knew anything. I betrayed you doubly, dear Alyosha, because I understood what a body could do. L. has amazing hands. And how amazing and sweet it is to be a woman in his hands!

Then, with you, Alyosha, it was painful, and frightening, and embarrassing. But with him everything was completely different. I'm grateful to him.

And you know the worst part, Alyosha? I told him about you. And he said, "That means he wasn't the one." At first I didn't understand at all. "What do you mean not the one?" "Just that. Not the one."

Alyosha, forgive me. I'm unworthy of you.

Only now did I realize, dear Alyosha, that you would love me forever. Forever! You will never have anyone but me.

I despise and detest myself.

14 April 1916. Thursday

I told myself there would be no more diaries, and here I was rummaging through my desk and found this empty notebook, which I had once prepared for a diary.

My nanny died. On Good Friday. She didn't last until Easter. She dreamed of dying on Easter.

In her last few weeks nanny suffered terribly. She looked awful, became dreadfully thin, and her face and neck were covered in drooping wrinkles. They laid her out on the table and put an iron washtub full of ice under the table. Overnight the deceased was transformed. All her wrinkles smoothed out as if there had been no terrible illness.

I was listening to the service for the dead and suddenly the words blazed up, alight: in a place of repose, a place of brightness, a place of verdure. Lord how nice, warm, and gentle: in a place of repose, a place of brightness, a place of verdure. Where is that?

Her husband died early on, and when I asked her once why she didn't marry a second time, she replied, "The dead see us, and rejoice, and grieve for us, and when we meet, what am I supposed to do with two husbands?"

Mama made the paskha, but it didn't come out like the real thing. Nanny, when she kneaded the paskha and put it in its tin, always handed me the wooden spoon: "Lick!" And I would lick it. And there was nothing more delicious! Now Mama held out the spoon to me and said, "Lick!" I didn't say a word to her and walked out. Mama and I have become complete strangers.

Everything seemed the same as usual, the bells rang festively and the candlelights flowed down the lanes, but there was no Easter mood. And the only person I wanted to ask forgiveness from was my nanny, and I couldn't.

In her last month my nanny read the Bible all the time, all kinds of prophesies: The end of the world was coming, brother will go against brother, there will be famine and pestilence. The time would come when people would go into the clefts of the rocks, and into the tops of the ragged rocks, for fear of the Lord. Might it have been easier for her to go like that?

At the funeral feast my father began talking about how Muslims don't bury their dead in coffins but wrap them in a shroud and carry them to the burial site on a special stretcher. They lower the body into the earth feet first and bury them facing Mecca, and if a Muslim has a Christian or Jewish wife who dies, and she is known to be pregnant, she has to be buried the opposite way, with her back to Mecca, so the infant in her womb is turned facing that holy place. I listened to him and suddenly saw that he was old. He had begun to take care of himself, tried to look younger than his age, dyed his gray hair, bought a Marengo suit in a stylish herringbone fabric, but all this only made him look even older. He is walking around with a bandaged finger; he had been helping operate on a complicated case and cut himself. Nothing like this had ever happened to him before. My dear, beloved papa—all of a sudden he is an old man. I couldn't restrain myself. I walked up behind him, wrapped my arms around his neck, and nestled up to him. But he said, "Wait a minute, Belka, don't interrupt!" And he said something more. And I became so frightened that he was going to die, too!

In a place of repose, a place of brightness, a place of verdure . . .

When my nanny's niece came from her village to collect her things, all of a sudden she started saying that we had deceived nanny, had shorted her wage, and certain earrings and brooches had gone missing. Mama drove her out.

Also a letter came from Masha. She described in detail going from Petrograd to Abo to see Boris. She wrote that you didn't feel the war there at all, you could have an excellent meal at any station en route. You dropped your ticket into a bowl at the buffet and took anything on the table—meat, fish, appetizers, any wine, and dessert. Boris took her to a restaurant in Helsingfors where they ordered bear paws and deer tongue! She also wrote that she was happy but terribly afraid for Boris. She kept having the same dream of him drowning. "I wake up in a sweat, but he's right here next to me. If he's not, if he's on the ship, I can't fall back to sleep." They have a tiny apartment, and she described in detail where everything was and how she tried to create comfort for Boris. The war there was different. Sailors perished with their ship or returned home to ordinary life.

In Helsingfors there was something you wouldn't see in Russia: they didn't ask for tickets on the streetcar and everyone put his own coins in the bowl.

Katya is planning to marry Viktor and move to Moscow.

There's been nothing from Sasha in a long time.

Nyusya came and left. I went with her to see Lehar's *Merry Widow*, put on by Krylov's troupe. I liked it very much, but Nyusya sneered. All Rostov is walking around humming tunes from it.

It's become lonely at home. Everyone's gone their separate way.

Look how much I've written.

Having completed the crossing at around midday, the Hellenes formed up and passed through the valley, ascending into the mountains, at least five parasangs. The host stretched out, articulating like a giant centipede. Near the river there were no villages, due to the wars with the Kardukhoi. The Hellenes made camp, but that night there was a heavy snowfall. It snowed for many hours, dense and heavy, and by dawn it had blanketed the weapons and the men lying on the ground and had fixed the pack animals by the legs. In the morning no one felt like rising because the snow warmed whoever lay beneath it. When Xenophon decided to rise undressed and started chopping firewood, one more man immediately got up, took the ax away from him, and started chopping wood. After him, others too began to rise, light fires, and smear themselves with grease. In this mountainous land there was a lot of grease, which was used instead of olive oil. It was made from lard, sesame seeds, bitter almond, and turpentine.

From here, for the entire day following, they walked through the deep snow, the hunger and cold exhausting many. The crossing was very difficult because a north wind was blowing directly in their face, slowly but surely freezing people and bringing them to a state of rigidity. Then one of the priests suggested offering a sacrifice to the wind. This was done, and it seemed palpable to all that the wind's force had waned. The snow's depth reached one orgyia, and because of this, many pack animals perished, and the people bringing up the rear, and as many as thirty soldiers. Xenophon, who was in the rearguard, collected the fallen with the idea of burying them with due ceremony, but that was impossible, and the dead were simply sprinkled with snow.

Their enemies followed on the Hellenes' heels, stealing the weakened pack animals and getting into scuffles with each other over them. The pursuers cruelly finished off anyone who lagged behind, cutting off his right hand, according to their custom. The mere thought of such an end drove the soldiers onward, nonetheless their exhaustion was so great that some did lag behind. Some began to experience snow blindness, others' toes froze. They had to keep moving constantly, not letting up for a minute, and take off their boots at night. If someone went to sleep without removing his boots, the straps cut into his legs and froze to them because the old footwear had worn out and their boots, their *karabatinai*, were made of undressed cowhide.

Because of these misfortunes some soldiers lagged behind and saw a patch of earth, black because the snow had melted from it. Indeed, it had melted due to the vapors coming from a nearby spring in a wooded ravine. They turned in there, sat down, and refused to go any farther. Xenophon learned of this and used every possible means and method to try to convince them not to lag behind, pointing out that they were being followed by the enemy, which had gathered large numbers, and finally he even became angry. But the soldiers asked him to put them out of their misery; they could not go on. Then they decided to try to frighten the pursuing enemy, so they would not attack those who were exhausted. It was already dark, and the enemy approached, talking loudly in their barbarous tongue. Then the hale soldiers of the rearguard prepared and ran at the enemy, and the sick soldiers raised a hue and cry and started banging their spears on their shields as hard as they could. In terror, the barbarians raced across the snow into the wooded ravine, and not one of them ever uttered another sound.

Xenophon and his detachment told the sick that they would come for them the next day and moved on, and before they had gone four stadions they came across soldiers who were wrapped up sleeping on the snow, over whom no guard had been posted. They woke them and reported that the lead detachments were not advancing. Xenophon continued on and sent his hardiest peltasts off with an order to learn the cause of the delay. They reported that the entire army was resting in a similar manner. Then Xenophon's detachment lay down right there to rest. The Hellenes spent the night by their fires. Wherever a fire burned, the melting of the snow formed a large hole that went all the way to the ground, and so they could measure the snow's depth.

At that same time, in the Muntenian land through which the Hellenes were passing, Red Army Day was being celebrated. In Grozny the residents were driven onto the main square and told that because the republic's population had given support to the Germans, the party and government had decided to resettle all the Gagauzes and traitors. They read decree number such-and-such to those assembled: "Resistance is futile because you are surrounded by troops, and anyone who tries to disobey or attempts to flee will be shot."

The crowd, dumbfounded and paralyzed with horror—Xenophon goes on to say—led by local officials, moved in ranks, four by four, to the market, where people were being loaded into trucks and taken to the railroad, not to the station but to the marshaling yard, where troop trains with cattle cars awaited them.

In other settlements they only arrested the men and ordered the women to pack their things and be prepared to take their children and leave their homes the next day. The Russian soldiers went from house to house helping the distraught mothers collect their things, telling them to take warm clothing and provisions, not gramophones or rugs, and helping them carry their belongings to the truck.

In the latter half of the day abundant snow fell, and there were difficulties dispatching the people, especially in mountainous districts.

They were being transported in Studebaker trucks that had come from America via Iran under Lend-lease. The trucks' engines were turned on, and their headlights lit up the fallen snow. The glow could be seen from afar—the powerful headlights of dozens of trucks.

The inhabitants of the mountain village of Khaibakh refused to carry out the order and abandon their homes. "We would all rather die!" the old women shouted, and they called on God to prevent this injustice and to take them quickly, so they would not have to die in a foreign land but could be buried in the land of their ancestors. They drove everyone in the surrounding auls who couldn't or wouldn't leave voluntarily to Khaibakh—the sick, the old, anyone caught on the roads, anyone grazing cattle, anyone hiding. The people were assembled in the kolkhoz stable. An icy wind blew through the cracks and penetrated their bones. The soldiers were ordered to lay hay around the long shed so that the people inside wouldn't be cold. That's what they told the people freezing in the stable. Then a Muntenian voivode by the name of Gveshiani ordered them to lock the gates and burn the shed down.

Fat wet snowflakes were falling and the soldiers ran around in the mud trying to set fire to the damp straw. One driver splashed gasoline from a canister. The straw burst into flames. A huge bonfire quickly rose to the sky.

There was panic inside. Under the pressure of the crazed people, the doors collapsed. Those running in front fell, barring the way to those pressing from behind. They began to fire submachine guns at those fleeing. So as to put a speedy end to it, the soldiers threw grenades through the windows at the screaming people.

The Muntenian voivode sent a list of the burned to Moscow. Here are the names, but you don't have to read them. Just turn the page.

Tuta Gayev, age 110;
Sari Gayeva, his wife, age 100;

Khatu Gayev, his brother, age 108;

Marem Gayeva, his wife, age 90;

Alauddi Gayev, Khatu's son, age 45;

Khesa Gayev, Alauddi's wife, age 30;

Khasabek Gayev, his brother, age 50;

Khasan and Khusein Gayev, Khesa's children,
      twins, born the night before;

Gezamakhma Gazoyev, age 58;

his wife Zano, age 55;

his son Mokhdan, age 17;

his son Berdan, age 15;

his son Makhmad, age 13;

his son Berdash, age 12;

his daughter Zharadat, age 14;

his daughter Taikhan, age 3;

Duli Gelagayeva, age 48;

her son Sosmad, age 19;

her other son Abuyezid, age 15;

her third son Girmakha, age 13;

her fourth son Movladi, age 9;

her daughter Zainad, age 14;

her second daughter Sakhara, age 10;

Pakant Ibragimova, age 50;

her son Adnan, age 20;

her daughter Petimat, age 20;

Minegaz Chibirgova, age 81;

her daughter-in-law Zalimat, age 35;

her son Zalimat Abdulmazhed, age 8;

her daughter Laila, age 7;

her daughter Marem, age 5;

Kavalbek Gazalbekov, age 14;

Zano Dagayeva, age 90;

Kerim Amagov, age 70;

Musa Amagov, age 8, from Charmakh;

Data Bakiyeva, age 24;

Matsi Khabilayeva, age 80;

the doctor Girikha Gairbekov, age 50;

Petimat Gairbekova, his wife, age 45;

Adnan Gairbekov, their son, age 10;

Medina Gairbekova, their daughter, age 5;

Zuripat Bersanukayeva, age 55;

her daughter Khanpat Bersanukayeva, age 19;

her second daughter Bakuo, age 17;

her third daughter Baluza, age 14;

her fourth daughter Baisari, age 9;

her fifth daughter Bazuka, age 7;

her son Mokhmad Khanip, age 11;

the family of Abukhazh Batukayev:

his mother Khabi, age 60;

his wife Pailakh, age 30;

his son Abuyezid, age 12;

his daughter Asma, age 7;

his second daughter Gashta, age 5;

his third daughter Satsita, age 3;

his newborn daughter Toita;

the family of Kosum Altimirov:

his daughter Zaluba, age 16;

his son Akhmad, age 14;

his second son Makhmad, age 12;

the family of Kaikhar Altimirov:

his daughter Tovsari, age 16;

his son Abdurakhman, age 14;

his son Mutsi, age 12;

Khozh Akhmad Eltayev, age 15;

Saidat Akhmad Eltayev, age 13;

Also perishing—Xenophon continues his story—was Pailakha Alimkhodzhayeva. I don't know how old she was; she too was killed in Khaibakh. When the soldiers left, the local residents who had escaped to the mountains recognized her body from her unburned braid. Her sister kept the braid all these years. Even now it lies somewhere, that braid.

The snowfall had cut off the roads in the mountains, and the soldiers reached the last aul, in Galanchozh District, the last before the pass, over a snow-strewn path, with a guide who was a local Party activist. The soldiers were afraid they would fail to carry out the order in time and were hurrying. They led the men away and ordered the remaining residents to prepare for resettlement, saying they would return as soon as the weather permitted. The men were led single-file down a narrow path over an abyss. One Chechen suddenly put his arms around the soldier walking next to him and plunged down with him. The other captives started doing the same thing. The soldiers opened fire. All the men of the aul perished.

Little boys saw what had happened in the gorge, and when they returned home they told how their fathers had perished. The old men gathered to decide what they should do. Then the eldest among them stood up and began spinning in the ancient dance of death his grandfathers and great-grandfathers had danced. Then all the old men and women, and the women, and the children of the aul joined the circle and began to dance. They all vowed to die rather than surrender to the Russians. Then the elders decided that they could not fight. They had neither weapons nor strength. But they would not wait for them to come and take them away from the land of their ancestors. All the remaining inhabitants of the aul gathered, taking only what was most essential, and went up into the mountains, to the pass.

It was difficult walking through the deep snow, and the wind kept knocking them off their feet. The women carried the small children and held them close so they wouldn't freeze. Not all made it to the pass: when people ran out of strength they sat down in the snow and froze to death.

They walked like that for a long time, losing track of time, exhausting themselves, and freezing in the blizzard. All of a sudden those walking in front looked down and saw lights where the valley began. Fires were burning directly on the snow, and men were sleeping around them. It was the Hellenes.

The aul's inhabitants went to them and asked whether they could warm themselves by the fires and get something to eat. The Greeks shared what little they had with the Chechens. Xenophon explained as best he could to these frozen, weary, starving people, who did not understand the Hellenic speech, that he was leading his Greeks to the sea. "Thalassa!" Xenophon pointed seaward for the elders. "Thalassa!"

And in the morning they headed out together to continue on their way.

26 July 1919. Friday

How nice it is to begin a new notebook! And with good news! That pushy Torshin has organized a variety show at the Soleil moviehouse! We are going to perform six times every Sunday, three matinees and three evening performances. The skit is terribly silly, but funny. "Hungry Don Juan." The scene: a declaration of love. A hungry schoolboy arrives for a tryst and in the end falls to his knees and admits he's hungry. Torshin made such funny faces it was impossible not to laugh. Wild laughter fell upon us and we just couldn't stop. We collected ourselves, started according to the script, and everything seemed to be going well, but the minute we looked each other in the eye—we split our sides laughing again. God forbid we get so worked up in public!

Six performances a day! We'll be rich!

And tomorrow Pavel is finally taking me to see Nikitina! The *crème de la Osvag crème!*

27 July 1919. Saturday

I am so angry at Pavel!

He finally took me to see Nikitina on Saturday. You'd think it was the salon of Princess Evdoxia Fyodorovna! High society! Natasha Rostova's first ball! What a nightmare!

Nikitina herself is an enchanting woman, but God knows who she invites! Some Mirtova, a poetess, from Kiev apparently, so affected, she talks louder than anyone and laughs at the wrong times in a deep bass, will not let anyone get a word in edgewise, and kept trying to recite her poems. Is behaving vulgarly and provocatively all it takes for everyone to like you, to be at the center of male attention all evening?

I was asked to sing. I demurred just a little, as one should, and right away felt the disdainful gazes of all the celebrities from the capital. That stung so! It swept away any timidity, on the contrary, to be replaced by a cheerful malice and ardor. Just you wait! I stepped out, one hand on the piano, my handkerchief in the other. And then a blow—Pavel told me not to worry about accompaniment—and who sat down at the instrument? Mirtova herself! She played terribly and did not listen to me. What choice did I have? I began to sing. Inside I was enraged at Pavel and at this Mirtova, who had the nerve to think this was her concert. The whole time, her chair kept creaking! I wanted the earth to swallow me up!

Nonetheless, it was a success! Chirikov himself came up and kissed my hand! He began purring about how I had a future and I would sing on the stages of the capitals. It is so nice to hear those words! He praised my voice especially.

The moment anyone gave me a stock compliment, such as these famous people always have at the ready, I would break into a smile. But I could feel it, too, that I sang well!

Pavel immediately became enmeshed with someone, some professor, I don't remember his name. But he didn't even come up to me after the applause! All right, fine, he didn't, but he should be slapped. He doesn't understand anything at all!

I'll write a few more words about famous people. You don't drink tea with greatness every day, after all. Chirikov read from his new novel. I was so excited I simply couldn't concentrate and it all flew past me. My legs were shaking and I couldn't calm down. And I was still hot, though the windows were open. I began perspiring, and it felt as though my cheeks and nose were shiny, but I couldn't go out to powder them. All I heard was the legend of a prisoner who sat in the solitary chamber of a prison bastion for many years and was supposed to stay there his whole life until his very death, and then one day he scratched out a boat on the wall with a spoon, stepped into it, and sailed away, and when they opened the door to give him his gruel, the chamber was empty. When Chirikov finished reading, after the applause, he suddenly said, "This novel is my boat. I'll write it, step in, and sail away." Everyone was silent, and the silence became somewhat awkward. Then Nikitina saved the situation and turned it all into a joke. "And this said by a man who has five children!" Evdoxia Fyodorovna is very clever, but she dresses in a terribly old-fashioned style. Paul Poiret taught woman to feel and love her body, but she . . .

Afterward everyone was invited into the dining room and treated to pies and cookies, baked by the hostess herself. We drank tea from cups that were gilded on the inside, which made it look like red wine. I was sitting with her husband. Just think! A former minister was paying court to me! Pavel was sitting opposite me and instead of throwing jealous, incinerating looks at his fiancée, he fell on the pies and kept up his conversation with his neighbor. And how did the state figure entertain his lady? With stories about cooperation! An incredibly engrossing topic! I noticed that the entire evening my cavalier, who kept offering me biscuits, did not exchange a word with his wife. Whereas she had something going on with that professor. Ladyzhensky, I think. Observing people is fun. She saved him from Pavel, leading him away by the hand and cooing about something with him in a corner.

Then everyone again turned their attention to Chirikov. He told stories about his prisons, tsarist and Red. Once he was imprisoned for his "Ode to the Tsar." He could write peacefully there: he had a room and everything essential for life, he was even given an allowance, and last year he was arrested in Kolomna and only a miracle saved him from execution. His *Jews* had never been produced in Russia before the revolution; only Orlenov had performed it on his foreign tours. He was told that *Jews* was being performed that year by Glagolin in Red Kharkov with Sinelnikov's troupe, moreover in the last act they released Christ on stage in the form of a policeman, and they beat him on the cheeks and spat in his face. They also sent out actresses from the Wolf studio completely naked, and the maidens ran through the hall, sitting on audience laps and so on. Even Valerskaya performed completely naked!

He was asked about Gorky. He cut them off: "The Smerdyakov of the Russian revolution!" How could he speak like that—about someone like that! Gorky! Might he simply be jealous of him, and thus this hatred? But for the most part Chirikov is cheerful, playful, even kind. You feel comfortable and at ease with him. It's as though he fluttered out from somewhere in the past with his bowtie and his gleaming, irreproachably white shirt. Lately men have let themselves go, become shabby, so quickly, but he has managed to preserve himself. He is married to the actress Iolshina. He is in Rostov without his wife, who is with the little ones in the Crimea, where they have a home, and the older children are scattered across the country. People are oddly made. Here he doesn't know what's happening with his son, whether he's even alive, and at the same time he sits here at the samovar, tucks away liver pies, and tells funny stories.

I wonder who makes sure his shirts are white in his wife's absence?

The pirozhki, by the way, are perfectly awful. Your teeth get mired in the half-raw dough. You can tell the salon's hostess began playing the democratic cook only recently. Nonetheless, everyone politely expressed rapture, naturally.

Also someone there with the face of an Old Believer merchant kept making jokes that weren't funny. Later I found out, at the very end of the evening, that this was Trofimov the film producer, who is now filming *For a United Russia* outside Rostov with OSVAG money.[25] I whispered to Pavel to introduce me, and he replied, "I don't know him myself!" "Well, think of something!" "Fine, Bellochka!" And that was that. Nothing is going to happen. I know what "Fine, Bellochka!" means!

In parting, Nikitina gave me her book of verse, which had just come out. *Dew of Dawn*. She signed it, "To enchanting Isabel."

The evening ended quite humorously. They were discussing what to do the next time, and Nikitin said he would like to read his memoirs, which he was working on now, about the siege of the Winter Palace and how the Provisional Government was arrested, but Mirtova interrupted again and began saying that that very evening, October 25th, she too had been in Petrograd and had gone to the opera, to see *Don Carlos* at the People's House, with someone she was having an affair with. Chaliapin was supposed to sing. At first it was all as usual. The theater was jammed, and each time Chaliapin appeared on stage the audience applauded furiously, and shouted, and the young ladies in the gods moaned hysterically, and when the last intermission was ending and the curtain was just about to go up, the lights went out in the hall and there was total darkness and quiet. Everyone sat in the dark and it was frightening. A wave of whispers began that something was on fire. There was a noise, as if they were chopping up the sets behind the stage. No one said anything or stood up. If a panic had been raised, everyone would have trampled one another. Then, in the dark, someone came out on stage and said that there was not a fire, that the electricity was just about to be restored. "And there, in that darkness, he proposed

---

25. OSVAG was the White Army's propaganda agency during the Russian Civil War.

marriage! Then the lights went back on and the performance continued. I thought they were chopping up the set, but this was gunfire. It was the chatter of machine guns! I will write about that one day, too, and that will be my revolutionary memoir!"

There are people who want to be the deceased at every funeral!

28 July 1919. Sunday

I awoke with the feeling that I have to clear things up with Pavel. Today, without delay. This conversation could not be put off any longer.

I went to his new laboratory, where I had never been before—where the former photographer Meyerson had been on Sadovaya, which OSVAG had requisitioned for him.

I arrived and couldn't bring myself to start. Pavel was printing photographs from his latest trip. It was awful. He kept telling me stories. He couldn't stop. He had to get it out. I just couldn't interrupt him. It was so awful! There was nothing human left! He had been photographing executions. Cossacks and officers had posed readily. They had hung two at once, throwing the rope over a crossbeam so that they strangled each other. One had been ordered shot, and they stood in front of the road, but he had cried, "Fools, put me up against the wall. There's the roadway behind me!"

We're standing in the light of a red lamp, and all of a sudden maimed children's faces start peering through the bath. It's awful. I closed my eyes. I couldn't look. While he told me stories about what he saw among the Kalmyks. Peasants from Russian villages had had their eye on that land for a long time, which is why they supported the Bolsheviks and wiped out the Kalmyks, slaughtered entire villages, which they call *khotons*. They killed everyone who didn't manage to run away. I think it was the settlement at Bolshoi Derbetovsky, I don't remember exactly. Pasha photographed the burned down Buddhist temples, the huruls. Everything was soiled and smeared with excrement. Smashed Buddhas. Ripped up holy books. Instead of icons they have silk canvases, which were looted, and all this is from Tibet. In one temple they dug up the ashes of some lama and threw his bones out on the road. Lord, people have turned into animals!

Pavel collected the remains of Buddhist statues with broken arms and heads and brought all this to Rostov. He wants to arrange an exhibit.

I picked up a small statue to hold. A little Buddha with its head broken off.

Pavel started kissing me. I couldn't. I pushed him away. He put his arms around me and said, "I understand." I felt like scratching him and shouting, "You understand nothing! Nothing!"

He also told me how they were riding on the steppe and noticed some pigs. They sent two men to catch a piglet. But the horsemen rode up, stopped, and turned around. "Why didn't they take the pigs?" "They were eating human corpses."

Photographs had been hung up to dry everywhere. I couldn't look at it all. I started to feel nauseated. My eyes seemed to stick to one: bare feet poking out from under the sand. Perfectly white. I couldn't tear away my gaze. I immediately thought of my brother and how when we were children they buried him in the sand at the river. Buried him so that his head, hands, and two feet poked out. Sasha shouted, "Dig me out!" And we laughed and tickled his soles. All of a sudden it felt as though it was Sasha lying there in the photograph. Pavel tells me, "Bellochka, calm down, forgive me! I shouldn't have shown you this! But who do I have to talk to? Please understand!" "Leave me alone!" I flew off, slamming the door. I ran home but kept seeing the bare white feet in front of me.

29 July 1919. Monday

Today Musya stopped by. I haven't seen her for such a long time. She's such a grown-up, beautiful young woman! She threw her arms around my neck. She was in tears! What's the matter? She held out a letter. "Dear Musya, I love you very much!" An entire love letter with grammatical errors and, at the end, threats to kill himself. "Do you love him?" "No." "Well, don't worry about it!" "But what should I do now? What if he does kill himself?" I stroked her head. "Let him!" "How can you say that?" She took umbrage and fled. I ran after her onto the front steps and called out, but I couldn't catch her.

I immediately thought of Torshin: "People rarely die from love, but they are frequently born from it."

Musya is still an utter child.

I practice every day and exercise my diaphragm. I warm up and imagine Koltsova-Selyanskaya standing behind me and I listen with her ears and make comments, the way she did. "Relax your larynx! Lift your upper lip! Don't let your chest drop!" It was as if I could feel her hand on my diaphragm. It helps so much! I am so grateful to her!

I need to clear things up with Pavel. It's killing me.

30 July 1919. Tuesday

Makhno is a schoolteacher. How strange everything is in Russia. Why do teachers lead gangs and pogroms?

I wanted to stop by Pavel's but didn't. Tomorrow.

31 July 1919. Wednesday

I'm so relieved! All day I've felt an inexplicable joy.

Before dinner I rehearsed at the Soleil. The room seemed enormous! But my voice sounds very good. Rogachev is the accompanist. He's from Moscow and worked as concertmaster at the Mamontov opera, too. At first he spoke to me disdainfully. Later, after I sang, his disdain flew out the window! He praised me sparingly, "I'm very glad. I hadn't expected this!" Coming from him, though, this means something!

You immediately sense the experience and artistry in him. I'm very pleased. We agreed which love songs I would perform in which *divertissement.* He said I should hold my temperament in check. "You need to keep a cool head."

After rehearsal I went to roam the city. Sun, a light breeze, so fine! On Sadovaya, between Cup of Tea and Filippov's pastry shop, there were so many people out for a stroll. It seemed as though everyone, not only I, had the sense that all the horrors were coming to an end and human life was at last beginning again.

And what shop windows! What silks, hats, ready-made suits, perfume, and jewelry! How elegantly the public was dressed! So many officer-dandies in their nice new service jackets! New cafés and restaurants are opening all the time. And the posters! Theaters, cabarets, concerts! God, it's so good that ordinary life is starting up again! War was a disease. And now the whole world has recovered. Russia, too, is recovering.

On the corner of Sadovaya and Taganrogsky, as always, there was a crowd in front of a huge window with a map. The tricolors creep higher and higher with each passing day. People come to look at the life of the fat yellow string. And they discuss everything so animatedly, all the strategists! The string has only a little farther to go and the war will be over! I'll see Masha, Katya, and Nyusya again!

I stopped in at the hotel where OSVAG is headquartered. There, some pompous general, the former director of a privileged educational institution, was explaining to all comers the picture of military actions. He would shift the little flags on a map and raise his arms, and the worn elbows of his gray double-breasted jacket would shine. Just like *The Three Sisters:* Moscow! To Moscow! To Moscow!

I bumped into Zhuzhu. She has a job there and takes OSVAG publications home for proofreading. She's flourishing. Wearing a green georgette dress. She never did have good taste. Really, why do blondes persist in wanting to wear that shrill green? It doesn't suit her at all. She's very proud of herself and boasts that she receives sugar, flour, and firewood from the warehouse and even liquor from Abrau-Durso! They wouldn't let me speak; the soldiers were shifting their heavy bundles of literature, and Zhuzhu was in a hurry. She said she had a job in the department with Professor Grimm and that if I wanted she would put in a good word for me. She clicked her heels up the very broad staircase going toward the sound of typewriters.

My goodness! I have nowhere to go now without Zhuzhu's protection!

If I wanted . . .

But I don't!

I know what I want. And everything is going to be the way I want it!

I saw on a poster that Emelyanova and Monakhov are coming! When I get my money, I'm going to buy the very best tickets!

1 August 1919. Thursday

Yesterday was so nice! And today, since morning, I've felt as though I've fallen into a black hole. I walked past the Soleil poster—with my name—and felt nothing but fear.

It's in front of people that I'm brave, while all my fears and tears are relegated to these pages. I'm afraid of failing, afraid I won't be able to sing well, that the hall will be empty. Afraid of everything. Most of all, afraid that everyone is lying to my face! They tell lies because they feel sorry for me! What if in fact I have neither a voice nor talent?

Last night I had the same gnat nightmare! Over and over again!

I can't do anything! I got it in my head that I was a singer—and have had my comeuppance. Yes, my comeuppance! Just what I deserve!

Everything I'd like to forget is exactly what gets into my head at night. I close my eyes and again I'm on stage at the former Merchants

Club. They announce me, I come out, I can't see anything, and I start singing my favorite song, from Plevitskaya's repertoire: "Above the field, the fields so pure"—and again this horror! I choked! A gnat landed in my throat!

There's a debut for you! If my braid were longer I'd hang myself from it!

I've written this to be free of it, to forget it.

Everyone is talking about the arrival of the Kachalov troupe from the Moscow Art Theater! Vertinsky was just here, and now we have Moscow Art coming! I'll see them all! Kachalov, Germanova, Knipper!

I bought a collection of Vertinsky's songs. My God, what a genius he is! I can see the poor legless girl among the graves asking for a spring gift from dear sweet God—two good legs—and the violet frock coat of the negro handing her her fur coat, and that madwoman kissing the blue lips of the fallen cadets.

It's so nice that we spare the money then and bought a ticket at the Mahsonkov in the third row—eighty-five rubles! In the first they cost a full hundred!

They could have used a bigger typeface.

How very vain I must be. Phoo!

Tomorrow I'm meeting with Pavel. It's our last day.

2 August 1919. Friday

Bad news. I immediately sensed that something had happened to Pavel. We met as usual under the Asmolov awning and then went to the Empire. Everything is returning to normal. Servants in tailcoats and starched linen, clean-shaven, smelling of cologne. Beautiful dresses on the women. Beautiful music. True, the musicians, Jews, have turned into blonds with the help of peroxide. Some visiting number sang horribly. Roza Chernaya! Her name says it all! Black! And they threw her flowers! They understand nothing! They just care about a cute face!

Pavel was silent the whole time. Then he said, "Let's get out of here! I can't stand this whole audience!" And I so wanted to sit a little longer! Again I said nothing. I rose obediently and left. We walked past the map on Sadovaya. I said to him, "I hope to God it's all over soon!" And he turned on me. "Nothing is over!" He started swearing at OSVAG, that they were hiding everything, and if anyone started saying what was really happening, he was immediately counted a Red agent. "Meanwhile, counterintelligence is full of robbers, thieves, and scoundrels. An honest person wouldn't go there! People are fighting for position and power, there's theft and bribery everywhere, and everyone is silent, trembling for their own skin!"

I realized something had happened to him. I began questioning him. At first he wouldn't say anything, and then he said he'd had some trouble at OSVAG. He had learned of one incident and had wanted them to print something in the newspapers, but they called him and threatened him to get him to be quiet. Trains coming from Novorossiisk were carrying goods for speculators rather than shells, clothing, and provisions for the front. At the same time, the front was receiving nothing from the rear but OSVAG woodcuts depicting the Kremlin and various knights. There weren't enough shells, but the commandant and his associates transported textiles, perfume, silk stockings, and gloves, attaching to this train one car with military freight and simply placing a crate of shrapnel in each car, thanks to which the train was allowed through unimpeded as military.

We walked for a long time. Pavel was very angry at our allies. They couldn't care less about us, in fact. They sent uniforms for either dwarves or giants. A few carloads of boots came with only lefts! They sent bamboo lances, machine-guns without cartridges and a belt our cartridges don't fit, and some cannons from the Boer war. I thought it was funny that the English had sent mules that never made it to the front, having been turned into shashlyk en route, but Pavel got angry at me.

Next week he has another trip.

When we walked past his laboratory, he said that old Meyerson, whose son had gone off with the Reds, was always coming by. He would come, look silently at his studio, and leave.

Pavel seemed more upset over some old man than me.

Again I couldn't bring myself to open our most important conversation. My heart sank. How could I tell him everything now? What would happen to him? How would he go to the front with this in his heart? No, we'll clear things up when he returns.

3 August 1919. Saturday

What a long day! Here is what happened.

Another evening at the Nikitinins'. I wish we hadn't gone!

I couldn't control myself with Pavel from the very outset. He came by for me when I was still dressing. He tried to hurry me. This simply enraged me! He doesn't care how I look! Just so he can start deciding the fate of the world as soon as possible! I told him the fate of the world would wait! A good entrance is necessary not only on stage, therefore we would be as late as necessary! He sulked. That's how we showed up, angry at each other. On the other hand, when we walked in, all eyes were on me!

Only what was the point? It never occurred to anyone to ask me to sing anything!

Chirikov wasn't there. Trofimov wasn't there. On the other hand, Boris Lazarevsky was! I have his book of stories. I remember how much I liked them, but Papa told me then, "Why write the way Lazarevsky writes if Chekhov already did?" Krivoshein from the *Great Russia* editorial office, which just moved here from Ekaterinodar, was there, too. But we know his kind! Bald, fat, stinks of sweat for a verst around, and immediately poking around with double entendres. That professor was there again, by the name of Ladyzhnikov. And once again Mirtova spent the whole evening showing off! Why invite people like that? I don't understand. There were also some gray scholar-mice. I don't remember their names.

Nikitin didn't recite and apologized, saying it wasn't ready yet. I was looking at Evdoxia Fyodorovna. Here is the moment! But she went to her professor and asked him please to tell us something interesting! And it began! A real circus!

Nikitin and Ladyzhnikov grappled. Oh, how they grappled! The sparks flew! Like two cocks over a hen!

Ladyzhnikov started saying that the Volunteer Army was no better than the Reds. "They're Temernik but so are we, only as children we were washed and cleaned and taught French, but at the first convenient chance we will degenerate and become just like they are! We already have! Power in Russia is held onto by the teeth, and the moment the tsar unclenched his teeth everything fell apart! The stronger the teeth, the more the Russian people give their permission: Eat us! Or else we'll eat you! And here we have the white knights of counterintelligence fighting evil, and we're carrying out executions in the same woods where they executed us!" He also said that we were going to lose this war anyway, even if we won it, because we've become just like those whom we were fighting. He banged his fist on the table so hard the vase nearly flew off, and he roared, "Good must lose out to evil. Therein lies its strength!"

And on and on in that vein, moreover no one was listening to anyone! Nikitin: "They're forcing us to shout hurrah when we should be shouting for help! Reports are coming into OSVAG from everywhere about how the mobilization has failed, the peasants are taking up arms and going into the forest, and they're filing them away!" He pounced on the Volunteer Army leadership. "The front is ragged, barefoot, and naked, while they sit here in their foppish tailcoats drinking champagne. Some shout about the speedy capture of Moscow and steal, while others have nothing but their conscience and lice, and they're going to their death! For what? Russia? What Russia? This one? Is it worth it?"

And the river began to flow: fatherland, duty, mission, holy sacrifices, the people! True, someone said quite handsomely that you don't lay out solitaire in a burning house.

I listened to all this and I felt like shouting, too: Lord, what mission? What duty? What people? People just want to live, rejoice, fall in love!

Lazarevsky tried to make peace between them and shifted the conversation to the calendar, saying it made no sense to abolish the Gregorian calendar introduced by the Bolsheviks. Really, how was the calendar to blame? He also said something amazing: "They wanted to cut thirteen days out of the calendar, but they tore a hole in time!" That is so true! We are at a hole in time. But no one was going to listen to him and they went on shouting. Lazarevsky pouted that no one was listening to him. He sat there for another half-hour and left.

Every once in a while poor Pavel tried to insert something about his Russian idea. He never did understand that the point for the debaters was the hostess, not the idea! How was he to understand such simple things! He only understands complicated ones.

There was shouting over tea, too. They started talking about tyranny and brutalities and about how the spirit of voluntarism had been driven out long ago. Nikitin on the Volunteer Army: "It rose up in martyr-like holiness and fell in disgrace, as does everything in Russia." And again it went round: the slogans were false, trust had been trampled, deeds spat upon! I listened and it seemed as though everyone was turning the handle on the same barrel organ! How tedious it is!

Toward the end of supper, when everyone had eaten their fill and was tired of arguing, a conversation began about chivalry. Ladyzhnikov said that we had never had chivalry, but we had had the virtue of humility, obedience, and dissolution in the mass: "The knight is always a solitary, a hostage of honor, not of the fatherland and tsar." Nikitin objected that it was in Russia that there was true chivalry because at chivalry's base lies the concept of duty. "Some have the beautiful lady; we have Russia. Their knights 'betrothed' their life to some unwashed fool wearing a chastity belt, whereas ours did to the people, the homeland! Isn't that genuine chivalry?"

Pavel managed during the pause, while the debaters were sipping their tea, to interject that there were only two chivalries in Russian history: the Oprichniki under Ivan the Terrible, and Pavel's short-lived command over the Maltans. Ladyzhnikov replied in a condescending tone. "I dare remind you, young man, that since 1894 duels have been permitted in the Russian army, and that speaks to something! Actually, I think this was before your time." I kicked Pavel under the table, to be quiet, because I could tell he was about to blaze up and say something he shouldn't. After this we left quickly. A spoiled evening.

Pavel saw me home, laying straight into OSVAG! "Conceited fools" and "hacks with an overly high opinion of themselves"! He especially could not forgive them this: "They receive huge sums from OSVAG and spend them on publishing their little poems! There it is, the Russian intelligentsia in all its glory!"

We walked past the Mashonkin theater. There are cafés, restaurants, cabarets, light, and music everywhere, people singing, laughing, and dancing! Suddenly I so wanted to dance! To cast off all these conversations! I pulled him. "Let's go, dear Pavel, please!" But he replied, "Right now I'm reading *The History of the Crusades*. A striking resemblance! A combination of idealism and animal egoism, and here we have the same thing. At the front ecstatic idiots are sacrificing themselves, while the smart ones are trying to wriggle out and flee to the rear, where there is a bacchanalia, a feast during the plague!"

I had been patient all evening, but at this I exploded! I grabbed him by the ears and shouted straight into his face. "Pavel, wake up! We're not in a book. We're here and now!" But he said, "Let me go, it hurts! I have to leave early tomorrow. I'm very tired and I want to go to bed." I turned and walked away. I couldn't go on like that! He straggled behind me like a dog on a leash. I told him, "Go away! Leave me alone! I can't look at you!" But he kept walking anyway. And so we walked all the way to Nikitinskaya. All of a sudden I began to hate myself. How could I let him go tomorrow like that? What if something happened to him? I ran up and embraced him.

When we parted he suddenly asked, "Will you wait for me?" Why did he ask that? Is he afraid I'll abandon him and not wait?

I will wait. And I'll tell him everything when he returns.

4 August 1919. Sunday

Today was the first performance at the Soleil. After the moving picture they raised the screen. I came out on stage and immediately realized I was wearing the wrong dress. I needed something dark, black or bordeaux. There was a strong light on me, and I couldn't see anything. I was blinded. This didn't happen in rehearsal! Suddenly I lost my presence of mind and didn't know how to move in this light or what to do with my hands. Right then I felt myself breaking out in spots, I was so agitated! It's a good thing I didn't fall off the stage! I had to sing to some one face in the hall, but there was a black pit. My throat closed and I started forcing my vocal cords. It was good I only sang three love songs. I couldn't have done a fourth. While the balalaika player was doing his number, I began to breathe the way Koltsova-Selyanskaya had taught me, to calm my nerves: three short, quick inhales and one long, deep one. And all the while counting my breaths silently. Rogachev, the good soul, supported me. He came up and whispered that I had sung marvelously! Then came our "Don Juan in Love." I was calmer now. Torshin said, "Look at me. Lock eyes with me. Everything will be fine!" And it was. The audience was falling about with laughter. Torshin is a comic genius!

Afterward they brought the screen down again and other viewers came. A full hall every time! We waited for the next show and watched the picture from behind the screen, inside out. I even learned to read the titles the wrong way around. Each time I took off my shoes, my only performing shoes, with high heels, to give my feet a rest. After that everything went well. I was dreadfully tired for want of habit. We got our money and were going to go out carousing, but I had no strength whatsoever.

Now I'm too tired to fall asleep. Overwrought. I close my eyes and once again I'm on stage with applause all around. And I bow to the pillow!

5 August 1919. Monday

I must write down this whole horror.

Tala has returned and is staying with us. She is a terrible sight. And then there are the lice. Mama and I took her to Katya's empty room, spread paper on the floor, brought a basin of hot water, washed her, and changed her clothes. We wrapped her clothes in the paper from the floor and burned everything.

Their field hospital fell to Makhno's men, or rather, his band was retreating and came upon their infirmary. They impaled the wounded officers with their bayonets. They led the medic away for retribution, and he asked them not to touch his wife because she was expecting. Someone said, "We'll see about that right now!" And he disemboweled her with his bayonet. Then they tortured the medic. Tala had potassium cyanide, which had been given out to the nurses for just such an instance. She carried the poison in an amulet on the chain with her cross. She wanted to take it but couldn't. They raped her. Then their commander came and took her for himself. But that night he helped her flee.

Tala recounted this calmly, then suddenly fell silent, as if she had collapsed into herself. We went to sleep under the same blanket and I warmed her icy feet. That night Tala had hysterics.

6 August 1919. Transfiguration

Tala told us something else as well.

Seryozha Starovsky died very foolishly and terribly, right on the hospital train. He was standing in the door of the heated car with his head poking out. At that moment switching was under way at the station. They gave his car a shove, the doors closed, and his neck was crushed.

Tala played the jaws or the drums during operations, as she put it, that is, she opened the drum of sterile material or held the jaw of a patient under anesthesia. She told us that holding jaws during trepanation was agony, especially if the head was on its side. Your fingers went numb, and how do you hold on when the surgeon starts chiseling? And their doctor shouted at her, too, if the head shook or if the nurse passed the wrong instrument! One time they'd been operating for days without a break, but they requested a report from her about how many men had been bandaged; remembering their number was impossible, so Tala set up one tin with peas and another empty one, and with each bandaging she moved a pea and later counted them all up.

They called for volunteers to execute Red prisoners. They shouted, "Anyone for retribution?" At first very few did, but later there were more and more. They finished them off with their rifle butts. But before the execution they made sure to torture them. There was no point trying to defend them. Tala did, but a volunteer, no longer young, told her, "This is for my daughter."

There was typhus everywhere, it just hadn't reached Rostov yet. They should expect it soon. Train cars full of sick people had to be locked for the night. In their insensible state, the sick would run away and roam through the station, some dressed, some in just their linen. Silovarzin is the only thing that helps. An immediate infusion halts the disease, but at the same time it destroys your immunity and you can get reinfected.

There is so much to write down every day, but my nerves and strength have run out.

The war is going on, and I'm singing. But I can't bandage up the wounded like Tala. I can, of course. But so can hundreds of other young women. Let the daring and decisive ones do it, not those like me. No, I'm daring and decisive, too. And I want to sing. It's not my fault that my youth came in time of war! I won't get another youth! And I'm convinced that singing when all around is hatred and death is no less important. Maybe even more important.

This is what I believe: If somewhere on earth the wounded are finished off with rifle butts, that means somewhere else people have to be singing and rejoicing in life! The more death there is around, the more important to counter it with life, love, and beauty!

7 August 1919. Wednesday

Today we were nearly blown to kingdom come. Through the fence, old man Zhirov saw the Pankov boys playing with English gunpowder. It looks like macaroni—long and hollow, only brown. Zhirov said that these macaronis get put into shells and possess the following property: if the air is compressed and there is pressure, this kind of gunpowder immediately ignites and fires, but if you just light it, it burns up and there's no explosion.

8 August 1919. Thursday

Today I spent the evening with Papa. It's been a hundred years since he and I talked the way we used to. I asked him about Elena Olegovna. He said he'd loved this woman for a long time, but he and Mama had agreed to preserve the appearance of marriage for our sake, until we grew up. He had come to collect the rest of his papers. I helped him gather his things.

He complained about the impossible conditions at the infirmary. The wounded are capricious and take liberties. They bring wine into the infirmary, stagger through town until the dead of night belting out songs, and there's no keeping them in check. What can a duty nurse do if even she is scared to death of them? There are no medicines, surgery patients don't have their bandages changed for days due to the shortage of bandaging material, and operations are put off from one day to the next. There is one needle for the entire department! The toilets are befouled, there are so few cots that the wounded are lying right on boards and on the floor, covered with their own rags. Poor Papa, he worries so and can't do anything! It's good that a widespread typhus epidemic hasn't broken out yet in the city, but it's expected. Everything's been stolen. The nurses themselves steal, taking everything they can carry, and go to the villages. Only the department heads remain. Papa got the mayor to announce a charitable collection and to print a decree in the newspapers for everyone to donate linen for the hospital. They did—and the laundries switched out the linen: instead of linen, the hospital got back rags. People steal and drink the alcohol, despite the smell of carbolic acid, which is added especially so it won't be used for drinking!

Worst of all is the department for the insane. Everyone's forgotten all about them.

They promise money but don't give it, and Papa feeds himself on his main specialty. He jokes bitterly, "Gonococci don't care which regime is at the door."

Everyone has been brutalized, even the staff. Papa told me about a terrible instance. A wounded Bolshevik nurse lay in the surgical department. The head nurse was Maria Mikhailovna Andreyeva. I remember her very well. She used to visit us. Her son was studying in the cadet corps and was tortured by Red Cossacks. This woman's wounds were rotting, but they didn't bandage her at all. Maria Mikhailovna wouldn't let them. She said, "A dog's death for a dog."

9 August 1919. Friday

My success at Soleil is already having its effect! Today I was invited to sing at the Mosaic!

Torshin has promised to arrange a performance at the Grotesque! He's already spoken with Alexeyev. Actors from Kiev's One-Eyed Jimmy will be performing there. I will be on the same stage with Vladislavsky, Kurikhin, Khenkin, and Buchinskaya!

As it is, I've already sung at the Divertissement and the Yacht. Right now the Soleil. And now there'll be the Mosaic! And the Bouffe on Sennaya has finally opened! There was a total rout there after all the rallies. I stopped by to take a peek and didn't recognize it! The hall's elegant decoration, the agreeable boxes, the electrical fixtures! And I'm going to sing there! Yes, I am! The Asmolov stage will be mine! And the Mashonkin! And the Nakhichevan! All the stages—mine! Wait and see!

I've reread this and even I find it funny. Exactly like some Khlestakov.

But I want it so much!

10 August 1919. Saturday

Mama and I went to Sasha's requiem. He's been gone a year.

Mama has become so lost lately. I feel so sorry for her!

We came home and remembered our Sasha. Mama took a sip, and so did I.

We remembered all kinds of things. As if it had all been in some-one else's life. We remembered how Sasha once ran into the room shouting, "What, you don't know anything?" Everyone got scared and Mama clutched her heart. It turned out the neighbor's dog had given birth the night before. I can picture it as if it were now. Mama walking to the sideboard where her phial of laurel water was kept and Katya and Masha and I laughing and running to look at the puppies. Later that day we found out the war had begun.

Mama has Avvakum lying on her nightstand all the time now. She keeps repeating, "The time for suffering is upon us. It behooveth you to suffer mightily." Today she said she'd read those words once and they'd stuck in her memory, but she hadn't understood. "And now it's all so simple. Punishment is meted out not for sins, not at all, but for happiness. Everything has its price: sorrow for happiness; birth for love; death for birth."

We recalled that entire horror we lived through last February when Sasha hid out for a few days at the Bratsk cemetery with some other students from General Borovsky's Student Regiment who hadn't left with Kornilov. The unlucky boys took shelter in the crypts. The freezing cold nights! One night, one of them made his way to town and let his parents know, and so the news reached us, down the chain. I went to see him and brought warm clothing and food. It was dangerous to walk with bundles, so I bundled up as much linen as I could and tried to crawl through a hole in the fence so as to avoid being noticed near the main gates. There were many officers hiding there, in the remote crypts. Sasha said one lost his mind and started singing—and they smothered him so he wouldn't give them away with his shouts. Through Dr. Kopia, whose husband had left with the volunteers, Papa obtained documents, so that night Sasha and a few of his buddies were able to leave. Then someone informed, there was a roundup at the cemetery, and those left behind, whoever was found, were all shot.

There were searches going on everywhere. We burned many papers out of fear, over Sasha—and my diary perished.

Mama collected all our gold things and buried them in a tin box—and later we never could find them. Someone had probably been spying and dug them up. For fear of requisitioning, Papa—he still lived here then—dismantled Sasha's nice new bicycle and stashed the parts in different corners of the apartment. I remember how proud Sasha was of his Dux. Before buying it he and Papa kept arguing over which was better, our Dux or a foreign Triumph or Gladiator.

Then Mama and I recalled the search when they burst in so drunk and nasty. "What do you know about your son?" And the nightmare began, with the ripping of wallpaper and breaking of floorboards. They also demanded tea, so we had to heat water for them. Before that I had heard about searches from Tosya Gorodisskaya, whose brother Petya had joined the Ice March and perished somewhere in the Kuban. When Tosya told her story, grinding her teeth, about what they took and how, I could only wonder at her attachment to things. Her father was a rich stockbroker. You could live without Persian rugs and silver, after all! What misfortune was it if people who worked by the sweat of their brow and had nothing took land, or a house, or furniture that they had earned with their whole life and which had, in essence, been stolen from them! Tosya's father hadn't exactly earned his mansions of stone through righteous labor! They themselves should have shared or done something for others. After all, it's shameful to live richly in a poor country and at the same time boast of your wealth! Retribution—it serves them right. The brilliant Blok explained it all in his poem! Only when they came to our place did I understand that it was not a matter of things or their value. Mama began imploring them, crying, when they started collecting everything that caught their eye, and I realized that it was a matter of human dignity. Better to stand there and say nothing! Papa saved us all. The search ended when they locked themselves in with him in his study and he examined them all. Leaving, they even thanked him. "Thank you, doctor!"

Those bicycle parts are still lying all over the house, just the way they were hidden then. And Sasha will never reassemble them.

11 August 1919. Sunday

I saw Zabugsky in the first row. The old man's quite off his rocker and gone to seed. Dirty and crumpled, but he was waiting for me with a bouquet of flowers. Poor Evgeny Alexandrovich! How can I forget the queer way he acted then? I'm drowning during his exam, and Zabugsky is constantly walking by. How can anyone copy anything! I make stealthy imploring signals to Lyalya to send me her crib, when all of a sudden Zabugsky imperceptibly places a neatly folded page on my desk. I unfold it and it's his handwriting! All the solutions, all the answers! After the exam he asked me to stop in at the mathematics room and made a declaration of love and proposed! I don't know whether to laugh or cry!

How pathetic he is! And how blind am I? I didn't see a thing! When he was pacing around the classroom and stopping at my desk, breathing straight down my neck, I always thought he could barely keep himself from grabbing my braid and tearing it off. But he probably wanted to touch and stroke it.

My admirers! First-class! You don't know where to hide!

Take that nameless boy, my silent, crimson admirer! He's been on the watch for me for a month but he's afraid to approach. I so want to lure him with a candy and give him a good spanking so he studies his lessons and doesn't waste his time on foolishness!

Or the dentist with his masterpiece: you open your mouth, and not a single filling!

And Goryayev! I did like him, I really did! Until the moment he and I ran into each other when I stopped by to see Papa. He was sitting there waiting for an appointment! He saw me and turned green. What does he have? Syphilis? Gonorrhea? That's it for love.

I know I can make people like me. I am constantly feeling those hungry, avid gazes on me.

But is that really what I want?

At night I weep and die, but in the morning I arise bold and strong once again. And then the night and fear once again. I cannot be alone. All of a sudden I start choking with longing, such a thirst for love, tenderness, and attention that I think I'll marry the first man I meet who asks me tenderly!

Sometimes, very rarely, I dream of dear Alyosha. And once again I'm a schoolgirl and all I have is this love. These are my purest, saddest, and brightest dreams. Afterward I go around like a sleepwalker, detached from life. All men disgust me, no matter who is by my side. This has to be a disease. The disease of love cut short by death. I will probably ache like this for Alyosha my whole life.

And then there's Pavel, too!

It's so good that Alyosha can't see this.

What if he does?

12 August 1919. Monday

Next week Pavel will return.

When I think of him my heart sinks from a strange sensation of guilt, longing, loneliness, and boredom that I cannot describe!

How can he be cured of this unnecessary love? Nonsense! There is no such thing as unnecessary love. But what can I do? I want happiness for him, yet I torment him.

Why do I torment him? Because I feel so bad myself.

Sometimes Pavel seems like my closest friend. I so want to nestle up to him, bury my face in his chest. But sometimes it's just the opposite and I feel that everything is wrong, that he is someone alien and incomprehensible to me.

Mama says, "Why are you torturing Pavel? Marry him!" He proposed the old-fashioned way, coming to see my father and speaking with Mama. As if they, not I, were deciding my fate.

Marry! I must marry someone. Must I? Why must I?

His infatuation stunned me. I was drunk with ecstasy. Love is infectious.

I know I will love just one man, but not this one man!

How long can I stand this? And if we part, what will become of me?

All these thoughts make me feel so awkward and empty inside.

And if not? If I don't love him at all? Why am I holding on to him? What am I saying, holding on—I've got him tooth and claw!

I'll be strong. I'll be cold. I'll tell him, Pavel, I love you very much, but love isn't everything.

No, that's wrong.

I must be direct. You don't like the fact that I want to perform, that I want to be the center of attention, that people admire me and pay me compliments, that I have admirers, but this is inevitable if you go on stage. What is the stage for, after all? To give your love not to one man but to many and to let the whole world fall in love with you! And this hurts you! Or rather, this flatters your vanity, but even more it scratches your self-possession. Yes, I like that they show me signs of attention, that they love me, but that is what life was given for, for me to be loved! On the contrary, what woman wouldn't be insulted if someone ignored her? I made you fall in love with me! Do you understand what happened? I made you love me, and now I don't know what to do with your love!

No, that's all wrong. I'll say this: we're very different. You're a very fine person, Pavel, good, courageous, and strong. But you have a heavy soul. You don't seem to know how to laugh at all. Whereas I'm lighthearted! I want to laugh and delight in everything, all the beautiful things in the world! Here Papa gave me a new silk blouse with real Brussels lace. It feels so good to put on over my bare skin! And you, do you have any idea of how to take pleasure in life? Remember, Pavel, you said, how can you sing and have fun when times are such and there is so much pain and misfortune, so much evil around! But I believe that if beauty and love do not suit the times, then you have to be beautiful and to love to spite the times!

He will ask, "What are you talking about?" As always, he won't understand me.

You see just yourself! For example, take the photograph, Pavel. If you want to be on view, on the stage, it's very important to have good photographs. I kept waiting for you to take my picture and make a beautiful portrait. After all, it's so important for me! But you never guessed until I asked. You apologized and cursed yourself for being a blockhead. You did it, but unsuccessfully. And you had no time to do it over. And I'm not going to ask you about it again.

You have more important things than me. And so I have been left without a good photograph.

No, I won't say anything about the photograph. I have to speak simply and without any explanations. He's not going to understand anything anyway. If I marry you, it would be a mistake, a painful one for us both.

Can I tell him all that? I don't know.

I think very well of him, and I feel sorry for him. I feel sorry for his feelings for me. Strong and courageous, he becomes defenseless and pathetic in love. And jealous. And touchy. Love and pity are opposite poles. This means I definitely do not love him.

Why don't I make this clear to him? Because I know I would be hurting him badly. Love is easy to give and hard to take away.

Pavel, the whole problem is that you need a wife who will create a home, comfort, warmth. All that is very important for me, too, and I too want to give that to someone! But besides that there is something else in my life, without which a home, and comfort, and all the rest lose all meaning! I can't imagine my life without the stage. I have experienced an amazing sensation that cannot be conveyed in words. I tried to explain those feelings to you, and you disdainfully called it theatrical ecstasy! You simply can't understand those moments when you feel like the mistress of the world, when it's no longer me singing, it's someone singing through me! I have to experience this over and over again. Otherwise I won't survive! Therefore I must be prepared for many, many sacrifices.

Nonsense. I can't tell him anything! All I can say is this: Pavel, you can make a woman happy. But not a woman like me.

13 August 1919. Tuesday

Dear, sweet Pavel, good Pavel, forgive me all this foolishness. I love you very very much! Only come back soon!

14 August 1919. Wednesday

I saw Zhuzhu. She's having an affair with an Englishman from the mission. "He's so unusual!" She's already forgotten her Wolf. He was "so unusual!" too. It's amazing how nobody even thinks about the Germans anymore! They went and amiably forgot. As if nothing had happened. The memory compliantly wipes away everything shameful! Yes, we fought, but when the German helmets arrived on the streets of Rostov, they weren't our enemies, they were practically liberators! How everything was transformed in a moment! Just before that people had dressed a little poorer, tried to efface themselves, appear inconspicuous, but then, overnight, they pulled out their best silks and jewels and the ladies went right home and put on hats! The men, ties, starched linen, gaiters. The shop windows suddenly shone, behind them were actual goods, colonial products, fabrics, shoes, watches! This after all the requisitions? Where did it come from? Everyone had just been hunting for food, and all of a sudden food was hunting for their wallets. The Germans banned selling and nibbling sunflower seeds—and the seeds were gone, whereas before, that was the only thing being sold! It was quite shameful to see everyone rejoicing at the Germans! Calm and order right away. All of a sudden janitors appeared out of somewhere and started assiduously sweeping the streets and sidewalks, which hadn't been swept in God knows how long. The thefts, murders, searches, and requisitions—cut short. How shameful and humiliating, that only the Germans could give the Russians order and liberation!

I still don't understand all this, since it turns out that we fought the Germans for order and sufficiency in our own country but were only able to get it when the Germans beat us. And what happened with the railroad! Overnight the train cars and stations were divided into classes, the trains ran on schedule, and there was order such as before the revolution! All of a sudden signposts appeared at intersections with precise indications of directions and distances—the way to the train station, to town, to the commandant's office—except in minutes: "10 minutes' walk." The municipal telephone started working immediately, and they gave us electricity so we didn't have to sit beside candles in half-dark rooms in the evenings. It is simply stunning the joy with which everyone is ready to accept the order— the German order, with the German flag waving over the city—and are incapable of doing anything for themselves! And how everyone rejoiced that they started playing German music in concerts that hadn't been played in a long time—Wagner! Though Wagner does make sense. But how are we to explain all the rest of it?

German officers have started coming to see Papa for treatment. I remember the bitterness with which he said then that Russia wasn't great at all but just a very large country of slaves, that it should be a German colony, and that if the Germans leave we'll all slaughter one another, bite each other's heads off.

Now the Germans are gone.

15 August 1919. Thursday. Assumption

Everyone around me has turned into an animal.

Today I saw a man hanged. People said it was someone named Afanasiev, a Red agitator. On Vokzalnaya Square. I had gone out for kerosene, and a large crowd had gathered there. They stood silently, pressed up close to one another. The peasant women were sobbing. They were leading him, pushing him in the back with their rifle butts. Twenty-five years old. Led to a tree. They didn't even build a gallows. Why should they when there are trees? One soldier slipped the noose over his head, took aim, and threw the rope over a heavy branch. The first time he missed. He gave it a few tries. The fellow was standing there looking straight ahead with his eyes wide open. He was about to shout something more but didn't manage to.

I came home barely alive. I opened Nikitina's little book. "Clouds twisting, streams spilling, windows ringing. Raindrops dropping—is this, isn't this how my life has passed?" Lord, what nonsense! "Dew of Dawn." "To enchanting Isabel." I flung it in the corner.

Why Isabel? What kind of Isabel am I to her? Everyone puts on airs on purpose, as if they were somebody. It's vile. And I am just the same. I won't go to see them anymore.

I think of Pavel constantly. How is he? And where? I'm so afraid for him. I can't do this anymore.

16 August 1919. Friday

Musya stopped by. Rivers of tears again. "What's wrong? Did he kill himself?" "No." "So why are you howling?" "He doesn't love me anymore!" "That's just fine!" "But now I love him!"

17 August 1919 Saturday

Pavel is back. Intact and unharmed, thank God. He just dropped by for a minute and said that Bredov's volunteers would take Kiev today or tomorrow. He was rushing to his laboratory. Haggard, unshaven, wearing a dirty greatcoat with golden spots, from dung.

I'm finishing this up tonight. I was just with him. He looks very bad. Again he's seen more than his fill of it all. He told me about riding with the gunners across a field where there had been battle and there were a lot of dead bodies. It was hard to get the weapons through without crushing someone. The Reds had fled or surrendered, but the Cossacks had slaughtered them. Drivers tried to run their wheel over a head so that it would split like a melon. Pavel started cursing them but they swore they'd done it by accident, and guffawed. He climbed down and walked off so as not to hear heads cracking under the wheel and their guffawing. "Some of the dead were twitching convulsively. They might still have been alive. And you know what I realized? I realized I hate everyone!"

We were standing in the red-tinted dimness. He was diluting his solutions, and I was stroking his back and head. He seemed to have a fever. I took fright. What if it was typhus? He began reassuring me it was a common cold. But I'm sick at heart.

Again I said nothing.

18 August 1919. Sunday

Today a full day at the Soleil. I made my way home just now dead on my feet, dog-tired. I want to write just a few words.

Torshin and I had finished the fourth *divertissement* and gone outside to relax, and who should show up all of a sudden? My Nina Nikolaevna! Utterly enraged, like a Fury. I hadn't noticed her in the audience. She said in a dissatisfied tone, "What were you acting?" "What do you mean, what? 'Hungry Don Juan.' A student is declaring his love to his flame but thinking about food." At this Nina Nikolaevna blew up. "No, that wasn't what you acted at all! All I saw was that you were hot and wanted to rattle off your part as quickly as possible and leave!" I implored her, "Nina Nikolaevna, please, this is the fourth show of the day!" She pounced on me. "What does the viewer care? You don't ask the hairdresser how many people he's served today or whether he's tired!" She went over the whole scene with us again and only then let us go to act it the fifth time.

Here is yet another unsent card.

It is the kind of card that fishing boats climb into from the rain, as if through a window.

The house was right on the shore of the small harbor at Massa Lubrense. In good weather you could see Capri on the left and Vesuvius on the right.

That day there had been no Capri or Vesuvius since morning, and there was nothing to do but take a walk under an umbrella or read. Isolde had gone for a walk with their son, and the interpreter had dragged out of the trunk the Migro paper bags with the two stacks of books he'd borrowed from the Slavic seminar library before leaving.

Through the kitchen window he could see how small the woman and child on the shore were and how big the surf's paws.

The interpreter wiped speckles off the cover of the top book, which was the lives of Russian saints, and started leafing through it. He came across the hagiography of Anthony the Roman and was drawn into the story of the Italian who became a Novgorod miracle worker.

"Saint Anthony was born in Rome in 1067 of wealthy parents and was raised by them in piety. He lost his father and mother early on, and after handing out his entire inheritance to the poor, began wandering in search of a righteous life but everywhere found only hypocrisy, debauchery, and injustice. He looked for love and could not find it."

The woman and child got smaller and smaller, as small as a drop on glass.

"One day he was lying on the ground, amid the flowers, and watching the white cross on the red petunias summoning a column of ants to storm their ant Jerusalem. Hearing the chiming of the hour, Anthony shuddered—and half a life had passed. So God can coagulate into any object, or creature, or the sound of a bell—like milk into curd.

"And then, despairing and grieving in his heart," the "Lives" author went on, "Anthony went out of the city. He walked without turning around, day and night, until he reached the sea's shore. That was as far as he could go, so he climbed onto a boulder that jutted out of the water. He stood on that boulder for an entire day with his back turned to the city he had left, gazing out to sea. Then night fell, but he still did not come down off the boulder or turn around. And so he stood for yet another day and yet another night. And a week. And two weeks. And a month. And then the boulder suddenly separated from shore and sailed away."

The legend drove Anthony and the boulder on the current and around Europe and cast them directly on the banks of the Volkhov.

Actually, then the life became banal, with the miracles of healing and incorruptible relics that disappeared along with a silver shrine in 1933. All that remained was the branch of sedge Anthony had brought with him from Rome, holding it in his hand.

Then Isolde came back and said that she and their son were leaving tomorrow because she couldn't go on living like this.

Isolde and the interpreter had decided to come to exactly this place for vacation in order to try to save their family.

But really, there was no more family. They just lived in the same apartment, growing more and more bitter. Isolde put the child to sleep every night between them. The interpreter's mama had done that once, taking him with her on the sofa in the basement at Staro-koniushenny, so that the child, who was supposed to bring them together, could serve as a barrier, a wall, a border.

They had decided to come here, to Massa Lubrense, specifically because it was here that they had spent their vacation a few years before this rain.

Everything had been different then. On the left, every day, you could see Capri and on the right Vesuvius. Fishing boats climbed through the bedroom window. Every night local fishermen went to sea and in the morning brought back fresh fish and *frutti di mare*, which frightened their son because they were alive and squirming.

The sea rocked slightly, hanging on the horizon like a laundry line.

Sometimes it rained, but brief, hot rains, after which everything sparkled and steamed. One day their son was digging in a flowerbed, wet after a downpour, and suddenly said that the rain worms were the earth's guts.

They swam every day. Sometimes foam and dirt washed up and there were seaweed and melon rinds all around, but if you swam out a little ways something entirely different began. There, transparency resided in water and sky, and you could see the wind on shore stirring up the grapevines and the church's gold acorn glittering in the sun.

The interpreter and Isolde had dinner in a restaurant at the shore where the child sucked up his long spaghettis every night. He was so tired after his day that he fell asleep right there in the restaurant, in the kiddie chair attached to the table, and for a long time they sat there and drank Lacrima Christi wine, from the slopes of Vesuvius, listening to the sleeping child's heavy breathing and the splashing of waves.

They had their own tree, a plane tree, and before going to bed they ran their fingers over its smooth skin. The air was fresh in the darkness but still warm.

At night, looking back toward Naples, you could see lights over the sea, like an enormous nest of flickering fireflies over the black water.

The stars were huge, angular, uneven, and crudely milled.

The interpreter and Isolde probably should not have come to Massa Lubrense again.

They had decided to give their family one last chance, as Isolde put it. That all of this was in vain was clear from the very start. They fought again—over an open window—back in a traffic jam before the Saint Gotthard and then rode the whole way in silence.

That night they talked until three. The same old same old. Meaningless, pointless words. Then the interpreter tried to fall asleep in the dining room on the lumpy sofa, covering his head with a pillow so he wouldn't hear Isolde's sobs.

In the morning they had no strength to talk about anything anymore. The child could tell the peace had collapsed, and he sat in a corner quietly, head down, drawing something. The water from his cup spilled and he made muddy designs over the wet, buckling paper with his finger.

After breakfast Isolde took him outside to play, and the interpreter read about miraculous healings and incorruptible relics.

And now they were back from the shore. Their son turned on the television and started watching cartoons, and Isolde said that she and the child were leaving tomorrow because she couldn't live like this anymore, and she asked the interpreter to go away right now because she couldn't be in the same house with him anymore, in the same space.

The interpreter said fine, it's true, we can't live like this, and they would all leave tomorrow in the morning and that he too could not be in the same space with her anymore. At this their son, who was sitting curled up in the chair in front of the television, whimpered softly. The interpreter also wanted to tell Isolde that they'd agreed not to talk in front of the child, but he didn't because all that was beside the point. And so as not to say anything more, he went outside quickly, forcing himself to close the door behind him slowly and gently.

The interpreter didn't know where to go. It was still drizzling on and off. People were watching him through their windows, and he wanted to be somewhere where no one was or could possibly be.

Breakers were passing over the sea, and the low sky was covered in blurry designs, as if someone had smeared the clouds with his finger.

The interpreter walked to their parking spot, got into the car, and started in the direction of Sorrento. Halfway there was a place where the cliffs went far into the sea and you could walk on them. There probably wouldn't be anyone there in this weather.

He had to drive through the village. Sometimes people's doors let out directly on the street, and the interpreter would brake and see how Italians lived—without any entryways, the family starting right past the open door. Here was an old woman in black with terrible, work-mangled hands sitting watching the car pass with the television flickering behind her. Children's voices could be heard through open windows. A dark-haired peewee in a white T-shirt and track pants ran across the street in slippers—carrying a pot with steam pouring out of it in the rain.

Each house had a family, if not several. How could they live together?

They couldn't! Behind each window, someone had told someone else, or sooner or later would, I can't go on living like this. We have to separate because I can't be in the same space with you anymore. And the other did or would reply, Fine, it's true, I can't live like this, either. And next to them their child would curl up in a chair and want to be very very small, blind and deaf, like a pillow, so he wouldn't see or hear anything.

When the interpreter descended the wet, slippery path to the sea, carved out here and there in the rock, he suddenly saw someone standing right by the surf. A short-legged, stout woman wearing a pink plastic rain poncho. She looked back, displeased. Obviously she wanted to stand here alone, and he was bothering her.

Her face seemed familiar.

"Buona sera!" the interpreter said.

She turned away without answering.

The interpreter wandered over the cliffs, but the woman still wouldn't leave, and her clumsy pink figure stood out against the sea and was impossible to block out.

She could have nodded back.

I came here to calm down, and again I'm breathing down someone's neck!

Then the interpreter decided he wasn't the problem, she was, and he told himself that on principle he was going to stand here until the pink poncho left.

He stood there, leaning against the cliff, to get out of the wind, and thought about who the woman reminded him of. This had already happened to him, coming across doubles of his Moscow friends in different countries. The person simply lived in a parallel world. The interpreter himself was now wandering somewhere through the streets of different cities.

He covered his ears from the wind and surf. It started growing dark.

All of a sudden the interpreter realized who the woman in the pink poncho reminded him of. Only many years had passed. Which was why he hadn't recognized her.

She looked like the girl who always slept as if she were swimming the crawl. That girl had been embarrassed by her breasts, too. She had a frogskin patch. As if there hadn't been enough human skin and they'd slapped on whatever came to hand. A princess frog.

That girl had once slit her veins in the bathroom—locking him out and swallowing some pills—when they were both nineteen. When he called the ambulance they asked him, "What, another sleeping beauty?" He didn't understand because he didn't know that was what the ambulance called young ladies who swallowed sleeping pills. As he bandaged her arms, the doctor said with a grin, "For future reference, if you seriously want to kill yourself, you have to slit them lengthwise, not crosswise." He had to wash the floor in the bathroom and hall. There were blood spots everywhere, and the medics had dragged in mud, and it was the middle of the spring slush. Later, many years later, the princess frog slit her veins the right way, lengthwise.

The wind was picking up. It started to rain again. The interpreter was soaked through and shivering. Dark fell swiftly, right before his eyes, as it only can in the south. The stupid pink poncho glowed against the sea's backdrop on the same surf-battered boulder.

Right then the interpreter felt like going home as quickly as he could to tell her all this. About the princess frog and about how he stood here and watched the burgeoning storm. And also to play something with his son. After all, they'd taken along a whole box of all kinds of board games. He so wanted warmth, coziness, home.

He wanted to go back, hug her, forget all the nastiness. To lie at night holding each other close and listen to the storm.

And in the morning the sun would shine again, as then, and the sea would sway a little on the tautly stretched horizon.

The interpreter started scrambling up the wet, slippery stairs carved into the cliff. While he was going up it grew completely dark, but the flickering poncho was still waiting for something.

The path took a turn and the interpreter turned around one last time to look at the sea. The boulder with the pink dot had separated from the shore and sailed away.

17 September 1924

It's been a hundred years since I've kept a diary, but I just saw this writing pad, not an attractive one, but I don't care. I so want to tell you everything, Seryozha! Don't be afraid of my letters. More likely you'll say you're afraid they'll get lost. Let them. Instead of letters you'll get this writing pad when we meet.

Here is what has happened to me. After the concert I drank a glass of ice water. I knew I shouldn't, but I'd done it a hundred times before and nothing had happened! I felt feverish all night. In the morning there was a tickle in my throat. It was terrible to feel myself getting sick. A cold. I wrapped up in a shawl, swallowed an aspirin, and drank lime flower tea with lemon. I felt a little better. I rubbed my chest with grease and vodka. I lay like that until evening. Vanya Delazari came by to pick me up for the Yar. It was sunny, and Vanya wanted to walk to the Seventh Line. Two steps away, down Sredny Avenue. But my legs were so weak. Only then did he notice that something was wrong with me. He was frightened. "Perhaps you'd do better not to sing today. We'll find a replacement." This enraged me! They're already prepared to replace me! How quickly all this happens with them! Replace? Me? With whom, I wonder? I told myself I would sing in any condition—with angina, with abscesses in my throat, with a sky-high fever. You can always shift the emphasis imperceptibly for the audience and compensate for a voice's lack

347

of resonance with your plasticity and temperament! If you can't sing, act. We caught a cab and were on our way. In the dressing room, as always, I put a drop of atropine in my eyes. What big eyes! During the second love song I could already feel the fever coming on, a roar in my head, a pain in my temples, and my throat all wrong. I finished singing blind and could see and hear nothing. Tears were rolling down my cheeks. This made a huge impression on the public. Real tears, and they thought, How divinely she acts! I hadn't had that kind of applause in a long time.

Once home I called the doctor. He examined my throat, ears, and nose for a long time and took a smear from my throat. By then I could only rasp: "What is it?" And he said, "Do you want me to be honest?" Everything grew dim. "In my opinion, it's bad, an inflammation of the vocal cords." I whispered, "But what can I do? I have to sing, I have concerts!" "You need to get better, not sing. You shouldn't even talk if you don't want to lose your voice altogether."

That was yesterday. What a terrible day! And night. I sat and wept. In the end I had no tears left. I lay in bed in a stupor. Devastated, senseless, exhausted. God, why have You punished me like this? What did I do? Why? What for?

Today everyone came running—Epstein, Vanya, even Klava stopped by later, and Maya. Maya will sing instead of me. She acted more distressed and sorrier for me than anyone, but she does a bad job of pity. Such a joyous pity. She concealed her happiness so clumsily. Iosif said Polyakov—Petrograd's's leading laryngologist—would definitely help me. He saved Sobinov. He treats all the greats. Epstein is a lamb! He's already made me an appointment to see him. He's booked months in advance—for vocalists there's no better. Let him treat their throats! And Iosif did everything to make sure Polyakov saw me on Friday. That's the day after tomorrow.

There, everyone's left and I'm alone. Not alone but with you, Seryozha! How I miss your words, your voice! How I wish you could whisper to me that everything will be fine. It will, won't it? I'll be able to sing again, won't I? Right?

I will. I must.

★

I'm writing at night. I keep getting worse. Swallowing hurts, each swallow of air scratches my throat's walls until I cry.

The coughing has begun.

Seryozha, I feel so awful, and you're so far away! I so want to embrace you, but I have to lie with my arms around my knees. I can do anything, I'm strong, but I can't do what's most important, Seryozha. I can't put my arms around myself and caress myself. I wish you could be here beside me now. I wish I could snuggle close to you and bury my head under your arm! I so miss your smell, your skin, your hair!

These pesky gnats are all that's interested in me!

I'm so happy to have you and so unhappy that in fact I don't!

★

1924 is the year of Venus—or so say the occultists—and I can feel that. This is our year. Everything will be good for you and me! Everything has to be good!

★

Nothing will be good!

I woke up this morning angry at myself for sniveling so yesterday. Ditherer! Just imagine, my throat! Everyone has a throat! No point wasting my time! I sat down at the piano. I have to work! I started reading the music Fomin sent me. Borya's a genius! It's awful if his gypsy ends up roping him in! I worked "dry," soundlessly. I can't open and shut my mouth. And the whole time, anger at my own throat: No, this can't be happening to me! Me!

And once again fear: Will I really never sing on stage again? I thought of unlucky Nina Litovtseva. She caught a chill, too, after all, and the cold turned into an inflammation of the middle ear and they had to lance the boil, and they did it in such a way that she got a blood infection! Paul told me this, and he knows Kachalov well.

It's so simple! One cold—and a whole life ruined.

I sobbed for another half a day. I felt so sorry for myself that the tears flowed of their own accord.

And still the same question: God, why me? If this is a punishment, then for what? Could it really be for you, Seryozha, could it really be for our love?

★

Friday is an entire eternity!

★

Klava stopped by and started complaining about Ivanovsky, who she did a screen test for at Sevzapkino. She was supposed to cry for a scene. She tried to think of something sad. The tears poured, but Ivanovsky shouted, "Wrong! Wrong!" And he started shouting at her vulgarly, saying she couldn't do a damn thing and she was trash, not an actress! At that she began howling from the insult and they immediately started shooting. He had set it all up on purpose! Insulted her especially so that her tears would be natural. I reassured her, "Dear Klava, sunshine, you yourself know that all directors are scoundrels and swine! That's their job!" At this she took umbrage for him. "You understand nothing! He is a genius!" I understand! Her role: lots of tears, and in the end she drowns herself and they carry her wet in burlap.

She also told me something strange, that snakes sense their partner's sex on stage, and so the male pythons "couple" with the actresses in the sketch and the females with the actors. Indeed, that actress performed with a male snake at the Hermitage.

The weather is getting worse. Someone told Klava there was going to be a flood.

★

After dinner I lay down, because of my sleepless night. I dozed off and jumped up bathed in sweat. I'd dreamt I'd come out on stage and my neck swelled up, like a real goiter. I'm singing, and instead of a voice—a rasp. I decided that if I can't sing anymore I'll kill myself. I decided and calmed down. I started thinking about suicide. Jumping off a bridge is frightening. I once saw someone who'd drowned. No! I don't want to die like that. Hang myself? Someone once said, and the words etched themselves in me, that if you want to hang yourself, first use the toilet! The bladder and colon evacuate on hanged people. Ever since, hanging myself has been ruled out. The only other choice is to swallow powders. And die like a seamstress, from veronal.

★

Lord, what have I written!

I'll put myself to rights immediately. Put on makeup, comb my hair. Put on my very best. For no one but me! I'll sit down at the piano and play!

★

I think I'm simply going mad.

I tore up my music. And scattered it around the room. There isn't

351

going to be any singing! Or music! There isn't going to be anything!

I rewashed the dishes. I'm sitting looking at my reddened hands and listening to the water running in the toilet. The toilet in this apartment runs constantly.

★

I've calmed down a little. I sat piecing the music together.

★

I was struck by Klava saying a few weeks ago that I'd become cruel. I asked her, "To whom?" She answered, "To yourself."

★

In some French novel a doctor prescribed that the heroine swallow chunks of ice as medicine for chest pain. I just can't remember which one.

I'd like to go out for a walk right now, but it's nighttime and I'm afraid. All the newspapers are about nothing but robberies and murders.

★

All of a sudden I thought, "What do I in fact do on stage? I love. I love those who have come and try to win their love. I have a love affair with the entire hall, hundreds of men and women. I know how to make them happy for one evening. Then I come home alone and lie in this icy bed."

This nocturnal loneliness, shot through with longing and fear, is so repulsive.

I took pantopon. Though I know it will give me a headache!

★

Phonasthenia!

Finally I saw Polyakov! Nothing good.

A functional illness of the voice. Developing on the background of a nervous breakdown. In severe instances, there is aphonia. That means I could be left mute altogether.

The old man first scared me, then he rubbed my throat with calomel and reassured me that it would all be fine. "I'll make you a nightingale's throat!" I have no doubt he tells everyone that. But one wants so to believe it!

Complete rest, absolute silence for several days, bromide preparations, and vitamins.

But what if this luminary Polyakov doesn't understand the slightest thing? Might he be one of those doctors who assure the patient that it will pass in a week with medicine but in seven days without?

Be that as it may, I'm strictly prohibited from talking. I'll have to explain myself with notes now.

I'm mute.

★

Polyakov also said that the glass of cold water had nothing to do with it. It was all from my worries. You see, Seryozha, it's all because you're so far away.

Horrible weather. Wind. Rain.

Once again I've gone and cried my portion of tears. It's a good thing you can't see me now.

★

What day is it? I've lost all track of time.

Longing, cold—it's silly to write this down. I also ripped my stocking on something.

My condition is extremely tense. I'm all tense inside. The slightest push or scare and I would go completely off my rocker. I can't do anything at all. I calm myself with a codeine bromide.

★

It's late. Vanya just left. We fought—for the first time. Nothing like this has ever happened before. He came to visit me, support me, and brought a bottle. I didn't realize at first that he was already drunk. My accompanist suddenly started saying such nasty things to me, but he may be right. Out of the blue he declared that when I sing on stage I'm a goddess, but when I'm saying something at the table I'm ordinary and I blather. Eventually I threw him out. When he drinks, he's mean. But there is probably something to it. Everything around me is unbearable, including me.

Who was it who said that artists and the public should not meet outside the theater? How wise! After the curtain falls, one should simply vanish, evaporate, with the wave of a magic wand.

★

It is strange, after all, I have success, flowers, admirers, and so forth, and still it seems as though this were some kind of mistake, as if they've taken me for someone else.

★

Of course, I am the most ordinary of women, and I need everything an earthly woman needs, and right now I need boots, a coat, a couple of winter dresses, a hat, perfume, my own apartment. But all this is foolishness. The real earthly me needs you! Right now, immediately, and every day! You are my salvation. I cannot live without you. I shall die here. Why are you with her now and not me? She is killing you after all. After all, you promised to leave her and come be with me! You did say that our love was more important to you than anything in the world! Why are you torturing me like this? Where are you?

Here I am playing with my agate beads, my June stone, which brings me luck. It brought me you. But do I really have you?

★

Shouts behind the door. All the linens have been stolen from the neighbors' attic.

★

It's been a week since I've had anything from you, and I want to receive your letters every day. After all, I live from letter to letter. Write! Sleep is sweet with your letter!

You also haven't written about whether you've seen Mikhail Chekhov's *Hamlet* yet. That production is all anyone here talks about.

Write something! After all, I don't need detailed reports from you. Just a few lines. Just your handwriting, your hand.

★

I'm sitting looking out the rainy window remembering how we roamed then, in April, forlorn, through Moscow. We wanted to be left alone, just us two, and we had nowhere to perch. How marvelous it was to hide from everyone somewhere in a museum. Remember the Morozov gallery? The Impressionists? Degas's *Printemps?* At the Shchukin I was struck by *Les Démoiselles d'Avignon* by Picasso. Monstrous, heavy, all angles. You explained something to me about Cubism. But later I realized it wasn't a matter of Cubism. This was just a woman abandoned by love. How terrible to be like that!

★

Fog outside. Autumnal, Petrograd fog. There is a wetness in the air, that special wetness without rain that you can feel here. But this is better than the summer's dust. All summer there was a stifling heat and columns of dust, they were repairing the sidewalks everywhere, whitewashing walls, you couldn't get anywhere along the street, everything had been dug up, there were tools, buckets, and shovels lying about, and it stank of paint and horse sweat.

Still, it is nice that all those terrible years are behind us. And so joyous that everything horrible and poor is in the past, the town is being cleaned, for the first time since the war buildings are being painted and sidewalks repaired, central heating is being restored everywhere, people are well dressed once again, you can buy anything for money, and in the summer people leave for their dachas again!

Everyone is still mixing up the money. I bought myself slippers at Gostiny Dvor, went to the cashier, and the young lady asked me how much I wanted to pay—on the chit the salesclerk had added indecipherably either *m.* or *t.* Millions? Thousands?

Everything changes so fast! What disappears fastest of all are the jokes. Remember the feeble joke about the plumber who repaired the pipes? "He walked in without a kopek and left half an hour later a billionaire." No one could understand what we were laughing at.

And it's all forgotten just as quickly. You know what I received from my sister Katya on my name-day in '21? A curtain for a winter dress! What happiness!

Now I have money. Sometimes a lot even. But what is it to have money in a poor country? Everything is in a jumble—wealth and famine. Eliseyev on Nevsky has game, and live fish, and tropical fruits, and gallant shop assistants, but there are beggars by the door. That's the way it's always been and always will be. You need to learn to live and pay no attention. Need to but cannot.

I walk through the city, but the ragged sleep right on the sidewalk, both singly and in families, all rags and lice. And there's a hat or torn cap on the sidewalk for people to toss in coins. You toss it in and later the money is stolen by the street children, or it all gets drunk up. And everyone barefoot. Those feet alone! You look and your mood is spoiled for a week and you don't feel like going to any restaurant. You walk past and there's nothing to be done. Except perhaps rejoice that you yourself aren't lying among them. And one so wants tomorrow to be not with them on the street but there, where it's beautiful, and clean, and warm, and gay. I can't understand how people once wanted to be simpler, to go among the people, the down-and-out. They must not have seen those feet.

And so many street children everywhere! One wants to pity them, but how can one if they gang up and attack? Nyusya told me how they tried to tear away her purse, which had her entire month's salary. She clutched it and wouldn't let go. A boy shouted at her, "I'll bite you, and I have syphilis!" She let go. And ran to me all in tears.

Should I be ashamed of my well-being when there is poverty and misery at hand? Or perhaps, on the contrary, should I rejoice that I'm not on the sidewalk in rags, that I have a pretty hat, and shoes, and rouged cheeks, and youth, and health, and love?

Lord, what am I writing about!

I walked over to the mirror again and opened my mouth, trying to get a look at something. A repulsive spectacle!

★

Rain. And how!

The pavement is covered in bubbly yellow foam. This is the pitch oozing from the wooden paving blocks. Why do Petrograders take such pride in their wooden paving blocks? Because there's nothing like them in any other city! The slightest rain and it's slippery, like walking on soap. Watch out or you'll break your leg.

★

The cannon went off. That doesn't mean it's noon, though. One time I wanted to set my clock by the firing, but Epstein said that you couldn't trust the cannon because the Pulkovo observatory didn't signal the fortress anymore when it was twelve o'clock. The signal only went to the main post office now.

★

I think of you constantly and remember your visit. What marvelous days those were! Everything here reminds me of you. Even the bread! Klava just stopped by. She brought a challah with raisins from the Filippov bakery, the kind you like so much. Remember, I took you to the corner of Staro-Nevsky and Poltavskaya? The bakery there.

How I dreamed of you coming! I imagined us meeting in Mikhailovsky Square, dining in the rooftop restaurant at the Evropeiskaya. And all of a sudden—you! No letter or telegram! What could be more marvelous in this world: I come home and you're here waiting for me! That was a miracle.

I was performing then at the Summer Theater, and there were rains, but each time we were sold out. I told you that this was all Utesov doing Zoshchenko, but you assured me it was because of me! How marvelous it was to sing for you! If only I could come out on stage each time knowing I would see you in the audience.

We never did get to the Hermitage that time. All roads led to this bed, so insignificant and empty without you!

Remember your handkerchief? I knotted its corners to make a little rag man. He lives under my pillow. Now I can only fall asleep if this little man is holding my finger.

★

Remember our trip to Strelna? How stones flew at us when we went for a walk in the park? They should warn lovers a verst ahead with big posters that there's an orphanage in Peter's great palace now!

And how we climbed St. Isaac's cupola and I got dizzy from the height?

And how badly I didn't want to get out of bed but had to think of something for supper, and you said, "Wait right there," and you ran down to the cooperative and brought back chocolate candies, Swiss cheese, grapes, and a bottle of wine! How marvelous that was!

I put a grape in your mouth, and you held it in your teeth! What divine teeth you have!

★

Epstein came and dragged me outside. He said that without fresh air I'd turn into a mummy altogether. We walked and walked until we reached the Piccadilly. We took seats and plunged into viewing the silliest German film—we came in during the middle of the third act. We couldn't stand it and left, heading out to tempt fate at the Coliseum. Before the show began the public was entertained by balalaikas playing foxtrots. We saw a drama, *The Prosecutor*. Foolishness, but it got me terribly worked up and, most importantly, distracted me. The prosecutor acts as the accuser of the woman he loves; she doesn't try to defend herself, in order not to mix him up in the case, and she is guillotined.

359

We were silent all evening. I out of necessity, and he, probably, out of nothing to say. Or rather, at first he chatted away endlessly, and then he suddenly said, "It's odd to talk all the time with a silent woman"—and he too fell silent.

Then we went to our Yar. We shouldn't have! We entered as Maya was singing. I started feeling unwell right away. Genuinely unwell.

I sit there and everyone around me is clapping for her.

Not for me anymore?

I said I had a fever and left. Iosif put me in a droshky.

But I do have a fever.

★

Seryozha, my beloved, remember I arrived all tear-stained because I'd climbed out of the streetcar, out of the crush, and only then saw I was covered in milk spots, even my shoes. You put your arms around me and started reassuring me, like a daughter. Where are you, dear Seryozha? Come, hold me, reassure me, rock me to sleep! It's so nice to be little with you! I so want to doze off in your arms! Forget everything in the world. Even the stage! I'm so tired of baring my soul on stage while hiding it deep inside behind the scenes because there what's needed are sharp teeth and claws, not a soul! Most of all, you need the hide of a rhinoceros, not skin. I don't have a hide! It hurts so much!

★

Today Epstein showed up with a bouquet of roses and again asked me to marry him. And you know, Seryozha, how my administrator from the Seventh Line thought to take me? You can't imagine! He is throwing all of France at my feet! They're planning to send him there as the Russia-Mezhrabprom representative!

Poor, naïve Iosif!

He thinks I ought to throw my arms around his neck over some Paris! I don't need any Paris, Seryozha. I need your love!

I've never before turned anyone down on a piece of paper. But I immediately tore a sheet out of this notebook and wrote in capital letters: NEVER!

By the way, here's an amusing episode for you. Imagine, Epstein even introduced me to his mama this week! I expected to see a matron run to fat, a biblical Rebecca, but this was a lively, dry wit speaking in a low, smoked-out voice. She kept asking whether I didn't have Jewish relatives! We took an immediate dislike to each other. Dislike at first sight, so to speak. On the other hand, the gefilte fish was wonderful! You'd lick your fingers!

Iosif also brought a tin of marvelous cocoa, Van Houten's! I drank it, treating my poor little throat. Remember how we argued which is better, Van Houten or George Borman?

Vanya Delazari came by, quite distressed. He lost at Splendid Palace. He borrowed some money.

★

Everything is a jumble. I sleep during the day and at night can't shut my eyes. I don't know today's date.

How I hate this room without you! My back feels as if it were going to break from this hammock of a cot. I'm gasping for want of fresh air, I open the window. I go to bed in socks, my feet to the wall, worried that cockroaches are going to crawl over me during the night. Dear Seryozha, save me! Knock on this door!

★

I can't sleep. I lie here thinking of you. I run through your words and gestures like beads. Here you are helping me take off my damp, heavy coat and pulling off my galoshes! Remember the day we got caught in that horrible snow mixed with rain? Over and over again I receive flowers and a bottle of Jicky by Guerlain for my birthday. Each time I wet my fingertip and run it behind my ears, a wave of tenderness for you rolls over me.

★

Remember how it all was the first time? You're a terrible deceiver! You invited me to some friend's birthday party, but there wasn't any friend or any birthday! How marvelous that deceit was! I came in from the cold. I knew it was all about to happen, which made it seem as though I was in a fog and not myself. I took a slow turn around the room, removed my hat and gloves, and threw them on the floor without looking. You walked up, took my hands, and whispered, "So icy!" And began warming them with your lips.

★

What are legal rights? I recognize only genuine rights, and by the right of love, you are mine. Oh Lord, how pathetic spousal rights are! What do they signify in comparison with my right to fall asleep and wake up with you every night and every morning? That right belongs to me, not her!

I have the right to you, but not you.

★

I reread these schoolgirl ravings, and suddenly it became so obvious that we would have nothing, that you would never leave her for me. How empty I felt inside! I lost all desire to live!

Only with you did I understand what it meant to gasp with fury. I imagined you with her. Kissing her hair, her lips, stroking her skin there, and here. I imagined you whispering to her—what? The same thing you whispered to me? I was consumed by jealousy.

★

No, I'm lying, that's all wrong! I know you haven't had anything for a long time. What truly hurts me is when I suddenly begin thinking not about you and her in bed but about you still loving her. It terrifies me constantly: What if you still love her?

★

That horrible night in Moscow when I came to your house for the first time pursues me like a nightmare. I want to forget it and can't. I walked in and immediately felt another woman's presence on my skin. She was everywhere, in everything. And everything was sterile, not like at my home. And the smell. Her smell. Her clothing, her perfume, her body. It was unbearable. Painful. I forced myself to say, "It's cozy here." And you answered, "This has nothing to do with me."

I lay down in your—hers, too, of course—bed. Her bed. In her room. I turned to stone. All desire vanished. I was afraid of offending you. I didn't say anything. But you could tell.

How humiliating! Like being thieves always. Are we really thieves, Seryozha? No, that's wrong, that can't be! You do love me, not her! You are my true husband, not hers! What belongs only to the two of us can't be stolen!

Again I'm saying it all wrong. It's not a matter of stealing. You know what it is a matter of? Her slippers. I was looking at her slippers by the door the whole time.

★

Klava is my closest friend. Do you know what she tells me about you? Of course, you don't. She tells me to leave you, that I shouldn't destroy another person's life. But the main thing is that if you truly loved me, you would have been with me long ago. If you truly wanted to leave her for me, you would have long ago. She's right.

I'm sure you don't remember that day. I've already noticed that we remember completely different things. That day I decided to leave you. To break it off. I decided, sat down in a corner, and cried for a long time without moving or blinking, staring at a flower in the wallpaper. Once when I was a child I learned how to cry like that from Bashkirtseva. I went to see you in the certainty I was going to tell you once and for all, No! I saw you and suddenly realized I loved you more than I had ever loved anyone and that I had been given this life for the sake of you. I saw you—and it happened all over again. How good it was to love each other! All I could think of was what happiness it was being yours!

You know, that had never happened to me before. I am constantly falling in love with you all over again. It sweeps over me—and I walk around as if blind, lips dry, eyes burning.

★

Am I jealous? Not a bit. How can I be jealous when nothing is left but ashes?

Remember at Shamkov's that impossible Runa-Pshesetskaya questioning you about your wife? "Why isn't she here? Is she very pretty? What is she like? Brunette or blonde?" I thought I'd rip her tongue out! This isn't jealousy for your Olya but for my not being your wife. Or rather for no one knowing that I am your wife. Why must we hide this?

And if I'm not your wife, who am I? Your mistress? What a vile word.

*

Tell me one thing: Do you still love her?
If not, then why aren't we together?

*

I know, Seryozha, everything will be good for you and me. In a
month I'll return to Moscow. I'll have a room. You'll leave her for
me. That will be our happiness.

*

You say everything rests on your son, that you are together for
his sake. I know it's hard for you with him. He's at the most difficult
age right now.

You were so distraught and beaten when you told me how he
stole money from you and lost it at the pari-mutuel with those
scoundrels.

I understand you when you talk about how hard it is for you to
leave because of Syoma. But he will still be your son. And we will
have one more child. Do you want me to give you a little girl?

I haven't told you this yet. Then here, know this: I very much
want a child by you.

Only you.

*

I keep asking myself this question: Why are you still with her?
I know the answer is not in those words about your son and duty.
And I can't ask you flat out what that woman gives you that I can't.
I can't? Me?

Maybe the problem is that I'm strong and you don't feel sorry for me. There are women who play the part of a little girl their whole life and force everyone around them to take care of them. Is she one of those? And you feel sorry for her?

★

I sift through my memories like precious seeds. Each sends up a shoot in me: the way we horsed around, pushing each other in the snow, and me throwing your hat in the snowdrifts. Then we went under the bridge and onto the ice, to the very middle of the river, and you stamped out our word in the snow. I remember the frost that gave you a gray mustache. And how we slept covered with both a blanket and your sheepskin jacket, which kept slipping to the floor.

And in the morning, in the mirror—a stranger, an unfamiliar, beautiful woman. Was this really me? You know how to make me beautiful with your love!

★

In my dream last night I kissed your clean-shaven cheek and smoothed your hair.

Once you went through my things on my table and suddenly said, "This perfume smells of you!"

I remember you by heart. I run my nails down your back. On your shoulder blades, my palms feel your downiness. I say, "Seryozha, you're growing wings! And for some reason the right is bigger than the left." And you answer from under the pillow that you flap the right harder. Why do you always sleep with a pillow on your ear?

This cannot go on any longer! I can't go on like this! We must be together, live together, sleep together, eat together! When you fell ill that time, my first impulse was to race to your side, look after you, save you! And I couldn't. I can't cross that line. Lies, nothing but lies! How unworthy this is of you, me, and her.

★

I'm tear-stained, and you don't like it when I cry. It's good you can't see my ugly, puffy face. I'm going to collect myself now so that you'll like it.

★

I ordered up a dream of you. Lord, it was a marvelous dream! You kissed me everywhere—everywhere! Understand? You drove me insane. I woke up all wet both inside and out! And happy! I was with you tonight!

Even now I still feel your hands on my skin. If a man has beautiful hands, truly beautiful hands, as you do, he cannot be ugly inside. Hands don't lie.

How I love your body, your hands, your feet, your toes! How I love to kiss and stroke all your birthmarks, scars, the big stitches on your belly! Lord have mercy, they gutted you like a fish in that operation! I adore stroking and kissing the black scar on your knee. The wound should have been rubbed with soot!

You like it so much when I run the tips of my nails over your skin. How famished you were for love and how divinely you know how to love! At night I relive over and over the way you kissed me below, lips to lips, and how your lips smelled of me afterward.

★

You're constantly talking about your family. You haven't had a family for a long time. How can you live together and not share what is most important and sacred, without which life is impossible?

367

I met Olya just once, and it seems to me that she immediately sensed, guessed. You should have seen how maliciously she narrowed her eyes. Your wife has predatory, curved little teeth. She is too smoothly coiffed, each hair neatly in place. She has the strong fingers of a musician with long phalanges that hold tight.

*

Iosif is funny. He's certain that a woman likes to be told she has a holy face and sinful eyes. Klava assured me that he told her the same thing.

And all these cheap tricks of balding lady-killers: "Careful, there's a worm on you!" I screamed and immediately realized there was no worm. "Don't move, I'll remove it!" He tried to put his arms around me. It's all so tedious!

Today Iosif criticized Zamyatin's *We*. Do you know what he discovered there? The heroes, you remember, instead of names have a Latin letter plus a number. But the Latin alphabet only has twenty-four letters. There are just 10,000 people per letter. That means there are a total of 240,000 people. That's our Vasilievsky Island. No more.

*

How good to have Klava! Today it all came pouring out on her! She scolded me for talking instead of keeping silent and protecting my voice, but I had already started having true hysterics! I can't have hysterics on a scrap of paper! Klava set about reassuring me and took in my fury so that she was infected and also flew into a rage. We were shouting at each other, she at full voice and I in a whisper, until we calmed down in tears and in each other's arms.

Tomorrow she is leaving for Moscow. How hard it is for her with her Igor!

Yes, I want the same thing everyone else does! I want to be famous, rich, and magnificent! Of course I want to go to Paris! Very much! But I need all this only so that one insane day, no, one marvelous day, the day life is worth living for, I can burn all this wealth and magnificence for the sake of the simplest feelings. For the human touch. For your love. Otherwise, why do I need all this?

Also for the sake of our child. He will definitely be. You and I in one body.

★

You know what Nyusya said once? She said terrible things. She said that the maternal instinct is just that, an instinct, and doesn't deserve our superstitious reverence. That's what she said. As if it were like the instinct of hunger or sleep. A physical exercise of the organism. And that the highest manifestation of the maternal instinct can be observed in the hen that sits so considerately on her porcelain eggs. I asked her, "You mean love is only an instinct? A porcelain egg?" And she in reply: "Love has no connection to the continuation of the breed. Love lives on its own—unreciprocated and entirely without progeny, but there can be progeny without love."

Since her divorce Nyusya has changed a great deal. And become bitter at the whole world. There's nothing to be done with her. I don't like seeing her now. I can't. It's too hard.

And it's terrible that she doesn't want to understand that she won't be able to concertize anymore. She'll lose touch—and go on doing finger flexibility exercises: place the thumb between the others first slowly, then faster and faster in the most various combinations. Then she seems to come to her senses and hides her hands.

★

A flood! Today is the twenty-second. Or twenty-third?

I was sitting at the window watching a huge puddle appear on our Sredny Avenue and the little boys running through it, getting their trousers wet.

All of a sudden the water started collecting very quickly. I kept looking at the clock. At six our sidewalk was still dry, but just after seven the lower floors began to flood.

The water isn't working. The electricity has gone out. All of Vasilievsky has been plunged into darkness. A bizarre kind of Venice. Boats are floating down the streets. It's awful.

All of a sudden it occurred to me that this is the flood! Yes, the very last flood. God's punishment. And you know what for? For us not being together.

★

A horrible night.

Loud explosions. A big fire somewhere. Its glow covering half the sky.

★

I've realized one thing about love: we shouldn't be apart for so long!

I will never agree to such long contracts again! I must be by your side always. I want to eat from your plate, drink from your glass, kiss you everywhere, and constantly smell your scent by my side! How crudely and simply I love you, dear Seryozha! And I'm not the least bit ashamed of it!

★

When you were here, with me, it was so fine! But the clock was ticking beside us. You had to catch your train. I felt like opening the glass and holding back the hand with my finger! Here I have everything, but when the hand gets to here—it will all vanish. And that's what happened. I burst into tears, and you couldn't understand what was wrong with me. After all, we were together, we were feeling good. I ran into the lavatory to wash my puffy, tear-stained face. I begged you to stay, was angry at you for still not leaving her to live with me, and said all this into the sink, letting the streams from the tap wash away my words.

★

Today it's been sunny since the morning. Everything is under water.

It carried off a stack of firewood from somewhere, and now that firewood is floating down our avenue, like fat dead fish. People are catching them from the balconies, using a basket tied with a rope.

I heard that a chemical factory's warehouse on Vatny Island exploded and burned in the night.

★

All day long I walk and talk to myself and you, like an old woman who has lost her mind.

All I want is to tell you how much I love you, and that turns out to be utterly impossible!

We must be together, if only so that we don't need any words.

★

I'm going to undress now and lie down. And gnaw the pillow so I don't sob loudly. It's good that your rag-man will hold my finger again.

The water has begun to subside. The firewood is floating back. The end of the world has been postponed! Serves them all right!

Iosif and I took a walk through the city. I just returned. It feels like a holiday on the streets! The entire embankment is heaped with firewood. Traces of the flood, mud, everywhere. The streetcars aren't running, the wooden paving blocks have been washed away all down Nevsky, and the water has jammed them into restaurant and shop windows. All the windows on the lower floors have been broken. Water is still standing in the Alexander Garden. We didn't get as far as the Summer, but people say trees there have been uprooted and many statues smashed. We saw a barge on the embankment.

My voice seems to be returning.

At a quarter to eight the interpreter was already ringing at the prison door. The usual summons: an interview between attorney and arrestee. It was early and cold, and he was sleepy. The intercom told the interpreter to wait for the lawyer and then they'd be let in together.

The interpreter shuddered, cursed the tardy lawyer, and having nothing better to do, walked over the lightly frozen puddles. The ice whimpered.

In these instances, lawyers are court-appointed and do not display any special zeal. They usually advise their clients to confess all their sins and ask the judge for leniency. Formalities. But they pay interpreters for that.

Finally, the lawyer showed up; she turned out to be a young thing, all red in the face from hurrying. Frau P. apologized for being late and gave the interpreter a firm handshake. She was trying to be businesslike and dry, but while they were waiting at the prison doors, she immediately informed him that she was graduating from university this year and was on her way to her brother's wedding today. Learning that the interpreter was from Russia, she exclaimed gleefully, "Und mein Bruder heiratet eine Slowakin!"[26]

She had wanted to say something nice to the interpreter. She thought that Slovakia and Russia were somehow similar, close. After all, one always likes finding something in common with a new acquaintance. The interpreter pretended to find this truly pleasant.

They were let in. They showed their documents, surrendered their bags and cell phones, passed through security, like at the airport, and found themselves in the prison.

They were led down a jointed corridor to a tiny cell that barely fit the small table and three chairs. They were locked in.

While they were waiting for the arrestee, Frau P. filled the interpreter in. A certain Sergei Ivanov, a refugee from Belarus, had received a "negative" long ago, but he was still in Switzerland. Moreover, he had landed at the police station more than once for theft and drunken brawls. One time he fought with a train conductor.

"Ja, ja, immer die gleichen Geschichten," the interpreter nodded to keep the conversation going. "Und immer heißen sie Sergej Ivanov."[27]

Frau P. tilted her head and her hair ended up right in front of the interpreter's nose. She kept tucking it behind her ear, which wasn't even pierced so she could wear earrings. She wasn't wearing make-up, either. How many years had the interpreter lived in Switzerland,

---

26. My brother is marrying a Slovak girl! *(Ger.)*

27. Yes, yes, it's always the same story. And his name is always Sergei Ivanov. *(Ger.)*

and he still could not understand: Why are the Swiss afraid of being women? However, here, in the room, the light smell of her perfume, barely discernible outside, dug deep into his nostrils.

"Ich habe bereits mit Albanern, Afrikanern und Kurden gearbeitet, doch noch nie mit einem Russen."[28]

"Und ich habe es nur mit denen zu tun,"[29] the interpreter joked.

"Aber Weißrussland, das ist doch nicht Russland?"[30] Frau P. asked.

"Wie soll ich sagen,"[31] the interpreter began, and he wanted to say something about the complexity of ethnic relations in his homeland, but Frau P. had already started saying she had never been to Russia and would like to take the Trans-Siberian railroad.

"Das muss sicher sehr interessant sein?"[32]

"Sicher,"[33] the interpreter agreed. For some reason, all Swiss wanted to travel across Siberia by train. When he'd lived in Russia, the interpreter hadn't. Even now he'd prefer a plane.

"Dieser Herr Ivanov ist ja immer wieder gewalttätig," she added, examining the documents she'd taken from the file and spread out on the table. "Schauen Sie, er ist in betrunkenem Zustand in eine Coop-Filiale gegangen, hat sich da allerlei Lebensmittel genommen, und ohne zu zahlen noch im Laden zu essen und trinken angefangen, vor allen Leuten. Dann belästigte er ein paar Frauen. Und schließlich widersetzte er sich auch noch den Beamten."[34]

---

28. I've worked with Albanians, Africans, and Kurds, but never before with Russians. *(Ger.)*

29. And that's all I ever get. *(Ger.)*

30. But isn't Belarus Russia? *(Ger.)*

31. That depends. *(Ger.)*

32. It must be very interesting, right? *(Ger.)*

33. Of course. *(Ger.)*

34. This Mr. Ivanov is constantly resorting to force. Look, he went into the Co-op intoxicated, took all kinds of food, didn't pay, even started eating and drinking

She looked at the interpreter in amazement, as if expecting an explanation for such strange behavior from his fellow countryman. "Verstehen Sie," the interpreter tried to justify himself, "die Russen sind im Allgemeinen gutmütig, ruhig, nur eben wenn sie sich betrinken . . ."[35]

She laughed, taking what he'd said for a joke.

"Das heißt, Sie feiern heute ein Fest," the interpreter said, to change the subject. "Ich gratuliere. Am Vormittag das Gefängnis und am Nachmittag eine Hochzeit?"[36]

"Sehen Sie, so ist das." She smiled, and with a heavy sigh added, "In diesem Leben ist alles beisammen. Der eine sitzt im Gefängnis, der andere tanzt auf einer Hochzeit. Die Welt ist nicht gerecht."[37]

"Ja," the interpreter nodded in reply, not knowing what to say.

When Frau P. smiled, she revealed her young, even teeth. The interpreter also kept looking at her lips. She was sitting right next to him, so the interpreter was looking point-blank at her. Usually people only look point-blank at people they feel very close to. Looking at this young woman, the interpreter suddenly felt old.

Right then the bolt clanked, and they brought in a young guy in a tracksuit. A sturdy lad with a crew-cut. An ordinary face. Someone like that might work at a suburban Moscow market or travel to Zurich as a businessman for negotiations. He gave off the thick, rotten smell of a body long unwashed.

Frau P. cheerfully held out her hand. He grinned and shook it.

---

right there, in the store, in front of everyone. He started accosting women. And then he also resisted the police. (Ger.)

35. You have to understand. Russians are usually quiet, not malicious. It's only when they get to drinking . . . (Ger.)

36. So, it's a holiday for you today. Congratulations! Prison in the morning, and a wedding after lunch? (Ger.)

37. There, you see? If it doesn't rain, it pours. One person is in prison, another is celebrating a wedding. The world is unfair. (Ger.)

The interpreter didn't try to explain to her that in his homeland men didn't shake hands with women.

First they were locked in after being shown the button for calling the guard. Just in case.

"Herr Ivanov," Frau P. began when they had finished with the formalities. "Ich rate Ihnen, sich in allem schuldig zu bekennen. Sie werden ohnehin aus der Schweiz ausgewiesen werden. Es ist in Ihrem Interesse, mit den Behörden zu kooperieren. Dann müssen sie weniger lang im Gefängnis sitzen und können schneller nach Hause."[38]

The interpreter interpreted.

The fellow grinned again.

"Who told you I want to go home?"

The interpreter interpreted.

"Aber in diesem Fall erwartet Sie eine Zwangsdeportation."[39]

The interpreter interpreted.

The fellow scratched his crotch.

"They fucking think they can scare me!"

Frau P. examined her client with curiosity. And he suddenly let it out:

"You think I haven't been around the block? On the plane I'm going to holler and kick so no one will take me. If the captain doesn't want to take someone like that, you can't order him to! And you only have the right to hold me in prison for six months. You think I don't know? Then you'll set me free as a bird. What, you won't? There you go! You don't have me by the balls, it's the other way around! Get it? I'm going to squeeze your Switzerland by the balls as much as I want!"

---

38. Mr. Ivanov, I advise you to confess your guilt in full. You are being deported from Switzerland anyway. It is in your interests to cooperate with the authorities. You will spend less time in prison and be on your way home faster. *(Ger.)*

39. But in that case you face mandatory deportation. *(Ger.)*

Both, the fellow and the attorney, looked at the interpreter expectantly. He interpreted.

Frau P. was flustered.

"Verstehen Sie, Herr Ivanov, ich möchte Ihnen helfen."[40]

The interpreter interpreted.

"She wants to help me! Spare me all of you who want to help but don't! You're all doing just fine here without me! Take you, interpreter, you phony, you've got yourself all set up here, but maybe I want to live like a human being, too! What makes you any better than me? Maybe you're even worse! Except you've got clean clothes and smell like cologne, while I have nothing to change into."

"Was sagt er?"[41] Frau P. asked.

"Das gehört nicht zur Sache,"[42] the interpreter replied.

"Ich möchte, dass Sie alles übersetzen,"[43] she said.

"Gut."[44] And the interpreter began interpreting everything the other man said for her.

But the fellow flew into a rage, obviously he hadn't bared his soul to anyone in a long time, and he shouted, "Maybe I wanted to live and work honestly, too, but all they gave me for my honesty was shit! Maybe I wanted an apartment and a family, to be like regular people. But where was I supposed to get the money? If you want money, go into trade. That's what I did! I'm drowning in debt. If I go back they'll rip my head off. That's the whole business. And why? What, are the Swiss better than the Russians? Were my ancestors any worse than yours? Maybe not, maybe they were better. You had Auschwitz smoking out your window, but you enjoyed life

---

40. Understand, Mr. Ivanov, I want to help you. *(Ger.)*

41. What is he saying? *(Ger.)*

42. It's not pertinent to the case. *(Ger.)*

43. I want you to interpret everything. *(Ger.)*

44. Good. *(Ger.)*

and multiplied. My granddad fought the fascists and lost an arm at the front. And my mother, meanwhile, a teacher, taught children geography her whole life, and what did she earn? A pension? She earned jack-shit! She takes her pension and sells vodka at night by the train station. What's she guilty of? You gobbled everything up here. That's what! You're a Russian, tell me. Isn't that so? Interpret for her, interpret everything!"

The interpreter interpreted.

Frau P. blushed and said that none of this was pertinent to the case.

"Verstehen Sie, Herr Ivanov, ich möchte Ihnen helfen. Aber Sie wollen mir nicht zuhören. Nun, es tut mir leid, aber in diesem Fall kann ich nichts für Sie tun. Möchten Sie noch etwas zur Sache hinzufügen?"[45]

The interpreter interpreted.

The fellow gave a crooked grin and spat on the floor. And scratched his crotch again.

"Pertinent? I'll give you pertinent. I want to fuck you in the ass, slut! You both must get it on every night with someone, while I jack off alone. I'm a human being, too! Do you understand that? Who needs me like this? I've got no money, and no one loves me. If you were sitting in my place, interpreter, no one would love you either."

"Was? Was hat er gesagt?" Frau P. asked impatiently. "Übersetzen Sie genau, was er gesagt hat!"[46]

The interpreter interpreted, trying to choose slightly milder expressions. Despite his efforts, Frau P. blushed, broke out in red spots, and silently pressed the button to call the guard.

"Hören wir auf. Das hat keinen Sinn."[47]

---

45. Understand, Mr. Ivanov, I want to help you. But you don't want to listen to me. Of course, I'm sorry, but in this case I can't do anything for you. Do you want to say anything else that's pertinent? (Ger.)

46. What? What did he say? Interpret it all exactly as he said it! (Ger.)

47. Let's finish this. None of this makes any sense. (Ger.)

The interpreter shrugged. They'd pay him for two hours anyway.

Frau P. commented drily to her client, "Auf Wiedersehen! Alles Gute!"[48]

They sat there for a minute in tense silence. All the air had been sucked out of that tiny room. The fellow was leering at the young woman, scratching his crotch. He winked to the interpreter, nodding at her, as if to say, go for it!

Finally the door opened. The interpreter followed Frau P. out of the room into the corridor.

The fellow suddenly remarked after them, "Tell her she looks like my little sister!"

They emerged onto Helvetiaplatz. They breathed in the fresh, frosty air. Frau P.'s face was still covered in red spots. She smiled embarrassedly at the interpreter.

He smiled in reply.

"Auch das kann vorkommen. Achten Sie nicht darauf. Gehen Sie auf die Hochzeit ihres Bruders und genießen Sie es!"[49]

Frau P. sighed.

"Nach so was ist es schwer, etwas zu genießen. Zuerst muss man wieder ein bisschen die innere Ruhe finden."[50]

"Sicher," the interpreter said. "Man muss abschalten lernen. Gut wäre jetzt ein kleiner Spaziergang, den Kopf auszulüften, dann geht es vorbei."[51]

They were still standing in front of the prison. The interpreter watched her nervously tucking her hair behind her ear. A streetcar rumbled past.

---

48. Goodbye! All the best! *(Ger.)*

49. It happens. Pay no attention! Go to your brother's wedding and enjoy life! *(Ger.)*

50. After meetings like that it's hard to enjoy anything right away. I have to regain my senses first. *(Ger.)*

51. Of course. You have to learn to switch off. You'd do well to take a little walk and let everything air out. Let it pass. *(Ger.)*

Frau P. said, "Meine Mutter war auch Lehrerin und ist jetzt pensioniert. Trotz allem ist die Welt ungerecht."[52]

The interpreter wanted to reassure her somehow, say something nice to her, only he didn't know what.

Frau P. reached out to shake his hand.

"Auf Wiedersehen! Und einen schönen Tag!"[53]

The interpreter held her hand in his.

"Wissen Sie was, nehmen Sie das Ganze auf die leichte Schulter. Das gibt es gar nicht, dass es allen Lehrerinnen gut ginge. Man kann sich auch nicht Sorgen machen wegen aller Lehrerinnen, denen die Pension nicht zum Leben reicht."[54]

This suddenly set the interpreter off, as if he'd been patient for a long time and had now found someone on whom to vent what had built up:

"Wenn es Ihnen und Ihrer Mutter gut geht, dann freuen Sie sich doch! Wenn irgendwo Krieg ist, dann sollte man umso mehr leben und sich freuen, dass man selbst nicht dort ist. Und wenn jemand geliebt wird, dann wird es auch immer einen anderen geben, den niemand liebt. Und wenn die Welt ungerecht ist, so soll man trotzdem leben und sich freuen, dass man nicht in einer stinkigen Zelle sitzt, sondern auf eine Hochzeit geht. Sich freuen! Genießen!"[55]

She looked at the interpreter rather oddly. She probably couldn't believe it.

---

52. My mama's a teacher on a pension, too. The world really is unfair. *(Ger.)*

53. Goodbye! Have a good day!" *(Ger.)*

54. You know what, pay no attention to all this! There's no such thing as all teachers having it good. And you can't worry about all the teachers whose pensions aren't enough to live on! *(Ger.)*

55. If you and your mama are doing well, then you have to rejoice in that. And if there's a war somewhere, you need to live and rejoice even more that you aren't there. And if someone is loved, there will always be someone whom no one loves. And if the world is unfair, you still have to live and rejoice that you're not sitting in a stinking cell but are going to a wedding. Rejoice! Enjoy yourself! *(Ger.)*

The interpreter couldn't much believe himself either.

Question: Who's there?

Answer: There's this parable. A weary traveler is walking—a riverbed for love, a thermos for blood, a walker for word problems, a destiny for an ant, a shadow for a road. He sees a hut. Something like the first little piggy's tiny house. Reed, hazelnut branches, and upturned stumps that look like the lines on your palm: you, stream, will have three children and a very long life, while you, ravine, will have two wives, and each with a mole on her right shoulder. The sunset sprinkles the straw roof with brick dust. Windows made of something transparent with a film over it, so you can't look in. You can't see anything, as if someone had stuck dragonfly wings on with his tongue. A front porch long in want of paint, and steps that breathe huskily: you step—exhale; pick up your foot—inhale. He knocks, softly, but no one answers. Cobblestones had been hung in orange nets from the apple trees, to make them grow broader. After the rain, the clusters of white lilac are covered in rust. By a birch tree, the grass under the sink is thickly spattered with toothpaste. An old brick by the phlox. He wonders, What if there's a key? He picks it up and finds a centipede. He knocks again—louder this time. Shuffling from the other side of the door, a stifled cough, creaking floorboards. A strange voice asks, "Who are you?" The traveler answered, "Me." And hears in reply: "There's no room here for two." The traveler stands watching a butterfly stumble on the air, land on the paint-flakey windowsill, look at him with its peacock eye, and then suddenly blink. The traveler knocks again and asks to be let in, but the voice again asks the same question. And it all repeats. And it goes on like this until the peacock eye flies away, and to the question, "Who are you?" the traveler answers, "You." Then the door opens. But you knew all this without me.

Question: I can well imagine that strange voice. I hear it every day. It's my neighbor mumbling incessantly. Before, many years ago probably, before he was a boy, he was a cheerful wooden puppet, Pinocchio. Then a bad fairy made him a person, leaving him with his puppet voice. Now Pinocchio had lived his life and grown old, and he walks around forgetfully in his grimy long johns, frightening people, to the mailboxes—ours are in the courtyard—and at night he sweeps our path of the pine needles and cones that have fallen. We live in a sturdy building, like the third little piggy's, except it has lots of one-room apartments that no wolf could get into. But the old men and women who live in them are quietly turning into pupae. Later, at night, they gnaw through their cocoons and fly off to the rustle of the broom and the muttering of old long john Pinocchio. And the pine needles keep falling. Only a lazy person could fail to make up a parable about a traveler, but it's all nonsense.

Answer: Why?

Question: Because hay and straw, tick and tock, paint and canvas, sole and path, mirror and room, meter and second, cliff and cloud, round-shouldered jacket and cigarette-smelling skirt, the string that vibrates, and the air that gives birth to sound.

Answer: Fine, you're a writing pistil and I'm a talking stamen. We can begin.

Question: How are you doing?

Answer: Everything's fine.

Question: That doesn't happen.

382

Answer: So what?

Question: What's new?

Answer: You watch the news!

Question: Terrific. The news! The latest news! You could never imagine the kind of news we have here! Turn on one program, and it's a society chronicle: Lysicles, a cattle dealer, an insignificant man, insignificant on his own account and of low birth, he became the number one person in Athens because he lived with Aspasia after Pericles' death. Change channels, and there Dionysius is walking through Montmartre carrying his chopped off head in outstretched hands and it's dripping. On a third the Romans have had Jerusalem under siege for six months. On a fourth some guy is saying he's the new kindergarten doctor and has come to check all the children in this courtyard for pustules on their bottom, and now he has to go with him to the clinic.

Answer: What news is that if I already told you about that guy in our courtyard all those years ago!

Question: You know very well. The news is what's left for your whole life and grows the way a word carved in bark grows with the tree.

Answer: But in fact all this is so unimportant.

Question: Why unimportant, when all this is in you and you're made of it? One time you found a condom stuffed with twisted rags under your mama's pillow. She was in the kitchen making breakfast. At first you wanted to ask her what it was, but all of a sudden you got scared and never did.

Answer: I remember, but all that really is not important.

Question: And what is important? How you acted out the fairy tale about the three sisters—one-eye, two-eye, and three-eye—and drew yourself a third eye on your forehead?

Answer: Yes.

Question: What else?

Answer: The doctor prescribed me salt rubs in the morning. I didn't like it, of course, but every morning Mama dissolved the sea salt and rubbed me down with a sponge. Once in school I fought during class change with the other girls, I don't remember over what now, and sat in the lesson and was so unhappy, lonely, and unwanted. And then I licked my hand and tasted the salt on my skin. A strange sensation shot through me. Does that mean there are people in the world who need these salt rubs of mine? That is, not even the rubs, but me. But I'm making this up now because at the time I just licked my skin and tasted the salt and felt the love.

Question: So tell me how lovers came to see your mother and you were supposed to do your homework in the kitchen, but your mother ran out in her robe, with nothing underneath, and shot off into the bathroom.

Answer: One, Uncle Slava, was funny, and Mama liked him very much. She liked them all, really. She didn't want to go south for vacation. She said you shouldn't have vacation flings—you got attached. Uncle Slava always said bizarre things. For instance, we're sitting at the table eating, but I don't want to. Mama says to me, "Why are you being so stubborn? Eat!" But I wouldn't. And then Uncle Slava defended me. "Tanya, lay off. A person isn't a gastrointestinal tract!" After the meal he suddenly started enlightening Mama as to how the world worked: "We men," he said, "are slaves to the hormones that are injected into our blood and slam at our brains. There's nothing you can do. They use us! God banks his fire with our bodies! Why is it laid down in the female instinct to take care of a man as if he were a child? Because for hundreds of thousands of years—forever—people lived in group marriage, and the male lovers were its grown children. For a woman, a lover is always her child!" And he winked at me. "Make note of that!" Mama liked him very much. He was married and visited Mama once a week, on Fridays. Mama waited for him, cooked him something tasty, made herself up. Sometimes she allowed me to paint her nails with bright red polish. She said that fingers should be like church candles, pale and slender, and the nails like flames. I liked to climb into bed with her. It was cozy to curl up there, snuggle with her, and prattle about something before falling asleep. Or she would read me something. Even afterward, when I was bigger. Then she would read me something of her own, not a children's book, that usually lay on her nightstand—novels or horoscopes. I remember her reading in a horoscope that she and Uncle Slava were simply counter-indicated for each other, and she got very upset. I tried to reassure her, "Mama, sweet Mama, but look, it can be all right with a Taurus or a Capricorn!" But she said, "I don't want anyone else, I only want my Leo—to comb his mane, and fiddle with his ears." Over her bed hung a Gauguin reproduction. Mama often lay there looking at it. She called it her window. I can see the palms and swarthy, half-naked girls as if it were now. Mama laughed. "I'll tie a vine around my waist and run away from here, from your winter, and go to my Tahitian paradise. Only you can't get lianas anywhere, there's nothing but snowdrifts all around!"

Question: Do you remember your father?

Answer: No. But Mama told me a lot about him. When I was supposed to appear, at first he didn't want me. Mama'd had a few abortions before that. This time, when Papa found out she was pregnant, he said they couldn't allow themselves a child right then. They set aside money for the abortion, which cost a lot then, and they had very little money. I must have wanted very much to live, though, because Papa suddenly took that money, tore it up, and said, "That's it. There is no money for an abortion. We're having this baby!" Mama loved him very much. She wanted the child to have his name, and she was very happy that he was Alexander because if the baby was a boy he would be Sasha, and if it was a girl she would be Sasha, too. She and I had no secrets. Before I went to sleep I'd snuggle up to her in bed and we would tell each other everything. I would tell her, and she me, absolutely everything, the good and the bad both. She suffered a lot over the fact that her younger sister died in childhood because of her. It happened in the summer, at the dacha, when Mama was eight. Her parents had gone somewhere and left her to look after her sister, whose name was Sasha, like me. She was a year and a half and she was sleeping, but when she woke up she started screaming. Mama tried to calm her down, but nothing worked. Then it started raining and Mama decided for some reason that if she took Sasha outside the rain would calm her down. So she wrapped their father's old raincoat around herself and her little sister, stepped off the porch, and sat down with her on a step under a lilac bush. The branches were bending, the trees were rustling, the puddles were gurgling, and Sasha quieted down from the sound of the rain right away. The rain was powerful and slanting, and Mama forgot to close the windows, so water came in on the veranda. She got up to carry the sleeping child to her crib and shut the windows on the terrace and started going up the front stairs but got tangled in the raincoat, stumbled, and fell, and Sasha's head struck the ground, full force. Mama got very scared and didn't know what to do. She ran to the neighbors, who took the child to the hospital, while she stayed behind to wait for her parents. Later, when they arrived, they went to the hospital, too. They never did bring the child home. A few days later, Sasha died. Mama was so upset she cried all night every night. She decided not to live anymore, to kill herself. She told herself, How can I live if little Sasha died because of me? And so when everyone came back from the funeral and was sitting at the funeral feast, she went into the garden and thought she would drown herself in the toilet, but she looked and saw worms there and got scared. I stroked Mama's hand, not knowing what to say, and said, "Dear Mama, don't cry, instead of that little girl now you have me! Maybe I'm that girl! I'm Sasha, too!" We would snuggle and fall asleep like that. It was wonderful to drift off to sleep together.

Question: You remind me of someone. A girl I knew many years ago. But it doesn't matter, she's gone. One time she and I had a fight, I don't even remember what over, and we said lots of hurtful words to each other, and she left after flinging a book at me. Half an hour later she came back and said softly, "Put your sweater on inside out!" I didn't understand, I just saw her sweater was inside out. I asked, "Why?" "When I was a child my grandmother said that if you get lost in the forest, you have to put your dress on inside out to find your way." I put my sweater on inside out and it was true, all of a sudden everything angry and cruel that had built up between us disappeared, and I felt like hugging her, squeezing her, never letting her go.

Answer: What happened to her?

Question:	What's the difference?
Answer:	Tell me more?
Question:	If you like. What are you smiling at?
Answer:	I remembered something. I used to think all my friends were pretty and I was ugly. I was horribly embarrassed by my body. I'd had boiling water spilled on my chest and neck as a child. I always wrapped up so no one would see. I wore a high-necked bathing suit to the pool and beach. But I so wanted to be like everyone else. So I remember, I decided to start smoking. All the girls smoked, but not me. My girlfriend kept offering, and I kept refusing. Then one time on the square I took the proffered cigarette, tried to inhale, and choked. Some old woman was walking by. She stopped, looked at us, and shook her head. Then she shouted to the whole world, "Now you're going to suck the devil's prick in the next world!"
Question:	Where's your scalded skin? In what spot?
Answer:	I'm not going to show you.
Question:	There was a bookshelf at the head of the sofa. She took out some picture book and started leafing through. Suddenly she says, "Why does she have a belly button?" I didn't understand. "What belly button? Who?" She shows me the two-page Cranach spread, and there's Adam and Eve, and Eve really does have a belly button. I wrote that down then. I had a fat notebook, and I thought it was important to write everything down. I also wrote down the way she set down the album—face down on her thighs, so it looked like a mini-skirt.
Answer:	I lived oblivious to myself. As a child. Then all of a sudden you realize you aren't just you but you're supposed to make people like you. Or rather, not supposed to, but want to badly. Everyone around you: men, women,

the mirror, the cat, the bus passengers, the clouds, the water from the tap. It's as if you've had an unwieldy sack dumped on you and been given a push—go. But you can't take two steps with a burden like that. I didn't like myself. Myself, my body. I absolutely couldn't stand me. I was disgusted that I existed as a body at all. I didn't like having breasts. That is true agony, being visible every day! And there's nothing you can do! I read in some book how the heroine cut off her eyelashes with scissors, after which they grew out so that you could rest several matches on them. I did the same thing, but the grown-out lashes were even worse than the old ones.

Question: I also remember, we were talking about something, and I said that God's existence couldn't be proved. And she objected, nothing of the kind, it was actually very simple. I said, "Prove it!" She was silent for a moment and answered that all it took was one line. She read the line from some poem about how a bird is the cross God wears. "Do you really need any other proof?" and she laughed. I can see her stopping as if it were right now. We were walking along the embankment late one evening, and she sat down on a granite parapet and started moving farther and farther down, rocking from side to side, taking little steps with her buttocks.

Answer: Something that wasn't me, something alien, seemed to be growing on my body's surface. I'm one thing, and this woman I'm growing is another. I was constantly blushing and didn't know what to do about it. Someone would start talking to me and I'd freeze, and I'd check, frightened, because it always seemed as though something was wrong with my clothing. A bolt from the blue—had my stockings run? I felt naked, I didn't know what to say, only my hands would sweat. I cried into Mama's pillow before going to sleep and she would try to console me. "Don't be a Gloomy Gus. Be cheerful!"

Question: We had nowhere to perch, so we would just walk the streets for hours on end. I remember, one peasant woman was by the subway selling cherries in a sweating glass jar. We bought some and wanted to sit somewhere, but all the benches were wet after the rain, so we walked to an empty playground with broken swings. I set my bookbag down on the edge of the sandbox and sat on it, and she sat on my lap. We started eating cherries. They were ripe and dripped juice. At first we spat the pits into the sand, which looked like gooseflesh from the rain and was littered with cigarette butts, broken glass, and beer bottle caps, aiming for a sand patty left by some child that had melted in the rain. Across the way was a venerable monument to the dead, a statue of a soldier with an arm broken off which had probably held a submachine gun—there was a rod sticking out from the stump. The dead soldier looked up with empty white eyeballs at the wet treetops, from which rain would fall with each gust of wind. With his remaining hand he was calling to someone to follow—us, evidently, because there wasn't anyone else in the little square, as if to say, Guys, let's climb those trees, and from there heaven is just a stone's throw! Then we started not just spitting the pits but squeezing them hard between our fingers so that they shot out and flew right at the soldier, leaving cherry scratches in the plaster, or whatever it was made of. We kept getting stained by the juice and pits and our hands were all cherry. She shot accurately, better than I did, and one time even hit him in the eye. A cherry pupil suddenly appeared in the white, so now the soldier was looking at us out of the corner of one eye, as if to say, I died for you and you're

390

shooting pits at me? We went into a laughing fit and set off to roam the streets some more. Now, after so many years, I know that the one-armed plaster soldier watching us go was thinking something very different: I died for something important and also for myself, and if you fired pits at me in this square drenched with rain and your love, then so be it, maybe that's part of what's important.

Answer: I get undressed and look at myself in the mirror. Here is someone's naked body in the middle of the room on the cold parquet floor. Scrawny, ugly, with a patch of frog-skin. A princess frog. And a star burning in her forehead. Not a star, an entire constellation. My whole forehead in pimples, and one is ready to pop on the tip of my nose. My cheeks are pale, but treacherously so. At just the wrong moment, they turned beet red. After a cold I get a sore on my lip. There is a draft in the room and my body, already turning blue, shivers. You run your hand over it, and it isn't smooth but covered in pimples. Breasts no bigger than a pincushion. Nipples as tiny as blackheads. On my belly, a red mark from my panty elastic. An ugly belly button, an outie, like an unripe grape. Below, curling hair. You could tug at the tufts. Why is there hair there? After that, invisible openings, which you can't examine without a mirror. How did people live before mirrors? Never seeing themselves once in their whole life? I stand and think, can this body that's turned blue, covered with gooseflesh, chinked, hollow, a body no one in the world needs, especially me, can this really be me? And what is this hair between my legs for?

Question: We were visiting a young couple, both musicians, who'd just had a baby, a boy. There was a piano in the room, inherited from a composer grandfather. The father, a conservatory student, my age, put his son on the piano lid between two pillows and played. Then he changed the baby's diaper himself, right there, on an oilcloth spread on the piano. We stood and watched how deftly he did it all with his long fingers. And how he tickled his son's tiny feet with his cheek stubble.

Answer: I didn't need anything, after all, just to love. It was as if I were a cup that had to be filled to the brim. Or a stocking waiting for a leg so it could become itself. After all, the whole point of a stocking is the leg. That's the only reason it was created, in its image and likeness. Everything in me was ready, but I was empty inside. Then one summer Mama and I went to the Riga coast for vacation. We agreed to be sisters. She looked very good for her age. That's how we went around, like two sisters. There was one Latvian there, a very young fellow, and I liked him very much. So did Mama. All of a sudden, for the first time in our lives, a chill ran between us. She was the swan queen and I was the frog. She was starting up an affair with the Latvian and I was getting in the way. Before that summer Mama had been practically everything to me, and I'd wanted to be like her. Now I suddenly looked at her with completely different eyes. And here one day at the beach Mama was playing volleyball and I was sitting in the sand by the water in agony because I had no one and nothing. I wiped the spray on my face and tasted the skin on my hand—salty, like when I was a child. And I decided that if a fourth wave licked my toes, I would have love—a tremendous, real love to last a lifetime. But the waves were puny, sickly, and kept stopping farther and farther from my feet, both the second and the third. But the fourth collected itself, buckled, and reached me. It took all my toes in its mouth and tickled my heel with sand! All of a sudden it was happening to me! I sat and listened, and saw, inhaling everything around me, sea, sky, wind, gulls, people, but this wasn't vision, or hearing, or touch, or smell. It was love, and I had nothing else of my own—no eyes, hands, or feet. It was all love's. I jumped up and ran across the water into the sea, literally flew, like a bird, the tips of my feet barely touching the water. Where could I put so much love? What should I do with it?

Question: One day we went for a ride on the river bus. It was about to rain, and she took her umbrella from home—big, antediluvian, faded, that didn't fold up but you could lean on it like a walking stick. We were sitting on the deck and it was frightfully windy. She slipped off her sandals and stuck her bare feet into the umbrella, hiding them there from the wind. She pulled up the umbrella and covered herself with its ribs and membrane. She shouted, "Look! I don't have any legs now. I have an umbrella instead!" She started lifting and lowering it, like a coiled tail slapping the deck. Then she said, "Hey, a half-woman-half-fish—that's a rusalka. But a half-girl-half-umbrella—what does that make?" I answered, "An umbrelka." She laughed. "You're the umbrelka! I'm a parapluika!"

Answer: Still, tell me, what happened to her afterward?

Question: She read somewhere that people are the branch we blossom on, like leaves from buds. The leaves fall, but the branch grows. She decided that some murdered child had migrated into her soul. Something had happened in their family, I don't remember. She said the only way to explain children dying was karma—that was why they were killed. A young girl's ravings. All sorts of things can happen any minute. Anyone can carry a child, stumble, and fall. That's it. It's that simple.

Answer: You don't understand a single thing! Here I was watching them doing experiments with dying people on television. When a person was dying, they set him on a very sensitive scale. A whole program of experiments. It turned out that after the agony and death the body's mass decreased on average by five grams. Or ten, I don't remember. Some a little more, some a little less. That is a person's net weight, without the body. Call it what you like—his soul, quintessence, pollen. And these few grams don't go anywhere. They're here somewhere. Multiply all that by billions or however many people have been looking at the sunset for tens and hundreds of thousands of years— quadrillions? These are the mountains that weigh on our shoulders. They tell us it's atmospheric pressure, but it's everything that happened to those who lived before us, that's why there's this weight. Sailors have a belief that the souls of the dead migrate into gulls, but that's not true. We are the branch, but for next year. And the soul of your father the submariner is not in some gull. It's in you. You're afraid of water, and everyone says that it's because in a past life you drowned. But that's ridiculous. There is no past life. Life is one, and in it is your father, he was nineteen, and he was lying with his boat at the bottom of the Baltic after a failed attempt to torpedo a German transport ship that was making a run at the end of the war from Riga to Germany with troops, or, more likely, refugees. He told you about that! Depth charges were exploding around them, and after one explosion the emergency light went off and in the pitch darkness he thought that was it, the end, that the next bay had been breached—they had started knocking at the hatch there, though they were supposed to sit in silence, no matter what. And your father got so scared that this fear

394

was now living in you. It's all connected, like with the tree, visible and invisible, rough and gentle, tops and roots. The roots are the mouth. The leaves are the baby fish. The pollen is love. It just seems that everything is on its own, that the record your father listened to in the basement on the player held together by electrical tape was one thing, and Dracula, who wanted to make people happy but didn't know how was another, and that chattering Pinocchio in long johns whisking his broom was again another. Naturally, besides those few grams, call it pollen, call it God, the name doesn't change anything, and man is not just animal but vegetable and mineral, too, simultaneously. Hair, nails, and bowels live by the laws of the vegetable world. The mineral is clear as is. The blind guts that just can't stop, and the stubborn hair that doesn't want to know anything, they really are different for everyone. But those flying grams, that's something completely different.

Question: How can something that isn't there be different?

Answer: Your gaze, which stuck to the lamp's reflection on the night window, your voice, which hides from you under the bed and jumps out the pane, the words you write, to say nothing of the milk teeth your mama collected in a vaseline jar—that's not you, but that doesn't mean there is no you. Just like this night, and the piece of bush out the window, white because the lamp's light is falling on it, and the drone of the plane, and your neighbor exchanging chirps with his key—as if neighbor and key were wishing each other a good night—all that will pass by morning, but that doesn't mean anything.

Question: And if I'd never heard anything about the Arunta tribe, which believes in a rock Eratipa, the haven for children's souls, which peek out of a hole in the rock at the

395

women passing by, confident that this is how a child ends up in their hot, wet fold, that doesn't mean there is no such tribe. And if somewhere in Colmar, known in Russia only as the homeland of Pushkin's murderer, the soap in one soap dish turned into a jellyfish, but I don't know anything about it, does my ignorance really prove the impossibility of soap turning into a jellyfish? And because the old lady hasn't thrown anything from the seventh floor for a week, that certainly doesn't mean she's gone.

Answer: You haven't changed at all. It's impossible to talk seriously with you about anything. And if someone once said I slept as if I were swimming the crawl, and in my sleep once I felt him touch my palm with his lips, cautiously, so as not to wake me, does that really mean it didn't happen if it did?

Question: I think I'm starting to see what you're getting at. On my way home today I saw a crushed cat. The car's wheels had rolled her out like a sheet of paper. It's in our world that it's as flat as a shadow on asphalt, but in fact it's got volume, three dimensions, like us, and on one page it catches snowflakes on the balcony with its paw.

Answer: Of course! The point sees the line, for the point is a line, and it thinks of it as a plane. Someone is reading this line now and seeing the page, a plane, but that is merely a reflection, the manifestation of some three-dimensional body, this old folder on the table here with the coffee stain, this moth here going crazy over the lamp, this lumpy pillow here, me, you. What are you thinking about?

Question: About how you aren't anywhere anymore, just on these pages.

Answer: You aren't listening to me at all!

Question:	Sorry, go on!
Answer:	So you see, a thinking shadow realizes that it is merely a reflection of the traveler, whom it can neither see, nor hear, nor apprehend. The shadow comprises the road, the grasses, the steps, the floorboards, the walls, whatever it falls on. The shadow can be animal, vegetable, and mineral simultaneously. But the main thing about it, you see, is the traveler. And here we are, merely the shadow of someone we can neither see, nor hear, nor apprehend. Our body is only the shadow of our other genuine existence, here, touch my knee!
Question:	Rough.
Answer:	Enough! Take your hand off!
Question:	But who is this traveler?
Answer:	What do you care? Traveler, snow, pollen—it's all words. All that's important is that where the traveler, snow, and pollen are, we are an intact whole. How can I explain so you understand? Here you smell something scorching—a moth's been caught, burned its wings on the hot light bulb—and outside a night rain has started falling again, but it's not drops falling from the sky but letters—d, r, o, p, s—you hear, drumming on the windowsill, and the smell of incinerated moth—it's all letters. And we are all an intact whole.
Question:	It really does stink of moth. We should open the window, to air it out.
Answer:	Go. I'll wait.
Question:	A soft, invisible rain. When drops fall right by the window, they blaze up in the lamplight. Large, intermittent, and long. It's as if the old lady were throwing utterly useless white pencils down at me from the seventh floor, picking them up by the tip one at a time and dropping them.

Answer:	Go quickly! I'm cold.
Question:	Wait, we were talking about something else entirely, after all. What?
Answer:	We've been talking the whole time about love. You and I never talked about that before. It's as if we've been avoiding the word because it seemed too much. Can you really gather up, funnel everything you're feeling into some narrow word?
Question:	So what should I do? Come up with another word? New symbols for the letters?
Answer:	You're teasing me again! This isn't about the word. Use any word—traveler, pollen, God, or even that same centipede. In one dimension it hid under a brick between the swollen, rain-laden phlox, but in the other, it's everywhere. Love is a special, God-size centipede, as weary as the shelter-seeking traveler, as omnipresent as pollen. It puts each of us on like a stocking. We're sewn to its foot and we take on its shape. It walks us. So here, in this centipede, we are all one. It doesn't have a hundred feet. It has as many as humanity. It comprises us, like cells, and each cell is by itself but can only live by the one shared breath. We just don't realize we're living in an invisible and intangible fourth dimension that is the love-centipede and see ourselves only in the third—that cat flattened on the road that is in fact alive and catching snowflakes with its paw.
Question:	You have icy feet.
Answer:	As usual, you weren't listening to me. Remember I said that ever since I was a child I was puzzled: "What is this hair below for?" But you answered so simply, "To be kissed."
Question:	I remember. It was very hot, and we were walking around the apartment naked. We'd gone swimming, and I was

sunburned all over. You said burned skin should be smeared with sour cream. There wasn't any sour cream, just kefir. You said kefir wouldn't do, but I said it didn't matter, the main thing was that it was cold! I lay on my stomach, and you rubbed my back with icy kefir from the refrigerator. We'd just remodeled the apartment, and there were newspapers spread on the freshly painted floor. We were walking around barefoot, and the newspapers were sticking to our sweaty feet—that was how hot it was—even as night fell. Then we went into the bathroom. There was a spider there, and you washed it away with a stream of water from the shower. I really wanted to take your bra and panties off your naked body, uncover your skin, so white it was almost blue compared with your sunburn. We drew a full bath, you climbed in and stretched out, and in the green of the water your legs looked short and crooked, like frogs' legs. I stroked them under the water, long and slender to my wet touch, and thought that this was how it should be because you were my princess frog. Then, when drops fell off me into the water, you leaned over to look and said, "Look, they've curdled like little clouds."

Answer: All my girlfriends had already done everything, but before you I hadn't done anything. Long ago my mama gave me these little balls you're supposed to insert into your vagina beforehand, but what was I supposed to do with these little balls? So they were lying in the refrigerator. You open it to get the milk and see the little balls, and it's enough to make you weep. How I wanted to love for real, to press myself to a body, flat, to stick to every piece of skin, to turn inside out, to pull you in me like a pillowcase. When you found out I was still a virgin frog, you suddenly fell still and were about to

399

say something, but I covered your mouth with my hand: "Quiet! I want to so much!" It didn't last very long for us, though; you ejaculated right away. I smeared it on my stomach, my breasts, the blotches on my neck, sniffed it, tasted it—and I still wasn't a woman. I started in the psychology department, failed, and got a job in the university vivarium. Before, I'd imagined that everything would have to be beautiful for me my first time with a man: a beautiful room, definitely with candles and beautiful music playing. Life should be beautiful. Then I realized that beauty was something completely different. I liked wandering between the jars of frogs, past the shelves of trays where white mice teemed. I liked that particular smell—warm, earthy, deep. There were also three monkeys, scared and mean. People were doing experiments on them. They were screwed into special clamps to hold them still and had electrodes inserted in their head. In intervals between experiments they sat in their cage with sad eyes. There were sacks of walnuts there. Remember, you held a nut through the grating and the monkey grabbed the nut and hit your hand as hard as it could. And looked at you with eyes that held malice, not sadness. In the courtyard there were rows of cages with dogs. When one started howling, the others would start in, and then the howling rose to the sky. I was supposed to drown the puppies, and you started helping me. We poured water into a bucket, threw the puppies in, and quickly covered it with another bucket of water and pushed down, so that the water spilled over, getting our feet wet. I got a hold of myself, but the tears still flowed. To console me, you said, "Hey there, don't cry! All this can get used later somewhere, in some story." You said something so absurd, my whole insides were pierced by such acute pity, such love for you, that I wanted to press your head to my breast and caress you like a baby. I had to bring straw to lay in the far empty cage. We went there, and before I knew it I'd wound myself around you, clasped you, kissed you, fallen on you. That was real beauty: the smell of the prickly straw, the heaven-sent howl, you inside me for the first time, and the pain, and the blood, and the joy.

Question: Do you remember the day the album covered your thighs like a skirt, and then you went to the bathroom and I thought you wanted a shower, but there was no splashing, and all I could hear was you looking for something in the cupboard where the shampoo, nail scissors, and different potions were kept? I lay there listening to the sounds from the bathroom, trying to guess what you might be doing there, looking at your sandal, now still in the armchair—you'd given your foot a shake to get it off fast when we were undressing and it went flying. I lay there thinking that once again I wasn't preparing for class; I was studying linguistics, and I was supposed to do exercises for every class, like high school. And there I was lying on my old sunken couch, which creaked at every movement, or rather, it didn't creak, it yelled, as if to say, Hey, you there, stop it this minute, you like making love here but I'm going to collapse any second, all my legs are teetering!, and waited for you and thought, Damn them, those irregular verbs! Right then you came out of the bathroom and stopped at the room's threshold. You smiled. "Don't you notice anything?" I looked at you standing leaning against the jamb, arms behind your head, elbows out, knee turned in slightly, the toes of one foot resting on the other's. I looked at the pink webbed patch under your collarbone, your nipple grains, the dark mass below your belly—as if you were squeezing something between your legs—a mitten or woolen sock—and suddenly I noticed you didn't have a belly button. I stood up, walked over, and figured out that you'd covered your belly button with a bandage. A flesh-colored bandage, unnoticeable at a distance. I swept you up and wanted to spin you around, but there was no room to in the tiny space. We lost our balance and fell on the couch. Remember the crack when it collapsed beneath us? You were dying of laughter, and I ripped the bandage from your belly, dying to tell you there, inside, to the grape poking out of your belly button, how much I loved you.

Answer: You scratched your lip on my earring that day, too. Show me! No, I don't see anything.

Question: I also liked visiting you at the vivarium. In that cage, our cage.

Answer: At first I liked everyone there, but toward the end I couldn't do anything anymore. They collected dogs all over town and brought them in frightened and half-dead. Different foods were issued for them, meat, but the meat was all stolen, and they fed the dogs dog meat. They would kill one, slaughter it, and throw it to the others. I told myself that on my last day of work, before leaving, I would open all the cages and free those wretches. One time I was held up, this was late fall, it got dark early, and it was as cold as winter. As it happened, that night all the cages were empty and only one dog was left. It started to bark a few times, but no one responded. And then it started howling. I ran away as fast as I could so I wouldn't hear that howling. It may have felt like the last dog on earth. I came home, to the one-room we were renting then in Belyaevo; you weren't there, and I started rummaging through your clothing, sniffing your sleeves, rubbing my face on your sweater, pulling on your shirt. There I was walking around the apartment and loving—and I couldn't do anything else. You weren't with me, but that was irrelevant, I was so filled with love for you that no other thought, even the teensiest, had anywhere to creep in. No matter where I looked, I saw you anyway. Just these rushes of happiness. There was the heat gurgling in the radiator—gurgling so cozily! The frosty air was slipping through the small pane—so good! Here was your scarf—so soft on my neck! Here I was looking out the window at two people standing under a street-lamp having a steam-puff conversation—what a marvelous language they'd invented! I got such pleasure from every sensation only because I was smelling, seeing, touching it. One might as well sob at the fullness of being, but I went to fry up potatoes and onions—you were coming soon—and sobbed from the onions, but for me, at that moment, it was the same thing.

Question: Wait a sec, my arm's gone to sleep. Lay your head on my chest.

Answer: It's not too heavy like that?

Question: No. Talk.

Answer: I thought about you and realized that this love was my first and last, it had never been before and never would be again. Never before us were there, and never after us would there be, those cherry pits, the kefir on your sunburnt back, the bandage on my belly that didn't want to pull off. Or remember that night on the Klyazma, when we were standing watching a horse under an apple tree reaching for an apple with its lips and the cloud that flew over, changing its color? Or how before bed you would read something cozy about myths out loud: first they decimated everyone there except for one boy, whom a she-wolf saved and fed, and then she became his wife and bore him nine sons. You reading and winding my hair around your finger. Me whispering, drifting off: "So I won't run off in my sleep?" You nodding and reading about some god who was born from under another god's arm. After all, it's me who was the newest newborn god! I curled up in a ball under your arm, pressing close to you, as if I'd just been born from under your arm. Through my sleep I hear someone conceiving from a dove striking her face.

Question: Tell me, where were you swimming in your sleep—one arm forward, under the pillow, the other back, palm up?

Answer: What do you mean where? To you! What I feared most was all this ending. Somewhere I'd read about the take-away game, and I started preparing myself: the fewer the attachments, the less it hurt to live. Medicine for dependence. The self-cure is to relax, wait a while, close your eyes. Imagine something nearby—an empty glass at the table's edge. Mama was taking her medicine, and she'd left lip marks on the rim. The glass fell on the floor and broke. Good luck. In the cupboard, an album of my childhood photographs. Someone might throw them out. Burn them even. Take a big skillet, put it on the burner, and burn them one by one. On my grandmother's pretty dish by the mirror, my rings and earrings. A burglar might come—and the dish would be empty. That's not so terrible. It means you won't scratch yourself on my earring post anymore. Skis in the toilet—due to the lack of space, but where else? If I come from the dacha in the summer, and they've been gnawed by a ski-eater, I could give the ski poles to the neighbor children, who would build wigwams from the poles and blankets. Here's my foot up against the wall: toes spread, then gather, as if my foot were scratching the wallpaper's back. I'm going to fall under a streetcar, my leg will get cut off, then I'll hop around on crutches, they'll make me a prosthesis so I can walk in trousers and no one will notice, but I'll get by without a leg. Here's my mama, my beloved, good, foolish mama. Her life didn't turn out the way she'd dreamed, and she felt that her life was a draft for me and I would rewrite it all anew, a fair copy: I'd get married and have everything like normal people, a family and a child from a husband I loved and who loved me, and all of it genuine. One of my first memories is my mama drawing a hot bath, boiling practically, that is, it actually was boiling water—she boiled the pot and kettle and filled the tub with the hot water—then sprinkling dry mustard in and getting in, squealing and keening. Then, when she got out she'd be all steamed, crimson. During one of these baths she accidentally scalded me. Mama used to tell me that when she was pregnant, and then had an abortion, she'd had mixed feelings: both pity for the unborn child and also something completely different. She felt like a full-fledged woman. On the contrary, if she hadn't got pregnant, she would have felt as though something were wrong with her, that she was inferior for not being able to give birth. For her, each pregnancy was a sign that all was in order, all was well. The next time she could prepare for a real birth, give birth to a child. And now I imagined my mama dying. Sooner or later this had to happen anyway, after all. My chest, where my heart was, felt like it was being crushed, but I would survive this, too. All of a sudden I saw a snowy, twilight funeral. Someone was saying that the earth should be her pillow. I threw a frozen clump of sand into the hole where she'd been lowered. It hit hard, ringing, and took a hop. As if I had thrown a stone at her corpse. For all her love for me. Tears welled in my eyes, but there was nothing you could do, that's how it was going to be and I'd have to live without her. That's when I started imagining losing you. But before I could think about what might happen to you, what disaster might take you away, everything grew dim, my insides knotted tight, even my temples cramped from the suddenly piercing fear, the instant void, the frozen loneliness. In one instant I ceased to be a person and became a stocking thrown on the winter's night garbage heap.

Question: It's hot. Let's not have a blanket. That's the way. Tell me, you did want to open all the cages before you left, after all. Did you do it?

Answer: Of course not. At least they were alive in those cages. Otherwise they'd have all been poisoned. There was so much of everything I wanted to tell you, but now that I'm snuggled up to you I've forgotten it all. You remember something else!

Question: Once you said that for a long time you thought children were born from behind, because in the village one summer you saw a colt born from under a horse's tail.

Answer: I probably smothered you with my love. It was just too much for you. It happens. One person loves, suspecting nothing, and the other suffocates from that love. Suddenly I was dying with longing for you and I called, and you said, "I can't talk to you right now!" and you hung up. I called back. You hung up again. I called again— and on and on. You didn't understand that I just needed to hear "I love you." That was it. I wouldn't have called anymore. As it was, I drove you and me both mad. You were writing some endless novel and would read me excerpts, and I didn't understand a thing, but I still liked it

tremendously. If you'd read me instructions for installing a washing machine I would have thought it marvelous. Once you wrote about me taking a white mouse
out of a tray by its tail and a whole cluster latching onto
it, and they had cranberry eyes, and you said, "As it is
you're going to disappear, but if I write you down, you'll
remain."

Question: And you laughed: "Where could I disappear to? But if
you forget your notebook in the subway, that's it! How
can you not understand that one hair of mine left on the
pillow when I leave in the morning is more real than all
your words put together!"

Answer: I thought constantly about our future and got scared;
after all, you can't fall in love for the first time and drag
that love through your whole life. That means it all has to
end someday. And I started playing takeaway with myself
again. Later I realized that this just prolonged the misery.
I was summoning it up by imagining it and by being
afraid. I really did break something—not my leg, true,
but my arm. I went around with a cast in a sling. It was
good for cracking nuts. Even later, when Mama died, it
was just as I'd imagined: a snowy cemetery at twilight,
and someone saying, "May the earth be her pillow!" I
threw a frozen clump of sand into the hole where she'd
just been lowered. It struck the coffin lid hard, ringing,
and took a hop, as if I'd thrown a nut. And when you
left, I howled exactly like that dog, left to freeze in its
cage. I suddenly understood Mama, why she used love
to save herself each time from that icy cold. After all, it's
impossible—being left alone with that universal loneliness, with yourself. She had to die of love every day so
as not to suffocate from the fear of the icy cage. I was so
afraid of losing you, and I kept thinking about the others

you would have afterward. Who were they? Could they really love you more than I could? I was beside myself with jealousy and envy. Here they'd be snuggling with you like me, kissing you like me, and touching you everywhere like me. Then a simple thought occurred: but they would just be copying me. Your love for me would be their template. Each time you would be loving me. When I realized this, I even stopped being jealous of them, and they became practically family. Even a little bit me, after all they would smell of you in the morning the same way. That is, they would be completely different, but a little bit me. As if you and I hadn't parted but kept meeting over and over.

Question: I really did lose that notebook somewhere. I thought it was the end of the world—that's how important everything there was. But everything there probably was unimportant. Those words are gone, but your hair on my pillow—here it is, I'm winding it around my finger.

Answer: Once, when Mama was already quite ill, she and I were talking about my father and some others, and she said you can only fall out of love if you didn't love, and that you would go on to love your beloved through many others. That's what she said. "If only I could gather them all up! I would hold them all close to my breast! I would seat them all at the table and feed them something tasty, like children!" She also said that it was only the distance between points A and B that was measured in kilometers, whereas life was measured in people, and you needed to absorb people into yourself, and no one you loved would go anywhere, they would live in you, you would comprise them. That's how you measure life. Then, after the summer on the Riga seashore, more than anything in the world I wanted not to be my mother.

I didn't want to resemble her in anything. Sometimes I caught myself thinking with horror that I understood and felt everything she once did. Here you and I loved each other, but in my head was the thought that maybe my mama loved my father exactly the same way when I was already somewhere near this world. And I'm holding you exactly the same way, running my fingers down your spine, wrapping my legs around you exactly the way she once did with my father. And I'm experiencing the exact same feelings she did. At that moment, she and I suddenly united, merged. You have exactly the same kind of mole below your shoulder blade as my father did. Mama said that all her life she searched for one man, her first love. Maybe he too had a mole below his shoulder blade?

Question: Maybe half of humanity has a mole below their shoulder blade. It's just that no one ever looked.

Answer: But tell me, you must have had the sensation at least once that you were your father, right?

Question: Never. Or rather, once, yes. Shortly after his death. I was somewhere on a train, it was winter, and it was late, night. It was too stuffy to sleep, so I was walking to the platform to stand a while and get some air. I made my way to the end of the second-class car—legs, arms, snoring, dream moans, stuffy air, stench coming from everywhere. The passage was narrow, the car was rocking, I grabbed the railing, which was cold and felt sweaty. I went out on the platform, where everything was grown over in ice, the door to the next car didn't shut, there was clattering, the buffers were dancing, the iron clanking. Not only that, but there was the darkness and not a single lamp on. All of a sudden I was gripped by such cold and crushed by such longing. For a moment the rattling car seemed like a submarine and I was him, my father. He and I became a single whole. Time and everything else suddenly turned to nothing, to dust. I was my father. The submarine was being tossed as if depth charges were exploding all around. I hurried back to my stinking, stuffy car. There, in the narrow passage, I ran into the conductor; he was holding an axe and coming right at me. I was taken aback, but he was on his way to chop the filth that had frozen in the toilet.

Answer: Do you know who lived in this apartment before you?

Question: No. Some old man.

Answer: You lived in your apartment before you. Nights you listened the same way to the sound of the broom and your neighbor's doll voice—he couldn't sleep again. Why don't you talk to him?

Question: I've already written about him.

Answer: He's lonely.

Question: That's how this building was conceived. All one-room apartments. Cells handy for quiet pupation.

Answer: But who does the old man share his concern or joy with? His tomorrow? And the fact that there's a storm coming? And it will be fall soon?

Question: What does the old man have to do with this? We were talking about love.

Answer: That's what we are talking about. Did you figure out who was throwing white pencils down at you?

Question: What time is it?

Answer: That's it exactly! Minutes and years, all these are units unknown to life and signifying what there isn't. Time is measured by the altered coloring of the horse that stretches its lips to the apple. Time, like a sewing machine, sews that overheated dog's cage full of straw in a jagged line with the empty subway car and the forgotten notebook, the rustle of falling pencils out the window, and that sheet twisted in a knot. And here this book that's lying on the floor, that you can open right away to the last page and read how the weary travelers, as they endure all their trials, losing and gaining, despairing and believing, killing their feet and scratching their souls, coarsening to the touch and maturing to love, come to the end of their long journey, to the very sea, which is hung on a tautly drawn horizon by distant sails, like clothespins, and, bathed in tears, rush to embrace one another and shout something ridiculous, delirious with joy.

Question: But if the period has already been placed on the last page of the future, can nothing be changed? What if you'd like to fix something in your life? Bring someone back? Love someone all the way?

Answer: On the contrary, even what's already happened can change at any moment. Every person you've lived changes everything that came before. A question mark or exclamation point has the power to turn a sentence around, or a destiny. The past is what is already known, but it changes if you live to the last page.

Question: Then can we page backward? Will the snow fall up? Will Akaky Akakievich cut each letter off the manuscript and shake it into the inkwell? Will generation after generation rise from their graves, and will Christ kill Lazarus? Will water and dry land, light and dark, return to the word?

Answer: Why don't you ever take what I say seriously? You understood what I meant. The same thing is always going to happen on the same page. If my mama were still alive and I had offended her badly once and then gone up and embraced her, hugged her close, and we stood like that in the kitchen, then we're standing like that right now, and

I've tucked my face into the warm triangle of tan above her flat white chest. If some February you and I watched the snow fall on a bronze horse and the flakes really did start flying up sometimes, then even today it has a horsecloth of snow on its back. If I've ever felt a surge of happiness over nothing, just because—over never having liked to comb my hair and here I am combing my hair after washing it, dropping my head and letting my hair fall forward, I'm running the wooden brush through and the strong match-teeth are raking through the density with a crackle, a crunch, a squeal—then now, too, I'm gasping with happiness in that bathroom over nothing at all, over the fact that you are, that the brush-matches are scratching me like sharp nails, the skin on my nape, over holding my head down and my freshly washed hair falling in a heavy, fragrant curtain, and also over it being so abundant, thick, wet, and tenacious, like life.

Question: But how can you not understand that this is all im-possible?

Answer: Why?

Question: Because you were taught to cut lengthwise, not crosswise.

Answer: Some crazy, hunched over old lady was standing on the street and hissing at all the passersby, "You're going to die soon!" I wanted to slip past, run away, become invisible. She was old and didn't know that the world is made in such a way that you can't disappear in it. If you did disappear here, then you'd show up somewhere else, in some other one-room cell for lonely people, in some hot, wet fold, in your own life many years ago. If you've disappeared from the surface, that means you dove head first and are just about to come up. Even after, a person still can't apprehend that he's gone. There's no sixth sense provided for that. My mama didn't find out, didn't understand, that she was gone. She died in her sleep, fell asleep and didn't wake up. She's sleeping now. And I won't learn, won't understand, that I'm gone. We don't have the freedom to disappear. You'll return in me. I'll return in you. And now here we're free to return to any point and any moment. The sweetest freedom of all is the freedom to return to where you were happy. To the moment that's worth the return. I leaf through my life and search in it for surges of happiness. And where I once nearly suffocated from love, I can stop and shut the book.

Question: You'll return to me?

Answer: No.

Question: What do you mean no? You already have. I'm holding you, breathing in the smell of your head. Here you are breathing, snuffling, dozing off under my arm. Here I am feeling with my fingertips the smooth membranes of the frog skin on your chest. Here you are scratching your belly where the bandage was. Here I am twirling your hair on my finger so you don't run away in your sleep.

Answer: No.

Question: But why?

Answer: Because right now I'm somewhere else completely. The beach—flat, Baltic, and half-empty. I'm sitting on the sand by a selvage of sea which is cold and barely alive. It's lapping just a little, sparkling just a little in the sun. Up ahead, seagull cries; behind, the sounds of a ball being hit, where they're playing volleyball. Someone is walking by, peering at the seaweed that's been cast ashore, searching for amber. Shells are crunching under his sandals. I know that there are just about to be three weak,

413

puny waves. And then mine, the fourth, the promised one will gather up, flex, and reach my foot, take my toes in its mouth, and tickle my heel with sand.

25 July 1926

Today at Printemps I saw this notebook in this marvelous embossed binding and couldn't help myself, I bought it. I'm going to keep a diary again. True, I'll try not to write down my ecstasies over the Seine, and Notre Dame, and the museums, and the Eiffel Tower, and all the rest. All those oohs and ahs have dried up after two weeks in Paris.

But I need a notebook to record the sensations that no one but me has ever experienced before or ever will! Because what is happening to me right now belongs to me alone! Me. I suddenly felt that the old me had begun to vanish, become transparent, and the other life was showing through me. My body suddenly belongs to someone else. I'm no longer on my own.

Sometimes it seems as though one act of my life ended with a sudden silence, without applause. A thick, heavy curtain separated me from everything past and present, which suddenly filled with all kinds of unnecessary rubbish. The most important and valuable thing there can be is already inside me. No one but Iosif and I know this yet. Everyone is chasing trivial things. I have my sweet pea inside me. That's what Iosif called it when we were trying to guess what was hiding deep inside me, a boy or a girl. A sweet pea. It already controls me and my body. None of my desires, whims, caprices, and oddities are mine anymore. My body is my sweet pea's language.

Mama used to say that when she was pregnant with me she had a craving for herring with grapes. Now I walk around Paris and inhale the smell of autos like a madwoman. Before, I couldn't stand it, but now I stop by the taxi stand and sniff and sniff. How marvelous the gasoline smells!

They say Jewish fathers are the best fathers in the world. He has so much patience and courage in him, my Iosif, and so much care!

I'm so glad that the nightmarish period of nausea ended before we left for Paris. I was horribly nauseated on an empty stomach, and the moment I woke up Osya would pour spoonfuls of sweet, strong, cold tea into me. Amazingly, it helped. But after breakfast, nothing did! It was revolting and humiliating to sit down in front of the basin Iosif brought me, like clockwork! Seemingly there's nothing left, and then everything turns inside out. Later, emptied and prostrate, I would take to my bed.

He went to the doctor with me, wrote down his recommendations, and demanded that I follow through on everything. That's when I started calling him Pcholik instead of Osik. Wasps are bad insects, and Osya was fussing over me like a bee.

*

I wanted to write the date and caught myself having lost all track of time here. Or rather, time is measured completely differently now. I know this is the eighteenth week, but everything else seems utterly inconsequential.

I bought a measuring tape and every morning measure how much my belly has grown. It's not very noticeable yet. Only to my shirtwaists.

Osya is at work, and I now face entire days on end on my own. I drink tea, straighten up, and go out wandering around Paris.

The first few days I couldn't pass the stores with equanimity. En route, in Berlin, I felt like a slattern; my shoes and skirt were horrid. And here not only are the palaces museums, so are the stores. I walked into one such palace the very first day and turned into a pillar of salt. All glass and chrome on the outside, a revolving door; all glass and chrome inside, too, and expensive wood. And so much of everything—vivid, colorful, beautiful! What a pleasure to walk through the endless halls and touch, stroke the waves of silks—the rustle, the shimmer, the flow! Most of all I wanted to buy lingerie: fine, elegant, in stitching and lace. There, in the store, I changed my clothes and threw out my horrid stockings, plain panties, and slip—with a grimace of disgust that I caught in the mirror—and burst out laughing. How good I felt all of a sudden! How important it is to feel like a well-dressed woman! And how nice it was to carry the bright packages and boxes home!

Osya gave me a guidebook, and I take it with me always, but I like simply walking, hit or miss, and looking at the shop windows and people. Today I came out on a street with a marvelous name: Cherche-Midi. How marvelous: Look for noon (at two in the afternoon)! We learned that saying back in school with our Maria Iosifovna, and now, all of a sudden, a street!

I like Paris so much when the sun shines! It's a cheerful bazaar, not a city. People sell everything on the street—fruits, vegetables, flowers. And their lovely long baguettes and croissants everywhere—airy and crusty! I can't stop myself; I buy. I'm hungry all the time. Crêperies at every step—that's the life! I stopped in at a café to rest, opened my guidebook, and it turned out to be the famous Procope!

Once at Lafayette I stopped in front of a window, and it seemed like a painting, not a window. This city was simply drawn by Impressionists! I love strolling through the streets where street artists exhibit their works. They set up screens and hang paintings on them. Entire street exhibits. Americans buy it all up. Osya explained that if you buy something cheaply today, in twenty or thirty years it will be worth a fortune. I keep wanting to ask him if we could buy something. Not to wait thirty years, of course. Why do we need a fortune in thirty years? In a few years there may be nothing and no one left. You just look, and sometimes you like them so much! But

I know how hard it is for him with money now. And he can't refuse me. My dear sweet Osik!

Today the artists were constantly glancing at the sky. Would it rain? I can picture what it's like for them to rescue their paintings. But I love the rain! In this city, the rains are special. Paris is very beautiful in the rain, especially, like now, in the evening, when reflections from the electric lights swim in the wet pavement.

★

A gray, gloomy day. It's been pouring rain since morning. I didn't go anywhere. I sang and read all day.

I sing not even for myself but for our sweet pea. They say that among gypsies the custom is to sing in front of the future mother's belly, inculcating musicality even before birth. Sweet pea! You should be very musical! When you get a little bigger, you and I will sing together, or I'll accompany you and you will sing!

I hope you're surrounded by everything beautiful there is in the world, not just music. I take you to museums all the time. You died from delight with me in the Louvre, and at the Rodin, and in the Cluny, right? Remember how much you and I liked the Lady with the Unicorn? How we sat in front of her for an hour! We'll go back to see her again, right?

Lord, how the day drags on! I wish Osya would come soon!

What a marvelous feeling, waiting for a husband. He comes home tired and hungry. My husband! How lovely that sounds: my husband. How happy I am with my Iosif! How he looks after me, me and our sweet pea! There's so much care and love in him! Every day before leaving for his office he gets up a little early to clean and grate carrots for me and our sweet pea. He's so touching!

★

I strolled for a long time, all the way to Trocadero. I was tired. I kept hearing thunder somewhere again.

I examined the shop windows and compared them with Berlin. Now everything there seems dry, tasteless, vapid. But here! The windows of ties are like gardens, landscapes, weirs, cascades, a flow of color. The perfume is the sea, spring. And all accomplished merely with contrasts of fabric, velvet, silk.

I try to take a walk every day, no matter the weather. My sweet pea needs fresh air. And the holidays. They are constantly having holidays here! Ever two weeks there are holidays in two of the forty arrondissements—street fairs, roller coasters, carousels, shooting galleries, Punch and Judy shows, magicians, jugglers!

How pleasant it was when the Parisians held a celebration in honor of our arrival at the Gare du Nord! The whole city came out on the streets! The crowds marched along singing their "Marseillaise." One should always arrive in Paris on July 14th! So many people, and no sentries or soldiers anywhere, couples walking with arms around each other, everyone smiling at everyone!

Usually I go to the Luxembourg garden. I think it the prettiest garden on earth, especially when the sun is out. It's so free and easy there! One person is munching sandwiches, another is giving someone a kiss. For the French, kissing on the street is apparently as vital a necessity as munching sandwiches. I wish I could sit there like that with Iosif, munching sandwiches and kissing! I like watching the old men playing their pétanque. I think I know them all now. They nod to me affably.

And so many young mamas with children! It seems all the women of Paris are either pregnant or recently gave birth, there are so many prams! Now, when I'm walking and come across prams, I feel like peeking inside.

Yesterday, a mother was reading to her child on the bench next to me. The pacifier fell out, the baby hollered, she picked it up, licked it, and stuck it back in. It's all so amusing. Are you and I really going to have all this, sweet pea?

But another tot, a little older, couldn't quite climb down the short steps in front of the fountain. He turned around and slid down the steps on his tummy.

This is a garden for royalty, not commoners. You stroll down the paths and keep encountering queens: Anne of Breton, Marguerite of Provence. Here is Bianca of Castille, and there is Ann of Austria. Yesterday I sat opposite Marguerite Valois. The sun peeked out for a minute, and sun spots started dancing on her dress, as if she had decided to straighten the long folds, and I thought that these women, when they were expecting their sweet peas, must have experienced exactly what I am now. All of a sudden it brought us so close, it united us! These queens, too, must have felt that every kingdom was an insignificant trifle compared with this sensation of a sweet pea growing inside. Inside, a world was growing that was bigger and more important than all the kingdoms and republics put together.

*

A storm woke me at seven. Now, as I write, there's another storm.

I live in Paris, the center of the world, and I have to spend my time with Lyubochka! We walked for two hours yesterday, and I had a headache afterward that lasted until evening. Lyubochka doesn't talk, she cheeps. And does so nonstop. But at least she's company.

She showed me where they killed Petlyura in May, at the corner of Racine and Saint-Michel.

She told me how they took her to the hospital in her eighth week with heavy bleeding, and everyone thought her chances of carrying the baby to term were few. They punctured her skinny buttocks until they were all black and blue, and the only thing that helped was applying cabbage leaves.

The first time, she'd leapt into matrimony "due to youth and foolishness" and divorced after her husband gave her gonorrhea. The baby was four months at the time.

She used to work at Gosizdat with an overripe lady who was constantly puffing away at a cheap cigarette. This was Blok's "Beautiful Lady," Lyubov Dmitrievna, who had been glorified by the poet. She told me this to make me laugh. But instead it made me horribly sad and distressed.

She is married to the trade mission secretary. I saw him one time, and he seemed pleasant enough, but after my conversation with her I got the impression that she didn't love him at all.

Lyubochka natters on so, and after half an hour my head starts to hurt and I can't respond. Not that she needs me to. Today she told me how she was ironing at home, here, in Paris, when suddenly the doorbell rang. A young man, a Frenchman, introduced himself as a poet. He was peddling his poems door to door. She felt sorry for him and couldn't drive him away. She haggled, and he gave her a very short poem for a franc. He left, she read it, and the poem was stunning! She fell in love with him immediately. She decided that he was her true love, the love of her life, because geniuses don't just drop by like that. She started searching everywhere, asking around, and was about to put a notice in the newspaper, but then someone told her it was a famous poem by Arthur Rimbaud.

★

My sweet pea moved! Just like the doctor said, in the nineteenth week.

In the afternoon, left alone, I create silence. I close all the windows. Stop the clocks. Lie down. Listen to what's inside.

That's what I just did, I lay down and listened closely. Nothing. I turned over on my belly. Fell still, held my breath. And all of a sudden—pop! like a tiny bubble bursting in my belly. And another, and again.

Whoo hoo! Who are you, my sweet pea?

Osya wants a girl, and I don't know what I want. Probably the same. I would love to weave ribbons in her braids and dress her in pretty clothes.

I'm glad about you, sweet pea, and I don't care whether you're a boy or a girl. If it's a girl, Lord, I hope she gets her papa's eyes and hands, but I hope her nose is mine. Please not his nose!

Today I noticed that my pretty new brassiere, which I bought at Lafayette, is too small. Overnight my bosom grew again, and again the right one—it's so amusing! First the right grows, and only a few days later does the left catch up.

I've started to like myself. All of a sudden I like looking at my body and stroking this skin. I've never had such a magnificent bosom before.

Sometimes my body doesn't seem like it's mine: heavy, alien. I spend a few days getting used to my new condition, but as soon as I do and stop noticing myself, something else happens to me. Tomorrow I'll buy a new brassiere, a special one that unhooks in front.

★

A heavy fog today since morning. I went for a walk and got as far as the Alexander III bridge. The Eiffel Tower looked only half-built. I thought that this must have been how Maria Bashkirtseva once saw it, unfinished. After all, this was her city. She lived here, sang, wrote her diary, drew, walked down the same streets I am now. She died here. I don't even know where she lies, in what cemetery.

★

Today I went to the Petrovs'. Lyubochka introduced me to the Soviet society ladies. In this Paris I've grown unaccustomed to people. At first I rejoiced at the new faces, that everyone spoke Russian, but half an hour later I wanted to flee! Lord, what an earful! First everyone boasted about what they'd bought where, and then they started discussing all kinds of taboos and talismens for pregnant women. Moreover, each started by saying it was all old wives' tales, and then would cite an example of some friend to whom that very thing had happened!

You mustn't kick or pet cats and dogs, otherwise the child will have a "bristle." Stuff and nonsense. If I see a cat somewhere now, I'm going to go up and pet it on purpose.

You mustn't step over a shaft, a rope, and something else, otherwise it will be born a hunchback. Where am I supposed to find a shaft in Paris?

And if you cross in front of a dead man, the child will have a birthmark—his blood will bake. Does that mean birthmarks signify the pregnant woman's encounters with death?

In the evening I told Osya. All this from savage folk lore! Osya explained it all. The ban on stepping over things, for example. It's because they weren't wearing anything under their skirt! In their ignorance, they were afraid that certain objects below would "see" their childbearing organs! So what if they did? After all, they believed there was a spirit in every object. What kind of spirit is in a shaft?

I bought a few books on pregnancy and motherhood. I'm reading them. How clear and simple it all is there! There's nothing to be afraid of. Only it's frightening anyway when you think that something might happen to the child in birth. It's also frightening that it's going to hurt.

I'm a coward and very much afraid of pain. That's what's frightening, that it's going to hurt physically and that has to be accepted. Osya said that pain is necessary in nature for self-preservation, to forewarn of death, to make us love life. How everything is arranged! They inflict pain to make us live. Drive us into life with a switch. If it didn't hurt, if they didn't stitch you up, who would be left to live?

About the pain, Lyubochka said that the pain and suffering are necessary, so you can love the child, so you can remember at what price he came.

★

Osya is a darling! I asked him to get me Bashkirtseva. I so wanted to reread her! Such a clever man, pure gold, he went specially to the library and found it! A very very old edition, read to tatters. I opened it at random and immediately came upon these lines: "What a satisfaction it is to sing well! You realize you are all-powerful, a tsaritsa! You feel happy thanks to your own merit. This is not the pride gold or a title gives. You become more than a woman, you feel immortal. You break away from earth and race to heaven!"

I leaf through and can only wonder at this girl. "Nothing is lost in this world . . . When people stop loving one person, they immediately transfer their attachment to another—without even registering it, and when they think they don't love anyone, that is simply a mistake. Even if you don't love a person, you love a dog or furniture, and with as much strength, only in a different form. If I loved, I would want to be loved as strongly as I myself love; I would not put up with anything, not even a single word, said by someone else. But you won't find that kind of love anywhere. And I will never love because no one will love me the way I know how."

When did she have time to experience and feel this? Were people once significantly more mature and wiser than today's adults?

Or: "I, who wanted to live seven lives at once, am living only one quarter of a life."

But a girl of fourteen can't write that!

423

I peeked at "today" from the last year of her life, an entry for August 30: "So this is how I will end . . . I'll work on my picture . . . no matter what, no matter how cold it gets . . . It doesn't matter, if not at work than on some walk, those who are not painting, they will die, too, after all . . ."

Two months later she was no more.

★

A letter from Katya! I read about their life in Moscow, and my heart sank. How I miss all our friends!

But I never expected her to be so superstitious! She writes that I mustn't cut my hair. It's a bad omen: it might shorten the baby's life. Tomorrow I'm going to go to the hairdresser and cut my hair and have it styled to spite all the omens. This is for all of you! I don't believe in omens!

It seems so recently I went to see them in Moscow for the first time. How many years have passed? Oho! Ten already! Yes, it was in January or February of '16. I dreamed of getting a job singing, but at the Hermitage—my Hermitage!—they wouldn't even listen to me! How amusing it is to recall all that now, when what had once seemed an unattainable dream has suddenly become a step taken. But then, my God, what a tragedy it was!

I wandered, unhappy, unneeded, through the center of snowy, wintry Moscow for hours, in the handsome, holiday crowd. Someone was talking about how Vertinsky had met Vera Kholodnaya. On Kuznetsky he had decided to flirt with the pretty young lady, and she said to him, "I'm married, the wife of Ensign Kholodny." He took her to see Khanzhonkov, the producer and she became queen of the cinema. And here I was, like a fool, walking and dreaming that someone would stop me and say, Wouldn't you like to be filmed or to sing?

I looked at the young ladies and they all had hairstyles like Vera Kholodnaya, and each dreamed of becoming a cinema diva.

How it hurt to hear some scrawny young lady come out of a store and comment to the clerk, "No, it's wrong, I don't like it. I may come back with my fiancé."

I walked by one shop window with hats and couldn't help myself—I stopped in to try them on. Parisian hats, desperately winning, whichever you choose, and I say, "No, it's wrong, I don't like it. I may come back with my fiancé."

Now all the hats in Paris are mine. What is important is something completely different.

★

More and more often I think, Could I sing here? I don't know.

My marvelous Osik takes me to *cafés chantants* and music halls. We have seen all the Paris idols—Mistinguette, Chevalier, and now Josephine Baker. They sing no better than ours, but in a completely different way. Lightly, freely. Whereas at home any song is performed in earnest, like an aria.

Yesterday we went to the Casino de Paris for Josephine Baker. A monkey, but as talented as an imp.

I also liked the Moulin Rouge very much. Where was I when God was passing out those legs?

But how am I to sing here? That is when you begin to contemplate the "Russian soul." It is when you can't frisk about the stage like this Josephine!

There are Russian dives here for the Russian soul. Iosif and I were in one of them on Montmartre. A terrible impression. Russians selling what is Russian for cheap: buy it for just a copper! It's disgusting to watch the Americans enjoying themselves, singing along with the gypsies, dancing. Drunks squat-dancing. And after their exaltation, without exception, they break a dish. They must think that's what the Russian soul is. There's something degrading about it all.

Later they turned off the light, and in the darkness they lit the hot punch and started a procession in some fantastic military style à la russe, triumphantly bearing shashlyk on rapiers.

The very thought of having to sing here is disgusting.

Lord, how I miss the stage!

You'll be born, sweet pea, and grow up a little, and we'll return home and you'll let me go sing again.

I wrote those lines and all of a sudden I wanted to go back, to Moscow, so badly!

We returned yesterday in a taxicab. The driver was Russian, from Tula. He said there were three thousand Russian cabbies in Paris.

What amazed me most at the Casino de Paris was a juggler carrying a tray on which there were forty glasses with forty spoons, each lying next to a glass. Alley-oop! and the forty spoons were in the forty glasses! With a simple alley-oop!

★

I was at the Louvre again.

Either I got up on the wrong side of bed or else my mood wasn't so gosh-oh-golly-gee. All of a sudden I was bored.

I looked at Aphrodite and remember how horrified I was when I read back in school the kind of foam she was in fact formed from. Just think: a son cut off his own father's member with a scythe!

I wandered through the galleries, and all of a sudden I was irritated. How many pictures on the same theme: immaculate conception! Why this bee in their bonnet over immaculacy? And what, actually, is depravity? What is bad about it?

Being born from a virgin and the Divine spirit is no less a miracle than from an ordinary woman and an ordinary man. Sweet pea, you are a miracle.

★

At last, a letter from Mama. The same thing. Complaints about everything.

The last time we saw each other was last year, when I performed in Rostov. Or rather, when I was fleeing Moscow; I simply could not stay there after all that happened then.

How aged and provincial both Mama and my father seemed after Moscow and Petrograd. They and all of Rostov. Or is it I who have been so mixed up over these years, so tousled, borne away?

Mama has let herself go. She always dyed her hair with henna, but this time, since she hadn't in a long time, her roots were completely gray. I'd never seen her like that before.

Papa was cheerful as ever, but now Mama writes that he is gravely ill. But he didn't say a word to me in his last letter. He's always like that!

I thought about them the entire day. As a child I so loved the way Papa played with me, as if he were a beast and wanted to eat me. His beard tickled my neck and cheeks.

Papa dear! How I love you! I will never tell you how I saw you then, in All-Saints, you who had laughed at priests and the church all your life, praying stealthily, hiding from everyone in the half-dark vestibule. Tanechka, your daughter by Elena Olegovna, my little stepsister, was dying of typhus.

I prayed for her then, too, or rather, for you. But Tanechka died two days later. My poor dear Papa! I can do nothing at all to help you from here. Just write a letter and think about you. And remember.

Memories are like little islands in an ocean of emptiness. On these little islands the people near and dear to me, all of them, will always live as they once did. On one such little island Papa is crossing himself stealthily in the half-gloom. Mama is dying her hair with henna. My Nina Nikolaevna is wearing her old-fashioned hat. I wanted to see her then, in Rostov, but she is no more. I never did get to her grave—there was no time.

In the first days of the revolution I met her on the street. I shouted to her, "Nina Nikolaevna, congratulations!" She asked in amazement, "For what?" "What do you mean what? The revolution! Spring!" She replied, "My dear girl! There is no reason to congratulate anyone on the revolution, and spring comes not according to the calendar but when I exchange my felt hat for my straw."

May she rest in peace!

★

Today, strolling across the Cité, I discovered a memorial plaque dedicated to Abelard and Eloise. And I thought of Zabugsky. My Rostov Abelard died of typhus in December 1919.

I recalled that terrible time, the war, the typhus. All that pain, yet all the warmth and light that remained! I recalled Christmas of '19. Everyone was fleeing Rostov. Papa had got train tickets for Mama and me. We waited somewhere outside of town on the tracks for five days. They kept moving us, and we were too frightened to leave the station to get something to eat. What if you were left behind? People would jump up and run off with their things for some other train, then return, and tell stories of seeing hanged men near the station, too. People said the engineers were sabotaging us, and indeed, we collected money for them, and only then did we finally leave. The air in the car was terrible because a child had a sick stomach. Someone kept consoling us, saying that after the heated freight cars our third-class car with benches was simply heaven. One woman kept shouting to her husband, "Sasha! A louse bit me!" And she would start unbuttoning, her teenaged son would hold the blanket, and her husband would take a long time searching for the bite to rub it with alcohol. A Frenchwoman and her husband, a Russian colonel, wounded, lost her head completely and rubbed her nursing infant with naphthalene to protect him from insects. He cried, and in desperation she started shaking him to make him be quiet, and to curse Russia and the Russians. It was a genuine nightmare. Everyone turned into animals and nearly went at each other with fists. And it was Twelfth Night. One woman decided to make a Christmas tree for the children in the car, amid the noise, stench, and hysterics. She found a branch—an ordinary one, not a spruce—and put it in an empty bottle. Someone laid out a green kerchief. They made decorations out of paper. Attached pieces of cotton wool to the branch. There weren't any candles, so they bought a fat lantern candle from a switchman. A few apples were found, and they were cut into thin slices. A Christmas party in the train car! The children gathered and the adults crowded around. I started singing with the children. Everyone's faces changed. They had been tired, angry, and tense, and they became joyous and festive! One little boy kissed me afterward and gave me his treasure, a button.

Where is that button now? Where is that amazing woman? What happened to those children?

★

How good it is to be wrong about people sometimes! In the very beginning I didn't like our landlady. The first day, when she started saying that the sofas and armchairs were upholstered in expensive "tissue Rodier," I immediately felt like spilling coffee grounds on them, on them and the landlady. She lives directly above us and invites us sometimes for coffee. How can you refuse? And the conversations are all about the horrible Russians to whom her deceased husband loaned so much money, buying tsarist bonds, and how they wouldn't repay her. It's an amazing feeling. Among your own you can curse Russia to your heart's content, but here, when strangers start speaking badly of my country, for some reason you immediately start defending it.

But for the most part she is sweet. She is always reading the Bible—she attends some Bible circle and is constantly inviting me to go. It's funny that for her all the prophets prophesied in nothing other than French.

★

I dropped by the chamber of wax figures. I'm still angry! I've become so sensitive to smells! The air there is so close, there's nothing to breathe. I couldn't bring myself to leave right away! I regretted having paid so much for the ticket!

I wandered around, confusing the live people with the wax. What is the point? Passing the dead off as living. A wax resurrection! They couldn't wait for the angels' trumpets! They've made an elegant morgue!

I couldn't finish and left, but the unpleasant sensation lingered. I went to Notre Dame to wipe out the impression. I like to sit there in the half-gloom, look at the enormous rose windows and the smoke under the ceiling, and imagine Queen Margot marrying her Henri here. She is alone before the altar, while he is outside the gates, on the street.

Would I like to be married here? I would like to sing here someday. Marvelous acoustics here.

I walked outside and stood for a long time on the Seine embankment in front of Notre Dame. What a huge shadow it cast today at sunset!

★

Today we went to rue Daru. Lyubochka and I went from store to store. She bought utterly tasteless things, and I had no desire to talk her out of it.

She assures me that next year it will be fashionable to wear skirts above the knee.

Lyuba chatters incessantly, I don't even have to nod, I can think my own thoughts, but it doesn't work. Today she was telling me about her lovers, as if it were nothing! Disgusting! She runs through her men like dresses on hangers in a cupboard.

Little boys were putting nails on the streetcar tracks. I could never understand that, but later I realized that they were making themselves toys that way. The nails were flattened, like little sabers. For toy soldiers? It was so dangerous! I felt like grabbing them and pulling them back by the ears! I'm glad a policeman scared them off.

Sweet pea, are you really going to be born a boy and also think up these foolish, dangerous entertainments?

Osya and I went to the cinema. We saw *Pat and Patachon.*

★

Today on the street I saw a little girl with a big red spot on her neck, and I immediately thought of those idiotic conversations. I couldn't help but think that her mama had probably been frightened and grabbed her belly.

I look at other children all the time now and think about how one day you, too, sweet pea, will play like that, the way the children were playing in the park yesterday, and we too will take either end of a long rope and make waves with it.

And if you're a girl, you'll play like those little girls I've been watching out the window for half an hour. They've dragged pots and cups out into the yard and are cooking soup from weeds and twigs, feeding their rag dolls sand porridge, changing their clothes, rocking them, spanking them, putting them in the corner, yelling at them.

I asked Osya how he imagined our child and what he would do with him. He answered, "I imagine myself teaching him to read.

Showing him how the letters are written. The word 'papa' comes out well, and so does 'mama,' but he writes the letter K backward." Sweet pea, how I love your papa!

★

Such a terrible day. It rained without letup from morning on. I stepped out briefly and got thoroughly soaked. And the filth everywhere! This must be the dirtiest city in the world. There is garbage covering all the streets and sidewalks—not even an army of street cleaners could deal with it all. And the stench! Is this really the Paris everyone is out of their minds over? They've invented a Paris even Paris misses!

Today I felt especially keenly how bored I am here, how much I miss my friends and family. What am I doing here? Why am I here?

It's like being in a gilded cage! And the cage isn't even gilded but the most ordinary—no matter what you buy, you shouldn't! There Lyubochka goes ordering dresses in fashion houses, while I buy ready-made, scrimping every franc.

It's not a matter of francs, naturally! Iosif leaves for work and I'm here alone. Alone the entire day with my thoughts and a Paris that no longer delights me. I need people! And not Lyubochka or the Petrovs! They absolutely cannot give me the normal human contact I need!

Here was Lyubochka today telling me that at night in the Bois de Boulogne automobiles gather on the lawn—they only let very expensive autos into the circle and won't take any old Citroën 10 cheveaux—and in them sit men in dinner jackets and cloaks and perfectly naked women under fur coats. All of them get out of their autos and indulge in orgies on the lawn. The automobile headlamps light the scene, and the chauffeurs sit behind the wheels as still as statues.

And I'm sitting listening to all this filth!

432

I leaf through Bashkirtseva for the umpteenth time: "When I think that you only live once and that any passing minute brings us closer to death, I simply go mad!" And I think about something else, about the fact that right now, as she's writing, she's still alive, still only fears death, while here I am reading her—and she's gone.

You know what else I thought about, sweet pea? Everything around us now doesn't exist for you yet. When you grow up and someday, maybe, you read these lines, this will all be gone.

Here I am now sitting by the window watching the little boys playing in the courtyard. They got a hold of crutches somewhere and have made up a game, jumping on them like on stilts. Where did they get the crutches?

Maybe even I will be gone.

How strange. For whoever reads this, the living me is gone, the way I read Bashkirtseva, who still only fears death and at the same time is long since dead. It turns out that all this is and isn't simultaneously, or rather, it is, but only because I'm writing about it now. About you, sweet pea. And about those little boys in the courtyard—now the older one has flapped the crutches to the side like wings and taken off, like an airplane. Everyone has run after him. They all want to fly, too.

In the end, is Bashkirtseva still alive only because she left her diary and I'm reading it now?

Are these lines really all that will remain of me?

No, that's all nonsense! There will be you, sweet pea!

★

I haven't written anything in a long time. I don't seem to be doing anything. I sit at home and the hours drag on, but there's not enough time for anything.

Sweet pea is already twenty-five weeks! Every day I try to do aerial gymnastics. The book for future mamas says that this is good for the organism. Maybe it is, but only when my mood is good. I strip naked, walk up to the mirror—we have a big mirror in a handsome frame in the foyer—all of me fits in it, and I examine myself for a long time, as if I were someone else. Then I seem like a beauty, a serene matron anticipating a mystery. This is me and not me but rather you and me, sweet pea. But when I'm bored and sad, I hate myself!

I've begun to tire quickly. After dinner I feel like lying down for half an hour, whereas before I never napped. And in the evening, after nine, like a young schoolgirl, I have to be in bed. And sleep! Children grow in their sleep!

Grow quickly, sweet pea. I'm tired of waiting for you!

I can feel you touching the walls inside me constantly.

★

Yesterday I stopped into a children's ready-made clothing store. It's all very beautiful, but they don't have things for the littlest. I bought some yellow wool and decided to knit a jacket, cap, and bootees. You're going to be as yellow as a chick, sweet pea! Winter babies need warm things. Just think, we'll be three for the New Year!

All morning I washed, straightened, laundered, and cleaned.

Where are you, my dear friends, Klava, Vanya, Borya, Ledya, Olya? There, in Russia, I couldn't even imagine how dear you were to me! How lonely it is here without you! And there's nowhere to go visiting! On Saturday I went to the Petrovs', took off my coat, and wanted to hang it on a tall hook, and all of a sudden everyone jumped and shouted that I shouldn't raise my arms or else the umbilical cord might wrap around the baby and strangle it! And on and on in that same vein. And these people are inviting us to greet the New Year with them!

I'm not going. I've decided we'll greet it as a threesome—Osya, Sweet Pea, and I.

How merrily we greeted the last New Year's! Osenin dragged in such a huge tree, it wouldn't fit anywhere. And how we all laughed when Danya and Mitya brought in a baby's bath filled with snow that had bottles of Champagne and vodka jutting out of it! And how Danya showed us his American brother's crowning trick: playing the violin with one hand while accompanying himself with the other on the piano! And how Sorokin depicted everyone on the guitar! How good it was to be together! My dears, how are you there? Where will you make merry and be silly this New Year's? Without me!

And what you came up with for my name day! The whole street came running to see that orchestra of tubs and pots, glasses strung on a rope by their bases, combs with cigarette paper, bottles filled with different amounts of water. It was the best concert of my life! My faraway friends, how I love you! Only now have I realized it.

★

At Printemps. I was tired. I came back in a taxicab.

At the store I happened to see myself in a mirror next to the other women and seemed unnaturally pale, deathly pale.

Now in the foyer I looked at myself again. How ugly I've become. Swollen lips, sharp nose. Puffy face. Owlish eyes. Belly as hard as a nut. Iosif walked up from behind, put his arms around me, looked at us in the mirror, and said, "How much prettier you've become!"

★

There are awful days when everything goes wrong.

The day began with me breaking a teacup. I can't believe that's good luck.

I bought a *dépilatoire*, which stripped my skin and left the hairs.

I sat on the toilet seat for a long time and my leg went numb.

Yesterday I saw a French performance of *Boris Godunov*. What a dreadful farce! The singer who sang Boris was imitating Chaliapin. At least he sang, but the others! And the direction! The sets! This is their notion of Russia! To top it all off, the deacon crossed himself like a Catholic!

Lyubochka just ran by and poured out her latest story on me. A real Parisian Decameron!

Yesterday she was riding in a taxicab. The driver was Russian. All of a sudden she recognized him as her love, the one who perished in Kharkov. And the driver kept looking at her oddly the whole time. But it couldn't have been him because he was too young. Or rather, he was as old as he'd been then. There she was riding and praying the trip would be longer. She twittered my ears off about how he held out his hand, what a slender, strong body he had, and how beautifully his hands rested on the steering wheel. "And all of I sudden I realized that if he had said then, 'Follow me!' I would have and would do anything he wanted!"

Fortunately for Lyubochka, the driver merely took her money in silence and drove off.

I said I wanted to go to the butterfly exhibit; I'd seen an announcement. But Lyubochka pounced on me. "What do you mean! Under no circumstances! They're dead!"

★

Tala! My dear, good Tala! A letter from Tala! How did she find me?

She's married, too, and already has two children! Her husband, a former officer, got a job as a worker at the Renault plant, then fell ill and lost his job, and now they were living by the sea. Poor dear

Tala! She was working as a laundress now and hoping for a better place in an old people's pension. What is this "better place"?

I wish I could see her! I answered her this very day, asked for her to come, and said I would send her money for a ticket. Or should I go see her? I don't know what Osya will say. He fears for me as it is.

★

I've been thinking about Tala all day. I even dreamed of her!

In school, before a history exam, she and I tried to guess what number question we would get, writing numbers on slips of paper and drawing them without looking. Tala drew a 2. She decided to re-check: another 2! The next day she drew a ticket with the number 22! Our divinations! How could we not believe in them?

Lord, how many years have passed!

For some reason I remember us running to see the toppling of the monument to Ekaterina. At the moment we latched onto the rope, something cracked, the statue shuddered and then came crashing down from the pedestal, right on the garden—and everything drowned in hurrahs! How good it felt! Then a team of carthorses hauled the statue off to the Sixth Precinct, under arrest, and coming toward us were students we knew with armbands that said "Militia." We fastened red ribbons on, too, and pinned red ribbons on the fur coats of all the passersby, while Tala even flaunted a policeman's club from a routed precinct. She'd taken it away from some fledgling policeman!

The universal rejoicing, everyone's shining faces: our great revolution! Bloodless! We rejoiced in the bloodlessness, and at the same time everyone said that there should be just one show execution—like in the French revolution. We should execute the tsar, who ought to pay with his blood for the people's blood, not simply by hanging,

437

but by having his head cut off or being set on a spike. Now it seems amazing that people spoke so calmly about that.

At the time, immediately after our bloodless Rostov revolution, a letter arrived from Masha in Finland—there's your bloodless revolution for you! Boris had been arrested, and the officers were being murdered on all the ships; there were an especially large number killed on the *Andrei Pervozvanny*, on which he served. A drunken gang broke into Masha's and searched for weapons. She had Boris's revolver. She managed to throw it in the garbage pail. They didn't find anything, but they broke the dishes and took the gold watch and cigarette case lying on Boris's desk. Masha found her husband in the morgue along with the other officers, disfigured, his teeth knocked out.

My poor Masha! Poor Tala! All our poor girls! Each has had her share.

And how good that all the horrors are behind. You, sweet pea, will have only the very best and nothing bad. All the bad has already happened.

*

I wanted to go for a walk, but the weather was disgusting again. Cold, repulsive rain and strong gusts of wind.

I slept poorly. I've had a headache all day.

I'm also upset for having shouted at Osya yesterday. He was tormenting me with his worries. All he said was, "Careful, there's a step!" And I exploded: "Leave me be, by all that's holy!" "Bellochka, my dear, don't get upset, I'll be quiet! I won't say another word, just don't skip down the stairs like that!"

I was ashamed all day.

What a marvelous man you and I have, sweet pea! And how unbearable I've suddenly become, out of the blue!

Here I've made myself comfortable in bed with a cup of tea and I'm writing. I'm going to think about something pleasant. Tala. I so wish I could see my dear Tala! Just one soul mate! In the morning I wrote a long letter and at the end asked about her husband: Does she love him? Is she happy?

And now I'm thinking about myself and what I would have told her. Do I love him? Am I happy?

Yes. Yes.

★

I'm in my thirtieth week. I'm awfully tired.

I was riding in the Metro and suddenly glanced at my feet. Lord, whose feet are those? Tired, ugly, dropsical. Only now do I understand what Andersen had in mind with his Little Mermaid, who traded her fishtail for women's legs. Now I feel as though I'm stepping on pins and needles. It's hard to walk.

I nearly felt ill in the Metro today. The Parisian Metro is simply a nightmare. White tile work, like a bathroom, and bathhouse air. Absolutely nothing to breathe. I dashed onto the boulevard from the steamy interior. Cold and wind. It didn't take long before I was sick.

I barely made it home, undressed, and took to my bed. I had a good rest and began examining myself in the mirror.

I've lost my looks! I used to be so proud of my white skin! What is happening to it? The doctor said this would pass, that the pigmentation intensified in all pregnant women. To hell with them all! And my belly button, my belly button spoils everything! For some reason it's poking out. As if someone were trying to pump up my belly like a ball, through that jutting belly button.

I'm embarrassed by my changes. Before I always felt a feline grace in myself, and now it seems as though I've been walking like a penguin my whole life. I'm so tired! Sometimes I feel like an unwieldy monster! I hope it's soon!

Iosif, my fine, good Iosif! He sat me on his lap and held my head to his shoulder. He talked and talked . . . About my inner beauty and special radiance from within. I don't believe him, but I felt better.

Notebook lost in the metro: The Flight into Egypt. He rose that night, took the Infant and His Mother, and went into Egypt. A white plain, full moon, light from heavens on high, shining snow. The green lights of the railway points. Locomotives screeching like gulls. First-class cars blue, second yellow, third green, now moon-like with snowy withers. The telegraph operator is lonely. A husk-crust of ice. Once in the winter the telegraph operator saw a family of wolves crossing the tracks. The father's midnight shadow walks along the lettered car, hammers at the blocks, bends over, as if he wanted to make sure it really said "Westinghouse Brake" or something else—and all's well, he swings his lantern, you can go. The silence swallows up the distant clickety-clack. The brief belch of a whistle. Back down the trench-path dug in the drifts. Full-moon breathing. The frosty universal crunch from his felt boots. The moon has frozen into the thin cloud and is peeking out from the ice. Star is silent to star. So many periods and not a single dash. It seems odd that Moses was once abandoned in a papyrus basket and sent down the Nile under these same stars. The life of Samuel Morse. Chapter one. Samuel Morse was an artist. The earth is a basket of humanity sent floating down the Milky Way. Returning from Europe on the *Sally Ann*, Morse looked at the future through his spyglass, correcting for the wind. A ripple in the eyepiece. He wrote his wife: "God looks upon us with the same eye with which we look upon him. My dear, how many words there are to denote the invisible! God. Death. Love. What are we to do if we must name that which is so close but for which we have no words? Or rather, those we do have explain nothing at all; moreover, they are painful, dirty, and vile. So few words we have for the condition of the soul and even fewer for the condition of the body! How can I describe what we had? Describe it in such a way as to convey at least a portion of what was genuine, amazing, and beautiful! Invent new words? Add periods or dashes? Lord, then what we kissed would consist of nothing but omissions! I once read, I do not remember where, that the soul, like the body, smells like itself and its food. How accurate that is. The smell of the soul. It is the soul that can have a dirty smell. But in love there can be nothing dirty; there is nothing there from us, there is only that which God has put into us. Therefore your smell (everything that I cannot put into words) is divine. And your taste. Each time, a little different. The body, like the soul, smells like itself and its food. A new alphabet ought to be devised to name the unnamable, so you're not ashamed to kiss something that still does not have a pure and beautiful name. The ship is empty, no one but me, just the sail—the wind's priest. The sunset dark red, in disarray. I am bringing you presents, my beloved, and the most marvelous of all is amber with a prehistoric earwig, and you can see all its feet and the jags with which it scratched ears God knows when. I focus my spyglass and see our kitten screwing up its eyes and stretching on your lap as it lowers its quote-claws." Morse's wife would die young, and the professor of the descriptive arts would long search for a deaf and dumb girl. And find her. They would marry, she would learn the alphabet he'd invented, and they would have long, happy conversations in periods and dashes. In the morning the plain is covered in a fair hand, in sweeps and drifts. A small cloud-shadow notarizes the snow with its seal. The words run over the frozen wires, but you can't convey silence. Children are building a snowman. The rickety columns stretch in single file to the back of beyond, in search of happiness, though not where they lost it, just as people look for their watch not in the ditch where it fell but somewhere better lit. When you glance at the column of fugitives, they freeze in a lambda. They won't get far. The edge of the world is there. You see, the world's brink passes through right here, where the words end. The world's outskirts are snow-blue and broad-boned. There is nothing beyond them. They are mute. And you can't go there, beyond the words. The former telegraph operator went as far as the border, and each time he ran into letters and beat against them like a fly against a window. On this side of the words, the linden in its lowered stocking leans toward a column; but on the other side, muteness. At sunset the drifts do not flex their muscles. And the smoke from the chimney has no heft. But here everything is literal. And there are no tenses—just the winter, continuous. In the deep snow—stout, hundred-mawed, howling, but here all are saved, here all are earwigs. Time is literal. Here I am writing this line, and my life is longer by these letters, but the life of whoever is now reading them is shorter. The light from the window on the snow is webbed. The world history of the ass. Chapter one. Born but not christened, dead but not saved, yet he carried Christ. Among the ancients the ass is the symbol of peace, the horse of war, therefore the prophet had to ride into Jerusalem on a white ass. Osiris's wife Isis and her infant son Horus flee Egypt and the persecutions of the evil Seth on an ass. According to Persian sources, the three-legged prime ass lets go a cry and all the female water sprites, Ahura Mazda's creations, are impregnated. The Asvins' chariot is harnessed to the ass which helped the Asvins win a race on the occasion of Soma and Surya's wedding. A golden ass. Buridan's ass. The ears wag the ass. Hair from the cross on the ass's back are a cure for infertility. Samson slays the unfortunate Philistines with an ass's jaw. Poisoned, Cesare Borgia, to save himself, split an ass's carcass in half and lay in the steaming entrails. If we are to believe Pliny, Nero's beloved Poppea liked to bathe in ass's milk. If you hear an ass's long cry in the distance in your sleep, that means you'll become rich due to the death of someone close to you. Who was it who said that time was an ass: lash it and it will dig its heels in, but if you want to hold it back, it will run without looking at you? If an ass could speak, it would ask this question: The Lord said

442

to Moses, "You may not see My face because man may not see Me without dying." Does this mean that the dead are those who have seen that face and all the temples and prayers are to that, to death? The snow tiptoed up to the window. It's nice to go out, breathe, and look at the smoke from the chimney. Quiet, windless, soon the ninth-hour would be snuffling nonstop. Some trains speed by holding their nose; others sniff at every column. The snow went farther down the road to Shablino, where milk is sold by weight—chopped with an ax—and people sleep on sacking without sheets. The teacher washes her sheets and hangs them up to try, and in the morning she looks and they're splashed with mud from the other side of the fence, so she washes them again. The Decembrist Zavalishin took note of the local customs: I look and a dog is lying there licking something bloody on itself. The bitch had its obscene lips sliced off, and quite recently, they were still bleeding, and Kashtanka was licking it up. The owner said that women seduce muzhiks that way. They cook the lips up with other meat, chanting spells over them, then it's all served to the man who would love the woman. On television the hostages' relatives plead for them not to begin an assault. The assault is about to begin. The people who are about to die in a few minutes are still alive. A machine operator, drunk on the occasion of Tankist Day and his birthday—he joked his whole life that he was born a tankist—fell asleep with a lit cigarette and burned up. He was afraid of burning up in a tank. That's what he was dreaming during his death, that he was burning in his combat vehicle. People sat at his funeral feast and ate up what was left from his birthday. Past the outskirts of the sea—snow, knee-high. The drift is a cape. Beyond that, smoke rises from the village's huts—snowy boats sailing in formation from river to forest. It was so dismaying that such important things, such great gifts as the Holy Mysteries, were served up in such crude form, a meal, something to be chewed and swallowed, or lowered into the water, expiated. How foolish the explanation of how a virgin gave birth and left no trace, no tear, no stitch, everything

443

stretched like the Red Sea, which parted for Israel's sake and then closed back up. Out the window you can see a woman walking down the street, another Maria, she stops in the middle of the road, pulls her skirt aside slightly, and without squatting, standing, freezes for a minute, then walks on, leaving a hole with yellow edges in the snow. A winter call-up, snow epaulets. The start of Broad Shrovetide, on the hill boys and girls sledding on something that looks like a skillet, with thick curved edges sculpted from manure, no bigger than half an arshin in diameter, doused with water, and frozen—I couldn't help myself, infected with the general merriment, I slid down the hill a few times, too. That's how to slide away from time, from Herod, downhill on frozen manure. Eyes watering in the cold, night clouds overlapping, the track sparkly, snake-bodied. There aren't so very many people on earth, in fact; on resurrection day it's really going to fill up. That's how I remembered that room: winter in one window, and branches of flowering lilac in another nudging a cloud. Bottles along the tracks, but no message in any of them. A railroad guard at the crossing: homespun coat, felt boots down at the heels, lambskin hat, two furled flags, red and green, under his arm, holding a doused lamp. The train picked up speed, the glass rode up to the bottle. The compartment door ajar, women passed by, holding on to the handrail, towels and soap boxes in hand and hair braided for the night. You could hear a folding seat knocking softly against the train car wall. But if Herod destroyed every infant under two, then Jesus would have had no one to play with, no one his age! Herod didn't kill any infants! They grew up and died on their own later. Across a white field, a factory's skyteat-stack. The locals didn't sell anything to the evacuees, and they poured out the left over milk, for show. A hut up to its neck in the spring flood. To the animals we're insane, best not to mess with us. Upon her arrest they let her say goodbye to her child, so she went into the nursery—he was sitting on his little bed—and said, I'm going away for work. Stay with Klava and be a good boy! And he said, First Papa went away for work and now you. What if Klava leaves, too, who will I stay with? The traditional Twelfth Night dishes—barley porridge without milk or butter and stewed dried fruit—remind us of the Holy Family's flight into Egypt. Compassionate people still let them into their homes to spend the night, but not into their heart. She hung a double cherry on her ear, held her umbrella to her shoulder like a rifle, and shouted: Don't move! To save a drowning man you have to deafen him with an oar's blow to the head. A game was under way in the room, everyone was scratching, reaching under their shirt for lice, which they immediately smashed on the notepaper, so that by the end of the game you couldn't read the numbers for the bloody commas. The ship set sail, briefly chasing down the winter. One riverbank flows by quickly; the other slowly. They were throwing chocolate to the gulls. During the war, Russian Germans were taken by barge into exile across the Caspian: the heat, a line for the water tank, cursing, fighting, and one woman says, Stop this. You're not Russians! A lunar umbilicus on the sea. After dinner, croquet, a battle 'til night fell and you couldn't tell the balls apart anymore, and Roza was cheating, too, adjusting her ball with the hem of her skirt every now and then, moving it into good position. The artist Fu Dao dissolved in the fog he depicted: he drew the fog and walked off into it. In her cell she collected burnt matches and scratched something with them on the piece of paper she was given for the toilet, or sculpted something out of chewed bread. They went to the smith to see him reshoeing horses and a smelly brown glue being boiled from bits of hoof. She rode back on a hay wagon—marvelous!—fell on her back, and felt as if she were rocking in a cradle of hay hanging right from the sky! So then he that giveth in marriage doeth well; but he that giveth not in marriage doeth better. When the Persian shah Aga Mohammed captured Tiflis, his soldiers tried not only to rape as many women as possible but to mark each one. They notched the tendon on the raped women's right leg so that even now, many years later, you come across old women limping on their right leg. I opened the hinged pane and the air leaned its brow on the curtain. Typewriters splash shafts of light in the sun. You can line your eyebrows with a burnt match, and instead of cream, women used their own urine—they were sure there was no better way to preserve the skin's freshness—and before interrogation they raked the chalky wall with their finger and powdered themselves with it. If your mother had too little milk, you'll admire large breasts, and if you were nursed until age two, you'll like women with a small, childish bosom. A relative, but not by seed. Coitus of circumstances. We know those ladies from proper families who throw themselves into a circus wrestler's arms. Death in a dream means a wedding. Rain is inopportune, the hay is being harvested. In the excavations at Pompeii they found people-voids. She looks at herself in the mirror; she's wearing his pajamas, unbuttoned, her breasts falling out, poking to the sides, flaccid, all the stuffing gone. He's sleeping, corpulent, white-lashed. The radio broadcasts the seven deadly sins: envy, greed, lust, gluttony, pride, sloth, and wrath. The numbskull son, into some kind of foolishness, melts cinnabar, tempers mercury, trying to find the elixir of immortality, and cares for nothing else in the world. Like a river, a child likes to suck stones. If a country is doomed, it has to be cleansed of everything light. The Polyubimov house on Bozhedomka, across from the big elm—she got so upset that when she wanted to unfold the note with the address, it had already turned into a damp lump in her fist. Our odiferousness is us giving away a piece of ourselves, mixing our self with the whole world, we become air, space, everything, multiplying by division. Death is life's most important, unrepeatable moment, on which so much depends in both the future and the past, but you can't let it take its own course; you must prepare for it, construct it. The rain fell sparse, gray, noiseless, brief, a hit-and-run, and by evening it had cleared up, the clouds dispersed, and every puddle was a star quotation. Dal, the famous physician-hypnotist in Moscow, cured Rachmaninov of drink by convincing him that vodka was kerosene, and out of gratitude the composer dedicated his *Second Concerto* to him. The letter got rained on, the ink ran, and the letters swelled and sprouted. Before throwing herself from the balcony, she dropped a slipper and watched it fly to the middle of the street. At Strelna you order sturgeon from the pond, they scoop it out with a net and cut a piece out on the gills with a scissors, and when they serve it, the removed piece has to fit into the incision. At the first frost she put on her fur coat; it had been packed away and retained the same smell it had had in Rome. Just as the pause between sounds belongs to music, so too the pause after death is inhabited. His wife hits the leg of the table the child hit himself on, Don't cry, There, you see? We made it hurt, too. A moon-soaked cloud. Her son died in the hospital, and after the autopsy they brought his things to the morgue and started dressing him, and lifted up his head, which was light as a matchbox: they had removed the brain. A rash down the river from the campfire. How good it was, after lovemaking, to lie on the twisted sheet, eat grapes, watch you braiding your hair, your shoulder blade moving under your skin, and then the braid being tossed back and striking that shoulder blade. An old woman, as dried up as a crust of stale bread, rummages over the scratched and burned oilcloth that is stuck fast to the kitchen table, searching for her loupe, and explains to the gas burner that bad things don't happen because mirrors crack; mirrors crack because bad things have to happen. Wooden barracks, the next room is the men's, and they scratched out a hole under the cots so that a hand could pass under, there was a queue under the cots. God fished the universe with his fishermen. Ladybird, fly away home, your children got hungry, the candy is none. The bird Eve is born only in the feminine and conceives by the wind. Pregnant, she walked rather oddly, gave a little hop, then ran up to a fence and threw up, wiping her lips with snow melt. She had a constant craving for overripe bananas, she'd buy them at the shop, and the salesgirl would say, Here, lady, take good ones, not the bad. They put a ladder in each and every entryway just in case, but

Jacob didn't come. A husband calls his lover at work and asks for Lena, but out of habit dials his wife's office and her friend answers, Just a sec, Andrei, I'll get Masha. Time is simply an organ of touch. A couple of days ago at this time, the moonlight lay on the rug by the door; today it's climbed onto the bed. Apples are lying head to head in the grass. The studio is in the cellar, and someone is constantly pissing on the stairs—the women downstairs, right by the door, but the men only go down a few steps. The baby fell asleep, and to detach him from her breast, she held his nose. The Germans here had just executed a Gypsy camp. At first the Gypsies begged, pleaded for their lives, tried to buy them off, and when they saw nothing would help, they began dancing and singing, and that's how they died—shot, while singing and dancing. I really want to wake you with a strawberry, fragrant and rough. I listen closely and can't figure out what that is, some strange sound, like walnuts, shell on shell. He was waiting for the bus under a street-lamp and opened his book—and snow started falling on the pages. Remember that night at the station, the rain, your curls escaping from your hood, and curling even more, I took you by the hood with my hands and started kissing your wet lashes, and a quadrillion years have passed since that night, a billion versts. The empty closet in the empty room magnifies the sounds. The post office has bad pens, an ink-spilled desk, he sent a registered letter and the snub-nosed young lady gave me a receipt, but it was returned—undelivered, wrong address. Now that I've had a son, I know how to object to Ecclesiastes. She opened her veins with curved manicure scissors, watched the blood drip, and lit a cigarette. I played too much ping-pong and now I can't fall asleep; the ball is jumping in my closed eyes, and spots of sun are flickering on the table. No, Valentina Georgievna, the most important thing in the Gospels are those three days when he was crucified and buried, he was gone, he had not risen, those three days have lasted until this day, and all this has yet to happen: that meeting on the shore, and someone also has to see that baked fish and fresh honey. Stems have broken through the asphalt like tusks. I need to go put down my old dog. All that exists is not creature but flesh; He created the world with Himself, His own flesh, and strained in exactly this position, the way acrobats strain in a pyramid, that is how He holds us, His flesh, by straining His muscles, therefore, since nothing on earth has changed, that means God exists. A stroll with my clouds, they never repeat, these are mine. Water for the vase ankle-deep. In the tale, the little girl runs away from evil forces and sacrifices everything to save her dear brother, but it is by abandoning her brother that she is saved, and they back off, but then the tale makes no sense, nor does the untale, and this girl doesn't need to live in this fairy-tale land at all. I was smoking on the balcony and watching her brush crumbs from the sofa with her hand, pluck something, and straighten the sheet along its crisp folds. It's odd to imagine something multiped, legless, or brainless implanting in me. Easter in the fog: the passersby go home at night holding candles in front of them, like dandelions. At last they brought in the piano, and everyone crowded around, but Mama wouldn't let anyone play because the piano had to rest from its journey. The tracks across the river melted and froze many times over until they were giants' tracks. She received his last letter simultaneously with the killed in battle notification, and in it he apologized because the paper might smell like fish, Mama dear, we are eating with our hands and washing our hands in another barrack; she stuck her nose in the envelope many times, and each time for a moment the smell really did seem to be inside there still. While we were drinking tea with our napoleon, Timka crawled under the table and tied all the adults' shoelaces. A soothsayer appeared in Novgorod and said he knew all that was to come, and he planned to walk across the river as if across dry land before all the people, and an uprising broke out in the city, and many believed the soothsayer and wanted to kill the Christian priests, and then Prince Gleb, in order to save Christ's faith, took an ax under his cloak, walked up to the soothsayer, and asked, "Do you know what is going to happen tomorrow and today before evening?" The soothsayer replied that he did and added, "I will create great miracles." Then Gleb took out his ax and chopped down the soothsayer. You are a widow and I a bachelor. One woman was struck by lightning because she decided to step over the grave of the Novgorod Saints Ioann and Longin during her unclean days. I did two watercolors on the riverbank, wetting the sheet of paper right in the river. There are elderberry branches scattered in the corners to ward off rats. The paints have such a fine, delicious name: honey watercolor—it just made me want to take a taste of those paint-cakes. I saw a lemon in a saucer on his desk, sliced and a little rotten, and I was about to throw it out, but he said, "What are you doing? I'm going to draw it!" On one stretch the lock flew off the door from all the shaking, and the freight car door slid to the side, and there was the sunset, the steppe in bloom, and everyone froze, and there was no more prison; the steppe's breath, the grass's smell, the sun's setting, and suddenly someone shouted that we had to call the convoy or they would think we'd done it ourselves and were trying to escape. Among the guests someone had brought two ancient ladies whom they called the granddaughters or great-granddaughters of Pushkin and, for some reason, Walter Scott as well, and they ate especially zealously and greedily. A city named after a Jewish fisherman, not a tsar. In the frozen car the conductor pulls the rope—a bell—and in response the driving car conductor pulls the rope—a bell—and the motorman steps on his bell—and the streetcar starts off. Suicides happen mostly during the White Nights. I was already running away, my bangle hopped out of my hands and rolled under the bed, I crawled under to get it and saw that the heels from someone's shoes had left dents in the parquet floor. The murder was discovered when the fig tree the dead man was buried under yielded unusual fruit. We were walking under a nighttime snowfall and came out on Palace Square, where bulldozers were scraping mounds of snow toward the Alexander Column. I'm stubborn as hell; when people talk to me forcefully, heatedly, about immortality, I'm certain that everything ends with this life, and on the contrary, when they try to convince me that it's all over, I start believing that since I am, so I will be. There is a wet, one-footed trail from a puddle. The building blew up in a gas explosion—in those days people still thought it was gas. On the balcony a feathery dawn has raised its elbows, and in its mouth—the Peter-Paul spire. Finally you have to understand, Tanya-silly-Tanya, it's not just that Christ extended Lazarus's four-day old age and agony from disease, since he died later anyway one way or another; no, it's all about the words that gave some Bethanian literal immortality: Get out! My puny sick little girl, the doctor said you're still on the mend, a little more treatment and we'll take you home! Ksenia's a rare name, but it suddenly became popular because of Alexander III, who called his daughter that on a whim. A meat pie, a wooden crust. Schröder-Devrien was appearing in *Il Matrimonio Segreto,* then, a magnificent singer, a favorite with the public and court (the memoirist is confusing her with the prima donna of Petersburg's Italian opera, S. F. Shoberlechner—*Ed. note).* The stocking wonders why it needs a foot when it's so stocking-y even without it! I fear for the sovereign, the empress is aging, and he needs a woman on a daily basis. The chow hall burned down at the camp, the area between the pump and barracks was fenced in, and inside they put the tables and benches. Now we ate outside under an open sky, and an old woman wearing a dirty pea jacket and rotted felt boots sighed: Just like Caffè Florian and Caffè Quadri on piazza San Marco! The route followed roads that belonged to various private companies, and new conductors kept coming on, each time punching the ticket with the sign of their road—a circle, a star, a horn. Without rings, her hands seem naked to her. En route I read *The Voyage of the Beagle:* pressed in winter by hunger, Fuegians kill and devour their old women before they kill their dogs: the boy, being asked by Mr. Low why they did this, answered, "Doggies catch otters, old women don't." People here don't lock eyes. The mumps started in Budapest and ended in Vienna. You have to arrive at unbelief yourself, and Russians get their unbelief for free, therefore they don't value it, they value faith. Alcyone turned into a bird because no one would kiss her lips, so they cornified. Letters don't reach their destination; those Tedeschi dogs are probably busy reading them. I'm afraid they've taken the cough tables for encoded documents. The bronze knight in armor living on the roof strikes his shield every hour. Rule no. 17: We despise the blinded world and everything in the world, we despise, too, any corporeal peace, and we reject life itself, for we are able to live in God's light. A kiss is full of single-cell creatures. In the moonlight, the grass shines white as alabaster. She was rarely in her cell but sat mostly in the courtyard in a pit filled with manure, which she always carried under her shirt. They build houses here a laundry line's length apart. Some lunatic picked up a stick, held it in one hand, and with the other drew the slender branch across it and hummed something under his breath—every bit as good as Tommaso da Celano singing about how beautiful God's world is. Losing their vault gave the columns meaning. We roamed among the ruins, and she broke off a fernlike twig: What's this? Maidenhair. Listen, the guidebook says that in Orvieto you absolutely must see Luca Signorelli's fresco, *Resurrection of the Flesh,* in the cathedral. Bernini's angels on the bridge want to soar into the sky, but they have stones on their feet. Fans buzzing in the Japaneses' hands, pocket mirrors for everyone to reflect how the first person creates himself a father in his image and likeness, muscular and springy, with the tip of his finger. A Jew races on the Corso. Now you, you damn kikes, you're going to know how our Lord was crucified! A christened kike is a sated wolf. Man out back, kike in the shack. Man is the Holy Sepulcher; he must be freed. Mary herself indicated where to build the church, and in the middle of August, snow fell on Esquiline. After the freeze the fallen leaves stiffened. Triton went crazy, like an angel trumpeting through the Eustachian tubes: Arise, arise, why are you sprawled out here! You wanted to go to the Eternal City, but it's not the real deal! We turned left from piazza Barberini into a dead end, Gogol started singing a dissipated Little Russian song, and at the end he went into a dance and started snapping the umbrella inside out over and over so that in less than two minutes he was left holding the umbrella handle and the rest had flown off. At night, the warm, stuffy wind bends the fountain waters. What touched that bit of air in Africa? Never odd or even. The mosquito is man's nemesis. Name now one man. Once in time of need, the good wife ate her seed. Drawn, I sit; serene rest is inward. In the gorge a path heaped with apples that never rot. He'd wanted a life an arm's length, not a hair's breadth. He did die, did he? Woe is you, little man. Dying is no bowl of cherries: he lay down under the icon and goggled. No devil lived on. Won't lovers revolt now? O stone, be not so. The moon rose and the reader expects a comparison to a nail paring—here, better catch it. Drab as a fool, aloof as a bard. Lid off a daffodil. O stone, be not so. Lend me some money, the wolf be my bond. The goat went at the bast, the nanny at the nuts. Stick to cabbage and cabbage you'll be. The muzhik drinks 'til he's tight, with his lady he fights, sees a pig and takes fright. Clouds aflutter in a skiff below water. Waves scrape its rotted side. A wolf sprawls in the sedge, belly bloated, flies glued to lids and maw, worms under tail. The goat stares, chewing all the while. Charon snaps off crisp, snow-white cabbage leaves to gnaw with his yellow teeth. A sunset sky infuses the mountain ash. Hark! Steps! He streaks to shore, darting among shoots of wild raspberries and nettles. Who are you? Just a little guy with God's sheaf of rye. Where have you come from? God. Where are you going? To God. Shem says a prayer, Ham sows the grain, Japheth has the power, and death owns them plain. Quit that, lad! Here, chew! He held out a torn leaf. A core piece, cruciferous. Noisy and succulent. The wall-scratch skiff floats downstream, rocking lightly on the waves. In it the fugitive sleeps curled in a ball, the handle of a prison spoon clenched in his fist. He's worn out. He floated under a willow leaning over the water, and a branch caressed his shoulder with its leaves. He smiled in his sleep.

★

Once again I have the time to sort things out. The last few months have left me so weary! Performances, tours, moves, meetings with people I do and don't need. I told myself I would spend these three weeks until Kiev without stirring from the dacha. I would do nothing, just lie in the hammock and look at the sky.

Here I am lying in the hammock and looking at the sky, but my thoughts are all on earth.

The last year changed my life completely.

After five years of silence, of harassment by fools and boors who understand nothing of music, of pointless sitting at home, of attempts to lead the life of a wife—and only a wife—after five years of enforced inaction, when I thought my life was over and it was time to go mad—all of a sudden everything resumed its normal course! Somehow I knew, felt, that everything would be fine, I simply needed to be patient and endure all the humiliations, clenching fists and teeth—and everything would be fine.

I'm on the stage again. And I know that I am different. It isn't a matter of my age or the lost years. My best years. I'm wiser. I probably shouldn't say that about myself. But I feel I've begun to sing about the same thing, but differently and about something different.

Soon my record will come out, at last.

People are writing me letters again and sending baskets of flowers. Admirers and the other unpleasantnesses connected with success plague me again.

I understand that I owe my success to my Iosif. A great administrator. He is climbing high. Director of the Hall of Columns! But for him this is merely another step. And I know this man will get everything he wants in life. For his anniversary he made himself a gift fit for a king: he bought a golden Chrysler from the Americans. There are only two like it in Moscow. Ours and the NKVD's. Now, when we meet on the streets, we greet each other with honks.

This anniversary cost me dearly! Out of modesty Iosif refused a celebration in the Columns—the boss felt awkward about using state property for personal purposes—and "confined himself" to the Metropol. But how he agonized over the guest list! He would get up at night, cross someone out, write down new names, constantly fearing he had omitted someone important. And naturally, he invited those who had ignored me these five years, forgotten me, pretended I no longer existed, during those terrible years when they ganged up high-handedly against "Gypsy music," when I so needed support or just a kind word. At first I said I wasn't coming. He begged me, as only he knows how. I still could not imagine how I was going to offer my hand to those people. But it turned out to be perfectly simple. And how utterly sincerely everyone rejoiced that I had returned to the stage, that I had concerts and tours, and how they congratulated me on my record! I still hadn't known a thing about the recording, whether it would happen, but they were all congratulating me already! I amazed myself. I never thought I could smile at them so easily, speak with them, laugh. I forgave them. I went and forgave them. They are unhappy people. It would be a sin not to forgive them.

How hard it turns out to be to hold a grudge and how easy and simple to forgive.

I watched as if at a remove, as if it were all just a film, as they made merry. As they rushed to have their fill of eating, drinking, and dancing. As if tomorrow it would all end. As if you had to have your fun while it lasted. Here they were carousing and drinking to the point of distraction, gluttony, vomiting.

Iosif did not stint: noblesse oblige. He chose the Metropol; another restaurant would not have the proper status. Carpets and crystal everywhere, the front door gleaming, doormen in gold braid. Women dressed by Lamanova, not the Moscow Dressmaking

Factory. Talk, laughter, the smell of expensive perfume. Caviar, sturgeon, bananas, tortes. A river of Champagne. And in the middle, the famous fountain that countless gentlemen and ladies had fallen into. With so many more to follow. The orchestra in tails.

Everyone kept asking me to sing. Iosif got down on his knees. His eyes held fear that I would refuse to sing and a plea not to spoil his anniversary with all these necessary people on whom his life depended. His, which meant mine, too. I came out wearing a long evening gown of crimson panne, sewn especially for this evening, and began to sing. I sang Prozorovsky. Everyone understood perfectly but pretended nothing had happened. Who is this Prozorovsky? Where is he? Maybe he never was! But the love song, this miracle, will always be! And who the author is and where? Better not ask! And what does it matter anyway!

The sound there is good. A huge expanse of music—a glass ceiling somewhere in the sky.

And under those vaults—vodka, gluttony, and drunken dancing.

I barely lasted until the evening's end.

When I was putting my coat on in the checkroom and standing by the glass doors waiting for Iosif to go home, I suddenly saw out the window that snow had fallen outside, out of the blue! And this was when everything in the city had already melted! I stood there looking and couldn't help myself. I went out into the falling snow. Everything whiter than white! How good it was to inhale that freshness after the hot, sweaty, drunken restaurant! Such silence, and huge snowflakes falling slowly, lit by the street-lamps. The snow covered the pavement—and melted wherever you stepped. I walked out right in my pumps across the snow-covered sidewalk—leaving a chain of narrow black tracks behind. I'll run away and he can follow my tracks! All of a sudden I felt so good, so wonderful! I scraped a handful of snow off a parapet, formed a little snowball, and ran it over my lips and neck! What a flood of wanton happiness! I hadn't felt this good for a long time. And all from ordinary snow.

Today it's been nine years.

I thought I'd cried all my tears in these years. You can't.

Suddenly you find so very few memories remain. I was with him a year and a half, almost never apart, and all I have left of his life is a few pictures to remember him by.

Volodya sucking his foot.

His smile.

This little piggy went to market—and I lightly tickle his big toe. This little piggy stayed home—I tickle his toe. This little piggy had roast beef—I tickle the next. And this little piggy had none. And this little piggy went wee-wee-wee all the way home—and I tickle his tummy. Little Volodya laughs.

It was here at the Paris clinic where they placed my baby on my belly, pressed colostrum from my breast, gave him a chance to lick it, and then took him away. But I'm hungry. They brought bouillon, and I was craving cabbage soup.

Iosif accosted me with an infusion of fennel, so there would be milk, and begged me, "Drink!"

Lord, what I endured then! Mastitis. Abscesses on both breasts. Cracked nipples. I'd give my baby son the breast and cry out in pain. And it was like that every three hours. No sooner did the wounds on my nipples heal up than he tore them open again.

A baby is as if your heart were somewhere outside your own body. You're here, but your heart is beating there.

At the time it hurt, but later I realized I would endure any pain just so my baby would live, and now nothing is left but my memory and the envelope I sent to Mama in Rostov. I pressed his little hand and foot to a piece of paper and outlined them in pencil. I measured his length with a thread and put the thread in the envelope.

Mama brought it with her and I've kept it. I opened it again today. Here's his little foot, and here's the thread. But my baby son is gone.

So many years have passed, and you remember a clot of blood instead of his soul.

Sometimes I feel eight hundred years old.

I never used to be able to understand why people in the Bible were five and six hundred years old. This is why!

★

I went to Sergiev Posad, which is now called Zagorsk for some reason. The monastery is quite desolate, the sanctuaries are closed and crumbling, people are living in the monastery buildings, there is linen hanging out to dry everywhere. Ugly linens, pathetic, impoverished.

The Bethany ponds where the monks raised fish are overgrown with grass and reeds.

I thought that if there have been centuries of prayer, then that prayer could not have gone away. It must be preserved here—in these stones, cupolas, and reeds, in this green, green grass.

People walk by—and cross themselves.

I prayed for my son to the cupolas, to the monastery walls, to the hundred-year-old trees, and to the green, green grass.

★

I was tired mainly from the moves, the trains, the drafty train cars that smelled of damp laundry, from the train stations, hotels, terrible beds, and sleepless nights. The nightmarish transfer in Kursk that night: people sleeping on the floor, lined up side by side, their arms around their bundles, the stinking toilets, the dreadful sadness. In Voronezh we wanted to take a walk through town, but one look at the crowd and we couldn't bring ourselves to. There were lots of beer stands, and torn and soiled people hanging about next to each. There were more drunks in town than sober people.

But everyone arrived at the concert elegant and beautiful, faces shining, eyes lively. As if they were going to a celebration.

Lord, for them I'm a celebration! They're the ones who have given me a celebration, not vice versa! What happiness, after all, to stand in front of a hall that radiates warmth, hope, gratitude, and love for you!

Then you go backstage and the fairy tale ends. Reality sets in. First, the driver is drunk, then they mixed up your tickets again, then the pipe broke in the hotel.

Thank God such marvelous people were picked! Thanks to Iosif! He knows how to do that. He got hold of Trosman from the Bolshoi Theater, and Khaskin, Lantsman, and Gladkov from the jazz orchestra. What marvelous musicians! And all with a sense of humor. Without that, just go try to come back alive from tours, while giving concerts almost daily and spending the night in filthy, bedbug-infested hotels!

Each time we rode into the next town, I would get agitated, worried. In those moments you feel like capturing the city, conquering everyone in it, making each person fall in love with you! Each time after the concert, at supper, Gladkov would say, "There now, Bellochka, and you were afraid! The town's ours!" And once Khaskin said, "You mean you still haven't realized that it's all the same town, just in a different place?"

After the concert in Tula, at the train station restaurant, Lantsman, already drunk, declaimed:

God said, "You've done nothing with your days,
Why have you lived? What sense your cheer?"
"Comfort I offered to weary slaves,"
And God let fall a single tear!

Everyone burst out laughing. At first he assured us he had made it up, and afterward admitted it was Garkavi.

Everyone repeated it, laughing. But we should have wept.

You're on the train looking out the window—field and stream—and you keep going over those lines in your mind.

When I was a child, Papa took us to the steppe to see excavations and showed us the stone women. These statues taken from a burial mound seemed in some way enigmatic, mysterious, eternal. But now I'd had my fill of looking out the window. Ordinary peasant women stood at every crossing all over Russia, only they were just like those stones ones, and they watched the train in their hemp rope shoes, padded jackets, and gray kerchiefs.

Letters came from the towns where I had had concerts. At first I answered each one, but now I don't know what to do with them. They ask me to send medicines. They write from prison. Admirers send photographs. Heart-rending stories. Or perfectly awful ones. An actress from the Kursk provincial theater is ill, three children, one, the girl, is an invalid—hot oil spilled, blinding her, and there's no one to help. Sheets torn from school notebooks, postcards. Admiration, assurances of love, requests for favors for someone, for a hospital bed. Iosif laughs. "That's what fame is. This is good! This is what you wanted!"

No, it isn't.

What am I supposed to do with all this? Throw them out, burn them? God would never forgive me, but there's nothing I can do.

Our only good lodgings were in Leningrad. Iosif took a room at the Astoria. I still remember how it was turned into a workers' dining hall. And now it's a fashionable hotel again. A marvelous room with a view of St. Isaac's.

Most amazing of all is that the same people are still there. Maitre d' Baron Nikolai Platonovich Wrangel. He seems to be the sole person who still knows how to wear tails off stage. I was even more struck when I saw the same elevator operator, Dina, with those same bangs, an exact copy of Anna Akhmatova from the Altman portrait, only she had aged and put on weight.

Here is what I wanted to write: I'm struck by how everything changes but the people stay the same.

That time, in the Astoria, I drew myself an enormous bath. This is the kind I want for our dacha, so that I can step, not climb in, lifting my legs high.

When I was a child I had this game: I imagined that when I grew up I would have a big house with lots and lots of rooms, and then I would furnish them.

And now I've grown up. And that is what I'm doing.

Everything you dream of comes true. Only what of it?

*

Today was a scorcher. Everyone crawled off wherever they could. The straw blinds were lowered. An old cherry tree grows in the garden right in front of the balcony, and if you lean over the railing you can pick the fruit. Through the narrow slit between the straws you can see the hot air rising, serpentine. The sound of hammers and axes coming from everywhere: Valentinovka is going up full tilt.

It's been hot since morning. The thermometer says twenty degrees Celsius in the shade, and you can fry an egg on the windowsill.

After my morning coffee I sat in the swing on the terrace looking through fashion magazines from the Baltics I'd borrowed from my dressmaker. Masha was banging pots in the kitchen, and Mama was listening to the radio. Iosif is in Moscow and won't arrive until Saturday.

Lugovskoi, my dacha admirer, stopped by on his motorcycle and sidecar and we went for a swim in the millpond. Riding is horribly uncomfortable, and the shaking is terrible, but it was fun and we laughed a lot. It's quiet and nice on the Klyazma. Lugovskoi played the fool like a little boy, despite his rank, and caught minnows with his forage cap. Then he put it on full of water.

On the way back we stopped at the former Zagoryansky estate to look at the ruins of the abandoned grounds. A large and beautiful park, but the statues have been smashed and toppled. The pond, horseshoeing the garden, has long since turned into a stagnant swamp. The trees have rotted from the inside and are holding on by their bark. The footbridges have collapsed. The surrounding residents have broken and dragged off everything they could. I can imagine how it all was there before. Someone had tried to make it all beautiful, after all. In tangles of goutweed Lugovskoi found the grave of the estate's last owners, who died back before the revolution: "God's slaves, the Bychkovs." It's good the Bychkovs can't see any of this.

We got back by five, and Mama and Masha were making jam on a brazier in the garden. I wanted to taste the foam, brought the spoon to my mouth, blew on it for a long time, and that insolent Lugovskoi nudged my elbow so my mouth and cheeks were all smeared! "Aha! Then I'm going to kiss you all right now!" Everyone ran away from me helter-skelter. I chased them through the garden and around the brazier, shouting, "The sweetest kiss of all! Where are you going?" We were laughing so hard we nearly died.

Why am I writing all this? After all, absolutely zero happened that was important or noteworthy. An ordinary dacha day, in the middle of a decade of some century.

Excerpts from Mozart's *Don Giovanni* were being broadcast over the radio—in fact, Don Giovanni's aria before Elvira's balcony.

★

The weather has taken a drastic turn. Rain all day since morning. We played lotto. Boredom. I didn't feel like reading. Dark fell quickly. As soon as the rain stopped I felt like a walk. I'm glad I convinced Osya to lay brick paths. That way you can go for a walk after the rain—no puddles, and you don't drown in mud. I went out into the cold, wet garden. I was shivering so, you'd think I'd had to put my damp woolen jacket on my naked body. No matter where you put your foot, you stepped on a snail in the darkness. There's a positive snail invasion this year. I stood there looking at the trees, the sky, the swift clouds, the apples, the strip of light from the blinded window in Mama's room. The branches were dripping. Wet rustlings everywhere. Treetops swishing softly. After the rain the phlox have a penetrating smell, sweet and intoxicating.

I went up to the empty terrace and sat in the swing. I didn't turn on the light. I so wanted someone dear to be sitting right beside me. To tell him in a half-whisper, "Look, the apples are shining in the dark, as if they were lit from within!"

I thought about different things. I remembered going to Khamovniki with Masha for Easter. Few churches remain, and there was a crush inside. The candles and crowd made it horribly stuffy. We stood squeezed in on all sides, so that I started feeling ill. Afraid somehow. We barely fled into the air.

The streets were full of people that night because on Saturday of Holy Week the theaters had announced performances starting at ten o'clock in the evening, and the movie houses were open all night.

We were walking home, and the marvelous Easter motif lived on in our ears: "Christ is risen from the dead, trampling death by death . . ." Masha suddenly asked me whether I believed in the future resurrection of the dead. "Now, I believe in God, but not in resurrection." "But why, Masha?" "I just don't. My dear departed grandma, you mean she is going to be resurrected to eternal life as a moldering old woman? Then everyone should die young. No, it's all fairy tales!"

Masha, Masha! Let it be fairy tales.

If God gave each person his own life, then He will give each person his own special resurrection.

If God performed one miracle and gave me this rushed, elusive life, then he will think up a way to give me another that lasts. And there will be this Easter night there, too. And today's evening after the rain. And Masha, who doesn't believe in her own resurrection and who is already breathing noisily in her little room. And Iosif, who is somewhere in Moscow with I don't know who. And my mama in the room upstairs, reading probably, her light still on. And Papa. And my little baby. All of it. All all all.

★

Iosif arrived this morning. He brought all kinds of delicacies from Eliseyev's and arranged a long lunch under the lilac. He let Masha try an oyster—and she spat it out. It reminded me of the Alexandrov pineapple. They gave their housemaid a pineapple as a treat for her family in the village, and they didn't know what to do with it, so they made soup.

Masha went to the store at the station, and Mama began a conversation about a servant stealing. She said she shouldn't be indulged and so on, but Iosif came to her defense. "I never count the change Masha brings. She took it out of need, so never mind."

Is he really sleeping with her?

He told us that in Moscow it was so stuffy it was quite impossible to breathe, that there hadn't been such a hot summer in a long time. There were heel marks in the asphalt. He cursed the newly opened Moskva hotel. The newspapers are writing that it's the best in the world, but in fact, it's like always: luxury on the outside, marble, malachite, and jasper; but in the rooms the commodes don't flush, the door to the bathroom doesn't shut, and there's no stopper in the tub and you have to rig something to plug it.

He always has a reservation for rooms for his guests, and I know that Iosif brings his music hall girlfriend there. I give him his due. He would never bring anyone home, to our bed. And thank you for that! Although what does "our bed" mean? There is no "our bed."

Iosif has been cheating on me for a long time. He looked me in the eye and said there wasn't anyone, but I could tell right away. I didn't know whether or not to believe him. I tried to persuade myself that of course I did. I'm always obligated to give my beloved the benefit of the doubt. But no matter what he told me, I didn't believe him and pretended I did. Even when he told me the truth I didn't believe him, and when he lied that he loves me alone, I did.

I went to the music hall especially to look at the thirty Moscow girls under the direction of the impotent Kasyan Goleizovsky. All the beauties were choice, in leotards sprinkled with sparkling powder, wearing chic high-heeled shoes and with ultra-fashionable hairdos. I tried to guess which one of them. Then I thought, What's the difference? They're all identical.

We have returned to biblical times, when a man had as many wives as he could support—like today.

★

I know it was my own fault. During those horrible years, when I didn't want to go anywhere or see anyone, all my anger and all my irritation spilled onto Osya. He stood between them and me. He protected me from that world, saved me as best he could, wanted to do everything to soften the blows so that it didn't hurt so much. But I was losing my mind, and all the rows, all the hysterics, it all spilled out on him, my poor Osik. I hated those people, and my husband suffered in their stead. I couldn't sleep with him anymore. I simply couldn't! All the attempts to make things right, to fix things, to talk, would always end in a row. I don't know how we managed to live like that, in an atmosphere of perpetual discord.

We didn't need any special reason. A few days of irritation would build up and press on me—and boom! I'm saying something and he isn't listening, he's getting dressed to leave, he looks at the alarm

clock on the dresser and says casually, "You have three more minutes." I pick up the clock and fling it to the floor.

Then we fought, not stormily and noisily, like lovers, but coldly,
furtively.

Our understanding had been severed. Like a broken telephone.
We talked, but there was no getting through the crackle and static.
Each heard only himself, his voice bouncing back.

And in exactly the same way I suddenly noticed that I didn't even
have a connection with myself, my body. Only then did I see the
nail marks on my palms. Apparently I was constantly clenching my
fists and hadn't noticed I was hurting myself.

I remembered our most recent row, over a vase. When was that?
Last year, in the spring. And this wasn't just cups and saucers. I
broke an expensive Chinese vase from some century that he had
proudly dragged home from the antique shop. And suddenly I had
the strange sensation that this wasn't me and that I was somewhere
far away. This was some other woman shouting in fury and smashing beautiful expensive objects for some reason. I myself had calmed
down long since and had no pain or pity left inside. This person was
too far distanced to cause me genuine pain.

But most of all, I was horrified at myself. I realized I hated myself
like this.

★

My first thought was to kill him and her! And blow up the house.
And obliterate the whole world. And then suddenly I ran out of tears
and the strength to be upset. I became calmer and pretended not to
know anything and that nothing in particular was going on in our
relationship.

How I hated his voice when he called out, "Bellochka, darling,
I'm going away for a couple of days!" And how he would go on and
on about business matters. But in fact he was calling from the room

he took to spend the night with his lover. And she may have been sitting next to him, stroking his knee. I responded, trying to keep my voice from shaking. "Of course, Osik, don't worry! Come back soon! I love you very much and look forward to it!"

I look at myself in the mirror. I have wrinkles here on my neck. And she doesn't.

But girls like that are not really frightening. There's nothing to fear from those prancing beauties. You need to fear the calm, quiet ones with the eyes of an astonished child. Like Masha's.

She really is still a complete child. Once I came home and Masha dashed out of my room. I went in and immediately realized she'd been luxuriating on my bed.

Suddenly I imagined myself in her place. After all, I too would probably try on all my mistress's dresses when she was out, her stockings, shoes, and hats.

A hard-working, clean, reserved woman. Still waters.

She refused her salary, saying she would just spend it all, and if she needed money for candles I'd give it to her, so I should keep the money or she'd lose it.

I must go buy her shoes or God knows what she'll be wearing.

*

I couldn't take the seclusion at the dacha and traveled with Iosif to Moscow. It was dusty and stuffy, but at least there were people.

We visited Dneprov and Milich. We talked half the evening about the reburials in Moscow. Everyone had been struck by the almost life-like look of the body of Nikolai Rubinstein, the composer. We also talked about the paintings from the Hermitage. Dneprov had heard that Grabar had said that eighty percent of the most valuable paintings in the Hermitage had been sold abroad and that soon they would start buying them back at a large profit.

Alexandrov himself deigned to appear. He was asked how he

managed to make the bull drunk in *Jolly Fellows*. It turned out that in Gagri, during shooting, they bound the bull's legs with wire. The ladies were outraged. "But that must have hurt it!" Alexandrov laughed. He recounted how for Meyerkhold they'd had to fight on stage for real and break each other's noses, and real blood spurted out. He declared that if you took art seriously, then, like Abraham, you had to know how to sacrifice not just a bull but your own son.

I looked at him and had not a moment's doubt that this man— yes, he would make the sacrifice, and his hand would not shake. He would sacrifice his son, his wife, and everyone at that table.

He sat there chasing his vodka with mushrooms and sprats and simply radiating success. He talked about meeting Chaplin and how in Hollywood all the celebrities were falling over each other to invite him to dinner. God knows, maybe they truly did.

They say he built Orlova a dacha in Vnukovo based on his own design, with little heart-shaped windows. The epitome of bad taste and wretchedness.

★

It's good to be back in Valentinovka after Moscow! Moscow left a strange impression: life is getting better, and you can feel it literally. They've canceled ration cards, closed the humiliating trade syndicates, where people brought their teeth, there's plenty of food, more and more even, and the theaters and cinemas are packed. But everything else is as before. People are the same! The Dneprovs boasted of their new Swedish table and new radio. Their home is a full cup. And they have all of it on view, just to cut a swath. Milich sent the cook to Eliseyev's, in front of her guests, to buy some cold pork for her Pomeranian. Afterward we were driving away and I saw out the window how poorly the women on the street were dressed and how everyone was carrying something, laden with some great weight:

cans of kerosene, bags, sacks, baskets. They board the streetcars with their sacks. And look at me with envy and malice.

Why does everyone hate each other and bend over backward to have something to boast of—apartments, fur coats, servants, lovers, autos, a fat, full life?

What if the punishment comes before death, not after?

★

The living room mirror condescends to me, shows me as I want to be; the bedroom mirror is pitiless and betrays me from the head down, my wrinkles, my sagging stomach. Am I really getting old already? There's no hiding my aging anymore, as before. Old age seems not to fear me any longer. It's brazen. It's entered me as if I were its home: gray hairs discovered after a sleepless night, wrinkles that weren't there yesterday. The fold by my mouth—just like an old lady.

Now, like Mama, I add a little bluing to the water so my gray hair doesn't yellow.

But I especially feel time's passage when I run into someone I haven't seen for a long while. The last time I was at a concert at the Great Hall, I ran smack into Taskin. He's quite old, but he struts about and, naturally, has some fresh talent on his arm, a blonde, of course. Ever since *Circus* came out, Moscow has filled up with dyed blondes. But their parts darken quickly, treacherously.

The last time I'd seen Taskin before that was in Leningrad, a couple of years ago, during my most difficult time. At the time he was cold and in a hurry, but yesterday he rushed to kiss me, paid me all kinds of compliments, the meaning of which boiled down to him saying, See, I discovered you, sweetheart, you haven't forgotten, have you?

How could I forget! It's as if I were standing in front of that building right now: 7 Kabinetnaya Street. My first contract. My first fee.

An ecstatic and self-confident schoolgirl, I had come to Petrograd to enter the conservatory. Only the conservatory! Why had I decided the conservatory was for me? I was all it needed! Nyusya got a voice professor to agree to listen to me, which he did, and said, faltering, "Your voice . . . is more of a mezzo contralto . . ." And he rejected me with the sense of his duty to art fulfilled. I was in tears, while he began consoling me, saying my voice was a natural and training would only spoil it. If it were made higher, it still wouldn't reach to opera, so sing as you do, child!

There went all my dreams! Out the window. Sing as you do, child!

Now I think, thank you to him!

I recalled my first odd impression of Petrograd. Not the palaces or the Neva, but the fact that, unlike Moscow streetcar conductors, who carried a board with a stack of tickets attached to it, in Petrograd the conductors had a purse on a belt with coils. Moreover, I was struck by the fact that the conductors were mainly women, because of the draft. And behind me someone was distressed that before the war a ticket cost three kopeks, and now it was a whole five. Nyusya and I were riding to a student concert—applause for her, she bows, and my heart sank with envy. Yes, envy. An insignificant failure envied her sister's success. In the mornings she studied at the conservatory, and in the evenings, to earn extra money, she played at the cinema. Nyusya knew singers and impresarios and offered to take me to see the famous Taskin, who had made Vyaltseva. I guessed this was my last hope. If he drove me out, I would go drown myself from the new Palace Bridge—it had just opened, and I would give it its first try.

I anticipated someone majestic, but he turned out to come up to my shoulder. Carrying his napkin—he had just eaten, and he belched up his roast. First he took my hand and purred, "A woman begins to please with her hands"—whereas he had stumpy fingers. His bald spot shone. Paternal patting all over. I turned around and went to the corner, so he couldn't get at me, and sang. He went into ecstasy.

"You're a ready-made singer! Learn three songs, any you like, and Godspeed onto the stage! Of course, you lack experience, but you have everything that can't be learned."

We agreed I would come to see him a few more times to consult on my choice of repertoire and manner of performance. I flew out as if on wings. Indeed, he did pull strings for me. The next time I came I learned a few love songs with him. On the piano were some papers and an envelope. My first contract and first money! Pressing them to my chest, I ran to see my sister, and on the corner of Kabinetnaya hugged a column and kissed it in broad daylight!

I began to perform at the Coliseum, and Taskin would call: "How are things, Bellochka? Everything all right? Are you satisfied? That's just hunky-dory. Come by this evening. A very important matter!" I went by, and the important manner was squaring accounts for the engagement. It nauseates me even now to remember his stumpy fingers and him breathing into my ear: "You aren't a Bella, you're a *baiser!*" I grabbed his hands. "Stop, I beg of you!" He tried to get a kiss. I slapped his cheeks and bald spot and dashed out of the apartment. He shouted after me, "If you change your mind, come by!" That was the whole engagement. I lost the job right away, as expected.

Twenty years have passed! We meet and pay each other compliments!

Wondrous are your works, Lord!

*

Last night I dreamed of Papa. I awoke in tears.

We're walking through our garden here, in Valentinovka, and I'm showing him the currant bushes, the strawberries, the young apple trees. I want to show him our cherry trees, left over from the former owners—there are so many cherries that from far away the trees look red—and all of a sudden they're gone, only pecked at, dried ones remain. I get terribly upset over this, but he reassures me and pats my head as if I were little: "There, there, don't cry! You mustn't! Everything's fine! You have a record coming out soon! People will listen to you all over the country! Everyone's going to love you!" But I wail even harder. "I don't need anything, Papa! My beloved papa! How good you didn't die!" And right then I woke up.

At the mere thought that I never saw him before he died and did not attend his funeral, I felt like sobbing desperately.

The last time we saw each other, he already knew everything about himself, but I knew nothing at all. At the time he said, "Why do we leave this life right when it feels as though we are just starting to understand something, to figure things out?" But I wasn't about to listen. "Don't say such foolish things! You're going to live another hundred years!"

All I have is a photograph from his funeral. He's in his coffin without his glasses, looking not at all like himself. They set him on the table, right where we always had supper.

Papa had kept certain ancient objects from excavated burial mounds. Sometimes he would show me his treasures, and each time he said, "Just imagine, thousands of years have passed since the artist's hands made this clasp!" Now it seems even more years have passed since the moment Papa handed me that clasp.

I keep trying to remember what we talked about that time before we parted. After all, these were his last words to me. And I can't remember anything. I was thinking about something else. If only I'd known then!

I agonize over never once having had a real talk with him about what is truly important. Whenever we met, he would always start a conversation about trifles. At least once, father and child should have an important conversation about the main thing in life. Papa's been gone a long time, and I will never have that conversation in my life.

Mama, my old mama! How I love you! And how little I know how to show you that love! With you, too, each time, we talk about trifles.

Yesterday she spent half the day walking through the forest breaking up anthills with her cane. Her legs hurt. Someone told her she needed to soak ant eggs in alcohol and spread this mixture on her knees.

Last week she got it into her head to sew herself a funeral dress, the dress she should be buried in. She looked at herself in front of the mirror to see how it fit.

Her main activity now is reading, but she doesn't read anything new, only what she's already read. Sometimes, looking at Mama from behind, I see her back suddenly start to shake. She is overtaken by sudden storms of weeping at reading something memorable, and even more often when she listens to music. Just today she teared up when Lakmé's aria flowed out of the loudspeaker, "Where is my young daughter rushing . . ."

Our SI-234 picks up foreign airwaves, and I love to twirl and listen. The whole world is broadcasting American jazz. When I have no more strength for anything, it's nice to turn it on and listen—and somewhere you find the will to live and you feel like dancing. But Mama can't stand that music. Every evening they broadcast operas for her: "Act two. The countess's bedroom." But when the news comes on, she turns it off.

Mama, are you and I really never going to have the one conversation?

Or is talking about trifles in fact the most important thing?

★

I went for a walk after dinner through the village, and a dog accosted me. I took it home and fed it. Masha sulked that here I was bringing in all kind of vermin and you couldn't feed all the hungry dogs in any case.

Since you can't—because you can't—you have to feed the one you can. This one.

It's like with happiness. Since everyone can't be happy anyway, whoever can be happy right now, should. You have to be happy today, right now, no matter what. Someone said there can't be a heaven if there's a hell. Supposedly it's impossible to be in heaven if you know suffering exists somewhere. Nonsense. True enjoyment of life can only be felt if you've known suffering. What would the leftovers from our soup be to this mongrel if it hadn't had a whiff of hunger?

It's always been this way. Someone's head is being cut off, while two people in the crowd on the square in front of the scaffold are knowing first love. Someone is admiring the picturesque sunset, while someone else is looking at the same sunset from behind bars. It will always be thus! It should be thus! No matter how many tens or millions have their head cut off, at that very moment someone should know first love. Even that adolescent. I can see his face before my eyes. We were returning from the Crimea by train and had stopped at some junction, and directly across was a Stolypin car, and there were bars and someone's almost childish face in the narrow window. While on our little table we had food, flowers, bottles.

We only stopped for a minute. Everyone in the compartment fell silent. And when we moved on, our gaiety was gone.

Or should it all be the reverse? After that should we all have lived even more gaily? And should the food have been zestier? The sunset prettier?

All the world is a single whole, communicating vessels. The more intense the unhappiness for some somewhere, the more intensely and keenly others should be happy. They should love more intensely, too. To balance out the world, so it doesn't flip over, like a boat.

Lugovskoi sent two soldiers to saw firewood, as promised. Two Vasyas. One Vasya is a sturdy lad; the other Vasya, tall and slender. They sawed stripped to the waist. I lay nearby in the hammock, swinging slowly and looking at their boyish cropped napes, tanned backs, and muscles. They carried a chock past me, and suddenly my nostrils were filled with the smell of freshly sawed wood and male sweat.

No one would ever admit that this could happen, that the smells of wood and sweat could be that arousing. I was so aroused, I got all twisted down below.

★

I agonized over my husband's betrayal as long as I wasn't betraying him myself. Or rather, until I realized it wasn't a betrayal.

Last summer. The Crimea. A vacation romance.

Palms, whiteness, distance, bare mountains. The Monk, the Camel, and the Siamese Cat, which slips seaward, arching its back like a cat.

Every day on the shore, early in the morning, he walked on his hands, turned somersaults and cartwheels, and stood on his head. The trained, tightly wound body of a gymnast. First I wanted him to like me out of mischief. We had climbed high up the mountain. On the narrow path I grabbed his arm—not so much to hold on as to touch him. A half-joking conversation. "I would steal you and take you away forever!" he said. "And I would give up everything and go with you!"

I awoke in the morning and realized I'd fallen in love, but I didn't know what to do about it. The delicate fever of love, as if I'd tested a battery's charge on my tongue.

Every day we went for a swim. We sat on the shore. I swung my beach slippers and felt young, strong, and frivolous.

He gave me back my body; through his love I came to love this body again. He also said, "You should talk during love, but you're silent."

Each time I wanted to undress him myself. To kiss him where his smell had collected. To love his whole body without fear of being misunderstood. Not to love but to be made of love.

After the madness and ecstasy, when I have to come back to myself, wet from sweat, with hairs stuck to my lips, I have a surge of strength and such tenderness for him, helpless, powerless. He takes my hand and puts it over his eyes. I nestle under his arm and feel his heart beating through my temple. Or I look at him, my elbow propped on the pillow. And I feel so good, so carefree!

In the morning he wakes me by nibbling on my earlobe and whispers words of love—and I don't care whether it's the truth or a lie. Because there cannot be a lie in love, only in words.

One night we took a boat ride over the sea. I had never seen the night glow of the Black Sea waters before. You row, and the wave touched by the oar begins to glow. Calm water no longer glows. A truly amazing spectacle! Not only did our boat leave a fiery trail, but every fish, down to the smallest, glowed when it moved. We came out on the open sea after a couple of kilometers and there observed a sumptuous scene: dolphins catching fish and leaving behind patches of glow. Patches of glow were scattered all over the night sea.

★

One day I came home with one earring and noticed only when I was undressing to go to bed. But Iosif didn't notice anything.

He generally doesn't.

Or maybe he knows everything and says nothing. My Iosif. My good, wise Iosif.

I'm just afraid I won't manage to give all I have in me. The body passes so quickly.

I've wanted a child from every man I've loved. I do now. I'm not old yet, I can give birth. I know time is running out.

I was afraid something was wrong with me, and no matter how many professors I turned to, they merely shrugged.

God has not seen fit.

Why haven't you? Are you waiting for me to grow quite old? Can you only perform miracles? Are you trying to test me? Are you trying to prove something to someone? Do you want me to live a hundred years and only then give me a child, the way you did Sarah?

I am not Sarah. I don't want to live to a hundred. I'm alive now, here.

★

They cut off the light to the whole village because of the storm. All the dachas are dark. I'm sitting with a kerosene lamp.

Today, July 28, the newspaper has a decree on the complete ban on abortions. And right there is an article about how they imprisoned some "Maria Egorovna Morozova, age thirty-five, a worker at the Nazievsky peatery, who in the last three years performed seventeen abortions on different peatery workers in unsanitary conditions by injecting a soap solution."

Sonya, Iosif's cousin, works as a visiting nurse at Otto's hospital. When she and I saw each other the last time in Leningrad, she told me all kinds of horror stories she had encountered through work. The things those unlucky women are brought in with after self-abortions! The poor women cripple themselves with crochet hooks, pencils, goose feathers, birch chips; they all have complications, infections, death from sepsis. They come asking for an abortion, they're turned down, then a visiting nurse comes to the house and they don't let her through the door. "You're pregnant!" "The pregnancy didn't hold." The usual explanation: she lifted something heavy, stumbled, her belly started hurting, and so forth.

★

A Kiev tour.

Changes for the better are noticeable on the railroad. We traveled quickly, without delays. International train cars, very comfortable and clean.

We're staying at the Continental. Prerevolutionary, sumptuous, antique furniture. The key on a heavy wooden bulb—nothing you could hide. This is so people don't carry it off. The Continental makes tiny éclairs that are famous all over Kiev. They're baked for twelve o'clock—it tastes so good to swallow them whole!

I ran away from my people and headed for the Monastery of the Caves.

I came out on the Dnieper—such beauty! So it was from here, from this hill, that Kievans watched the idols floating down the river and prayed fervently to Perun to rise up.

They so wanted their god to show them his full power against the impious! But the idols neither surfaced nor came to shore, they punished no one, they just kept floating, like logs, onward, obedient to the will of the waves.

I got to talking with some woman. She told me to definitely go and pray at Kiev's Sophia to the miracle-working icon of Nikolai Wet. She said his name came from a miracle. A husband and wife were living in Kiev with their only son, Nikolai, still an infant. When they were crossing the Dnieper in a boat, the baby fell out of his mother's arms and drowned. In despair, the parents started reproaching Saint Nikolai for not helping protect the child, then they came to their senses and began praying for forgiveness and consolation for them in their grief. In the morning, before the service in Kiev's Sophia, as the sexton entered the church, he heard a child's cry. He and the guard went up to the choir loft and there, behind a firmly closed door, which had not been opened, in front of the icon of Saint Nikolai they saw that very infant—and he was wet, as if pulled from the water.

★

I've just returned from the municipal children's home. I spoke with the director, Dr. Gorodetsky. I said I was thinking about taking a child and asked for his help.

He and I talked for a long time, then he led me through the rooms and showed me everything. He said that during the '33 famine there were a great many foundlings. The police picked them up by the dozen on Kreshchatik. Gorodetsky took in five hundred children. They began opening shelters for them. Many died of starvation and disease. And I'm looking at the children, who are now all plump and clean, the little girls in identical little dresses, all shaved clean, so you can't tell them apart. I glanced into a ward where the children's eyes were dirty, covered with festering incrustations. I asked, "What's wrong with them?" "Trachoma." We went on. It turns out they aren't told they're living in a shelter for foundlings; they're certain they're living in a sanatorium. "My mama's going to come and take me home." Gorodetsky said that many did come and adopt. In the last six months they had taken away thirty children. The children also choose parents for themselves. Gorodetsky laughed that if someone who isn't rich wants to adopt them, they say, "We won't go because you didn't come in an automobile." While we were standing in the courtyard talking, a crowd gathered around us. They stood looking at me. There was a question in everyone's eyes: Who am I? What if you're my mama?

"Galina Petrovna!"

She doesn't hear. All around him, noisy Piazza Mignanelli drowns out his voice.

The interpreter walks up very close, but she doesn't notice him. She's getting her fill, head back, of the immaculate virgin placed on an antique column pulled out from under some emperor.

Galpetra is the same as ever: the violet suit, the white mohair hat, and the winter boots with a half-lowered zipper. Even the same museum scuffs. And a slip of paper taped to her back. The very same.

The interpreter calls out again, "Galina Petrovna!"

She shudders and turns around.

"Lord have mercy, how you frightened me!"

She straightens her hat.

"I was just standing here thinking, Great, they've put up a monument to conception! There's just one thing on their mind!"

She takes a crumpled handkerchief out of her sleeve, blows her nose, and tucks it back in her sleeve.

"While you're riding the subway from our Vykhino, everyone sneezes all over you!"

The street is filled with a ringing that's harsh and feathery. Someone has caught a bird-stocking in the sky and is pulling it on his foot.

A dyed old lady, coming out through the Tabacchi doors, glances up and opens her umbrella just in case. Other passersby have umbrellas, too, because of the birds.

"Well, let's go!" Galpetra says, once again straightening her mohair hat.

"Where?"

"Anywhere. Why stand here by this column? Only look both ways carefully! They race around here like madmen!"

Galpetra lets a herd of scooters pass and crosses the street, in no hurry, waddling and scuffing her slippers over the Roman paving stones. Her boots' unfastened tops click against each other at each step.

The interpreter catches up with her, and they walk side by side. Galpetra stops at every shop that sells souvenirs, postcards, and

T-shirts with celebrities' names. Shoulders her way up to the stalls. Examines the windows of shops with Madonna-Barbies and Barbie-Madonnas. She shakes her head at the prices.

Tourist groups overtake them. Japanese. Germans. Japanese again. Above the heads in the crowd, there are umbrellas everywhere and the guides' sticks with varicolored scarves that say, Don't get lost, follow me and I'll show you, in this bustling, muddle-headed city something genuine, important, and eternal, which is why you came here, after all, you weren't here before and won't be here after, but you're here now!

Someone steps on Galpetra's slippers. She snarls, "Are you blind or something? Watch out!"

Passersby look around at her museum slippers, at the paper with the naughty drawing on her back, but here they've seen worse. They're used to everything.

"What's there? Let's go there! Gosh almighty, I'm really here in Rome! Who would have ever thought!"

They turn onto via del Tritone. Coming toward them is a group of schoolchildren, each holding a Big Mac. One throws his wrapper on the sidewalk. Right in front of Galpetra.

"What have we here!"

She grabs him by the scruff of his neck and makes him pick it up. Crazed, he picks it up and runs off with the wrapper in his fist and keeps looking around. He isn't used to being grabbed like that, by the scruff.

Looking at her own reflection in the boutique windows, Galpetra keeps straightening her hat, tugging at her skirt, and trying to see her back.

She stops by a shop window with plaster statuettes and rubs her temples.

"I was just going to tell you something, and now it's slipped my mind! Lately I've been having these memory lapses. You carry what you don't need around with you your whole life, and what you do need—just try to remember it! Look, the Laocoön! I dreamed of seeing the real Laocoön my whole life! But you know, he was found without an arm and they made a new one, and Michelangelo took a look and said the hand should be holding the snake from behind, by the head, not the top, or maybe it was the other way around, from the top instead of behind, I can't remember now. Later, centuries later, they found the actual hand—and it was all exactly as he'd said. Let's go. Enough counting crows!"

They've stopped at an intersection.

"Just look! Even here everyone crosses on red!"

She gets her handkerchief out of her sleeve again and wipes her puffy nose. There are papillae on her upper lip; she's probably been tweezing the hairs.

"Tell me, have you seen the real Laocoön? In the Vatican?"

"Yes."

"What did you think?"

"It's all right."

"What's that? What did you see? How could you? That's the Laocoön! The Trojan horse! Enraged Athena! The ancient Greeks! And how beautifully the ancient sculptor depicted the sufferings on the face of the father, who watches both his sons die! This is deathless beauty itself! This is beauty captured in stone for the ages! And his arm, tell me where his arm is reaching—up or back, over his head?"

"I don't remember."

"But how can that be? Why did you come to Rome?"

They come out on the piazza Colonna. The smell of leather from the purses laid out on the sidewalk strikes them in the nose. No sooner has Galpetra leaned over to feel one of them, when the negro seller, scooping up a dozen purses in both arms, runs away. They've probably tipped him off that the police have come. Purses under his held-out arms, like outstretched wings.

"I'm tired. And my feet hurt. Shall we sit right here a bit?"

We perch on the railing of the iron fence around the column of Marcus Aurelius. The tourists are examining the bas reliefs through binoculars. In the bas reliefs the Romans conquer the Sarmatae, and above is Paul with a sword. Galpetra, groaning, bends over and unlaces her scuffs. Pigeons all around. Some flap their wings over her head, lifting the taped slip of paper for a moment. Galpetra waves them off.

"Fancy that, flying off!"

She pulls off her boots, which have dried salt stains. She kneads her toes.

"What are you doing sitting in Rome and not going anywhere?"

"Why? I am. Yesterday I went to the old Appian way."

"Well, and what's there?"

"A road. Stones. Old and worn. Wheel ruts in the stones. The Spartacists were crucified along that road. I walked along and remembered how when I was a boy I saw the movie *Spartacus* at our house of culture on Presna and how later we played gladiators and our shields were bucket lids. In those days there were buckets for food scraps on each floor. We stole the lids, and the janitor's wife yelled at us.

An old woman crawls up, the same one, from Elektrozavodskaya. "Prego! Mangiare!" Her hand shakes. Her fingers are black.

"Oh no, I don't have anything to give," Galpetra sighs, pulling her boots closer, just in case. "Well, is that all? There wasn't anything else on that old road except where the Spartacists were?"

"There's also a church called Domine Quo Vadis. Sienkiewicz has a novel with that title, *Whither Goest Thou.*"

"I know. And so?"

"I went in. There wasn't anyone inside. Just a bust of Sienkiewicz. I wanted to go farther, but then in the aisle I saw a white slab on the floor under a grating. I went a little closer and saw tracks, the imprints of bare feet. On that spot Christ appeared to Peter, and his tracks were left in the stone. I leaned over to get a better look. Huge feet, bigger than mine. And perfectly flat. Sharply expressed flat-footedness. All of a sudden I so wanted to touch them. I was about to reach out, but all of a sudden I felt bad."

"Why was that?"

"If it's all a fraud and this is the work of some stone dresser who placed his own foot there, drew around it, and carved, then why touch it? But if these really were His feet? He whose last words were, 'Father, why have you abandoned me?' Right then I heard steps. A priest in a black soutane emerged quickly from a side door still chewing something. He saw me with my outstretched hand. I got flustered and pulled my hand back, and he smiled and nodded, as if to say, That's all right, touch it, you may. Touch it! And he added that it was a copy anyway."

"I knew it!" Galpetra sighs. "What did they do with the real stone?"

"That's what I asked. Turns out, people kept sneaking into the church and trying to steal it, so they moved the original to a different church, San Sebastiano, fairly close, farther down the Appian. I went there. It's not a church even, but a huge cathedral. I wandered through it and just couldn't find where the stone was displayed. A giant with golden hair hung near the ceiling. It hangs there and looks out the window: what's there? And out the window the sky is swept by clouds, old and worn, like slabs from the Appian Way. I asked some padre about the footprints. He nodded to a side altar to the right of the entrance. There was the grating and glass. It was dark, and you couldn't really see anything because of the glare. I looked for a box to drop change—they have them here in church—for a candle to be lit for a minute you have to pay—but didn't find it."

"And that's all?"

"That's all."

"So you never did see it?"

"No."

Perching next to the interpreter on the railing is an old guy with a backpack, wearing shorts, a T-shirt, a Panama hat, and hiking boots. And binoculars around his neck. His white, flabby legs are completely hairless. He smiles and offers the interpreter his binoculars, as if to say, want to look? The interpreter aims the binoculars at the column. A powerful zoom. Immediately he bumps into someone's lopped off head. A Sarmatian, no doubt. Then someone on a horse and a curly beard—maybe the emperor-philosopher himself, who said that more than anything in the world he wished the dead would come to life, not to sentence the living to death. Higher up, Paul with his sword. A long sword. The kind that's probably good for cutting off Sarmatians' heads. The interpreter hands the binoculars to Galpetra. She looks at the column just a little and then starts examining the street, building windows, passers-by, pigeons.

"Look there! Just like Moscow's!"

The pigeons dart about underfoot.

"Galina Petrovna!"

"What?"

"I keep wanting to tell you something."

"Well?"

"It's pretty silly, but . . ."

"Quit hemming and hawing and tell me!"

"You know, all those years I . . ."

"Are you talking about the paper on my back?"

"Yes. Or rather, something completely different. I wanted to ask you this: Why did love us while we hated you?"

The old guy in shorts is getting ready to move on, he gives his fat knees a resounding slap—and the pigeons shy away. Galpetra gives him back his binoculars and the strap catches on her sleeve button.

"You loved me, too, you just didn't know. I wonder, was Korczak in Rome?"

The interpreter shrugs. "I don't know."

Some demonstrators are assembling on the square, frightening off pigeons and tourists both, unfurling their posters and banners. One of them checks how the megaphone is working and sings into it to the whole of piazza Colonna: *Amore, amore, amore!*

Galpetra puts her boots back on and ties the laces on her museum slippers.

"There. Now I'm going to agonize over where the Laocoön's arm is reaching."

"Galina Petrovna, this isn't the Laocoön."

"What do you mean it's not the Laocoön? Who is it?"

"Korczak."

"What on earth are you saying?"

"This is Janusz Korczak and the two children he took by the hands as they were going into the gas chamber. They're dying of suffocation. This isn't beautiful at all. What does the play of muscles have to do with anything here? And what difference does it make where Korczak's hand is reaching?"

"You're mixing everything up! You always mixed everything up! You're a bungler. The Laocoön is one thing, and Korczak something completely different. An emperor can't be a philosopher, and a philosopher can't be an emperor. Sevastopol officers are one thing, and Bernini's angels something completely different. The ancient Greeks are one, the Chechens another. Felt museum slippers in an unheated Ostankino are one, and the child who was inside me another. You have to understand, the boy from Belarus who sniveled into the telephone receiver is a separate thing, and the bird-stocking, that—look!—just turned into a nose, a separate thing. Peter's foot is by itself, and the photographs of lepers by themselves. Remember, in the Vatican, on the square in front of the cathedral, near the obelisk, they were collecting money for lepers and all around were posters with photographs of children and adults without fingers and toes? She turned away, too, so as not to look."

"Yes, we were standing in line for Saint Peter's. Gusts of wind were scattering water dust from the fountain. Everyone was searching for the Pope's window: there, the second on the top floor. In front of us was a group of Polish schoolchildren wearing Boy Scout uniforms, with neckerchiefs like Pioneer ties, white and red. And behind us was a group of little Indian girls in novice's habits from some order, white with blue. I wanted to see the Swiss guards with their halberds, but guards in sunglasses and black suits were checking everyone at the barrier. She was stopped; they wouldn't let her in because of her bare, suntanned shoulders. Dark scarves were heaped in a huge plastic bin. She wrapped up. She laughed and pretended to be an old woman with trembling hands. They let us in. At first we walked through the cathedral together, but then she said she wanted to light a candle and I left her alone. I got in the line for pilgrims for the statue of Peter, which they wanted to hold by the foot and ask their dearest wish. Now ahead of me in line were the white and blue little Indian girls, while the Polish Boy Scouts were somewhere behind. I stood there reading in my guidebook that in fact this was not Peter but an antique statue of Jupiter the Thunderer. At some point they made it a new head and stuck a key in his hand instead of a sheaf of lightning bolts. The line moved slowly; each little Indian girl held Jupiter's foot for a long time. Behind me stood a woman dressed in black with a son of about ten, who was blind. The boy kept squeezing his eyelids shut, and his face muscles kept twitching. Finally it was my turn—and the sacred foot turned out to have no toes, as if they'd been eaten away by leprosy. I touched them and felt the cold of the bronze and the sticky sweat of hundreds of people. I involuntarily pulled my hand back. The thought flashed through my mind that I never did make my wish, but by then the mother had placed her blind son's palm on the toe-less, leprous stump. I moved on to roam through the cathedral. She was still standing in the same place holding a candle. They have these silly, fake candles here, the kind they put on restaurant tables, in red glass holders. With this shining red cup cradled in her hand and dark borrowed scarf on her shoulders, she suddenly seemed old and hunched, with tousled hair. I walked up to put my arms around her and again smelled the acrid stranger sweat on my fingers—and wished I could go somewhere to wash my hand."

"You never did understand anything. You're all so smart, you think you're Solomon, you make everything complicated! They think up Rome, and then they're surprised there is no Rome, just some bones lying around the Forum, sucked dry by time and grown over with green, green grass. They think up the Tiber and expect who knows what, but in fact it's something muddy, Tiberian, and real. You have to love that Tiberian world! It's all simple. You were supposed to be her Tristan. You needed to be him, to give her back that day in Izzalini. This is you lying with a book under a tree on an air mattress, and hanging from the branches on invisible threads are black caterpillars, nimble and quick. They throw themselves on everything that breathes: leaves, shadows, stones. They're goddamn Tatars, not caterpillars. Now it's not bad, but last spring, this rose-bush here was chewed down to the nub. Everything around is alive. You just put your book on the grass to pull off your T-shirt, and when you picked it back up there were ants crawling over the page like scattered letters. In heaven you have to be on your guard, make sure a scorpion doesn't crawl in your purse or boot. You have to walk through your garden with a stick, tapping the earth, because there are snakes. A house on a hill, a village below, invisible because of the treetops, only from the balcony can you see the *castello's* tower and the church roof. From the village comes the buzzing of power saws, and when it dies down the birds, the leaves, and the scuffling of bare feet chime in. Twenty minutes ago, her breasts were chilled and tight from the icy water in the shower. Now it's baking hot and she keeps trying to creep into the shadow, out of the sun: the over-grown path, the hose forgotten by the Etruscans, and the worn sandal that smells like your foot. In shorts and bikini top she hangs the laundry on a line: your boxers and her panties, socks and anklets, side by side, rubbing, caressing each other. She puts her foot on the edge of the air mattress, raising you up, rocking you. Her leg covered in bites. She holds out a tube for you to rub it on. Here the mosquitoes are tiny and nasty; before you can hear or feel anything, you're scratching. And her leg, slender, tanned, light, not yet twisted by iron, not yet overgrown with scars. Scratched red bites on her instep, her shin, her calf. You want to kiss and lick each bite—but she pulls her leg away: 'Don't do that! It's dirty!' You grab her heel and kiss her ankle, and Isolde laughs, hops on one foot, smacks your shoulders and head with the tube, loses her balance, falls, grabs onto your neck, and the mattress bucks and rears and dumps you on the grass. And in the sky the boxers and panties, socks and anklets, each creature two by two, drying in the postdeluvian sun, and for all the days to come of sowing and harvesting the earth, cold and heat, summer and winter, and day and night never cease. Later you're going to go see the frescoes of Luca Signorelli. The road swings its hips. Somewhere below is the Tiber. Sometimes the river comes into view behind the trees, and Isolde says, 'Look, what an odd boat!' But you're watching the road. Between Todi and Orvieto there are little African girls sitting on the shoulder every kilometer. They shield their eyes and peer intently at the people in the passing cars. They jump up if someone brakes. They're dropped off along the road in the morning and picked up at nightfall. Isolde is indignant that the poor women are forced to sell themselves this way, like dogs, under bushes. You joke: They're the whores of Babylon. She answers, There is no such thing as a whore of Babylon. Around the turn yet another little African girl follows your car with her gaze. In Orvieto all the parking spaces are taken, but you're in luck; someone is just leaving. You walk to the cathedral, but there's a mass and confirmation going on and the chapel with the frescoes is closed. You have to wait for it all to be over, and not only that, it's a holiday: you came on Palombella. Over people's heads you can see, in the depths of the church, in front of the altar, two nuns directing a girls' chorus. The girls are wearing pink and white dresses. They're singing something cheerful, as if they were performing a scene from an American musical. Everyone is swaying to the beat, clapping, and raising their arms first to one side and then the other, wiggling their fingers. Soon the festivities begin on the square. Above the crowd are the plywood clouds the dove is supposed to fly out of and announce something important without which life is impossible. Rumble and salute. Peals of thunder. Fireworks around the immaculate Mary and the crucifixion. Mary and the crucifixion drown in the rocket smoke. From the other end of the street, also with a crack and shots, a cage is lowered down a cable, trailing blue smoke. There, in a clear cylinder, a poor bird quivers and beats its wings, scared to death. The Italians are clapping, shouting ecstatically. We can wait out the festivities in a restaurant. Through the open windows, peals of thunder—real ones now. The dove, released from its cylinder, probably flew to where it could lodge a complaint. Beat them! And here comes the storm and hail. It drums on the tin roof. You're sitting by the window watching huge hailstones spilling on the asphalt and hopping higher than the windowsill. People run into the restaurant from the square, shouting and laughing. You say you hope it doesn't crack the windshield, and Isolde sighs about those women along the road. Poor things, what's it like for them there now, in the bushes! Ice pellets fly through the open door. The waiter drives them back with a broom, smiles at you, winks, and pretends he's a hockey player driving the puck into the goal. Then the hail stops and you go outside, where there's sun and steam. The hail was egg-size, and now it's melted to peas. You joke: Look how many leaves it's killed! Not much life left. But it's always that way. Because you were her Tristan, you just didn't realize it. Resurrection of the flesh. Out of nothingness, out of the void, out of white plaster, out of a dense fog, out of a snowy field, out of a sheet of paper there suddenly will appear people, living bodies, they rise up to remain forever, because they can't vanish, disappearing is simply not an option; death has already come and gone. First the contours, outlines, edges. Period, period, comma makes a crooked little face. Cross-out. The man stretches from this crack in the wall to that spot of sun. Stretches from nail to nail. Arms, legs, heads, breasts, bellies—all this is found in the snow, fog, and paper white, and has now been set out for identification. The bodies are still as transparent as an empty glass's shadow on the wall. Reality is malleable. Flesh is gradual—missing arms here, missing legs there, like the statues in the Vatican museums, and hammered off between the legs. Plane shifts into volume on the back right where the shoulder blade juts if you twist your arm back. The play of muscles, of epithelia not yet healed over. They creep, their drawing unfinished, their writing unfinished, they rise to their knees. Raspy breathing, indistinct muttering. They go back under the skin. They look around with still blind eyes. They sniff. They clamber here out of nowhere. And where the dimensions meet, the wall, snow, fog, and paper collapse in time: he ate pomegranates with bitter membranes and husks and said it helped against plaque; she tried to open the door, but it wouldn't yield, the wind was pressing from the other side; we drank from weightless plastic cups on the street—and you had to pour it all in at once so they wouldn't blow over. His buttocks are growing fur again. Superstitious, he again puts his sandals on left foot first, then right. Squinting, he pours a glass of ass's milk—prescribed for him by the earwig-doctor for breast disease—in himself every morning. And this one with the nostrils flared from singing is on his way home, carrying a hundred shekels of silver for his wife and singing, his horse casts its blue eye-whites on the cows with their dung-smeared udders, and to the person he meets who possesses knowledge about how the hens and hogs strutted over the site of the fire and hopped with a childlike cry when they stepped in hot ashes, with half a day's journey still to go—he came out early in the morning to the shore, grown wild overnight, just a pinch of people in the distance, and on the sand after the rain a firm crust—he steps and his bare foot breaks through. And there's the woman who loved a married man. When he stayed for the night the first time, she covered the icon with a scarf, but afterward, just the opposite, she took it off. She sorted through her things and poked her finger through a moth hole. She washed the floor—and steam rose from the rag. All her mother said when she was going away was defrost the refrigerator—instead of important words about love. Her hair was thinning and starting to fall out. Someone else's husband embraces her and says she has the amazing feline gift of turning any point in space into a home, of giving birth to coziness, of shutting out drafts with love, and he explains that this is because a woman has drafts in her soul, because she has no home inside, she's a stranger to herself there, and that emptiness can only be plugged up with something male and strong. She loved to sniff his flaxen beard. Somewhere she'd read that what happened at night never kept anyone around during the day. She sits in line at the clinic, looks at her feet, and thinks: An isosceles triangle truncated by my knees. What can the doctor say? He said that diseases are caused by grief and resentment and are cured with love. He asked, Did your mother kill the children inside her? Yes. There, you see? She killed love, and now you're paying for her. Her old neighbor drank his tea and was getting ready to leave, tucking his beard under his coat, and she saw he had hidden her panties in his pocket, and she didn't say anything, she just imperceptibly replaced them with a pair that hadn't been laundered to death. And this was the same soldier who had come home from war alive, only with his jaw messed up, so he went around with a silver straw inserted in his throat. When he was four he was beaten up in the courtyard by some boys. The future soldier went to complain to his mama, who was washing the linens. She left off her laundry and said in a compassionate voice, Poor little boy! Then she wrung out his father's long johns and lashed him on the back as hard as she could: Never come snitching to me! In Poltava there weren't any firs, so they brought a pine in for New Year's. A child is the warmth wrapped up beside you that is so easily hurt. There is nothing temporary. Here, in your childhood, you write something random in the water with a pitchfork as you rake up a ball that's fallen in the pond, and it turns out to be forever. The pop-eyed neighbor threatens to beat you with the washing machine hose, and his wife has a goiter spilling from her outsize collar, like a huge pear. He sliced a frog open with a razor and watched its tiny gray heart contract. He also got the idea of giving frogs shots: he would take its leg, poke a pen through the skin with a crackle, and inject ink. Little girls are playing in a may-flower bush near the shower stall, making dinner—you can prepare three dishes from dandelions: macaroni, fried eggs, and herring. They lick the petals of a little scarlet flower and stick them to their nails, and it looks like a manicure. They run into the outhouse to sit over the hole, which is drafty. In winter the dacha is constantly being burglarized, so he wrote a note: 'Comrade thieves! You have found out for yourselves that we keep nothing valuable or alcoholic here. Please don't break anything, including the windows, we are not rich people.' He came one weekend, walked in the twilight from the gate down the frosty path blanketed with stars, and every-thing in the house was smashed and shat upon, and his note lay on the floor held down by a pile. He started cleaning up with a dust-pan, and the frozen pile clattered. Man is a chameleon: if he lives with Muslims, he's a Muslim; with wolves, a wolf. Russians don't eat doves because the Holy Spirit appeared in the form of a dove. Grievance from Corinth: we took a passenger on board, and he turned out to be a prophet, he brought a herring back to life, which skittered over the slippery deck and overboard, and one little fish would have been all right, but it was a whole barrel, as a result of which the crew was left without provisions. It's better to eat than starve, better to live than die. Souls, Heraclitus teaches, come from moisture, but this means they have a tendency to dry out. You have to say yes to angry people, strangers, and no to your own, your near and dear. And how can you be certain of something if tomorrow the Thunderer gets up on the wrong side and you have to sacrifice your father's house for a trireme, or you start out for Syracuse to see your aunt for pancakes and you come upon pirates, or a runaway slave slits your throat while you're asleep? Wanderer, where are you going? To Sparta, you think? The snow has fallen so hard again that the streetcars aren't running. The resurrection of the flesh. Bashmachkin is the soul; the overcoat, the body. Leave him his coat and he won't chase passersby. Drop everything and we'll go to Rome—it's so close to the sky there! Gogol suffered from insomnia. At night he would often come to see me in my room when I was already lying with the candle snuffed out, sit down on the narrow wicker sofa, lower his head on his arms, and doze for a long time. In the middle of the night he would move on tiptoe to his own room, sit down on his own sofa, and remain there, half-dozing. With the dawn's coming he would muss up his bed so the maid wouldn't worry and would see that the lodger had spent a good night. He was afraid of dying in his sleep and so tried not to sleep at night. What air! Sniff the air and it seems as though at least seven hundred angels have flown up your nostrils. You believe that you often violently desire to turn into one big nose and nothing more—no eyes, arms, or legs, nothing but one honking nose, with nostrils as big as two good-sized buckets so you can take in as much scent and spring as possible. When I went up to Gogol's body, it did not seem dead to me. The smile on his mouth and his not-quite-shut right eye gave rise in me to the thought of a lethargic sleep, so that all of a sudden I could not make up my mind to take a mask. He had been afraid of not dying. That straw-wrapped bottle has to be resurrected: we drank dry wine over our game, and Gogol deftly poured off the upper layer of olive oil that served as a stopper and protected the wine from spoiling. Objects are flesh, too, after all. That mossy brick in the dacha phlox bushes that the centipede was under. That gramophone with the handle wrapped in blue electrical tape, in the cellar on Starokoni-ushenny. And the frost all those years ago when the subway grew icicles, and the janitor spread salt and sand from a bucket, which made it freeze even harder—that's flesh, too. And the paints. On the windowsill, in a glass, color felt markers—all of them black against the light. The sink is rusty from the iron in the water or from rusty pipes. My gums are bleeding; the toothpaste makes a pink foam. And those honey watercolors. And the sounds. All of a sudden I could hear the clocks, as if they had broken through, as if they had been silent and had now started, first the wall clock, unhurriedly, followed by the alarm clock skipping along. Old records crackle like logs in a stove. At the cinema an empty bottle rolled across the floor. You also need to resurrect the laughter in the rubber factory, when they had to stop the conveyor belt. Both the silence and the void. The voids of the people found in Pompeii. The sojourn that went missing. The whores that aren't. Absence is flesh as well. After all, silence is as much a word-created creature as the void locked in a room, or the reflection of street-lamps on the wet nighttime paving stones that propagates asexually, by grafting. Or like these finger-prints in the sky, although no, those are just birds breaking up now into several flocks. They named the man Ash and the woman Wil-low. Adam was master of the eastern and northern sides of heaven, while I guarded the western and southern. Adam was master over beasts of the masculine gender, while I was master over beasts of the feminine. On Judgment Day they will torture the whores and machine operators. I saw a river ablaze with fire, and many men and wives, like mustard seeds, submerged in it to their knees, others to the waist, others to the mouth, and the last—to the hair on their heads. Question: Who are these people in the fiery water? Answer: Those who blow neither hot nor cold. For they did not end up among the righteous, although they finished out the days of their life on earth, for they spent some of their days at God's will, and other days in sin and adultery, and so they lived without cease.

Question: Why are you naked? Answer: Don't you know that you yourself are naked? For you wear the pelt of worldly sheep, and it is rotting along with your body. While I, having looked at the sky, see my face and clothing as they are, in their true form. Question: How many parts does the soul have? Answer: Three: word, fury, and desire. Question: How many gods are there by rights? Answer: Seven hundred seventy-seven. Question: And even more correctly, how many? Answer: One hundred fifty. Question: But in fact? Answer: One. Question: Tell the truth! Answer: Less than one. Question: Should you tell a mother that her son has drowned at sea or say he went far away and never came back? Question: Tell Me, Shadrach, from the creation of the world and down the ages, how many drops of rain have fallen on the earth and how many have yet to fall? Question: And if there are snowdrifts all around—then the red stripe on your skin from your underwear elastic—how is that not a vine? Answer: There won't be any Day of Judgment. There's nothing to fear. There won't be anything there hasn't already been. They're trying to scare you! And how can you scare an old woman in a blind mirror? Me, who was scared to death of growing old and now has been punished for this with a long life, how else can I be punished? Well, I lost my loupe and looked for it all day, but she, the rogue, watched me from the stove, gawped at the old fool. The old gray mare she ain't what she used to be. Fingers bent by arthritis. Skin sagging like a gathered curtain. I've become small and shriveled—like a sickly monkey. I get lost in my bed. I dig in the past through sleepless nights. I excavate my Troy, which may never have been. Sand and dust by the shovelful. Suddenly, a gleam of something china—here I need to be cautious, use a brush. After excavating it I examine what I've found from this angle and that, and in the light, and sniff it, and scratch it with my nail. My first love was a china puppy. Papa brought me over to the sideboard and said that this was no ordinary puppy, it was magic. He loved me and would have a candy for me every day if I behaved well. I took the puppy and removed its head: it was hollow, and inside was a candy. I tried as hard as I could to behave well, and every day my favorite china puppy gave me a magic candy—delightful, unusual, incomparable, the most delicious in the world. One day I ran into the room and saw my father squatting, holding a paper wrapper, and next to him on the floor the headless puppy. My father saw me, was embarrassed, and handed me the candy he was planning to put inside. I put it in my mouth but it didn't taste very good. I had an allergy to cats; it came on suddenly when I was six, but no one could figure out what was wrong. I knew but didn't tell anyone. Or I thought I knew. I had a cat when I was a child, she got old and ran away to die in a field. Cats hide when they're dying. And here I was gasping if the cat was in the room. And because of that, the first time everything was supposed to happen with the man I loved, but he was married, I had an attack. We'd gone to his house. His wife and children were out of town. He was kissing me, and after a while I started gasping. I ask: You don't have a cat, do you? He answers: No. But I can tell. They did have a cat, but they took it with them to the dacha, and its fur was everywhere. So I told him, I can't, I feel awful, but he thought I was flirting, thinking up silly things, playing. He started undressing me, but I could barely breathe. Before that I just couldn't understand how all this could be happening to me simultaneously: here I am now, loupe in hand, and at the same time I'm there, holding him close and feeling that I'm about to pass out, dying, I can't catch my breath. But now I understand that it's all simple. Everything is always happening simultaneously. Here you are writing this line now, while I'm reading it. Here you are putting a period at the end of this sentence, while I reach it at the very same time. It's not a matter of hands on the clock! They can be moved forward and back. It's a matter of time zones. Steps of the dial. Everything is happening simultaneously, it's just that the hands have gone every which way on all the clocks. There's a dither because the sun is rising in the kitchen window and setting in the other window, in the room behind the lemon on the sill—she stuck a seed into a pot of dirt and now a little tree's shot up. It's like New Year's. In London they're still laying the table, while in Japan everyone's already drunk. Here I am waiting for my pension on Friday, while at the same time the Friday clouds are still somewhere in the water supply. There, in his cell, he's still just scratching a boat on the wall—and at the same time he's going down the Tiber toward Orvieto. Here I am telling you, my darlings, during class, that only old women believe in God, and at the same time I whisper into my pillow, 'Our Father, Who art in heaven,' and I'm thinking how beautiful that is: 'art in heaven.' And I'm thankful for every day lived and love known. I beg forgiveness for telling you that there is no proof of God. A pack of lies! A miracle is proof. Death is a miracle. I'm going to die. What other proof does anyone need? That's just the way they draw him, with a beard and a mantle. In fact, he might not be a menacing old man on the Friday clouds in the water supply but a vacationer roaming the Baltic beach with a matchbox, peering at the seaweed cast on shore, searching for amber, and the cockleshells crunch under his sandals as he walks along. Or the salesgirl who once told me, Here, lady, take the good bananas. Why choose the bad ones? Or the bungler himself. But more than likely it's neither one nor the other nor even a third. It's something very simple, some kind of grass. Green, green grass. Just growing. Lowering roots into every crack. People once knew it was a god from the cryptogamic family, but later they forgot. Now they survey temple ruins and miss the point: the temples merely marked where a sacred hill or grove was, after all, the menacing old men, vacationers, and bunglers lived in the treetops, wind, and grass, not in the altars. It's all about the green, green grass. If people stop believing in a primal god, he doesn't disappear, he just goes to live off on his own, unobtrusively, invisibly. Remember the house built for all the gods? Since everything is happening simultaneously, then even now you're walking with her—whether with scars on her legs or not, it doesn't matter—down the via

Pastini, and then you come out on the piazza Rotonda, and there it is, the temple of temples, lost in the crush of buildings, squeezed in on all sides by architectural ragamuffins. Ancient Romans in plastic armor—disguised Streltsy from Red Square—accost tourists under the colonnade. When you enter through the narrow crack in the tremendous, bronze doors, green from the ages, a draft runs over your bare sweaty skin, as if someone had darted between your legs, some invisible cat or the god of cats. You go from the heat into the murk and cool. The *oculus* draws all eyes. It's propped up by a slanting column of light—dust and haze. Insects are flying under the ceiling and blazing in the beam. An old photograph on a stand: during the flood there were boats floating in the temple, or the gods of boats. You keep wanting to look up, into the pupil. Somewhere there, high overhead, under the resonant, tessellated vault, lurked those whom naïve Theodosius thought to abolish with his decree, having decided to consolidate them into the immaculate Mary and martyrs, and ordered twenty-eight cartloads of bones brought from the catacombs. No point in you fattening up there. Just look what palaces! We have sweat, you have bread! What used to be yours is ours! The more the merrier! Honest work will not earn you palaces of stone! Why wash if there's no one to kiss? Love it like a soul, shake it like a pear! There's a deportation order, but how do you deport them if you can't see them? They could be right here in the corners hanging upside down, like bats. Wings furled, ruffled up, squeezed into living wisps, awaiting their finest hour. But the main one, the almighty, waits for no one, which is why he is the green, green grass. Only you can't see him right away. You have to go out. Let's go. I'll show you. You go first, and that woman who simultaneously does and doesn't have scars on her legs will wait on that side of the doors for the next tourist group to pass. And while you're standing between the columns waiting for her to come out—whether for a minute or all these years—and she's standing and waiting for everyone to pass, so as not to get jostled in the doors, I'll show you the most important thing, right here, where the side and back brick walls are, and then all of a sudden, a cliff of pink limestone, and on it, column capitals, frieze fragments with dolphins, and all of it dressed in moss and healed over, see, by a god, something light and curly. For us, this is a house plant, otherwise it wouldn't survive, without human warmth, but here it's a weed. So you see, this is in a dead language, signifying something alive: Adiantum capillus veneris. Venus hair, genus Adiantum. Maidenhair. God of life. The wind barely stirs. As if nodding, yes yes, that's true: this is my temple, my land, my wind, my life. The greenest of grasses. It grew here before your Eternal City and will grow here after. And those beards in mantles who dreamed up the wanton conception, draw and sculpt them all you like. I will grow through all your canvases and break through all your marble. I am on every ruin in the Forum and under every brick under the phlox. And my pollen is where you can't see me. I have been and will be where I am not. I am where you are. You are on the piazza Colonna—and so am I. Demonstrators have put on white coats and are chanting into a megaphone, 'Morire con dignità!'—these are doctors from the cancer clinic threatening a strike if they don't get a pay raise. They're accosting passersby with a long petition, just sign here, after all, today or the next you, too, will be getting tested for cancer! You, mister, everything still all right with your prostate? Come come. I'll be seeing you! And here, on the Corso, where the crowd is and the ties are so cheap you could eat them, the running of the Jews. They have to run naked. The way they crucified our Lord, as they were brought into the world. Carnival. Carnivalissimo. Merrymaking and rejoicing all around. The sorriest case, who has nothing to wear, turns his jacket inside out, rubs coal on his face, and runs there, too, into the colorful pile. And this gaiety is straight out of nature. Eat, drink, be merry and take a pretty girl to wife! The Jews were all ransomed, of course, leaving one Oroch. A tailor without coat or pillow, though there is a wife and children and the appropriate grief. Now the Tunguses are leading the Oroch here, to the Corso, and his wife and children are weeping loudly, saying goodbye to their father, because no one finishes alive. They hand out rods to the crowd. The Oroch removes his trousers, and the whole street dies laughing. He is standing there naked, covering his shame with his hands, and saying, "They're going to kill me now, and I want to say that I love you very much, Zhenechka, and you, Alyosha, and you, Vitenka!" Ready, set, go! And so he runs, and so they beat him. Have mercy, brothers! He's running, and they're beating him. Have mercy, brothers! He's running, and they're beating him. Have mercy, brothers! That's all. He can't run anymore. He's fallen. Now he's supposed to die. And suddenly he sees someone else running after him, naked and skinny. Who is it? Skin and bones, sweat and blood, beard shaking. It's obvious he's kaput, too. Only his nose isn't like mine, the Oroch thinks, which means it isn't me. But the Oroch knew all the Jews in Rome. This was some stranger. 'Where are you from?' the Oroch asks. 'Your face looks familiar, but where do I know you from? I've never left Rome, never stuck my nose outside the gates. All I know is that the white birch under my window was covered in snow, just like silver. And why are you running? After all this is for me to run, for me to die! Maybe I already died?' And the other answers, 'You cannot know me because I died long ago, whereas you are still alive. I seem familiar to you because we are all made in his image and likeness: hands, feet, and pickle, but the soul, like the body, smells like itself and its food. And the main thing is to remember where my arm was reaching—up or back, behind my head. Only I probably never will remember that. But for you this doesn't mean anything now. You have to live, you have Zhenechka, Alyosha, and Vitenka. I'll run for you.' The Oroch is astounded. 'But you aren't a Jew!' The other smiles in reply: 'Don't you know that in the kingdom of King Mateusz there is no Hellene, there is no Jew? You go on home, have your supper, turn on the television, play with your children, read to them about Urfin Jus and his wooden soldiers at bedtime, and then set your alarm and go peacefully to sleep, and I will run for all of you. For the Jews, the Sarmatians, the Orochs, the Tungus, the emperors, the philosophers. Well, go on, they're waiting for you at home! And be more careful! Look both ways! They're all rushing around here like madmen.' And he ran at a trot. Overtaking the passersby and tourist groups. Leaping over the hatches under which the Senate and people of Rome are hiding. He runs down the Corso toward the piazza Venezia, where he can't cross the street until a gallant guide dashes across traffic holding his bamboo stick like a sword. If you go up the steps and turn around, all you can see is the tail of Victor Emmanuel's steed, and under its tail the horse's balls hanging over Rome. The birds over the Capitoline have again flown up Gogol's nose—and seven hundred angels are flying up the bucket-size nostrils. Augurs follow their flight in order to predict events. A one-eyed cat races into the Forum. On the via Sacra the slabs are squared, one is convex, the next concave, so the victor must have been severely shaken in his triumphal chariot. The sacred Lacus Curtius is much smaller than the spring puddle at our Fryazino market. And this here is the Carcere Mamertino. Tell me, where did they kill Caesar? Wait, don't rush, we haven't got that far yet, he still hasn't been killed, he's still alive. So you see, this was the empire's main political prison. The prison seems small to us, just two rooms, upstairs and down. You could only get to the lower one through a hole up top. The upper room has an altar consecrated to Peter, who, according to legend, was held here before his execution, but this has not been confirmed by any documents, whereas in the Annals of Tacitus we read the story of the killing of Sejanus, prefect of the Praetorians, who had attempted to organize a plot against Tiberius. The body of the botcher-rebel, already dead, was thrown to the crowd to tear apart and into the Tiber three days later. But that was the least of it. They brought his children here. His younger daughter understood nothing and kept asking what transgression they meant to punish her for. She promised never to do it again and couldn't they punish her the way they punished children, simply giving her a couple of lashes with a rod? Inasmuch as the lawyers noted that in the history of Rome there was no precedent for the execution of a young girl not yet a woman, the executioners dishonored her before strangling her. But no one is going to put up an altar to that girl. Because Peter was not in Rome, but she was. Because if there is something real somewhere, then people don't look for it where they lost it but in Rome, where something is the matter with time, which collects rather than going away, fills this city to the brim as if someone had stuck the Coliseum in the drain like a plug. Because if there was love, then no one could make it not have been. And dying is utterly impossible if you love. Here I am lying on a sleepless night and remembering everyone I've loved. I'm blind, but it's as if I see them before me. How difficult it is to spend one's last years in solitude. How I wanted a child! The child who was then, at the Ostankino Museum, inside me, never born, became a fish and swam away. How I prayed: Green, green grass, give me another little baby! It replied, But you are old! I: So what? It: Judge for yourself. Everything female you had ended long ago! I: So what? What does that have to do with this? Everything had ended for Sarah long before, too, but you gave her one! Is that too much to ask? What do you care? Then the green, green grass said, All right, you're impossible. As you wish! Go to the bakery for a Borodino loaf and you will have a sweet pea! Here I am going to our bakery, trudging with my cane, bent, and coming toward me is a Gypsy who has three hands. She's soaking wet, as if she just swam in the river. She has a baby in one arm, also soaking wet, as if it were flowing off him, and in the other a pear with a bite out of it. Her third hand is stroking my head and she is saying, 'I just fled from brigands, which is why I'm soaking wet. Don't look on me as a Gypsy. I'm not just anyone. I'm pure, immaculate, and there's nothing left, not a seam, not a scar, immaculate as the Red Sea, which parted and then closed back up. She spat on the pear and gave it to me. Here, take a bite!' I took a bite, and I had never tasted anything sweeter in my life than that pear. Here I was trudging on for bread and all of a sudden I could tell I was pregnant. I was nauseated. I grabbed the fence and vomited and started wiping my mouth with snow melt. The next morning I woke up and thought, I must have dreamed it all. I look at myself in the mirror and can't believe my eyes: I'm young again! My breasts have swelled. And my belly has already grown. I was frightened. What would the neighbors say! That old lady is off her rocker! I began hiding, and hiding my belly, from everyone. How do you do that? It's growing by the hour, not the day. And inside, everything is alive. A live belly. My sweet pea has come back to me! I listen to myself and the baby stirs. I tried so hard to hide my pregnancy from everyone, pulled my belly in, but you couldn't hide it any longer, it expanded so. I started hiding from everyone and not going out. I lie in the bed and don't get up. But I'm going to have to give birth someday. And now, in the middle of the night, it's started. This is it, I can't anymore. Contractions. Terrible, intolerable pains. I suffer and suffer, but I'm afraid to call for someone. Then all of a sudden it shot out of me like a cannon. Boy? Girl? I can't see anything, I need to turn the light on. I started feeling around on the nightstand, hit the wire, and the lamp crashed to the floor! I tried to get up but didn't have the strength. I slipped on something and fell, hitting my head. I lay there and heard everything and saw everything, but oddly, it was like through a window, as if I weren't lying on the floor but standing on the balcony and looking into my room and seeing myself; there's a puddle by the bed, next to the broken lamp. Someone runs up and says, That's it! Her ordeal is over! Around me, deep night. Everyone is asleep. The wind, too, is asleep. All the boots, sandals, and shoes that ran their fill today are asleep. The fish have gone to sleep in the garden. The birds have gone to sleep in the pond. Rome, the city of the dead, where everyone is alive, is asleep, too. Calm now, embraced by eternal sleep. Only in one little window can a light still be seen, where a lieutenant newly arrived from Ryazan, a great fancier of boots, is trying on a new pair, walking toward his bed for the umpteenth time in order to shed them and lie down, but he just can't. He lifts his foot and admires the marvelously stitched heel. A stomach digests Berne. A baton glows. If you pull the hair stuck to the piece of soap by the end, the continents spread apart. The earth's guts are asleep. The white pencils are asleep. The young women are asleep, as if they were swimming—right arm forward, under the pillow, left back, palm up. At night the fountains are louder. No one by the Barcaccio. No one by the Trevi. The fountain of fountains, the admiral, the flagship, leads a fountain flotilla over the sleeping sea of stone. No one is there for the water dust to land on. No one is drinking the delicious Aqua Virgo, no one tossing a coin over his shoulder: here, ferryman of goats, wolves, and cabbages, take your Peter's pence, now the debt is yours! From the opening in the Pantheon's cupola, having awaited their finest hour, the bats slip into the night and dart in and out. Under the bridge leading to the Castello San Angelo, the boat scratched on the wall floats down the Tiber— empty. It's quiet, empty, in the Forum, only the cats sit, eyes riveted to the nailed hands. Soon it will be growing light. The architect of the sky picks up his scissors, he's just about to go and cut out everything superfluous: St. Peter's colonnade, the bridge with angels. He's a bungler, too; he tries to cut out angels and gets Sevastopol officers, they want to surface and, tied up, they shoot upward, and their shirt shreds rise like wings. Maybe it was he, Bernini, who mixed up everything in the world! They ordered him to sculpt an old woman from marble, a woman who did not conceive and did not let others, but before her death she mumbled: Here it is, the long-awaited hour, my lord and master! Now the time has come for us to see each other, my groom, my death! But the bungler came up with a young bride. And her groom is maidenhair. It's growing light. Piles of yesterday's garbage on the Spanish steps. Someone shouts from the direction of Monte Pincio, Eloi! Eloi! Lama sabachthani? The black angel froze on the corner of piazza del Popolo, unfurling its wings of purses.

Galpetra runs down the Corso, bumping into the first morning passersby—she, toilet-papered, mustachioed, naked, swinging her heavy, slapping breasts, she has a sweet pea in her belly. She's rushing, she wants to chase down the one running ahead at a trot to the kingdom of King Mateusz, and calls out, "Wait, take me with you to run for everyone, let's run together!" And at the end of the street a lonely guide raised her furled umbrella high with a kerchief attached the color of dawn, as if to say, don't get lost, follow me and I'll show you the most important thing in this fleeting city! This is the Egyptian obelisk with a pink cloud tied to it calling out: Where are you? Follow me! I'll show you the green, green grass!

Zurich-Rome, 2002-2004

M ikhail Shishkin has worked as a school teacher and a journalist. In 1995, he moved to Switzerland, where he worked as a Russian and German translator for asylum seekers. His novels have been translated into fourteen languages. In addition to winning Le prix du meilleur livre étranger (2005), he has won the Russian Booker Prize (2000); following its publication in Russia in 2005, *Maidenhair* was awarded both the National Bestseller Prize and the Big Book prize. Shishkin splits his time between Moscow and Zurich.

Marian Schwartz is a prize-winning translator of Russian. The winner of a Translation Fellowship from the National Endowment for the Arts (2006 and 1998) and the Heldt Translation Prize (2011 and 2002), Schwartz has translated classic literary works by Nina Berberova, Yuri Olesha, and Mikhail Bulgakov, as well as Andrei Gelasimov's *Thirst*.